FOREST VILLA

SUMMER

Karen KINGSBURY

Summer

Doubleday Large Print Home Library Edition

TYNDALE HOUSE PUBLISHERS, INC.

Carol Stream, Illinois

Visit Karen Kingsbury's Web site and learn more about her Life-Changing Fiction at www.KarenKingsbury.com

ISBN-13: 978-0-7394-8608-5

Printed in the United States of America

**This Large Print Book carries the
Seal of Approval of N.A.V.H.**

Donald, my prince charming

Sometimes I think of all we've been through together, the brief and brilliant seasons. You and I sitting at a picnic table outside our garage apartment, you playing praise songs on the guitar, and both of us believing that we needed nothing more than God and each other. And the baby days, strollers and high chairs, when whispered conversations over a sleeping baby were magical. I remember you and me walking through the grocery store with a kindergartner trying to keep up and a toddler sitting in the cart. Older couples—couples in their forties— would look at us and smile, and there was something wistful in their eyes. Now we're those people, smiling through the slight pain in the heart as we see young couples with kids. The years fly, but I've learned something lately. As our children grow and become, and a little ways down the road as they leave home, even so I see the subtle pinks of a new day, a new sunrise. A time when you and I might sit outside our bigger home with just a picnic table and a guitar, singing praise songs and knowing there is nothing else in all of life we could ever need. I love you more each day.

Kelsey, my precious daughter

You are very nearly eighteen, a young woman all grown up. Gone are the pigtails and braces, the middle school moments and high school heartaches. College life beckons, just as we always dreamed it would, and I'm breathless from the ride, from the speed of it. But I've learned this, my precious daughter: When I look at you, I see more than the beautiful, godly, grown-up girl you've become, more than the one-in-a-million girl we always knew you to be. I see the four-year-old blonde, blue-eyed pixie who almost never left her baby brother's side. There you were, standing atop a step stool after your bath, Bible in your hands, giving your brother an impromptu sermon. You couldn't read, but you knew the truth then as much as you do now. I see too the kindergartner all girly with pink ribbons and puffy bangs and the eight-year-old with tears on her cheeks asking Jesus to forgive her for lying and making a promise to love Him forever and always. I see you and your daddy in the waters of baptism, your eyes shining with that unearthly light, the light that still shines from them. I love your friendship with your brothers, especially Tyler. You and that younger brother still rarely leave each other's side. I've loved every minute of your childhood, Kelsey, and I love this time on the bridge, as you figure out what's next and prepare to make your way. Oh, and congratulations on your Triple Threat award, sweetheart. I'm proud of you even more because you weren't expecting it. Keep taking the stage for Jesus, and if you ever get lost, check back with the little girl inside, the one who has believed in the truth from the beginning. I'm cheering for you, honey. I love you so much!

Tyler, my beautiful song

Somewhere along the way we switched places. Once upon a yesterday you could run to me and jump into my arms. Now you are a six-foot-two teenager, and when we watch a family movie, I can rest my head on your shoulder. Just thinking about that makes me smile through teary eyes, because I love this—I absolutely do. I love the confident young man of God you're becoming, Ty. And I love that somewhere inside that grown-up-looking body is the heartbeat of a wide-eyed, happy kid, a boy who still bursts into song as he walks through the house. One of so many things I love best about you is that you're so kind and loving, that you care about the Lord and others. And of course I love how you are with Kelsey. Could a brother and sister be better friends? When I thank God for all He's given me, that special laughter and like-mindedness you share with Kelsey is high on my list. The sound of you two dancing and singing in *Pocahontas* will stay with me forever. Keep using your gifts to glorify Jesus, Ty. I love you, precious oldest son. Always.

Sean, my wonder boy

At the end of a day of writing or when life has sometimes thrown me something I wasn't expecting, I can always count on your hug to lift my cares. Years from now when I look back at our short season of raising children, the picture of you will always be one of your arms outstretched, a smile across your face as you come to me for one of our hugs. God knew you belonged in our family, and I will be grateful forever. It's that way on the soccer field, too—you leading the way in kindness and team unity. "Strange," one parent said at our team party. "This group of kids has been more closely bonded than any my son has been with." I wanted to wave my hands and say that I knew why. It's because of that special something you bring to the group. It's the same something special you bring to our family. Your enthusiasm is contagious even on a rainy Monday morning. Keep Jesus first, Sean, and you'll always find your way. I love you so, dear child.

Josh, my tender tough guy

I've watched you shoot up this past year, and I smile at the glimpse of tomorrow you're giving me. I love your easy smile, the way you are by nature a leader and a peacemaker and the picture of quiet confidence all at the same time. And your sense of humor, the way you jump out from the shadows to make Kelsey scream or your teasing way with your brothers when you're always getting a kick out of saying, "I'm just joshing you." At twelve years old, you think your name stands for Chief Jokester. But when I peek ahead at the things God may have for your future both in sports and in academics, I'm convinced you'll need not only humor but humility and a dependence on Christ above all things. I'm so grateful God brought you to us and that He knew which little boys from that Haitian orphanage belonged here with us. I love you, and I cherish the way our relationship is growing closer as the seasons pass. The hugs and smiles and back rubs, the connection between us is one that will take us into the next chapter of your life and the next after that. I'm so proud of you, Josh. I love you always!

EJ, my chosen one

What amazing changes in you these past months! Dad asks me which of our sons I think might've aced his math test, and the answer—more often lately—is you! You who struggled with learning when you arrived in our home now excel at it! Not only that, but you're the class cutup without meaning to be. You still mix up your words, but more often now I think it's so you'll get a laugh from your dad and your brothers. "Why is your shirt inside out, EJ?" Dad asked the other day. And you shrugged. "I don't know. I looked for the *flag*, but I couldn't see it." You make us smile, and you give us something fun to talk about at the end of the day. But beyond your academic successes, I'm grateful for your kind servant heart, EJ. You offer to help on a daily basis, and often you're the one handling a task before Dad or I know that it needs doing. You have a quiet way of showing that heart for God you've been given, and I'm so glad. I also love your way with our dogs, how you'll be missing and we'll find you outside sitting between Mandy and Reggie, singing to them in your own silly way. I thank God for you, EJ, for leading us to you at the very beginning of our adoption journey. You are my child through and through, no question. I love you forever.

Austin, my miracle boy

Last year when you celebrated that ninth birthday, I rested assured that I still had another year, another set of seasons before I needed to say good-bye to single digits. But here we are on the brink of your tenth birthday, and I feel dizzy at the thought. Dizzy and grateful in a way that cannot be defined by mere words. I remember how it felt when Daddy and I held you in that small curtained-off area at Children's Hospital, how it felt to have just a few minutes to say good-bye—maybe forever this side of heaven. I remember placing you into the arms of the heart surgeon and seeing that he too had tears on his face. Five hours later God gave you to us a second time, and I've been mindful of that fact ever since. We were given a miracle that day, and with each month and year that passes, I smile to see the zest for life that makes up that special heart of yours. You try hard at all you do, and I can see the gift of learning you've been given. Somewhere down the road I'll know more about the reasons God saved you that long-ago day. But for now I cherish every moment, knowing that none of them would've happened if not for the grace of our Savior. They had to sew your IV into your wrist in the days after your infant heart surgery, and even now the scar remains—a scar on the inside of your wrist in the shape of a cross. Never forget what it stands for, Austin. I love you always.

And to God Almighty, the Author of life, who has—for now—blessed me with these.

ACKNOWLEDGMENTS

This book couldn't have come together without the help of many people. First, a special thanks to my friends at Tyndale, who have believed in the Baxter family books and worked with me to get this next piece of the story to my readers in time for summer! Thank you!

Also thanks to my amazing agent, Rick Christian, president of Alive Communications. I am amazed more every day at your great integrity, your brilliant talent, and your commitment to the Lord and to getting my Life-Changing Fiction out to readers all over the world. You are a strong man of God, Rick. You care for my career as if you were personally responsible for the souls God touches through these books. Thank you for looking out for my personal time—the hours I have with my husband and kids—most of all. I couldn't do this without you.

As always, this book wouldn't be possible without the help of my husband and kids, who will eat just about anything when I'm on deadline and who understand and love me anyway. I thank God that I'm still able to spend more time with you than with my pretend people, as Austin calls them. Thanks for understanding the sometimes crazy life I lead and for always being my greatest support.

Thanks to my mother and assistant, Anne Kingsbury, for her great sensitivity and love for my readers. You are a reflection of my own heart, Mom, or maybe I'm a reflection of yours. Either way we are a great team, and I appreciate you more than you know. I'm grateful also for my dad, Ted Kingsbury, who is and always has been my greatest encourager. I remember when I was a little girl, Dad, and you would say, "One day, honey, everyone will read your books and know what a wonderful writer you are." Thank you for believing in me long before anyone else ever did.

Thanks also to my executive assistant, Tricia Kingsbury, who stepped in and took over this job with little notice. Tricia, keep dreaming big and reaching for your goals! And until God opens that door, thank you for using your talents to help me reach mine. Also thanks to my sister Susan, who helps me manage reader letters and who lends a great deal of spiritual and relational wisdom to the job. I appreciate you!

And to Olga Kalachik, whose hard work helping me prepare for events allows me to operate a significant part of my business from home. The personal touch you bring to my ministry is precious to me, priceless to me. . . . Thank you with all my heart.

And thanks to my friends and family who continue to surround me with love and prayer and support. I could list you by name, but you know who you are. Thank you for believing in me and for seeing who I really am. A true friend is loyal above all things, stands by through the changing seasons of life, and cheers you on not for your successes but for staying true to what matters most. You are the ones who know me that way, and I'm grateful for every one of you.

Of course, the greatest thanks go to God

Almighty, the most wonderful Author of all—the Author of life. The gift is Yours. I pray I might have the incredible opportunity and responsibility to use it for You all the days of my life.

FOREVER IN FICTION

A SPECIAL THANKS to Marla Selby-Stone, who won the Forever in Fiction item at the Kings Way Christian school auction. Marla chose to honor her daughter, Tatum Renee Selby, by having a character in this book named after her.

Tatum is eight years old and is proud to have Jesus in her heart. She cherishes her friendships, enjoys trying new foods and places, and loves a happy ending. Tatum is involved in gymnastics, and she also enjoys singing and dancing. She is a good friend to many and is known for her compassion and discernment. She is the oldest of three siblings and is part of a very close extended family. She and her mother and siblings live next door to her maternal grandparents. Tatum's favorite vacation spot is Hawaii— maybe the only place where she couldn't take her precious poodle, Princess. Tatum has long blonde hair and blue eyes and makes frequent visits to Bulgaria, her mother's homeland.

In *Summer*, I chose to make Tatum a special friend of Brooke and Peter's daughter Maddie. She is also the first girl Cole Blake gets a crush on—something that makes his mother, Ashley, feel how quickly her son is growing up.

Marla, I pray that Tatum will be honored by your decision to name her Forever in Fiction, and I hope that whenever you read this book, you'll see your daughter as part of the story.

In addition, a special thanks to Amy McDaniel, thirty-seven, who won the Forever in Fiction item at the Northshore Christian Academy in Everett, Washington. Amy wanted to be a character in one of my books, and I chose to make her an obstetrician in *Summer*. In real life, Amy's life revolves around her love for family. She has five kids—Kobe, Kaden,

Kalvyn, Kami Rose, and Karson. She is married to Brad, the man of her dreams, and together they own a hardware store, where they enjoy chatting it up with the regulars.

Amy has been a teacher and a bungee jumper. She's good at water sports and helping her friends decorate their houses. She loves snow skiing, scrapbooking, and Hawaii. More than anything, Amy loves Jesus, and she loves being a wife and a mother, but she still misses her younger brother and her father. Amy lost her brother when she was a senior in high school, and her grief led her to a relationship with Christ. Her father succumbed to cancer shortly after he had the privilege of walking Amy down the aisle at her wedding. These losses have made Amy compassionate and understanding, the way Dr. Amy McDaniel is in this novel.

Amy, I pray you will see a glimpse of yourself and your passion for family as you read *Summer* and that you will always be glad for the chance to be Forever in Fiction.

For those of you who are not familiar with Forever in Fiction, it is my way of placing you, the readers, into my stories while raising money for charities. To date this item has raised more than $100,000 at charity

auctions across the country. If you are interested in having a Forever in Fiction package
donated to your auction, contact my executive assistant, Tricia Kingsbury, at Kings-
burydesk@aol.com. Please write *Forever in
Fiction* in the subject line. Please note that I
am able to donate only a limited number of
these each year. For that reason I have set
a fairly high minimum bid on this package.
That way the maximum funds are raised for
charities.

CHAPTER ONE

FOR KATY HART Matthews, all her life—every successive year of her adolescence, every season of pain or joy, all the lonely days and weeks and months without love—had only been the path that led her to the here and now, her honeymoon with Dayne Matthews.

With every breath she was convinced that this brilliant moment in time would shine forever like the brightest star in the night sky of her memory, a time that would always make her certain that this—this man and this time and this shared faith—was the reason she'd been born.

Dayne had surprised her with a two-week

trip to the Bahamas. They'd spent the first week in a secluded beachfront bungalow not far from the well-known Atlantis resort and this second one on a private island a thirty-minute ferry ride from Nassau.

Wilma Waters, the wedding coordinator, had handled the details so Katy and Dayne had a personal staff complete with a chef, a cleaning crew, and a recreation coordinator in charge of providing scuba gear, Jet Skis, and whatever else the couple might need.

Only Wilma and Dayne's agent knew the phone number at the bungalow, and both had promised that, short of an emergency, they wouldn't call.

It was the third day of the second week, and Katy woke next to Dayne, amazed as she had been every morning since the wedding that this was her life, that she and Dayne were forever going to wake up this way.

Sunshine streamed through the sheer curtains and shone across the white, downy comforter. Katy drew a long, slow breath and looked at her husband . . . her *husband*. The word still made her feel like they were pretending. The idea had felt impossible for so long; through every brief visit and every long good-bye, while they fled the paparazzi and while Dayne recovered from his car accident, they'd agreed time and again that love could never work for the two of them. *Would* never work.

But somehow here they were on a brilliant blue day, sharing a bed and a brand-new marriage and a love that simply could not be denied. Not for any reason.

Katy rolled onto her side and studied the man beside her, the gentle rise and fall of his chest. Whatever his past, it was behind him.

"Fifty years from now, I'll look back on this time," he'd told her during one of their walks on the secluded sandy shoreline, "and I'll know that my life didn't really begin until now. With you."

Dayne didn't spout pithy lines or tired phrases. So when he told her his life only really started on their wedding day, he meant it. Every word.

Since their first night together, each whisper and quiet conversation over a candlelit dinner had been marked by words that crossed his lips the moment he thought them, words that seemed to take even him by surprise in their depth and intensity. When he took her in his arms and kissed her, when their bodies came together in a show of love Katy hadn't known possible, she was convinced she was meant for this, to find her way to Dayne Matthews. And so the honeymoon was more than Katy could've imagined because she had never known love like this. Overnight her ability to feel seemed magnified a thousand times over. That's what loving Dayne had done to her. She could only imagine what love would become as they shared the months and years, as they journeyed through the seasons of life together.

Dayne stirred and took a deep breath. He rolled onto his side, facing her, and slowly opened his eyes. "Mmmm . . ." A slow smile filled his face even before he was fully awake. "Good." He reached for her hand. "It's not a dream."

Katy was about to tell him that no, it wasn't and that she'd had to remind herself of the same thing when she first woke up, but before she could say a word, the phone on Dayne's bedside table rang. The sound of the ring was foreign after so many days without an interruption from the outside world.

Dayne frowned and sat halfway up. "This better be big." He picked up the receiver, and as he pressed it to his ear, he slid closer to

Katy, erasing the inches that separated them. "Hello?" He paused, his expression serious. "That's okay. What's up?'"

Katy watched him, waiting for his reaction. Since Wilma and Dayne's agent had been instructed to call only in case of an emergency, she felt her breath catch in her throat. It could be her parents or one of the Flanigans or the Baxters . . . almost anything.

"And he needs to know in an hour?" Dayne raked his fingers through his hair and rolled onto his back again.

Katy breathed out and felt herself relax. Whatever the news, it wasn't tragic. Based on Dayne's reaction, it was probably business.

After throwing on a robe, she climbed out of bed, slid the curtains over, and opened the window. She drew in a long breath of ocean air and gazed at the sandy stretch outside their room. The beach looked like something from a calendar, so beautiful that no camera could ever really do it justice. Behind her she could hear Dayne wrapping up the call.

"Right. I've seen the show." Dayne didn't sound short, but he wasn't happy either. "I don't know. . . . I mean, do we need that sort of publicity?" He sighed, and for a while he said nothing. "Okay . . . I get it. I'll talk it over with her and get back to you."

Katy turned and dropped into a chair near the bed. "Your agent?"

"Yes." Tension was written across Dayne's brow, a tension that hadn't been there since their wedding day. He sounded tired and uncertain. "Word leaked out that you took the part in *But Then Again No.* I'm sorry, Katy."

"It's not your fault. They would've found out."

"This is a little different." He hesitated, almost as if he didn't want to finish his thought. "*For Real* wants to feature us in a twelve-episode segment. It'd run once a week when our movie opens."

Adrenaline shot into Katy's veins, and her heart skipped a beat. She blinked and stared at the tile floor. *For Real* was one of the most watched reality shows on TV. "You mean like . . . follow us home and camp in our living room?" Reality shows had done that with other celebrities, usually with terrible results.

"No." Dayne sat up and leaned against the headboard. "They'd stick to the set." Doubt flashed in his eyes. "My agent thinks it might make the whole movie thing easier for us."

Katy gripped the arms of the chair. She couldn't shake a sudden surge of fear. "Having us the subject of a reality show?" The idea was enough to make her change her mind about the part.

Over the next few minutes, Dayne explained the offer. The camera crews would document Katy and Dayne working together, giving the country what it would so desperately want anyway—an inside look at Dayne Matthews and his new bride.

"Sort of like my idea." Katy was starting to understand. "Smile for the cameras rather than run from them."

"Right. Only on a much bigger level." The fine lines around Dayne's eyes were proof he didn't like the idea, but his tone said he understood where his agent was coming from. "Make the story more available and because of that less desirable."

Katy stood. A reality show? About the two of them? She turned and walked out onto the balcony. Behind her, she could hear Dayne climb out of bed, hear him slipping on his shorts. The touch of his arm as he came out and stood beside her sent chills down her. For a while neither of them said anything. Then Katy rested her elbows on the railing and met Dayne's eyes. "Think it'll work? Take the heat off?"

Dayne looked at her, and the weight of their decision colored his expression. "My agent thinks so."

"What about you?"

"Maybe." A warm breeze drifted up off the gentle surf. "The producers want a commitment from us in an hour. They need to put together a package and present it to the network execs."

Katy didn't want to make the decision. Too much rested on how it went. "If we do it, what's the worst thing that could happen?"

"The press could get more interested." He narrowed his eyes, concentrating. "But I've only seen that when the crews follow celebrities 24-7."

A fine layer of salt lay on the railing, and Katy dusted off a section with her fingertips. "It isn't a long commitment, I guess."

Again they were quiet, and Dayne slid his bare foot next to hers. He breathed out long and hard and stared into the clear, blue sky. "We don't really have a choice. They'll follow us one way or another."

"It'd be good publicity for the movie." Katy still felt slightly sick at the thought, but Dayne was right. If they turned down the offer, they would be dodging paparazzi every hour of the day. At least with a reality show, there was a good chance the story would feel overplayed. The press might find another, more secretive, celebrity to focus on.

"Exactly." Dayne allowed the hint of a smile, his first one since the phone call. "That's what my studio's saying. Obviously."

In the end, they prayed together, and when neither of them had a sense of peace over the proposition, Dayne tried to call his friend Bob Asher, who worked as a missionary in Mexico. Bob always seemed to have the right answer for Dayne, but this time Dayne couldn't get ahold of him.

His last attempt was a call to John Baxter, his dad. The call didn't last long, and afterwards Dayne sat in the chair near the phone, his expression more confused than ever. "He said the idea worried him."

"It worries me." Katy went to him and put her hand on his shoulder. "So what should we do?"

He stood and eased his arms around her. His eyes searched hers. "We have no choice about the scrutiny. They'll take pictures with or without our permission."

At the end of a restless hour, Dayne and Katy agreed. Letting the paparazzi have full access to them during the filming of the movie was the lesser of two undesirable situations. They would have nearly one month to savor their privacy, to return home from their honeymoon and help Katy move into their lake house. They would have quiet mornings overlooking Lake Monroe and dinners with the Baxters, and come early May, they would fly back to Los Angeles, roll up their sleeves, and get to work.

Dayne made the call. His voice still held some of the doubt from earlier. "We'll do it." He gave Katy a wary look. "The cameras can only be on the set, and it will only be for twelve episodes."

After the phone call, Dayne and Katy tried to put the news behind them, tried to find their way back to the easy laughter of the past few days. But they compared notes several times that morning. All they could think about was the reality show and whether agreeing to it had been the right decision.

An hour after breakfast, they walked out to the sandy shore and toward the supply box stationed near a pair of beach chairs. They'd arranged to snorkel today, and even with so much on their minds, Katy couldn't wait to hit the water.

Positioned at either end of their private beach were lifeguards with radios. Their first role was one of safety and protection, but they were also available if Katy and Dayne needed anything from a box lunch to towels or additional gear.

Dayne held Katy's hand, their legs brushing against each other as they walked. When they reached the wooden box, he stopped and turned to Katy. A breeze blew in from the ocean and swirled around them. "For the next few hours, there's no thinking about movies or reality shows or paparazzi." He crooked his finger and placed it gently beneath her chin. He seemed to find a deeper place in her heart. "Too soon we'll be headed home." He leaned close and touched his lips to hers. "We didn't come here to talk about business."

She felt the corners of her lips lift. "Okay." She shifted her gaze to the white, sugary sand and the blue-green water beyond it. Honeymoons came once in a lifetime, and a honeymoon like the one she was sharing with Dayne Matthews was beyond anything she had ever dreamed. She kissed him again and grinned. "The gear's in the box?"

"Let's see." Dayne released her hand and lifted the lid. The hinges creaked, and as he

opened it all the way, a pair of moths flut-
tered free and drifted toward a bright pink hi-
biscus. He reached inside and pulled out a
snorkel, a mask, and a pair of fins. He
handed them to Katy and took out another
set for himself. "All we need is a little water."

Her laugh mingled with the sound of the
surf. The ocean spread out as far as she could
see. "I don't think that's going to be a problem."

They slipped on their gear and moved
into knee-deep water. Dayne pointed toward
an area fifty feet out. "There's a small reef
that way."

Then without saying another word, they
eased into the water and started swimming.
The water was clear and warm and silky
against Katy's skin. Neither of them was in a
hurry. Even before they reached the reef,
they spotted schools of fish, some of them
as large as Frisbees with orange and black
and white stripes.

Dayne took Katy's hand, and the feel of
his body moving through the water beside
her did what nothing else had been able to
since the phone call from Dayne's agent. It
made her forget about the reality show.

They spent most of the next two hours
along the shallow reef, marveling at the coral

and stopping to study brightly colored exotic fish. A ways off, they spotted a four-foot shark moving slowly along the reef. Their personal guide had told them that the sharks in this part of the ocean were small and had plenty of food. Even so, Katy felt her heart skip a beat. She reached for Dayne's hand, and he gave hers a couple of reassuring squeezes.

Before they finished for the day, a trio of dolphins swam past them and jumped out of the water in unison. The moment took Katy's breath, and she and Dayne hovered at the surface, watching the threesome swim in playful circles, breaking the surface a number of times before they left the area.

Not until they were back on the beach eating lunch did Katy even remember the phone call and the commitment they'd made.

"You're quiet again." Dayne set his fork down and studied her.

"Thinking about the show." She took a long breath. The air tasted faintly of seawater. "I can't decide if we made the right decision."

They talked again about the pros and cons, about giving the press what they wanted and avoiding the sort of situation that had led to Dayne's car accident. And they talked about privacy and how they wouldn't have any with a reality show following them around the set. They agreed that since the interest was limited to the filming of the movie, maybe it wasn't a bad choice.

The conversation faded, and they stretched out on their beach chairs along a shady section of sand beneath a cluster of palm trees. Katy thought about what lay ahead. Other couples had broken up after being the subject of a reality show or dropped out before the full run of episodes in an effort to salvage what remained of their relationships.

By the time they sat down to prime rib that night, Katy had warmed a little more to the idea. It wasn't as though they were committing to a twenty-six-week season, after all. And it would certainly give the press what they wanted without a chase. Which made the show a good choice all on its own. Anything to keep Dayne and her from always running.

Along the way they might even have the chance to share their faith, the beliefs that now drove both of them. God would use the next season in their lives, because while Katy and Dayne might be newly married, they weren't like other Hollywood couples.

They would grow closer through the experience. A reality show wouldn't hurt their relationship; it would make them stronger.

Katy was sure.

CHAPTER TWO

ASHLEY BAXTER BLAKE could hardly wait to start walking the track at Clear Creek High again.

She had been tired for a week after the trip to Mexico for Dayne and Katy's wedding. Same as her sister Kari. Both were four months pregnant, and now that they'd been home for two weeks, they were ready to resume their afternoon walks at the track.

The routine today would be the same as it had been before the wedding. Ashley and Kari would meet in the school's parking lot with their kids and strollers and a pair of small bicycles. Kari and Brooke had swapped girls earlier in the afternoon so Jessie could play with Hayley and Maddie and her little school friend could hang out with Cole. RJ and Devin—the younger boys—would most likely fall asleep in their strollers, and Ashley and Kari could get in an hour's walk before calling it quits.

Kari's husband, Ryan, was head coach on the school's football team. Today he would be in the boys' weight room, helping get the players ready for next fall. In the month leading up to the wedding, when Ashley and Kari walked the track, Ryan had occasionally stepped out for a quick hello.

Ashley arrived at the school first. She parked her van and at the same time noticed Kari's car pulling into the lot.

From the backseat, Cole released a pensive sigh. "I've been thinking, Mom." He leaned up and took hold of the back of her seat.

Ashley smiled. "Thinking's a good thing."

"If the new baby's a boy, we'll have more than half a basketball team. 'Cause you only need five for a team."

"And if the baby's a girl?"

"Well—" disappointment rang in Cole's

voice—"I guess we could let her play. But it wouldn't be the same."

Quiet laughter came from Ashley. Cole had just finished his first season on a youth basketball team, and her husband, Landon, had put a hoop up at the end of the driveway after they returned from Mexico. Cole spent an hour shooting baskets every day— regardless of the cool temperatures this spring.

Ashley reached behind her and placed her hand over Cole's. "What if this new little sister doesn't like basketball? What if she wants to dance or sing or be in Christian Kids Theater?"

Cole unsnapped his seat belt and slid along the backseat so he could see Ashley better. "Maybe she might do both."

Before Ashley could respond, Kari pulled into the spot beside them.

"Aunt Kari!" Cole gave Ashley a look. "If me and Maddie race today, I might let her win. Otherwise she'll get bored and stop riding with me."

Ashley raised her eyebrow at him. "I wouldn't tell her that."

"I won't." Cole's eyes sparkled, the way

they did whenever he had a chance to tease his cousin. He jumped out of the van and headed for the open back door of Kari's car.

Ashley laid her fingers on her abdomen. After just having a baby last year, she was already showing. But that was okay. Kari was showing too. The small bumps beneath their jackets only served to remind them that this was the rarest of chances. The two of them being pregnant at the same time, together going through morning sickness and doctor appointments and dreaming about names.

Brooke and Erin, their other two sisters, had both expressed a mock sense of jealousy.

"Imagine how much fun it'll be once the babies are born," Brooke had told Ashley a few nights ago. "You'll do everything together."

But the truth was, they all would. As much as Brooke's schedule as a pediatrician would allow and as often as Erin might come home from Texas, the whole family would get together. These newest babies would be the same age, and for that reason they were bound to share a special bond. But all the Baxter cousins were close—even when the relationships between them involved a little competition.

Ashley waved hello to Kari, stepped out of her van, and opened the back door, where Devin was sleeping. Kari was helping her kids out, and Ashley noticed the other little girl, the school friend Maddie had brought. When the girls were out of the van, they faced Cole.

"This is Tatum Selby. She sits next to me in school." Maddie put her arm around her friend. "And she's the fastest bike rider in the third grade. Plus she's good at gymnastics."

Cole sized her up. "Really?"

"Yep." Maddie stuck her chest out. "She's so fast you won't see her ride past you."

"Let *her* tell me." Cole looked at Tatum. "Are you fast?"

Tatum giggled and shrugged one shoulder. "I guess so."

Ashley kept an eye on the conversation. Tatum was darling, shorter than Maddie with long blonde hair and blue eyes.

"'I *guess* so' means you're not that fast." Cole cocked his head, studying her.

"Actually . . . it's true. I'm the fastest bike rider in my class." Tatum flung her hair over her shoulder. She was missing a few teeth, and her smile never quite left her eyes. But when she talked about her bicycling skills, a mix of determination and compassion colored her expression. "Anyway, I'd rather sing."

"There you go." Ashley scooped Devin into her arms, shut both doors, and joined Kari and the children. "Tatum can sing and be athletic. So you're right, Cole. Your sister can probably do more than one thing."

Kari raised her eyebrows. "A sister? I thought your ultrasound was in two weeks."

"It is." Ashley laughed. She pulled Devin's stroller from the back of her van. "We're assuming here. Cole wants a basketball player, and I was saying maybe the baby will be a girl."

Cole crossed his arms and made a face. He met Tatum's eyes. "A boy would be better."

"Not always." Tatum didn't blink. "Girls can do everything boys can do."

"Yes." Kari had her stroller out now too. "Our friend Tatum is living proof that you can't put little girls into a box. She's trying out for the next CKT show."

They opened their strollers and began moving toward the track. The whole time, Maddie chattered on about how Tatum was going to Hawaii for spring break and had been to Bulgaria five times and had a poodle named Princess.

Every now and then Cole looked over his shoulder and shot Ashley a look that said he wasn't interested in the girl talk and couldn't understand why Maddie felt compelled to keep reciting details about her friend. Even so, he kept his steps even with Tatum's.

When they reached the track, Tatum turned to Cole. "Do you have Jesus in your heart?"

Cole looked taken aback. "Yeah. For a long time."

She grinned, and her missing teeth became more apparent. "Then I guess the bike race doesn't really matter." She patted his shoulder. "Right?"

Cole's cheeks grew red. If Ashley didn't know better, she would've thought maybe Cole was enamored with this little girl, a girl who could play sports and dance and find the compassion to talk about Jesus.

He opened his mouth, and for a few seconds nothing came out. Then he quickly looked away and hurried to his bike. "Enough talking."

The three of them climbed onto their bicycles and peddled off, with Cole shouting something about a few warm-up laps.

Ashley watched them go. "Interesting." She zipped up her jacket and fell into step beside Kari. "Almost looked like my little boy had a crush for a minute there."

"Apparently lots of little boys have crushes on Tatum." Kari looked thinner than usual and pale. Pregnancy was always hard on her. She smiled. "Brooke told me that Tatum and Maddie sort of lead the pack when the boys start chasing the girls at recess."

"Makes me feel old." Ashley found a steady pace and kept her eyes on Cole and the girls. "Like I better not blink or he'll be calling to tell me he's getting married."

Kari laughed. "I think we have a few years."

"Still . . . they grow up too fast."

"They do." Kari's laughter faded.

They let the conversation drop for a few minutes. The air was crisp, the sky above them bright blue with only a few puffy white clouds on the horizon. Already the sun was making its way down, casting shadows over the track.

Their pace wasn't as fast as it had been before the trip to Mexico, but it felt good.

Ashley sucked in a deep breath. She liked the way the cold air filled her lungs. Back when she was pregnant with Cole and later with Devin, she had wondered about the women who said they never felt better than when they were carrying babies. But this pregnancy was different. She was at peace with God and her family, energetic and strong and healthier than ever.

So maybe this would be the little girl she and Landon had rarely talked about, the one that would complete their family. She was even carrying the baby differently, lower than before. She drew another long breath and glanced at her sister. "You feeling okay?"

Kari kept walking, but she pressed one hand to the small of her back. "I'm fine. Just tired. I'm not sleeping great."

Concern rippled the calm waters in Ashley's heart. "Just the baby . . . ?"

"I think so." Kari made a face. "This one seems to be permanently lodged on my bladder."

Ashley didn't want to pry, but she had to ask. "You and Ryan—everything's okay with the two of you?"

"Definitely." Her eyes softened, and her smile crept up her face. "I love him more now than ever before. He's busy—coaching football and working on his side business, helping former pro athletes find life after sports. But his first concern is always me. Whether I need help with Jessie and RJ or if I just need an hour nap." She peeked around the stroller and checked Ryan Junior. Then she looked at Ashley again. "I don't know what I'd do without that man."

Ashley sensed it again, the wonderful feeling that all was right with the world. She felt fantastic, the afternoon air was invigorating, and she and her sister were married to a couple of good guys, men who took their roles seriously, who made life one incredible love story.

All that, and they were about to have babies at the same time. Ashley looked up, beyond the distant trees to the sky. *Thank You, God, for this season in life. You led Kari and me through the storms, and now You've blessed us with lives that seem too good to be true. Thank You, God. . . .*

Daughter, in all things I work for the good of those who love Me.

The verse filled her head sure and clear, and it made Ashley hesitate before moving her feet again. She'd read it before, of course. But mainly in times of trial. So why here, now, in the midst of the happiest time in her life, would that verse be the first to fill her mind?

Cole and the two girls whizzed past on their bikes, with Cole in the lead.

Maddie was shouting after him, "We're still warming up! This isn't the race, Cole!"

Ashley watched them, and a chill passed over her arms. Was God trying to tell her something? Was another trial waiting around the bend, or was the verse merely affirmation that after everything she and her sister had been through, this, finally, was the good God had worked out for them?

"What are you thinking?" Kari's voice was quiet, thoughtful. These walks did that to both of them—made them think about life, all that had passed and all that lay ahead.

Ashley found her pace. "The future, I guess."

"Me too." Kari ran her hand over her middle. "I can't wait to go through the next years together. What a dream."

Again Ashley was quiet for a moment. "You ever wonder . . . whether we've ridden out the worst trials or whether there are more ahead?"

"Sometimes." Kari kept her focus on the distant track. "The other day Jessie asked me about her first daddy, whether she would know him when we all got to heaven."

"Hmmm." Ashley kept her eyes on the kids, now halfway around the black oval. "You don't talk about Tim much. Does Jessie know the details?"

"Not everything. Just that before he died, he loved Jesus very much." Kari straightened her shoulders. "I told her yes, I thought she'd recognize him in heaven. That's when she asked me the question I've been dreading. 'How did Daddy die?'"

Ashley made a face. Innocence and security marked the lives of their children. Kari and Ryan had hoped to avoid talking about the specifics of Tim's death as long as possible. "What did you tell her?"

"I said a mean and sick man hurt him. That's how he died."

"And that was enough?"

The kids passed by again, their legs flying as they pushed the pedals.

Kari sighed. "For now. Someday she'll want the details, and I'll have to tell her. Tim's affair, the college kid who had a thing for Tim's girlfriend, and the fact that Tim was gunned down outside the girl's apartment. All of it." She blew at a wisp of her hair and gave Ashley a sad smile. "Yeah, I'd like to think the hardest trials we'll face are behind us."

"Me too." Ashley noticed the three kids stopping ahead of them.

"This is it." Maddie climbed off her bike and held her hand out in front of Cole and Tatum. "One time around. First one back to this spot wins."

"Sometimes I think Brooke should've named her Lucy." Kari chuckled.

"True." Ashley felt the nerve-racking thoughts from earlier lift. "But only if I would've named Cole Charlie Brown."

"Ready, set . . ." Maddie put her hands on her hips. "You're cheating, Cole. Back up."

Cole mumbled something they couldn't hear, even though they were drawing closer to the kids. He backed his bike up a few inches. "There. Is that better?"

Maddie tilted her chin up. "Yes. Much." She smiled at Tatum. "Mark, get set . . . go!"

The bicyclists were off, tearing down the straightaway and rounding the first turn. Cole was fast, but Tatum kept up with him around the curve and all during the next straightaway.

"Go, Tatum! Go!" Maddie stayed in her spot, jumping up and down and motioning for Tatum to pass Cole. "Faster!"

Ashley and Kari stopped walking and turned so they could see the race. Cole edged in front of Tatum, and gradually a full bike length separated them. Then, without warning, Cole's front tire began to wobble, and before Ashley could warn him, both tires slid out from under him, and the bike crashed onto its side.

"Cole!" Ashley took a step in his direction, but at the same instant, she saw him sit up and brush off his arms.

"He's okay." Kari touched Ashley's arm. "Wait a minute."

The instant Tatum realized what had happened, she braked hard and jumped off her bike, dropping it to the ground. She was at Cole's side in seconds, lifting his bike off him and waiting until he was on his feet and could take it from her.

Kari was right; Cole was fine. He might have skinned his elbow, but he could walk, and he didn't look like he was in pain. The accident had happened just ten yards from where Ashley was standing, so she could see that Cole's cheeks were red again as he brushed himself off. But she could also hear Tatum's clear, sweet voice.

"Are you okay?" She pointed to his elbow. "I think you're bleeding."

Cole twisted around and looked at his arm. "It's okay. Just a scrape." He filled his cheeks with air and released it slowly.

From a ways down the track, Maddie was running in their direction. "It's a do-over. That doesn't count!"

Tatum giggled when she heard her friend. She looked at Cole and shrugged. "You win. You were going to anyway."

"Nah, Maddie's right. I fell, so that means you woulda won." Cole pulled his bike close and climbed on it. He was careful to anchor his feet on either side, steadying himself. He grinned at Tatum. "How 'bout it's a tie?"

Ashley's heart soared. Cole was actually bending a little, letting his competitiveness go, at least for a few minutes. "That a boy, Cole," she whispered.

A smile lit up Tatum's face too. "Perfect."

Maddie ran past Ashley and Kari, and after a few more strides, she reached her cousin and her friend. "A tie? Tatum, not a tie! You coulda won." She reached Cole and patted him on the back. "Even if you didn't fall, she coulda won, right?"

Cole smiled at Tatum. "Maybe."

"But it doesn't matter." Tatum climbed back on her bike. "Let's do more warm-up laps."

Maddie ran alongside Tatum and Cole, and the topic turned to their respective plans for summer vacation in a few months. When they reached Maddie's bike, Cole and Tatum stopped, and then—without any further talk of racing—they continued on their way.

"I think you're right about Cole." Kari began walking again. Inside the stroller, RJ was stirring.

"That he's actually making progress being nice to girls?"

"No." Kari laughed. "About the crush he has on Tatum."

Ashley rolled her eyes, and the conversation shifted. This time they didn't talk about trials past or those that might still lie ahead. After all, in just a few weeks, she and Kari would know whether they were having boys or girls. Then they could begin planning their nurseries and getting ready for a couple of August birthdays.

Whatever God had intended her to gain from the Scripture verse, she was sure it wasn't some sort of ominous sign. Truth was truth, for the past and for every tomorrow. God Almighty would indeed make good out of everything for those who loved Him. Whether that meant a bike spill in the middle of a race around a high school track or figuring out how to let a child as precious as Cole take the next step toward growing up.

One way or another, there would be trials.

But for now, Ashley wouldn't spend another minute thinking about that. Not when the spring stretching out before her and Kari was nothing but sunshine and smiles; not when her favorite time of year was right around the corner—another warm, endless summer.

And with Dayne a part of their family and the babies on the way, Ashley had a feeling it would be the very best summer of all.

CHAPTER THREE

JENNY FLANIGAN SET her stadium seat firmly on the third row of the bleachers behind home plate and focused her attention on the Reds, who were warming up in the field. Specifically she watched Ricky, the youngest of her six kids. He was playing shortstop today, and there was no question he had on his game face. Only a bit of his blond bangs fell onto his forehead from beneath his baseball cap.

"Over here, Cole!" Ricky shouted at Ashley and Landon's son. He bit his lip and held up his glove. Cole winged the ball at him, and Ricky grabbed it, pretending to tag out a runner before he fired it to the catcher.

"Come on, Reds," Ricky yelled to his teammates. "Let's do this!"

Jenny smiled. Sports would always be a part of their lives, the way they had been since she married Jim. She'd gone from sitting in the stands cheering for her NFL-playing husband to cheering for her kids, but it was a role she wouldn't have traded. Already Ricky had swapped his T-ball uniform for coach pitch and his coach pitch gear for the official Little League uniform he wore now.

Cole waved his arms, and Jenny turned. Ashley and Landon were making their way up the hill toward the ball diamond. Landon pushed a stroller, and Ashley wore a camera around her neck. She waved back.

Cole was playing first base, so he and Ricky would work closely together today. It was the last Friday in March, and the sun beat down on the field, warming it up enough that the fans needed only light jackets. At least until the sun started to set.

"How long's the game?" Bailey, her oldest and only daughter, was sitting beside her, texting someone on her cell phone. She wore a thin sweater and sunglasses, her long, light brown hair pulled back in a ponytail.

"Hour and a half, maybe two." Jenny smiled. "You brought a jacket, right?"

"I did." She pointed to her backpack a row beneath her. "Is Dad coming?"

"After weight lifting." In Jenny's perfect world, the entire family would be together this afternoon for Ricky's game. But Connor was with the Reed family, shopping for sheet music for the upcoming CKT auditions, and her next three boys were working out with their soccer team, getting ready for the summer tournaments. For now it was just her and Bailey.

"Is Dad bringing Cody?" Bailey lowered her phone and leaned against Jenny's shoulder. "I miss him now that weight lifting's started."

"I think so." Jenny put her arm around Bailey's shoulders. She and Jim had watched with caution the friendship growing between Bailey and Cody Coleman. He'd been living with them for nearly a year, but last November he'd nearly killed himself through alcohol poisoning. He was still attending his rehab classes, and he'd made tremendous progress in every area of his life—his grades, his social decisions, and his commitment to sports. His turnaround had been so complete that he might even have the chance to play college football after all—at a junior college in Indianapolis.

But he wasn't the guy for Bailey, at least not the way Jenny and Jim saw things.

Bailey was texting again, her fingers flying over the keypad on her flip phone. Jenny was about to ask who she was chatting with when Ashley and Landon reached the bleachers and took their seats.

"Good." Ashley sighed and situated herself on a thick blanket. "We didn't miss anything."

Landon lifted little Devin from the stroller and took the seat beside his wife. "I'm trying to schedule my shifts at the firehouse around the games." He smiled at Jenny. "Cole doesn't think he can hit the ball if I'm not here."

The teams were each gathered around their coaches, standing outside their respective dugouts, listening to whatever last-minute advice might make a difference in the game. The Reds were in the field first, and the fans around Jenny and Bailey clapped and cheered.

"Let's go, Reds!" Jenny stood and raised her voice. "Give it your best, guys!" She noticed that Ashley stayed seated, her clapping more subdued than it had been during basketball season.

Landon gave Jenny a wry look. "I've toned her down a little."

"I can see that." Jenny sat back on the bleachers. "Better to start small in these things."

Ashley and Landon laughed and turned their attention to finding a bottle for Devin.

Bailey was still texting. "Makes me so mad," she muttered. "How stupid can you be?"

"Something wrong?" Jenny leaned closer to her daughter. She couldn't read the text window in Bailey's phone, but she didn't need to. Bailey shared everything with her. Especially now that Bryan Smythe was no longer in her life.

"Marissa." Bailey hit the Send button and snapped her phone shut. "She went to that clinic by the university, the one that gives out free birth control pills."

"Marissa Young?" Jenny felt the shock to her core. Marissa and Bailey had grown up together, friends since their first day of

Sunday school at Bloomington Community Church. They'd been inseparable until Bailey started doing theater with CKT her freshman year. At that time, Marissa had played volleyball and run track. But this year she'd dropped out of both sports—at least that's what her mother had said when they'd run into each other a month ago.

Bailey ran her fingers through her bangs. Their conversation was quiet enough that even Ashley and Landon couldn't hear them. "She's dating this college guy, someone she met through Facebook."

"I thought Facebook was just for college kids." Jenny knew about the Web site, same as she knew about MySpace. Lots of Bailey's friends had gotten in trouble one way or another from having profiles on MySpace.

"Not anymore. Now she's got this college boyfriend, and it isn't good."

Jenny winced. "She wants birth control?"

"She does now. The guy talked her into sleeping with him last weekend."

The hurt in Jenny's heart was as strong as if she'd heard the news about one of her own kids. "Oh, Bailey . . . I'm sorry. Marissa was a virgin, wasn't she?"

"One of the last." Bailey dug her elbows into her knees and stared at the baseball field. "Sometimes I feel like I'm the only one who cares, Mom. The only one left."

Jenny was careful with her answer. Her daughter's feelings were real and couldn't be easily dismissed with assurances that she wasn't the only teenage girl desiring to save herself for marriage. Jenny ran her hand along Bailey's back. "The right choices are never easy, honey."

"Yeah, and then there's Alec. He smoked hookah with half the baseball team every weekend, and now that the season's started, he's switched to taking speed." She looked at Jenny. "Speed! Can you believe it? How crazy is that? He says he's stopped, but whatever. He always lies to me."

The blood drained from Jenny's face. Alec's parents were also friends of hers and Jim's. "That's serious, Bailey."

"I know. In health class we learned how you can have a heart attack or a stroke taking the stuff. You could even die right there on the spot." She crossed her arms and straightened again. "It's like I have fewer friends every week."

Jenny had to agree. "What about Tim Reed? He's trying out for the next CKT show, right? He's always been a good friend."

"He's trying out, but I don't know." She waved her hand in the air. "I barely hear from him anymore."

On the field, with runners at second and third, the batter connected with the ball and sent it straight toward Ricky. He caught the ball off its first hop, tagged out the runner leaving second base, and fired the ball to the catcher.

"Double play!" Jenny was on her feet again. "Way to go, Ricky! Good work, Reds!"

Cole and the other Reds were hooting and howling their approval at Ricky. Those two outs made three, and the Reds were up to bat.

Jenny sat back down and thought about what Bailey had told her. A quick phone call and she could be in a conversation with either Marissa's or Alec's mother. She'd want them to call her if it were Bailey making those kinds of choices.

But Jenny had no real proof other than what the kids had told Bailey. Once, two years ago, Alec had lied to his parents and gone to a party where there was drinking.

Jenny found out about it and called his mother. The woman's response had not been what Jenny expected, and she would always remember the hurtful comments spoken that night.

"I can handle my son, Jenny Flanigan." Alec's mother's tone was beyond irritated. "With six kids, you might have enough to worry about without keeping tabs on other people's children."

It was the last time Jenny had ever betrayed her daughter's confidence. When Bailey told her about the kids at school, she didn't hurry to the phone to call one of their parents, and she wouldn't. Not unless one of Bailey's friends was in danger. If Alec had promised to stop with the drugs, that would have to be enough for now. Same with Marissa. At this point, telling Marissa's mother would only bring a heartache Marissa apparently wasn't ready to share with her mother.

Even so, Jenny wanted to stay up on the situation. She drew a long breath. "Marissa needs to get away from the guy, and she needs to tell her mom."

"I know. I told her that."

"And?" Jenny slid closer to her daughter, her voice still low.

"She says she's going to marry him. And she'll tell her mom when she's ready."

A sigh slipped from Jenny's heart. Ricky was up to bat, and Jenny glanced over her shoulder. Jim and Cody were jogging over the hill, trying to reach the bleachers before Ricky took his first pitch.

Bailey clapped. "Let's go, Ricky! Keep your eyes on the ball."

Jim hurried across the grass, his eyes on Ricky. "Like I told you, buddy. Nice and easy."

In an instant, everything about Ricky's posture looked more confident, more determined. He glanced back at Jim and grinned; then he squared up to the plate and squinted at the pitcher.

Jim reached the chain-link backstop, a few yards from the batter's box. He stayed quiet as the first pitch flew over the plate for a strike.

"Way to get a look, Ricky." Cole's voice came from the dugout. "The next one's yours."

The words and sounds and springtime air were as familiar as breathing, and they made Jenny relax, made her forget for a few minutes the battles Bailey was facing. This was the favorite time of year for the Flanigan family. A time when the rigors of football season were still half a year away, and the boys had only the weekly soccer practice and baseball games. Summer was within reach, and the days grew longer and warmer with every passing sunset.

Years of following her family through sports had helped Jenny have perspective. She would cheer, but she would forget the details as soon as she left the park. The games were fun and exciting, and like today, they were the highlight of their week. But still, they were just games. The outcome didn't matter nearly as much as the experience.

Chatter came from the opposing team's dugout. "Hey, batter, batter, batter. . . . Hey, batter."

The next pitch was another strike.

Ricky stepped out of the batter's box and practiced his swing a few times. Then he positioned himself over the plate once more. This time he swung with all his might and connected with the pitch just enough to send it bouncing toward third base. Ricky dropped his bat and raced for first, beating the throw by less than a second.

"Way to go, Ricky!" Jim pumped his fist and gave a few hearty claps. Then he turned and jogged up the bleachers to his place on the other side of Jenny. He kissed her cheek and smiled at her. "How's the most beautiful woman in Bloomington?"

"Hey . . ." Bailey gave him a pretend frown. "What about me?"

He blew her a kiss. "You, my dear, are the most beautiful *girl* in Bloomington. The other honor—" he looked at Jenny again—"will always go to my wife."

Jenny laughed. "Must've been a good day in the weight room."

"Cody helped a few of the juniors, and I must say, the guys are looking good. Much stronger than the team last year at this time." He slipped his hand around Jenny's waist. "Maybe the no-drinking policy's actually making a difference."

"I hope so."

The team had ridden a roller coaster of emotions since Cody's near death from drinking. Other players had come forward and confessed to drinking, and Jim had held a meeting, making each player sign a contract that he wouldn't drink again or he'd be kicked off the team. Things had looked good until Jim caught a few of his players drinking at a New Year's Eve party. They were eliminated from the squad, but rumor had it their parents had formed an angry voice, calling for Jim's job.

All of it was speculation at this point, but Jenny was worried. Not that Jim needed the coaching job at Clear Creek High, but he loved it. If the administration buckled and let him go, Jim would have to seriously think about returning to a coaching position with the NFL, and that would mean moving out of Bloomington.

Jenny didn't want to think about it. Not yet.

Cole was up, and though he tipped a few of the pitches, he struck out. He started to walk back to the dugout, dejected, but his eyes caught Landon's.

"Good job, Cole." Landon gave his son a thumbs-up. "You'll get it next time."

Like Ricky had, Cole stood a little straighter, and a smile tugged at his lips. He nodded and returned the gesture to his dad.

Again Jenny felt reassurance. The ritual of sports had its downsides, its ugly moments and times when anyone involved might wonder about the point. But watching these little boys and their dads build closer bonds made it clear that good came from sports too.

Much good.

Since Jim arrived, Cody had been standing off to the side, watching the game. Now he caught Bailey's eye and motioned for her to join him.

She slid her phone into her jeans pocket and stepped lightly down the bleachers and over to him.

Cody gave her a side hug and a smile that clearly came from deep inside him. His eyes sparkled as he said something to Bailey that Jenny couldn't hear above the noise of the game.

"How come Bailey's eyes didn't light up like that when I talked to her?" Jim was teasing, and his tone said as much. But Jenny knew him well enough to know he wasn't entirely kidding.

Jenny slid a little closer to her husband. "Pray for her. Things aren't easy right now."

"More trouble with friends?"

"Yes." Jenny turned her attention back to the game. One of the Reds hit a triple, sending Ricky around second, third, and sliding into home.

The Reds fans were on their feet. It was the first run of the season, and all the games lay spread out before them like so many possibilities.

Jenny waited until the cheering died down. Then she leaned in so only Jim could hear her. "Marissa Young told Bailey she's sleeping with some college guy, someone she met online."

Jim slumped forward and sighed. He closed his eyes. "She was over at Christmastime. Talking about how glad she was that she and Bailey shared the same values."

"I know. She wants to tell her mom when the time's right, but maybe I should say something to her mother first. I want to talk to Bailey about it later." She waited a beat, then told Jim about Alec and the experiments he was doing with drugs. "He says he's stopped, but the situation has Bailey down. All that and her CKT friends haven't called in a while. She's feeling lonely."

"Which leaves Bailey a lot of time for Cody." Jim looked at their daughter and the young football player beside her. The two of them were laughing about something.

At that moment, Bailey glanced up at them. "Cody and I are taking a walk to the playground." She smiled. "We won't be long."

Jenny opened her mouth to say something, but Jim gave her a gentle nudge. "It's okay," he whispered. Then he waved to the teenagers. "Don't be long. You'll wanna see the Reds' next ups."

Bailey nodded, and then she and Cody were off.

Jenny groaned. "Really, Jim. We should at least try to discourage them."

"They're just friends. I've seen the way Cody acts around girls he's interested in, the way he looks at them." Jim narrowed his eyes and watched his daughter for a few seconds. "It's different with Bailey. Cody respects her. He's treating her like a friend, even if he might like to think about dating her."

"I hope so." Jenny's doubts made her feel guilty. Cody was a nice kid, but he was an alcoholic, and he'd always be one. Whatever girl married Cody, she would spend the rest of her life praying that he stayed away from drinking. It wasn't a role she wanted Bailey to have to play. Not now or ever.

"It doesn't really matter." Jim looked at the field again. "Cody's still planning to enlist after graduation."

"I thought he had a chance to play for a junior college?"

"He does." Jim shrugged. "I think the army thing's gotten into his blood. Maybe it matters more to him than football."

Jenny pondered that for a few minutes.

The Reds were in the field again, and a play was in progress. Cole stretched as far as his legs would go to catch a throw from third base for an out. The Reds celebrated the play, the cheering and clapping and little-boy voices filling the air. Again the sound was comforting.

With Bailey getting older, so much of life felt unsettling and new, taking Jenny and Jim into territories they'd never walked through before. When Bailey was little, the answers had been easy. *Yes, you can stay up late to watch a movie,* and *no, you can't go out to play until your room is clean. Yes, you can spend the night at this friend's house,* and *no, you can't walk to the park with that one.* Jenny could hear herself meting out wisdom as quickly as it was needed.

But now things seemed so much more complicated. How could she help Bailey get by in this difficult season, when following God's plan for her life made her feel isolated and friendless? And should she do more to discourage Bailey's friendship with Cody?

Jenny closed her eyes and sucked in the cool air. *God, send the answers. Please . . .* She let the silent prayer sit for a while, echoing in the hallways of her heart. Somehow direction and wisdom would come, because God would bring them. He would walk her and Jim down the unknown path before them and give them the answers that seemed so elusive.

She opened her eyes just as Ricky caught a pop-up for the third out. A smile filled her soul. God wouldn't only give them answers; He would give them a reason to cheer.

Now and always.

CHAPTER FOUR

JOHN BAXTER SETTLED into his favorite booth at Grazie! and stared across the restaurant to where Elaine Denning stood just outside the door, talking to her daughter on her cell phone.

John didn't mind waiting. Every once in a while, a few unexpected minutes alone like this were good for him, a chance to take stock of his life and how God was bringing all of the people he loved into a season of warm days and sunshine.

Not just with the upcoming summer weather. But in life.

From outside the Italian restaurant, Elaine

peered through the glass and found him. She was still on the phone, and she held up one finger and made a worried face. He waved at her, silently telling her he was fine, and she could take her time. She nodded and focused again on the call.

John exhaled, and the blessings in his life filled his heart and head. His oldest son, Dayne Matthews, had married the woman he loved, the one he'd been taken with since the day he first saw her. They were home from their honeymoon, starting life in the house they owned on the shore of Lake Monroe. His daughters were all married to wonderful men, raising families and providing him with a constant stream of humorous stories and charming anecdotes about his grandkids. And his son Luke was a full-fledged attorney, working in Indianapolis exclusively on Dayne's affairs. On top of that, his middle daughters, Ashley and Kari, were both expecting babies within a week of each other at the end of August.

John watched Elaine snap her phone shut and hurry through the door. He leaned forward, his elbows on the table, and studied her. The dark clouds of his past were lifting, and maybe the strongest reason was the woman coming toward him.

She reached the table and took the seat across from him. "Sorry." She was breathless, and she shook her head. "All that to say my granddaughter's out of the hospital."

"The pneumonia's gone?"

"It's better. She's on antibiotics. Getting lots of rest." Elaine set her purse on the spot beside her.

"Out of the woods, anyway."

"Yes." Elaine looked around. She drew a long breath. "I love this place."

I love being here with you, John thought. But he stopped himself from saying so. Instead he smiled. "Me too."

They checked their menus and talked about what they'd eaten the last time they were here.

After the waiter took their order, Elaine sipped her water and looked at him. Her eyes danced, the way they did more often these days. "What are you thinking about?" She tilted her head, her words unhurried.

"You." John smiled. "How much I enjoy being with you."

The lighting made it impossible to tell if

she was blushing. But her cheeks seemed darker than before. She set her water down and laughed.

"Oh, good." John pretended to be hurt. "Just the reaction I was looking for."

"No." Elaine waved her hand. She was laughing harder now. "It's not that." She worked to find her composure. "It's just . . . it's taken a lot of work."

John blinked. "Meaning . . . ?"

She covered her mouth, stifling another round of giggles. "Sorry." She forced a straight face, but her eyes still twinkled. "Meaning we've been doing this—" she looked around as if the answer hung somewhere in the air above their table— "whatever it is we've been doing, for almost two years. Between your kids and mine and the busyness of our own lives . . ." She shrugged. "I don't know. I guess it feels like it took a long time to get here."

"Here?" Understanding dawned on the horizon of John's heart. He hesitated. "At a place where I can tell you how I feel?"

"Yes." Her tone was tender, blending with what remained of the humor from a moment earlier. She reached across the table and took his hands. "I wasn't laughing at you, just at us. Two adults in our sixties afraid to tell each other how we feel."

The feel of her hands around his did strange things to him. She wasn't being critical or complaining. Only recognizing the situation for what it was. He cocked his head. "It's complicated."

"That's true." Her laughter dropped off. She paused, studying him. "When we dreamed about our separate stories all those years ago, we never planned that the main characters would be missing."

"No."

"But here we are." Elaine gave his hands a squeeze and then released them. "And I couldn't agree with you more, John Baxter. I enjoy being with you also."

Long into the meal John wondered about her statement, about her laughter at his admission that he enjoyed spending time with her. He'd nearly lost her friendship once—when her closeness had scared him away. But now, in light of her reaction, he wasn't afraid of her. He was afraid of himself, afraid he might've given her the permanent impression that he wasn't interested in her outside of being her friend.

When the fact was, that had changed. He

was interested and getting more interested all the time.

Their meal was unhurried and marked with easy laughter over Cole's latest challenge to his cousin Maddie—that he'd hit more home runs this season than her—and concern about Dayne and Katy and how their participation in a reality show might actually hurt their relationship more than it would create a peace offering for the paparazzi.

When they were finished, John drove Elaine home and walked her up the brick path to her house. He held her hand, the way he did more often these days. It would be an early night; he had work in the morning, and she had to make phone calls for a charity auction she was helping chair. Still, John didn't want the day to slip away without his saying something to clarify how he'd come across at dinner.

It was almost sunset, and April's mild afternoon had given way to a cool breeze. The smells of roses and fresh-cut grass lingered in the air between them as they reached the door. John's heart beat hard against his chest, and he thought about telling her later.

But before he could bid her a quick good-bye and hurry down the walk, she turned to him. "Your hands are sweaty."

Heat shot through his veins and into his cheeks. He let go of her fingers and wiped his palms on his pants. "Sorry."

"It's okay." Elaine searched his eyes. Her voice held a calm that gave him the courage to stay. "What's on your mind?"

John swallowed. Maybe he wasn't ready to share his feelings. Maybe they weren't feelings at all but fleeting thoughts. But then why did he want nothing more than to hold her hand again?

She was waiting patiently for his answer, her lips slightly curved in a smile that told him perhaps she already knew what he was trying to find the nerve to say.

He cleared his throat. "Earlier, when I told you I enjoyed being with you . . ."

Elaine took hold of his hands and ran her thumbs along the sides of them. "I didn't mean to laugh."

"I know, but . . ." John closed his eyes and drew a long breath. When he opened them, when he saw her standing before him, a sudden burst of knowing filled his heart. He straightened. "Elaine, I care a great deal for you." He paused, and for a moment he didn't breathe. "Far more than I would care for a friend." Cars passed by on the street behind him, and a few houses down, a group of children were jumping rope in a driveway, their voices loud and happy. But John barely heard any of it. He gently squeezed her hands. "Do you understand what I'm telling you?"

"I think so." A blush warmed her expression, and a smile crept up her cheeks. She suddenly looked more like a shy schoolgirl than the confident woman she'd been just a few minutes ago. "Are you saying you have intentions?"

Intentions. John's soul soared at the word. That was exactly what he'd been feeling. A chuckle started low in his gut and became a full laugh.

"Oh?" Elaine raised her brow, and a teasing look came over her. "Now I'm the funny one?"

John shook his head and found his composure again. "Sorry, it's just . . ." He shrugged. "All night I've been trying to find a way to say that. Maybe for a few weeks now. And it took you three seconds to figure it out."

"Really?" Elaine's expression softened. "You do?"

"Yes." He slipped his fingers between

hers. "I don't know what my intentions are just yet." He didn't want to make her angry or ruin the mood, but he wanted to be clear. He carefully chose each word. "But I have them, and they remind me all the time that I feel more for you than friendship. I wanted to tell you before another day went by."

Elaine looked deep into him, beyond the silliness and awkward moments that had marked this turning point for them. "We can take our time."

Something about the idea didn't sit well with John. If he and Elaine were going to get closer, if they were going to share something beyond friendship, then why would they take their time? They'd known each other for more than a decade, and they shared everything that mattered—their faith, their love for family, and their feelings for each other. He thought about saying so, but the admission felt like too much for now.

Instead he smiled at her. "I have intentions toward you, Elaine Denning."

A sparkle lit up her eyes. "And I toward you."

John pulled her close and hugged her, and the warmth of her worked its way through him, to the coldest dark corners of his heart. He wasn't going to kiss her, had never planned on it when he thought about how this night might end. But as he drew slightly back, before he might release her, he touched his lips to hers and she responded.

Their kiss didn't last long—a few heartbeats at the most. But it ignited in John a sense of hope and love and longing he hadn't expected to ever feel again. He brushed his knuckles tenderly against her cheeks. "Talk to you tomorrow."

Elaine cupped her hand around his. "Good night."

He must've floated back to the car, because he didn't remember taking a single step. He was halfway down her street before he reminded himself to breathe. He wanted to laugh and cry and shout out loud in thanks to God that somehow—through the darkest of nights—the Lord had led him to a place of new life, new love. He never would've chosen this. Elaine wouldn't have either.

But it was here all the same.

He had told Elaine his feelings and finished the night with a kiss, and now his whole world felt different. Fresh and full of possibility. His mind raced with the implications. Even though all this felt strange at his age, and even though he'd never intended to do this again, he and Elaine were officially dating.

The statement settled from his heart to his gut. That meant his kids would need to know, and what about the rest? If he had feelings for Elaine and intentions toward her, and if he was aware they didn't have any reason to wait, wouldn't something far more serious be right around the corner? If he and Elaine married, changes would be inevitable. The way they marked Elizabeth's birthday and their anniversary and the day she died. And what about Christmas and Thanksgiving and the Fourth of July? Over the past few years, Elaine had been a guest with the Baxter family, but she would be entitled to her own traditions and ideas.

And something else would have to change. He and Elaine could never start their marriage in the old Baxter house. Not with memories of Elizabeth filling every room, her presence woven into the colors on the walls and the things she'd collected over the years. He pictured his belongings in boxes, a For Sale sign anchored in the ground in front of the old house.

Suddenly his intentions felt flimsy and uncertain. John slowed his car as the lights from his front porch came into view. He turned in and rode the brakes up the driveway, his eyes on the house. The changes ahead of him felt like so many towering mountains and this—the familiar and warm and loved—like the oasis he never wanted to leave.

He opened the garage, parked, and trudged through the house to his bedroom. No matter how much fun they'd had tonight, no matter how badly he didn't want to lose Elaine, the reality lay here. In the home he and Elizabeth had spent a lifetime building.

The house was too quiet. John turned on the radio in his room and checked his four favorite channels. All commercials. He flicked the machine off and let out a long breath. He had work in the morning, but it was only eight o'clock. And the idea of watching something mindless and numbing on TV did nothing for him.

Then, the way he had done so many times since Elizabeth died, he remembered her letters. The box full of correspondence between him and Elizabeth over the years. Most of the letters were written by her, and a number of times he'd meant to copy them and put them in scrapbooks for his kids. He had even planned to compile the scrapbooks for Dayne and Katy's wedding, but he hadn't finished. The task always seemed too daunting, too emotionally draining.

But here, at the brink of a new season, he owed it to his children.

He went to his closet and moved the box onto their bed. Even still it smelled like her, his precious Elizabeth. He peered into the box at the letters on top—the ones he'd found and read in the years since her death. Nothing would make the job an easy one, but he needed to go through them. He would take each one, read it, and decide whether it belonged in the pile of letters to be copied for their kids.

And in the process he would hold on to Elizabeth a little while longer.

He sat on the edge of the bed next to the box and went quickly through the few letters on top. Each of them needed to be copied, and he placed them on the bedspread. Those first letters talked about her ten rules for a happy marriage and her love for her children, her hopes and prayers and plans for them. Peace surrounded him, because this was the right thing to do, the best way he knew to keep himself from thinking about what had happened with Elaine half an hour earlier.

Now that he'd cleared away the top layer, John spotted an envelope slightly larger than the others. The paper was thicker, and he wondered if it was one of the birthday cards Elizabeth had given him. He reached for it and smiled. She had been a celebrator of birthdays, a maker of moments. No birthday had passed without her marking the occasion with her thoughts on the year past.

He opened the envelope and pulled out a card, one that looked nearly brand-new. The front said only *My lover, my friend. . . .*

Pain and a sense of betrayal over his dinner with Elaine pricked at John's heart. Elizabeth had indeed been his lover and friend.

The card was similar to most Elizabeth would pick out. A brief birthday greeting with a full page of her own handwritten sentiments. He checked the date. The card wasn't old. Which meant . . . when she wrote it she might've just had the first signs that her cancer had returned.

He steadied his hands and found the first line.

Dearest John,
How blessed I am to be celebrating another year of your life. Even the act of buying this card made me smile, because I never take the years for granted. Never.

John ran his finger over the words and pictured Elizabeth browsing the cards, looking for one with plenty of white space. He kept reading.

I think of how many couples don't get the years God has given us, and I am grateful beyond words. Because you've spent your years defining life for me, John. The way you laugh with me and hold my hand on our long Sunday afternoon walks. In some ways with you it feels like we never get a day older. But that's what birthdays are for, I guess. Little reminders that as good as this is, it won't last forever.

John's throat felt thick. Had she known about the return of her cancer when she wrote this? He looked at the framed photo of the two of them, the one that had stood on their dresser for as long as he could remember. *No, Elizabeth . . . it won't last forever.*

He found his place again.

And so my wish for you this year comes from Deuteronomy, my love. You know it, because you've shared it with me and the kids so many times. Here it is: "I have set before you life and death, blessings and curses. Now choose life, so that you and your children may live."

We're not as young as we once were, and I want you to know, whatever happens in the years to come, you must choose life. We both must. Every day we wake up with another twenty-four hours.

Happy birthday, sweetheart.

I love you always.

Elizabeth

Choose life?

A shiver ran down John's arms as he

reread that last part. She was referring to their lives together; she must've been. But that's not how her words came across now, in light of the day's events. *Whatever happens in the years to come, you must choose life. . . .*

John lowered the card to his lap and closed his eyes. This had happened before—times when he needed wisdom, when he was missing Elizabeth, and God had led him to one of her letters, the exact one he needed to find peace. But this . . .

He opened his eyes and found her photo again. Had she known? Had she imagined a time down the road when she might no longer be here and he would need more than anything to hear this very Bible verse?

He returned the card to the envelope and placed it at the top of the stack of letters to be copied. Her picture was calling to him, so he went to it and took it in his hands. Her eyes were just as he remembered them, blue enough to fall into. She was like no other woman, no other friend or lover he would ever have.

But she was gone.

And her letter reminded him of what he desperately needed to hold on to. The knowledge that Elizabeth would've wanted him to do exactly what he'd done today— share his feelings with Elaine, tell her about his intentions, allow himself to move forward. In that moment he knew what Elizabeth would be doing if somewhere in heaven she could know the intentions he had toward a woman who had been one of her friends.

She'd be smiling.

CHAPTER FIVE

ASHLEY BABYSAT FOR little Ryan Junior the morning Kari went in for her ultrasound. The minutes passed slowly even though Devin and RJ kept her busy. Kari was having a girl. Ashley would've bet on it. They both were. It was something she'd thought since the beginning.

Finally, just before noon, she watched Kari and Ryan pull up outside and climb out of the car. They were both grinning, and Kari hurried Ryan along. Ashley held her breath. RJ and Devin were sleeping, so she moved quietly from her place at the window to the entryway.

Kari's words were out the moment Ashley opened the door. "We're having a girl!" Kari rushed inside and hugged her; then just as quickly she drew back and gently placed her hand on the small bump at Ashley's waist. "Maybe you're right and you're having a girl too!"

"You've got Kari convinced." Ryan stepped inside. He laughed and shook his head. "She already has the two girls dressing alike for the first day of kindergarten."

Ashley giggled and placed her hand over Kari's. "I can't explain it." She lifted one shoulder. "I just had this feeling we were both having girls. I even told my doctor that at my appointment last week. I asked if it was true that sometimes a mother just knows what she's having."

"And?" Ryan seemed amused by the planning and dreaming going on between the two sisters.

Ashley made a face. "She said there was no way to tell until the ultrasound."

"Which is in a week." Kari kept her voice low. The sleeping boys were across the living room, side by side. "I can't wait."

"Landon says I'm obsessed. I'm counting down the hours." Ashley grinned. She and

Kari talked for a few minutes, and then Ashley left.

Over the next few days when they walked the track, Ashley allowed herself to dream aloud about the possibility that they were each having a girl. "They'll be closer than sisters. Like twins almost."

Kari easily got caught up in the excitement. "I can picture us helping them buy prom dresses and remembering back to this time."

They talked about everything from the babies' first steps to the weddings the girls might have in the same year, and as the days grew closer for Ashley's ultrasound, she was convinced. Something about this pregnancy was different, and that could leave just one explanation. She was having a girl.

The night before Ashley's test, Kari called before she turned in. "Jessie's thrilled about having a sister. Well, actually, thrilled doesn't touch it. She was bouncing all over the house. She made up a song about finally having a sister."

Ashley was already in bed, more tired than usual, but she smiled in the dark. "I wish I could've heard it." She thought for a few seconds. "If I'm right about this one, Cole's reaction will probably be a little more subdued."

"Hmmm." Kari's laughter faded. "He still wants a brother?"

"He wants an entire basketball team."

They both giggled, though the topic stayed with Ashley after the call ended and as she tried to fall asleep. She'd even tried to broach the subject with Cole again. "God might have a sister for you, Coley. That would be okay, right? Even if she didn't play basketball?"

"Well—" Cole had been digging into a bowl of Cheerios—"I already asked God for a brother, so thanks, Mom, for trying to make me ready for the bad news. But I think you're wrong." He pointed to her stomach. "That's a boy in there. I'm pretty sure."

Landon told her not to worry. "Cole would love a girl. He'd be the best big brother ever."

She fell asleep praying that her son would understand if the news in the morning wasn't what he was hoping for.

When the alarm went off Monday morning, Ashley hit the Off button and reached for Landon's hand. "It's here. The first ultrasound."

"Mmmm." He turned onto his side so he

was facing her. "We don't need the test, Ash." His eyes were still closed. "It's a girl. You already called it."

Ashley grinned and put her hand on her abdomen. She felt like shouting for joy. The day had finally come. Today she would know whether she was right. She climbed out of bed and slipped into a pair of stretch pants. She was ready in half the time it usually took, but even in her rush, she felt calm and relaxed. Cole might be right. She might be having a boy. And even if she was carrying a girl, Cole would of course get used to the fact. She had nothing to fear.

Ashley was buttoning her sweater, checking her look one more time, when the phone rang. From the kitchen, where Landon was making breakfast for the boys, she heard him call, "I'll get it."

Ashley smiled. Landon was a great dad, a great husband. He never complained about helping with the boys or going the extra distance to make her feel comfortable. He was always one step ahead of her.

"Ashley." He walked down the hallway and into their bedroom. His brow was knit, his eyes veiled in concern. "It's the doctor."

She wrinkled her nose as she took the

phone. The doctor would be seeing them later this morning. Why would she call now? Ashley pressed the receiver to her ear. "Hello?"

"Ashley . . . this is Dr. Amy McDaniel." She paused. "You're still coming in today for your ultrasound, right?"

"I am." Ashley's heart pounded, and her throat felt dry. Landon was waiting a few feet away. "Is something wrong?"

"Well, I'm not sure."

Ashley braced herself against the dresser and hung her head. Nothing was wrong; it couldn't be. She refused the doctor's words and forced herself to listen for the explanation. The explanation that had to be coming.

"Your alpha-fetoprotein test came back high." The doctor's tone grew reassuring. "That might not mean anything, but with a high AFP test, we like to make sure you're not alone at the ultrasound. In case we find a problem."

Ashley's mind was racing. "AFP? That's the blood test I took last time I was in?"

"Yes." Dr. McDaniel was a mother herself. She had five kids and a fantastic bedside manner. She had delivered several of the Baxter babies. But her normally upbeat attitude was greatly subdued today. She sighed. "We use the AFP as a way of screening for a number of issues."

AFP. Ashley closed her eyes and thought back to the days when she'd returned from France, pregnant and single and afraid, and sat in a doctor's office with her mother. Yes, that's where she'd heard this before. "Wait." She opened her eyes. Landon moved closer beside her, his face paler than before. She reached for his hand. "I had a high AFP test with my first child—with Cole."

"And he was healthy?"

"Very much so." Ashley felt herself begin to relax.

"Okay, good." The doctor sounded somewhat relieved. "Ninety percent of the time a high AFP test means nothing. Either way, you'll be bringing someone today?"

"Yes." She looked at Landon. "My husband."

"Very well. We'll see you at eleven, then."

Ashley hung up and tried to give Landon a reassuring look. "My AFP test was high, same as it was for Cole."

"Oh." Landon blinked. He still looked nervous. "I haven't heard of that before."

"Me either. Not before Cole, anyway." She set the phone down on the dresser and slipped her arms around Landon's waist. "That time I was with my mom at the doctor's office. I remember being scared to death when they told me." She thought for a moment. "My mom called my dad, and he told me not to worry. Just because it's high doesn't mean anything's wrong."

Landon linked his hands near the small of her back. "I'm sure it's nothing." He leaned in and kissed her, his lips lingering on hers. He smiled. "Let's not let it bring us down. This is the big day."

"Right." She found a tentative smile. "Exactly."

But there was no way to escape the shadow the doctor's call cast across the morning. They saw Cole off to school, and as he headed toward the front gate, he turned and waved at them. "When I get home you can tell me what my brother looks like."

"Get to school." Landon grinned and waved one last time.

They headed toward Kari's house, where Devin would spend the morning. She loved having him over, loved watching the way her own little RJ doted on his younger cousin.

The idea was that Ashley and Landon could experience the ultrasound without interruption and then go out to lunch afterwards to celebrate. But after they dropped Devin off, Ashley couldn't help but think that maybe they'd need time alone for another reason.

"You're supposed to be bouncing out of your seat with excitement." Landon was driving. He glanced at her. The hint of a smile lifted his lips. "Remember?"

"I am bouncing." She took a quick breath. "On the inside, anyway."

"Don't worry, Ash. It's nothing."

She tried to take a full breath, but it wouldn't come. "You don't know that."

"I do." He gave her a sheepish glance. "I called your dad."

"You what?" She shifted in her seat, studying him. "This morning?"

"You were taking care of Devin, and I had to hear for myself. Your dad said not to worry. He agreed with Dr. McDaniel. Ninety percent of the time a high AFP test means absolutely nothing."

A warmth filled her, soothing the anxious places in her soul. "You did that? For me?"

Landon turned into the doctor's office

parking lot. "For both of us. I trust your dad, and I knew I wouldn't stop thinking about it until I talked to him."

Ashley waited until they were parked before putting her hand on his shoulder. "Thanks, Landon. That means a lot."

"I want today to be special. We can't go in assuming the worst." He nodded toward the front door of the office building. "Let's see who's right—you or Cole."

Four other pregnant women were in the office. Ashley and Landon found two chairs together in the corner and waited for nearly a half hour before a nurse opened the door and called them in. By then Ashley had ridden a roller coaster of emotions enough times to feel nauseous about what lay ahead. Good or bad. Her father was right, of course. She'd had a high AFP test before, and it had meant nothing. There was no reason to expect the worst. But it was there, like a smell she couldn't ignore no matter how much fresh air filled the room.

Landon took her hand and led her along behind the nurse into the examination room. When they were alone and she had changed into the white cotton gown, he smiled at her. "Very attractive."

"I'm thinking about getting one for around the house." Ashley laughed, but the sound didn't ring true.

She sat on the edge of the table and crossed her bare legs. She was shivering, but the room wasn't really cold. Next to the table was the ultrasound machine, already turned on and waiting for action.

Landon took the seat across from her. "Maybe Cole's right."

"It's a boy?" She angled her head. If the doctor would just hurry so they could get past this moment, so that even the slight possibility of bad news might be something they could completely dismiss.

"Right, because a whole team of basketball players wouldn't be so bad." He rested his forearms on his knees. "Besides, I already have one princess. I couldn't dare hope for two, right?"

Before she could answer, there was a knock on the door, and Dr. McDaniel came in. She was in her late thirties, blonde and attractive. She'd delivered Devin, and at various appointments Ashley had been impressed that the doctor's office was filled with pictures from home. Her children hugging her, her family together in a boat with

Dr. McDaniel skiing behind it, and vacation photos from Hawaii. The doctor and her family went to the same church as the Baxters, and Ashley understood that her role as a doctor was something she saw as a ministry.

Even so, Dr. McDaniel was professional, and today her expression was more serious than usual. She nodded at Landon and then at Ashley. "How are we doing?"

"Good." Ashley's answer was quick. "Anxious for the test."

"You told your husband about the AFP results?" She looked from Ashley to Landon.

"Yes." Ashley shivered again. She reached back and pulled the edges of her gown a little more tightly together.

Landon cleared his throat. "I talked to Ashley's dad, Dr. John Baxter. He agreed that most of the time high levels mean nothing."

"It's true." The doctor's voice was laced with compassion. "But we have to look carefully at the ultrasound to make sure there's nothing unusual going on."

Ashley had wanted to check the Internet before they left, do a search on high levels of AFP and see what it could possibly mean. But she'd resisted the urge. It was one thing to have the high test results in the back of her mind this morning. If she had a list of possible problems, it would ruin her mood completely.

"Why don't you lie down and we'll take a look." Dr. McDaniel went to the sink and washed her hands.

Ashley did as she was told, but a lump filled her throat. *Please, God . . . not my baby. Don't let there be anything wrong with her, please.* Ashley gripped the sides of the table and realized she'd done it again. Prayed for her baby as if she knew for certain the child was a girl.

A nurse entered the room and handed the doctor a tube of gel. The younger woman smiled at Ashley but otherwise kept quiet.

Dr. McDaniel lifted the gown off Ashley's abdomen and opened the tube. "This'll be cold but only for a minute or so." She squirted a blob of the clear gel onto Ashley's stomach and reached for the ultrasound paddle.

The nurse turned up the volume on the machine. Immediately a familiar *fwup, fwup, fwup, fwup* filled the room.

A thrill raced through Ashley. She looked at Landon, and they shared a silent celebration. The baby's heartbeat sounded strong and healthy. Ashley moved her head so she could see the screen. Little feet took up the circular image. *Thank You, God . . . two feet, what looks like ten toes.* There was nothing to worry about.

Landon came to her side. He put his hand on her shoulder and stared at the screen.

"There're the feet and legs." Dr. McDaniel kept her eyes on the images. "There's nothing more beautiful than that." She clicked a button and the picture froze. She pointed to the feet. "Looks good." She shifted the paddle, and Ashley felt a sense of movement.

In the past week, she'd felt a fluttering, like butterfly wings against the inside of her belly. It had happened often enough that she was sure it was the baby, and now the feeling returned. Ashley watched the images as they changed. Movement had to be good. A baby that moved around as much as this little one must be healthy.

She checked the doctor's expression. She wasn't smiling, but then she was probably too focused on the screen to worry about how Ashley might be reading her.

Dr. McDaniel adjusted the paddle so that the image changed to the top of the baby's legs. With a few shifts in either direction, she stopped and clicked the picture frozen again. "Congratulations." She looked over her shoulder at Ashley and then at Landon. "You're having a girl."

Ashley sucked in her next breath and covered Landon's hand with her own. "I knew it."

"You have two boys already, right?" Dr. McDaniel was clearly happy for them.

"Yes. Cole and Devin."

"We have four boys and a girl." The doctor grinned. "No question, there's something special about having a little girl in the house."

Ashley couldn't respond. Tears stung her eyes. She was having a girl, her first daughter. A love like no other filled her heart, and she pictured her own mom, how close they'd grown in the years before her death. Ashley loved having sons, but a daughter would be so different. A girl who would look up to her and hold long talks with her and learn about love from her. Two tears slid down the sides of her face.

Landon bent down and kissed one of them. He whispered in her ear, "She'll look just like you."

Ashley nodded, too overcome to speak. An hour ago all she could think about was that maybe, just maybe, there was something wrong with her baby. But now she knew better. She was having a little girl, and everything was going to unfold just the way she'd pictured it.

The doctor moved the paddle and settled it inches from where it had been. The baby's spine came into view, and it looked normal, as normal as Ashley could remember the image looking from her ultrasounds with Cole and Devin. At the same time, a round shape appeared on the screen.

The baby's head.

Ashley stared at the roundness, and she thought she saw her daughter's profile. A tiny nose and high cheekbones. The technology was overwhelming, giving her this first look at her little girl. She dabbed at another tear and held her breath. They were almost finished. The doctor needed to snap a picture of the baby's head and measure it— the way Ashley had seen it done with her two boys. Then Dr. McDaniel could smile at them and tell them everything was fine. The high AFP test was nothing.

But instead something changed in the doctor's posture. She straightened a few inches, then shifted the paddle again, studying the picture. Ashley might've imagined it, but she was almost sure that Dr. McDaniel's next breath was more of a sigh. A heavy sigh.

"Everything okay?" Landon knew better than to ask. Doctors preferred going over the specific results of a test like this later on, after the test was finished.

Dr. McDaniel ran her hand through her blonde hair and moved closer to the image. "Just a minute."

The grip Landon had on Ashley's shoulder grew tighter. She didn't dare move or say a word. She had to remind herself to breathe.

A minute passed and another, while the doctor adjusted the paddle and clicked a series of pictures of their little girl's head. Ashley squinted, trying to see what might be troubling the doctor. But the baby's head looked normal as far as she could tell. Round with various shadows on and near it. Ultrasound pictures were always like this, right? Her daughter's head looked the same as Cole's or Devin's.

The nurse was still standing on the other side of the machine, watching the test also. And only then did Ashley realize that the young woman's face was ashen, her eyes deeply concerned. She exchanged a look with the doctor and took a step closer to the door.

Dr. McDaniel nodded at the nurse, and the nurse excused herself.

Ashley peered up at Landon. He was pale and tense, and though his lips were parted, he remained silent.

Dr. McDaniel wiped off the paddle and turned to them. "Ashley, why don't you get dressed." Her expression was impossible to read, except for one very obvious thing. She was no longer making small talk about her own children, no longer smiling. "I'd like to see you both in my office."

When she was gone, Landon helped Ashley up and cradled her head against his chest.

"Landon, what's happening?" Her heart raced at double its normal rhythm. "Did you see anything?"

"No. She looked . . ." His mouth sounded dry, his words clipped and filled with fear. "She looked beautiful."

Ashley clung to him, nodding. She wanted desperately to agree with him. "She did, didn't she? Her profile was perfect."

"Maybe the doctor's just being cautious."

Landon stepped back so she could get dressed.

She didn't answer, didn't say anything that could shatter the hope his words had placed between them. That was it. Dr. McDaniel was just being cautious. Of course. The AFP test had been high, after all. Now the doctor had to tell them the possibilities. That even with a normal ultrasound, there was still a chance of some rare problem. And that was her job, to tell them about the possibilities.

But when Ashley was back in her clothes, she didn't make a move for the doctor's office. Instead she turned to Landon and fell into his embrace. As long as she stayed here in his arms, as long as she didn't leave this room, they could hang on to everything that had seemed certain just moments ago.

"We're having a daughter." There were tears in her eyes, but she smiled despite them.

"She'll have your eyes."

She kissed him, and the wetness on her cheeks spread to his. "And your heart."

They stayed that way for what felt like ten minutes, clinging to each other and to every hope and dream they shared for their daughter. Because the moment they let go, they'd have to take the next steps beyond the examination room door. The doctor would either give them news that would confirm the results they'd seen with their own eyes, that their little girl was whole and healthy, or she would give them the results they dreaded.

Results that could change their lives forever.

CHAPTER SIX

DAYNE COULDN'T SHAKE the bad feeling.

He was hanging another of Ashley's paintings in the dining room of the lake house, and Katy was in the bedroom on the phone with her mother. Everything about their lives was exactly where he'd always dreamed it might be. They'd returned from their honeymoon, stopping by the Chicago retirement home where Katy's parents lived, and after a few days they'd flown to Indiana to settle into the house on Lake Monroe. They had three weeks before they needed to be in Malibu for the movie.

But Then Again No would begin with

meetings and interviews in Los Angeles, after which Stephen Petrel, the director, had
made some changes. Instead of starting the
project in Los Angeles, the shoot had been
moved so that most of the filming would take
place in Santa Fe, New Mexico. Only the last
few weeks would happen in LA. Stephen
wanted more than strong acting. He wanted
strong cinematography. He'd moved the location shots because he was convinced that
areas outside Santa Fe would bring more
emotion to the film.

Dayne picked up a nail and positioned it
at the center of the wall. What could be better? He and his new bride, starring in a film
with a director whose passion for art was un-
equaled? Dayne grabbed the hammer and
knocked the nail firmly into place. Eventually
he wanted to have Ashley's artwork framed
to match the rugged wooden beams in the
dining room. But for now a simple nail would
hold up the canvas.

The painting was of a bride and groom
standing barefoot on Malibu beach. Ashley
had given it to them when they returned
home from the Bahamas.

"Your wedding present," she'd told him.

Today she and Landon would find out if

they were having a girl or a boy, so by tonight there'd be more good news to celebrate.

Every area of his life was better than ever, so why the sense of doom, the feeling that wouldn't leave ever since they returned home? He paused and the answer became clear. Maybe it had nothing to do with being back in Bloomington but more with the commitment they'd made to the reality show.

Dayne balanced the painting on the nail and stood back. Perfectly centered. He took the box of nails and the hammer and returned them to a shelf in the laundry room. A few of the leaders from Christian Kids Theater were coming over this afternoon for a meeting. Things didn't look good for CKT, and today, among other things, they'd get a report on the sale of the downtown theater.

He entered the dining room, and a breeze filtered through the screen door. It smelled of fresh grass and new life, and it called him outside. He slipped on his flip-flops and went out to the railing at the edge of the back deck. The early afternoon sunlight cast diamonds across Lake Monroe.

Dayne breathed in, and suddenly a memory flashed in his mind. The way he'd felt lying in the hospital bed after coming out of his coma. He wasn't sure he'd ever walk again, let alone find his way to a place like this, a life like this. God had given Katy and him the impossible, so why put everything about their future up for grabs? Why place their personal lives on a platter for the world to gawk at—even if the show wanted only what they could capture on the set?

A pair of geese flew by, flapping hard and honking. In the distance, from somewhere down the hill near the shore, came the sound of a couple of battling frogs.

Dayne closed his eyes and took a long, slow breath. This was what he wanted, nothing more. To live here with Katy and figure out a solution for her theater group. They should call his agent and tell him to forget it. Forget the film and the next one after that and what was left of his contract.

He was home, and he wanted to stay here.

The screen door squeaked behind him. He looked over his shoulder and smiled at Katy. "How's your mother?"

"Worse." She frowned. "Dad too. The retirement home moved them both to the nursing wing."

He turned and rested his back on the railing. "I'm sorry."

"Me too." Katy slipped her hands around his waist. "I'm glad we spent some time with them."

"We can go again." He studied her. "Whenever you want."

"Thank you." She smiled, and some of the sadness lifted from her eyes. "They loved you."

He grinned. Her parents were simple people, the kind that weren't ruffled by celebrity.

"They liked you because you married me, not because you're Dayne Matthews."

"I could tell." He gazed at the sky over their log house. "Another gorgeous spring day."

Katy relaxed into his arms. "Makes me wanna be out on the lake."

"You and me and a rowboat. Floating along the shoreline."

"Mmmm." She looked deep into his eyes. "Sounds perfect."

Dayne paused, letting his senses fill with her presence. "So tell me once more why we're leaving in three weeks?"

She took a half step back, and a crooked grin played on her mouth. "Not that again."

"Well . . ." He exhaled hard and turned to face the water. He felt her snuggle in beside him. "That's all I keep asking myself. Why are we leaving if this is home?"

"Your word, for one thing." Katy gave him a slight bump with her hip. "The studio would sue you if you broke the contract. You know that."

Dayne lifted his chin. The breeze washed over his face, clearing his mind and some of the tension he'd been feeling. She was right. His contract left no room for escape, and Stephen Petrel had already spent a million dollars in preproduction on the film. God wouldn't want Dayne to bail out now. To do so would be wrong and illegal.

"You're worried about the reality show again." It wasn't a question. Katy knew him well. Because he'd let her farther into his heart than he'd ever let anyone.

"Remind me again—" he looked at her— "what good could come from it."

"We'll basically be an open book—at least professionally." She'd recited the list to him several times a day since they'd been home. "The paparazzi won't have a reason to chase us, because we'll be giving them exactly what they want."

Dayne looked out at the water again. The contract with the reality show acknowledged that the cameramen capturing their relationship on the set also worked for a few of the tabloids. The images caught could be used in magazines leading up to the release of the show—as prepublicity. So in that sense, Katy was right.

He dropped his voice a notch, more pensive than before. "And you think that'll do the trick, take away their desire to chase us?"

"Dayne, we've been over this." Katy put her hand on his shoulder and massaged the muscles at the base of his neck. "Don't you think so? I mean, if you're this worried, maybe we should change our mind."

He thought about that. The problem was, they could never exactly predict the whims of the paparazzi. Sure, they'd be on the set, spending ten or twelve hours a day with Katy and him. It made sense that they might've had enough after that, that they'd head for their hotels or the bars or wherever they wanted to go when the day's work was finished.

But maybe it would only make them more determined to see what happened in Katy and Dayne's world *after* the cameras stopped rolling for the day. There was no way to tell until they were smack in the middle of the action. "We won't know until we get started."

"It makes sense though, right? If we give them photo ops all day long, they're bound to be bored of us by nightfall."

"I hope so." He angled his waist into the deck railing and faced her. "Sorry."

"For what?" Katy must've sensed that he was letting go of the issue, because there was the hint of teasing in her eyes.

"For being such a downer."

"You're worried." She swayed slightly with him. "After all you've been through, that only makes sense."

"All *we've* been through." Dayne kissed her forehead. "I couldn't have gone through a day of it without you."

For a little while they said nothing, just looked at each other.

"They'll write a hundred different lies." Katy brushed her cheek against his. "We have to stay strong, not let them get to us."

"We won't." His heart was growing light, the way it always did when she was in his arms. He wasn't worried about the dirt, though she was right—the paparazzi would be relentless with wrong information, whatever they could make up. But the love he shared with Katy wasn't like other Hollywood relationships. Tabloid headlines couldn't touch what they had together. Dayne's fears centered around the danger, the idea that somehow the reality show wouldn't satiate the paparazzi's interest—it would fan it into hot, searing flames.

He exhaled. Either way, the movie was weeks away.

"Know what we should do?" Katy batted her eyelashes at him. She peered over the deck railing and down toward the rocky path that led to the water.

"Stay here forever?"

She wagged her finger at him. "No, today. After the CKT meeting."

"What?" Dayne moved in to kiss her.

"Listen." She giggled and slipped away. "We should hike down to the water and watch the sunset from that rock, the big one at the end of the trail."

He gave her his best suggestive look, the one he'd used in a dozen different films. "That could be interesting."

She tilted her head back and laughed. "Dayne Matthews, that's one thing we never have to worry about. Whatever else happens, life with you will definitely be interesting."

The doorbell rang just as Dayne was making a promise to himself. He wasn't going to waste another hour of this precious time with Katy worrying about what was coming. She was his wife, his best friend. This wasn't the time to live in fear over what might happen. It was a time to do what he wanted to spend the rest of his life doing.

Celebrating every minute with the woman he loved.

Katy took a few steps toward the door, turned, and gave Dayne a quick kiss. "That's for the one that got away," she whispered.

The doorbell rang a second time, and she hurried across the deck and into the house. This was the first time she'd meet Chad Jennings, the new assistant director just in from Cleveland. The leaders of CKT had been talking about him for weeks. She quickened her pace. "Coming!"

Breathless, she answered the door and found CKT area coordinator Bethany Allen, with Rhonda Sanders and Chad, on the front porch. Dayne joined them near the entryway, and the group moved into the living room.

Chad fell into place beside Katy. "I've

heard so much about you, your work with the kids. I hear it's a very talented group."

"It is. You'll love directing them." Katy studied him. He wasn't quite six feet tall and had dark hair with a tanned complexion that made him handsome in a rugged sort of way. More than that, he had kind, compassionate eyes, eyes that quietly spoke of a faith tested and true. Katy felt an immediate connection with him.

"Rhonda and I've been meeting nearly every day." He smiled. "We have a lot of ideas."

"Good." Katy felt a sudden lump in her throat. No matter how much she liked this new director, he was here for one reason. Because Katy was no longer directing CKT—at least not for now. She took a seat next to Dayne and felt her heart pound out an erratic rhythm. Whatever lay ahead, the changes were going to hurt more than she'd let herself believe.

Bethany waited until everyone was seated. "Let's pray before we start."

Peace filled Katy and calmed her. God already had the answers. He knew what was coming and whether CKT's time in Bloomington was ending. He knew the way through it, the way beyond it. She slid closer to Dayne and linked her arm through his while Bethany prayed.

It wasn't until they finished praying and Bethany handed out the agenda for the meeting that Katy noticed what was happening across the room. Rhonda—one of her closest friends and confidantes—was sitting next to Chad, their heads bowed together. He was whispering something to her, and she giggled in response as she pulled out a pad of paper and a pen.

Rhonda was twenty-nine and certain that somehow God hadn't heard her prayers about finding a godly man, someone who could laugh with her and lead her, a man who would be her friend and someday her husband.

Guys had come and gone from Rhonda's life, but no one ever fit the bill; no one ever made her eyes light up when the two of them were together. At least not as far as Katy had ever seen.

Until now.

The chemistry between Rhonda and Chad was so strong that Katy wondered if everyone in the room could sense it. The way they leaned slightly toward each other and the way everyone else seemed to disappear when their eyes met. Katy couldn't keep the smile from her face, and at that moment, Rhonda looked her way.

In her expression was a message Katy could read perfectly. What she was sensing about Rhonda was indeed true. They would talk about it later.

First on Bethany's agenda was the fact that the spring play had been changed from *Seussical* to *Godspell*. "We took into account several things." Bethany looked at her notes and then at Katy. "Primarily the mission statement of CKT, which is to glorify God through musical theater. I discussed with the national board how we would want to go out if this is the last CKT play." She hesitated. "With a message to the community, obviously."

Katy focused on the notes in front of her, willing herself not to cry. Bethany hadn't said anything about this for certain being the last CKT show in Bloomington. But the possibility hurt. She kept her gaze down, even when she felt Dayne's arm around her shoulders. *Godspell* was good. No, it was perfect. She'd seen a video of the CKT version back when she first came to Bloomington to do Christian Kids Theater. It was a series of vignettes illustrating the parables of Jesus.

It would be fitting for the kids of CKT whether it was the last show before summer or the last show ever.

Rhonda and Chad shared their vision for the play, how they pictured the sets as minimal and the costumes being whatever street clothes the kids felt most comfortable in.

"The point, if I get this right, is to show a modern-day picture of what it would look like if Jesus were telling His stories to a group of kids like the ones in CKT." Chad glanced at Rhonda, then Bethany. "Is that right?"

"Exactly." Bethany smiled. "It'll be the perfect show to bring the kids close together and remind us all why we do what we do."

Guilt pricked at Katy's soul. Why they did what they did? Shouldn't she be asking herself the same question? She was about to film a movie with Dayne that would bring no overt portrait of faith to the viewers. Was that what God wanted of her? Was it enough to simply star in a film with Dayne without looking at the project in light of eternity?

Dayne must've sensed what she was feeling, because he gave her shoulder a light squeeze.

Katy took a long breath and looked up. She had to stay focused on this meeting.

Bethany moved past the next few items quickly. Auditions would take place at the end of this week, on Friday, and already more than a hundred kids had signed up for classes. The CKT budget was in good shape with plenty of funds to pay a small stipend to the directors and cover the cost of renting the theater.

Bethany sighed. "That brings us to the real reason we wanted to meet with you, Katy."

"The theater?" She leaned into Dayne and held her breath.

"Yes." She paused and glanced at everyone in the room. "I'm afraid the owners have made up their mind. They've been contacted by a number of developers, and it's no longer fiscally sound for them to hold on to the building. They can make far more money selling it to someone who'll tear it down and build condominiums than they could ever make renting it out to groups like CKT. They have approval from the city council."

Katy blinked back tears. "What's their time frame?"

"They still want to list the building in June, right after *Godspell* closes." Bethany lowered her notes to her lap. "I'm sorry."

A tear rolled down Katy's cheek and onto her shirt. These were her worst fears realized. Months ago, when they'd talked about the possibility, Katy had felt sure something would change. For one thing, the city was looking to protect an atmosphere of arts and culture in the downtown area. She sniffed and found a level of control. "Can we appeal to the council? I mean, there're enough houses and condos going up around town. An old theater isn't something they can replace."

"I know. I met with them a few weeks ago and told them exactly that." Bethany made a face. "Apparently the builders' proposals include a new movie theater complex with architecture that'll match the renovated look of the downtown area."

Katy's shoulders sank a few inches. "That's not fair."

For a few moments no one said anything. They were all in agreement. The kids of Bloomington needed a program like CKT, but without the theater, the group wouldn't survive.

Finally Bethany said, "It isn't fair, but it's a fact. We'll have to announce it after the last show. Until then, the owners of the theater have agreed to keep the sale quiet."

The rest of the meeting passed quickly, and before they left, they formed a circle, held hands, and prayed again.

Chad led them this time. "Give us a miracle, God. Show us how we can keep the theater open. We ask in Christ's name, amen."

When the group was gone, Katy wandered back onto the deck. Uneasiness settled on her shoulders, making her doubt every decision she'd made in the past year, except one. Marrying Dayne was something she would never regret. But agreeing to take part in his Hollywood life? Leaving Bloomington to star in a movie?

She heard Dayne step onto the deck and come up behind her. He wove his hands around her waist and kissed her cheek. For a long time he didn't say anything, just stared out at the sky and the gray-blue water stretched out beneath it.

Finally he spoke softly against the side of her face. "It isn't your fault."

"It is." She lifted her chin, angry with herself. "I never should've agreed to leave."

"Okay, so let's say you stay here." His words were kind, unhurried.

"I stay here and we find a place for the kids to perform." She leaned back and rested her head on his shoulder. "No one's more passionate for CKT than me, Dayne. I've seen kids from broken homes find a family in this group and kids from great homes sharing the experience of a lifetime with their parents." Her voice cracked. "I've seen them learn how to love and learn how to forgive. I've watched them come together for a show that was so much greater than what any of them could do on their own."

"I know." Dayne pressed his face against hers. They were both still staring straight ahead, soaking up the incredible view from their back door. "I've watched you be a part of it."

Katy turned and faced him. "Those kids need CKT."

"They need God, and they need each other." He smiled, compassion warming his expression. "They were lucky to have CKT as long as they did."

"But if I stay—"

"It won't matter." His interruption wasn't rude; it was firm. "Bethany's looked all over the city for another theater." His words hung on the afternoon breeze. "There's nothing you could do, Katy. Whether you stay or go, CKT won't have a place to perform."

She breathed in sharply through her nose. "Why, Dayne? Why would God let this happen?"

"Maybe CKT's served its purpose." He brushed a lock of her hair back from her face. "Maybe so you'll feel good about spending this next season with me."

Katy rested her forehead on his chest and let her mind wrap around the possibility. The timing was certainly interesting. She and Dayne heading off to Hollywood for what could be the beginning of a time of acting together, just when the theater was being sold out from underneath the CKT kids.

"If I had my way, we'd stay right here, and CKT would head into the sunset performing musicals in that old theater."

"Ah, Katy." Dayne ran his hand along the back of her neck, soothing her nerves. "I love that you're a dreamer."

"But I'm not." She lifted her head. "I'm a doer. Only this time you're right. There's nothing I can do to change things for CKT." Another sad thought hit her. "I'll be gone for their last show."

"We'll fly back for closing weekend. The director won't have a problem if we tell him ahead of time."

She hated thinking about all the good-byes to come. "We'll be here for auditions."

"And the first couple of rehearsals."

She tried to picture Tim Reed, Bailey and Connor Flanigan, the Shaffers, the Picks, the Weils, and so many other families and kids when they heard the news about CKT. The ache in her heart doubled. Sometime in June, the theater would go up for sale, and a few months after that it would be demolished, leveled to make way for high-rise condominiums. Old theaters weren't profitable, not in today's market. And so there was no way around it, no matter how they prayed. They would have to walk through the days and trust that if God had brought these kids something as wonderful as CKT, He would replace it with something better.

Even if for now Katy could think of nothing better than the magic and memories they'd built together inside the walls of the lovable old brick theater, a building she would always see on the edge of the park in downtown Bloomington.

No matter what they built in its place.

CHAPTER SEVEN

LANDON RELEASED HIS hold on Ashley. "We have to go."

She nodded, but she said nothing. What could she say until they met with Dr. Mc-Daniel, until they found out whatever it was that had darkened her expression a few minutes earlier?

Just as Landon reached for the door handle, there was a knock from the other side. "Ashley?" It sounded like Brooke.

Landon exchanged a look with his wife. "Don't say anything."

"I won't." Ashley gave a sharp shake of her head. "It might be nothing."

Landon held on to that truth. Even if the meeting ahead of them was only protocol, this wasn't the time to visit with Ashley's sister. But they couldn't avoid it, either. Brooke was a doctor, and her office was one floor above Dr. McDaniel's. She knew about Ashley's ultrasound this morning, and she was bound to stop by. All of the Baxters knew about Ashley's ultrasound, and everyone had their opinions about whether she was having a boy or a girl.

"Come in." Landon glanced at the clock on the wall. This had to be short.

"Hey, Brooke." Ashley found a smile, but her face was still pale.

"So . . ." Brooke beamed. She held out her hands and looked from Ashley to Landon and back again. "Like Maddie said, I need to find out if I'm going to be an aunt or an uncle."

Landon chuckled, but it sounded forced. He nodded to Ashley. "You tell her."

"We're having a girl." Ashley lifted her shoulders and grinned. As she did, tears filled her eyes. "Isn't that great?"

As if she was just cluing in to the atmosphere in the examination room, Brooke's smile faded. "Wait . . ." She looked at Landon. "Is everything okay?"

"We think so." Landon reached for Ashley's hand. "Her AFP test was high." He hated this. He wanted to be alone with Ashley, hurry her down the hall to the doctor's office so they could hear the news that everything was okay. All this worrying was for nothing.

Brooke's eyes grew wide. "What about Dr. McDaniel? What did she say?"

"She wants to see us in her office." Landon shrugged. "We were just about to go."

"AFP tests are high a lot of the time. Did she tell you that?" Brooke put her hand on Ashley's shoulder. "Some pregnancies just run high."

"Cole's was high." Ashley's voice was shaky. She patted Brooke's hand. "Thanks for coming by. I guess we better . . . we better go."

"Amy's a friend of mine." Brooke seemed to be working to sound confident. "She's very cautious; your baby's probably fine." She took a few steps toward the door. No doubt her words were meant to be reassuring, but the alarm in her expression said that she too feared what the doctor might tell them. "Call me later, okay? We're home tonight."

Ashley gave a quick nod. "Thanks."

With a final look, Brooke turned and headed back down the hall.

Landon exhaled. Whatever the news, he wanted to face it without an audience. Just him and Ashley and God. From the moment he'd heard about the high AFP test, he'd felt a strange knot in his gut, a knowing that the news today was going to be almost more than they could bear.

When Brooke was gone, he led Ashley down the hall to the small office where Dr. McDaniel was sitting behind her desk. Photos of smiling little boys and a precious girl filled her desk. For a split second, Landon wanted to turn and run, take Ashley far from the medical office to a place where their future was still full of promise.

Before he could take another breath, the doctor looked up. Her expression told him that his feeling had been real, a warning sent from God. It was the sort of feeling he'd had once before, back on September 11, 2001, when he watched the Twin Towers collapse with his firefighter buddy Jalen inside.

That certain, horrible feeling that after today life would never be the same again.

Ashley willed herself to take in air as she and Landon sat next to each other opposite Dr. McDaniel. This whole buildup was nothing more than a figment of their imaginations. How crazy they were to read into a doctor's sigh or her expression. The woman did ultrasounds all day long. Of course she wasn't going to smile through every one of them.

Breathe, she told herself. *Keep breathing.* Ashley folded her hands on her lap and pressed her arm against Landon's.

Dr. McDaniel turned to them, and her eyes glistened. "I'm afraid I have very bad news." She turned her computer so they could see the screen. The ultrasound image that appeared was of their baby's head. The head that had looked so normal just minutes ago.

"See here?" The doctor touched an area that appeared cloudier than the rest. "This is where the spine meets the back of the head, and it's where something called the neural tube should naturally close up during development. But for some babies, this process doesn't happen."

Ashley squinted at the picture. What was she talking about? Neural tubes? How come she'd never heard of such a thing until now? Next to her, Landon was breathing harder than before. Ashley forced herself to listen.

"You can see here—" Dr. McDaniel pointed at the shady area again—"unfortunately your baby's neural tube did not close properly." She looked about to cry, and she shook her head. "Because of that, she will definitely have a neural tube defect."

Landon slid to the edge of his seat. "Is this . . . is this something that can be corrected inside the womb?"

"No. I'm afraid not. This type of birth defect is fatal 100 percent of the time." Dr. McDaniel's shoulders fell, and she looked down for a moment. "The condition is called anencephaly. I've seen only two other cases in all my years of delivering babies, but I've researched it extensively." She folded her hands and shook her head. "I'm sorry, Ashley . . . Landon. Many babies with this type of neural tube defect die before birth."

A fog fell over Ashley, and she stared at her lap. The information was wrong. It had to be. She'd already begun feeling the baby move. In some far-removed corner of her mind, Ashley could hear the doctor going on, talking about the baby's brain developing outside her head and how a few hours or a few days was the longest a baby could live with . . . whatever it was the woman thought her baby had. *Anen*-something. And more information . . . too much information.

Ashley closed her eyes. She felt sick, and suddenly she stood up. "I need a bathroom."

The doctor was instantly up and opening the door for her. "It's across the hall."

Landon stayed by her side, holding her elbow so she wouldn't fall. She barely made it to the sink in time before losing her breakfast.

"Ashley," Landon whispered close to her. He held her hair back from her face. "We'll get through this. The test could be wrong."

And there it was. The single ray of light in the darkest cavern Ashley had ever found herself in. The test could be wrong. Her stomach was still warring against the news, but after a few minutes, she straightened. Her knees shook and her hands trembled, but she found the strength to grab a nearby roll of paper towels and clean out the sink.

Landon helped, and he pulled a paper cup from a wall dispenser and filled it with cool water. "Here. Take small sips."

Ashley homed in on his voice, like a person lost in a blinding snowstorm. She took the water and brought it to her lips. The test was wrong. That had to be the answer. Her baby girl was fine. Her arms and legs and hands and feet were perfect. The shadow near her head might've been an air pocket or the way the baby was lying. That was possible, wasn't it?

She dried her mouth and looked at her reflection. Her cheeks were gray, her eyes wide with fear. Dark spots danced before her, and she steadied herself on the sink. "I feel . . . like I'm going to faint."

"I'm here." Landon placed himself behind her, supporting her elbows so she wouldn't fall. "We can get a second opinion, Ash. We can't be defeated by one ultrasound. God's bigger than this."

Ashley nodded. Yes, God was bigger. But God allowed some women to walk this path, right? She remembered a woman who had come to church for the first time a few weeks ago. Her four-year-old had cancer, and the illness was tearing her family apart. And that woman loved the same Lord, so it was possible. She turned and gripped Landon's arm. "What if . . . ?"

His expression told her he was already there, already imagining the same thing. "Whatever happens—" he gritted his teeth— "God will lead us." He pulled her into a desperate hug, clinging to her. "If we don't believe that now . . . then we won't believe it ever."

His words breathed strength into her. She grabbed a few quick breaths and eased back from him. Her hands were still shaky. She reached for the paper cup and drank enough that her mouth was no longer dry.

"You ready?" Landon looked as though he felt the same way she did. As though the last place he wanted to go was back into the doctor's office, back to the results that—if they were true—would be devastating. But this was one of the reasons she loved Landon. In his expression was the same resolve that made him a great firefighter, the resolve that wouldn't let him give up on her all those years when she was being stubborn. He was the sort of guy who rushed into a burning building, not out of it. And when his friend was buried in the rubble of the Twin Towers, Landon had been the one who put his own life on hold while he spent nearly three months digging through the pile until his friend was found.

Whatever the truth about their little girl, Landon would stand strong in the journey. And he would do so not just for himself but for her. She held tight to his arm and nodded.

They returned to the office, and this time Dr. McDaniel met them on the other side of her desk. She hugged Ashley and then Landon before they were seated. "I'm so sorry. I can only tell you that God has a plan for every child. No matter how brief the life."

Ashley felt sick again.

"We'll meet in a few weeks so we can talk about the details. For now, I understand you need time." She handed Landon a pamphlet. "Anencephaly is described here. We can do another ultrasound in a few weeks, but the results of today's test are conclusive." She leaned against her desk and folded her arms. "I'm so sorry."

Ashley pursed her lips and exhaled in short bursts. She refused to let the doctor's words penetrate to her heart. The woman wasn't saying this about her baby, about her first daughter. No, she was merely reciting a list of medical facts. Nothing was conclusive until a baby was born. God would have the final say. Period.

Landon took the material and assured the

doctor they would schedule another ultrasound for two weeks from now.

"I don't think this will interest you, but I must tell you all the same." Dr. McDaniel looked beyond sad, as if the news she was delivering had indeed touched her in a personal way. "Many women choose to abort babies with anencephaly. It's—" she seemed to struggle to find the right words—"very difficult emotionally carrying a baby to full term knowing that the baby will die almost immediately upon birth. Obviously an abortion isn't something I would do, and it's not something I would recommend. But I'm obligated to tell you."

Another wave of nausea washed over Ashley. She gripped the arms of her chair, and for a moment she was back in France, back in the abortion clinic ready to rid her body of the tiny life growing inside her. A shiver ran down her spine and her arms. At the last possible moment, she had decided her mistakes weren't her baby's fault, and she'd listened to herself, her instincts, instead of the technician at the clinic or the married artist she'd slept with months earlier.

Her decision to choose life had resulted in one of the greatest gifts ever. Her son Cole.

The words stuck in her throat for a few seconds, but then in a rush they came out loud and certain, interrupting the doctor even as she was talking about various counselors they might visit and how anyone could understand having an abortion under these circumstances. "There won't be an abortion. Not ever."

Landon looped his arm through hers. His voice was calmer but just as certain. "We wouldn't consider it."

"I know." The doctor dabbed beneath her eyes. "The road ahead will be marked with great joy as your baby grows and great sorrow. But I must say, even a short life can be very significant."

"Doctor." Landon stopped short of interrupting the woman, but frustration sounded in his tone. "The test could be wrong . . . because all tests can be wrong. And if not, we'll be praying that God will heal our daughter."

Dr. McDaniel opened her mouth to say something, but then she stopped herself. "I'll be praying too." She hesitated. "I'll see you in two weeks."

Landon stood and shook her hand.

Ashley watched him, her head spinning. Everything about the moment felt surreal, like something from a strange and horrible dream. She leaned into her husband, and he helped her to her feet.

The moment they were outside the office, he inclined his head close to hers. "Are you okay? To walk, I mean?"

"Yes." Her eyes were dry. They'd been dry all this time. She steeled herself against the news, against the sick feeling still welling up inside her. They walked in silence, the fog that had clouded her earlier back again. What was happening, and why weren't they smiling and laughing the way she had pictured them looking when they left this appointment?

When they reached the van, Landon helped her inside and then quickly moved around to his door and joined her.

"The test could be wrong." Her heart raced, and there was nothing she could do to calm it.

Landon didn't start the van. He rested his arms on the steering wheel and stared straight ahead. "Tests are wrong all the time."

Ashley placed her hands on her abdomen, as if she could somehow protect her daughter from the doctor's declarations, from whatever it was the woman had seen on the ultrasound. Her mother's face came to mind, her mom who always seemed to have the right thing to say in a situation like this. It was the verse, the one that had flashed in her heart while she was walking the track with Kari that day. A verse her mother had quoted often. She pressed her fingers to her throat, trying to find the strength. "Mom would tell me that Romans 8:28 is true no matter how dark the storm clouds."

Landon looked like he'd been punched in the stomach, but he put his hand on her knee. "'In all things God works for the good of those who love him.'"

"Yes. All things."

Landon turned the key, pulled out of the parking space, and headed for the driveway.

He was halfway there when the fog in Ashley's mind lifted. Quickly and certainly, the reality loomed like a jagged cliff, one they were speeding toward with no sign of stopping.

Tears rushed into her heart and soul and built up in her throat. They were having a little girl, and she didn't want anything to be wrong with her. But suddenly, as clear as the trees that lined the driveway, she had to wonder if maybe it was true. Maybe her little girl had anencephaly, and maybe she wouldn't live more than a few days.

Panic circled her and grabbed at her until she couldn't contain her fear another minute. And why couldn't she breathe? Her mouth was open, but her lungs were screaming for relief. She couldn't get the image of her baby's shadowy head out of her mind, and she held up her hand. "Wait!" Ashley panted, desperate for air. "Landon, stop!"

He pulled over and slammed the gearshift into park. Her fear was instantly contagious as he turned to her, alarm thick in his expression. "What is it? What's wrong?"

"I . . ." She shook her head in short, fast movements. A birth and a funeral in the same week? "I can't do this, Landon." She kept one hand on her stomach. "I don't want to. Nothing can be wrong with her."

"Oh, baby, come here." He leaned across the console and took her into his arms. In the process he spilled a nearly empty bottle of water in the cup holder, but neither of them made a move to clean it up.

"Maybe . . ." Ashley was gasping for air now, hyperventilating. She dug her fingernails into Landon's shoulders. "Maybe . . . I can't handle it."

He held on to her. "We can handle it together."

"Landon." A burst of air slipped into her lungs, and the ability to breathe somehow released her tears. An ocean of tears. She clung to him and sobbed for her little girl, who might—just might—even now be fighting for her life. "Help me."

"Ashley, I am." Futility rang from his voice, and then—as if the idea had come to him all at once—he began to pray. No, it wasn't merely a prayer. The words he lifted up to heaven on behalf of her and their baby were a desperate plea for help. "God, You are the Creator, the Healer. Nothing is impossible for You. So breathe life into our little girl, and please let the tests be wrong. Help us to never . . . never doubt that You are the giver of miracles." There was an angry cry in his voice as he continued. "And if the tests . . . if they aren't wrong . . . walk us through what lies ahead. Please, God."

With every word of Landon's prayer, Ashley felt reason returning, righting her world once more. God had created the universe. Certainly He could heal their daughter—if the tests were even accurate.

Small sobs were still shaking her shoulders, but she pulled back and looked at Landon. "From this day on, I'm believing God for a miracle." She grabbed three quick breaths and dabbed her fingertips beneath her eyes. "I might be . . . afraid. But I won't doubt."

Landon hesitated, and for a moment it seemed like he might say something to correct her. Something about getting prepared in case the test results were right and God didn't choose to heal their baby. But then determination filled his eyes. "I won't either."

"We have to tell the others." Ashley sniffed. She put her hands back on her stomach, as close to their unborn daughter as she could get. "So they can pray."

"We'll call your dad when we get home."

"And Brooke." She straightened back into her seat. "One of them might know of something we can do, another test we can take."

Like that they set their course. They would move forward, stealing from fear as many moments as possible so they could enjoy Ashley's pregnancy and make plans for the arrival of their little girl. As often as they could, they would pray and believe and not doubt.

And they would ask everyone who loved them to do the same.

CHAPTER EIGHT

THE PRAYING WAS about to begin, but no matter how positive Ashley and Landon tried to come across, the mood was tense and somber. Ashley's phone call last night had prompted John to call his kids and ask them to pray. The prayer meeting was Kari's idea. She and Ashley hadn't talked yet, but Kari was deeply shaken. Like Ashley, she wanted to believe that the test was wrong or that if it was right, God was going to grant Ashley's baby a miraculous healing.

Now they were gathered in the Baxter living room, the way they'd gathered so many times before. Dayne and Katy sat in one corner next to Kari and Ryan. Brooke and Peter sat on the couch across from them, and Ashley and Landon were side by side in a pair of dining room chairs. John sat in his recliner and surveyed his family. The sense of shock was similar to what it had been after 9/11 or when they returned home after Elizabeth's funeral.

John stood and took a few steps toward the family room. "I'll check on the kids."

Ryan and Peter nodded, but otherwise no one responded.

John walked past the kitchen and into the next room. The kids were watching a cartoon movie, the volume turned down so it wouldn't be disruptive. It was eight o'clock on a school night, and even the little ones were quiet, cuddled up between their older cousins under a couple of blankets.

"Everyone okay?"

Cole looked up and wrinkled his brow. "How come everyone's so sad?"

"We're not sad." John's answer was quick. "We're just praying for your little sister."

"Why just for her?" Cole put his arm on the back of the sofa and turned enough so he could see John's face clearly. "Why not for Aunt Kari's baby girl too?"

John hesitated. Ashley and Landon hadn't told Cole anything except that they needed to pray extra hard for his sister. Now, though, Cole had a point. "We'll pray for Aunt Kari's baby too."

"Good." Relief filled Cole's eyes. "Every baby should be prayed for." He turned back to the cartoon and settled into the sofa once more.

John stepped a little farther into the room. "You kids stay in here, all right? We won't take too long."

Mindless nods went around the room.

He smiled at the kids and headed back to the others. As he did, the certain sadness came over him again. He knew all about anencephaly. Yes, God could miraculously heal Ashley and Landon's baby, but this much he understood clearly about neural tube defects: the testing was almost never wrong, and he'd never heard of a single case in which a baby was spontaneously healed.

He stopped in the hallway and gathered his strength. Ashley was looking for him to be strong, for his attitude to reflect hers or maybe lead it. Her call last night had been short and to the point.

He could still hear her voice, the way it left no room for debate as she rattled off what she knew. "Landon and I aren't settling for this diagnosis. We want everyone to pray and believe with us that the test might be wrong or that the baby will be healed." Her words were thick, and he had no doubt she'd been crying.

If she wanted a strong front from him, she would get it. There was no need to tell her the stark facts about that type of birth defect. Time would be teller enough. The problem tonight wasn't so much with Ashley and Landon as it was with Brooke.

Already Brooke had tried to pull him aside when Ashley was busy getting the kids set up in the other room. "Dad, she doesn't have to go through with this. You and I both know that—"

John had held up his hand. Was his oldest daughter suggesting abortion? If so, they would have to have a much longer talk about this later. "Not now. Ashley asked us to meet so we could pray for her baby." His tone left no room for negotiation. "You and I can talk later."

Since then, Brooke had been unusually

quiet, whispering on occasion to her doctor husband, Peter.

John clenched his fists and closed his eyes. *Here we are again, Lord . . . together with all the dark clouds of uncertainty lined up on the horizon ahead of us. The facts are shouting at me, so be louder, God. Let me hear Your voice tonight and only Yours.*

He opened his eyes and willed himself to act stronger than he felt. Elaine wasn't here tonight, but she was praying from home. They'd talked earlier today, and he could count on her support.

He was walking back to the living room when the front door opened and Luke and Reagan and their kids came in. Luke's eyes met his, and for a moment they both froze. Luke and Ashley had been particularly close as kids, and though they had a falling out in the years after Ashley returned from Paris, they'd been close again for years now.

"Where do you want the kids?"

"The family room." John nodded over his shoulder. "They're watching a movie."

Reagan tended to Tommy and Malin, removing their sweaters and leading them quietly into the room with the other cousins.

"Dad—" Luke came a few steps closer—"is it possible?"

"Ashley doesn't want to think so." John wanted desperately to protect Ashley from the skepticism that was bound to come from the others. Anyone who knew about anencephaly might think it better for Ashley and Landon to face the truth while praying for their miracle.

"But what about you?" Luke looked broken, as if he could cry for his sister at any moment. "What do you think?"

"This kind of birth defect is always fatal." He kept his voice low. "And the tests are virtually never wrong."

Luke put his hand on the wall in front of him and hung his head. "No." His voice broke. "How can this be happening?"

For a few seconds, John didn't answer. He put his arm around Luke's shoulders. "God has every life, every soul, in the palm of His hand. Tonight . . . that's all we need to remember."

Luke sighed and lifted his head. Then, as if he'd tapped into a strength that hadn't been there a moment earlier, he straightened. "Where is she?"

"In the living room with everyone else."

Luke led the way, and John watched him stop at the doorway to the room and find Ashley. Then without saying a word to anyone else, he crossed the floor and held his arms out to her. "Ash . . ."

She stood and allowed herself to be pulled into his embrace.

The scene reminded John of a thousand times when these two had helped each other through a hard time. He blinked back tears and cleared his throat. "The kids are settled. Let's get started."

Luke sat on the floor near Ashley and Landon, and Reagan joined him there.

John fought the thickness in his throat. "We've done this before, and I'm sure we'll do this again. But it's important, and it's what makes us a family." Left on his own, he might've picked a Bible verse from John 16, where Jesus said, "In this world you will have trouble. But take heart! I have overcome the world." But Landon had asked him to share a verse from Luke.

John reached for his black Bible, the one that stayed on the table next to his chair. He flipped through the well-worn pages until he reached the Scripture. "Luke 1:37 tells us simply this: 'Nothing is impossible with

God.'" He stared at the words for another heartbeat; then he shut the Bible and returned it to the table.

Landon was holding Ashley's hand. He looked determined to carry the burden of this alone. "That's the verse we'd like you all to keep in mind when you pray for us." He gave a confident nod, but it didn't hide the fear layered deep in his eyes. "We've asked everyone here so we could pray together out loud." He looked at each of the faces around him. "Whatever you're comfortable with."

"I'd like to start." Luke had his arm around Reagan's shoulders, but now he turned slightly and put his hand on Ashley's knee.

The others nodded, and hands were linked around the room.

When everyone was ready, Luke began. "Dear God, You've always been with us, no matter what situation has come our way." His voice sounded thick, and he paused. "Before Devin was born, we huddled around Ashley, waiting for a tornado to pass. You pulled us through then, and I know . . . I believe with my whole being that You'll pull us through now. Tests are wrong, and I pray that this test is one of those. A year from now—" His voice cracked again.

John opened his eyes and watched his son's struggle.

Luke pinched the bridge of his nose and gave a strong shake of his head. "Sorry." He coughed twice and tried again. "A year from now, I pray that we can sit around this same room admiring Ashley and Landon's healthy little girl. Thank You."

For the next half hour, prayers came from each of them. Dayne prayed that God would hold Ashley's unborn baby girl tight to His heart, and Katy echoed that prayer with a similar one of her own.

Kari was quick to pray next, declaring that she would believe for a miracle and that she looked forward to the day when her unborn daughter and Ashley's could play together. Halfway through her prayer, she started crying. But she kept on, undaunted. "Lord, these two little cousins have been planned for from the beginning; we believe that. Please let them have the lives we've been dreaming about."

Only Brooke's prayer hinted of a sense of acceptance and inevitability. "Lord, we don't always understand Your ways. Thank You for giving us options when we're faced with insurmountable odds."

Before the praying ended, John remembered Cole's request. "Lord, we also pray for Kari and Ryan's baby girl, that she might be developing into a healthy child and that her delivery will go smoothly."

When they finished, John opened his eyes and saw that Cole and Maddie had entered the room. They sat near their mothers, their heads bowed. Sometimes John and the other adults tended to think that kids didn't pick up on the more serious events that happened around them. That they had been blithely unaware of Elizabeth's cancer or the seriousness of Hayley's near drowning.

But as Cole lifted his face, John had no doubt that the child knew. Whether he'd been told or not, he could certainly sense that something was wrong, that once again his parents faced a terrible storm at the time when his mother was going to have a baby. The proof was there for all of them to see. Because Cole's eyes were no longer filled with the certainty John had seen earlier.

They were filled with tears.

The adults were standing, stretching, and

making their way over to Ashley and Landon. Luke and Reagan, Kari and Ryan all kept their comments upbeat and positive—like their prayers.

But Brooke walked discreetly past Ashley and headed for John. "Dad, we need to talk." She looked beyond concerned. Almost urgent.

Peter cast them both a knowing look as he walked past. "I'll get the girls."

"Thanks." She smiled at him, but just as quickly she turned back to John. "Please, Dad. Come into the kitchen."

With Ashley busy talking to the others, John agreed. He followed his oldest daughter into the kitchen and over near the stove, where their conversation couldn't be heard by anyone else.

Brooke didn't waste any time. "What I was trying to tell you earlier is that Ashley's wrong. There's no mistake with the test. Any doctor could spot anencephaly on an ultrasound." She was trembling, as if this news were strangling her. "You know that."

"Yes." He kept his tone calm. "But for every foolproof test there's an exception. Something a doctor mistook for a problem, when in fact it was a glitch in the imagery or the baby's hand covering its head. You have to admit that scenario is possible."

Brooke pressed her fingers to her chest. "It's possible the sun won't come up, but it's not very likely. Most people have to plan for tomorrow on the assumption it's coming."

"What are you saying?" Anger stirred in John's soul. "That we shouldn't pray? That it's bad for Ashley and Landon to ask for a miracle?" He studied her. "You of all people, Brooke. Every time you look at Hayley you should know that miracles happen."

"Of course they do. But if Ashley's baby has anencephaly, then her brain is already growing outside her skull. I researched it yesterday, Dad, and there's never been a case of anencephaly reversing itself. Not ever."

"I know about neural tube defects. I was a doctor before you were born, remember?"

"Okay, so why isn't someone telling her that now—before it gets any later—she should be considering an abortion?"

"Brooke, listen to you! You have no right to—" Before he could finish his sentence, something caught his eye and he turned.

Ashley was standing in the doorway, her mouth open. "Are you kidding me, Brooke?"

Her eyes were on fire. She took three quick steps closer to them. Shock and fury battled for position in her tone. "You think we should abort our baby now before it gets any later?"

"That wasn't for you to hear." The color drained from Brooke's face, but she didn't back down. "No matter what you want to believe, you need to consider your choices, Ash. That's all I'm saying."

A sound like a laugh but without any humor came from Ashley. "You think I would consider abortion? You really think that?"

Brooke sighed and seemed to make an effort at sounding compassionate. "People with a diagnosis of anencephaly do it all the time. It's not a morality issue. Babies with that type of birth defect will die anyway."

Ashley looked ready to roll up her sleeves and knock her sister to the floor. "*Everyone* dies anyway. Isn't that right?" Tears sprang to her eyes. "I can't imagine anything . . . anything so heartless in my life."

John was about to step in when Landon joined them and took his place by Ashley's side. "What's going on?"

"My sister wants me to get an abortion." Ashley gestured toward Brooke. "Just stop by a clinic and have a quick procedure. Just like that. No more problem."

Brooke gave Landon a defeated look. "A high percentage of people abort anencephalic babies to avoid the heartache. It's very emotionally damaging carrying a fatally ill baby to full term. That's all I'm saying."

Kari and Ryan peeked in, bid a quiet good-bye, and ushered their kids toward the front door. Dayne and Katy left at the same time, and Reagan returned to the family room with her kids.

"What's happening?" Luke walked into the kitchen and looked at the angry, hurt faces around him.

"Brooke wants me to get an abortion."

Before Luke could respond, Peter and the girls appeared in the doorway. He looked like he'd heard much of the exchange, and he shot Brooke a look. "We need to go. The girls are tired."

"You didn't really say that, did you?" Luke crossed his arms. "I mean, we just finished praying for a miracle, and you tell Ashley she should get an abortion?" His look toward Brooke spewed disgust. "That's the cruelest thing I've ever heard."

"It's not like that." Peter was still standing

in the doorway with the girls, but apparently he couldn't resist. "This is a medical issue, not a moral one."

"Not true." Ashley looked on the verge of collapse.

"Look—" John held up his hand—"it's late, and I think we're all feeling the strain of tonight." He put one hand on Ashley's shoulder and another on Brooke's. "No one is trying to hurt anyone else. That's not how this family works."

"Then maybe Brooke should leave now." Ashley leaned into Landon. "I asked if people would support us."

"Fine." Brooke turned to Peter and made a brushing gesture with her hand. "We'll all just sit around believing for a miracle." She stopped and faced Ashley once more. She seemed to force herself to sound calmer. "And while I'm at it, I'll pray for you and Landon. Because the road ahead will not be easy, Ashley. It won't."

"Thanks, Brooke." Luke stepped between them. His words dripped with sarcasm. "We've had enough medical advice for one night."

Brooke's face fell at the reprimand. Without saying another word, she walked past Peter and her girls and headed for the door.

"Brooke, don't leave like that." John followed her. "This will look different for all of us in the morning." He turned his attention to the others. "We came together to pray, not to argue."

"Sorry." Peter directed a sigh toward Ashley and Landon. "Brooke means well."

Without turning around, Brooke said good-bye and left with her daughters on either side. Peter followed, and as the door closed behind them, an awkward silence fell over the kitchen.

John was glad Cole and Devin were back in the family room with Reagan and Tommy and Malin. He slipped his hands in his pockets and leaned on the kitchen counter. He wasn't sure where to begin.

"Did you know that, Dad? That Brooke believed in abortion?"

John felt weary. "I don't think she believes in it. She's been trained to believe that where birth defects are certain and fatal, an abortion is sometimes the best option."

Shock flashed in Ashley's eyes. "You don't believe that, do you?"

"Definitely not." He gave his daughter a sad smile. "I've seen some amazing stories come from the short lives of babies with anencephaly. Every case I'm aware of defends the truth. That life belongs to God."

"Good." Luke moved closer and hugged first Landon, then Ashley. When he pulled back, he kept his hands on her shoulders. "I agree with Dad. Brooke was tactless, but that's Brooke sometimes. Just the cold, hard facts." He kissed her cheek. "Hold on to your hope, Ash. God's bigger than all of it."

"I know."

"Thank you." Landon nodded at Luke, and after a few minutes, Luke and Reagan and their kids left.

Ashley and Landon and their boys weren't far behind. But even though John asked Ashley again not to be angry with Brooke, he had a feeling the relationship between his two girls would be strained for a while.

When everyone was gone, he called Elaine and gave her the report.

The bottom line was that no matter how they prayed, there were tough times ahead. Ashley would have another ultrasound in two weeks, and if it confirmed anencephaly, then only a miracle could save the baby. At the same time, there was a bigger problem, one John hadn't known existed before today. The problem was with his oldest daughter, a bright and educated young woman who had given her life to Jesus Christ but whose value of life clearly did not align with the truth. That was the sort of change that wouldn't come easy, especially in light of all Brooke had been taught in med school. It was the sort of dividing line that could split Ashley and Brooke for a long time. Maybe even forever. John explained all of this to Elaine, and she agreed. In the weeks and months ahead, John wouldn't be praying for only one miracle.

He'd be praying for two.

CHAPTER NINE

THE NEWS ABOUT Ashley's baby was something they all agreed to keep quiet. So that Friday at CKT auditions, Katy was determined to act as if nothing were wrong. But the truth was, she felt uneasy. She and Dayne would watch the auditions, but for the first time since she'd arrived in Bloomington, she wouldn't be on the panel. The decisions would belong to Rhonda, Chad, and Bethany. Bailey Flanigan would help choreograph the show, but because she was trying out, she wasn't one of the judges.

Katy sat in the first pew with Dayne by her side. Maybe it wasn't uneasiness but more a lack of control. Her sister-in-law was entering what could be a very difficult trial, and she was flitting off to Los Angeles and New Mexico without a care. All while CKT was about to begin their last play. The very last one.

"You're thinking about Ashley?" Dayne leaned close. The kids had been great about not hounding him for autographs. They accepted him now, treating him like any of the other adults in charge. The normalcy of the atmosphere brought the only comfort Katy felt that afternoon.

"I'm trying not to." Katy snuggled closer to him. Ashley had already said she wouldn't be available to paint sets this time, and they still didn't have a music director, since Al and Nancy Helmes had moved away from the area. That along with the uncertainties of Ashley's pregnancy and the doomed fate of the theater combined to make Katy dizzy. She frowned. "When I don't think about Ashley, I think about this. How it's all coming to an end."

"When I'm done making movies, we could come back." He talked low and close to her face. "We could find some land and build our own theater and never leave Bloomington again."

She laughed, but she heard the discouragement in it. "You wouldn't be happy with that." She turned to him and met his gaze straight on. "Even if you stop making movies, you'll want to direct. You already told me that."

"I also said maybe I'll skip the whole thing and buy out the rest of my contract." He rubbed his nose against hers. "I'm serious, Katy. Don't think of this as the end of CKT. You never know what God has ahead."

Sadness wrapped itself around her shoulders like a wet blanket. "But the truth is, it's ending. For five years or forever, it's over."

His expression said he couldn't say anything to refute that, so he drew a long breath and smiled. "Then let's enjoy this audition." He poked his elbow lightly into her ribs. "I still can't believe they won't let me try out. I don't look a day over eighteen."

Katy giggled, and some of the sadness lifted. Life with Dayne would always be an adventure, but she would never doubt his love for her, his way of turning a frightening moment into something they could handle together.

The buzz around them was getting louder as kids filled the church sanctuary. They huddled together in groups, some of them singing bits of their one-minute songs. Others sat alone, poring over lyric sheets. In the past half hour, nearly every one of them had stopped by Katy and Dayne for encouragement or just to say hello. The recent CKT newsletter had explained that Katy was going to Hollywood to star in a movie with Dayne, so many of the kids also offered congratulations.

"I can't believe you're going to be a movie star!" Bailey Flanigan's hug lasted longer than the others. Standing next to her was Cody Coleman, the high school football player who lived with the Flanigans. He had given her a ride today so he could watch her audition. He smiled but let Bailey do the talking. She gushed about how she was going to miss them and how they better not stay gone for long. "And don't let it change you!" Bailey wagged her finger at Katy and grinned.

The warning was a joke, because no one in the Flanigan family was truly worried that Katy would let any amount of fame or attention change her. Katy had assured them that Bloomington was home, and it always would be, no matter how long and far away the adventure of making movies took her.

Bailey moved on, and Katy looked at Rhonda, ten yards away and setting up the judges' table next to Chad Jennings. Again they looked cozy, not so much in any sort of physical way but in the connection when their eyes met.

Katy jumped up. "I'll be right back." She hurried over to Rhonda. "You all set?"

"I think so. You sure you don't want to give the opening speech?"

"You're directing." She gave her friend a quick hug. "I'll be here if you need anything."

"I think you'll love what Rhonda's come up with." Chad tapped the *Godspell* notebook on the desk. "She's brilliant."

Rhonda gave him a playful push. "Half the stuff's yours."

"Well—" he grinned at her—"let's just say we make a good team."

Suddenly Katy had to wonder about the future of Christian Kids Theater. Even if somehow land could be purchased and a new theater built, most likely it wouldn't be Katy and Dayne running it. It would be these two. Their passion for CKT was unquestionable, and they'd have more time to devote to the kids than Katy and Dayne would.

A sense of uselessness passed over

Katy, a knowledge that she wasn't needed here anymore. The feeling should've given her a release that she was doing the right thing following Dayne to Hollywood to star in his next picture. But instead it only brought back the sad feeling from earlier. Despite that, she smiled at Rhonda and Chad, and as Bethany joined them at the table, she returned to her place next to Dayne.

Rhonda brought everyone to attention and started by talking about Katy and Dayne. "Lots of you already know that our Katy Matthews will be starring along with her husband, Dayne, in his next movie!"

An explosive cheer burst from the kids and families around the room. A few of them yelled, "Go, Katy!" and "Way to go!"

Rhonda smiled at Katy and waited for the applause to die down. "Katy will spend most of this show away with Dayne, but they'll both be here for closing weekend." She raised her eyebrows at Katy and Dayne. "Right?"

"For sure." Katy turned so she could see the crowd behind her and raised her voice. "You guys better make it good."

Another round of applause and it was time for Rhonda to get serious. That was always the hardest part of a CKT audition—keeping the kids focused when they were so wired they could hardly sit still. She started in about being courteous and not talking or leaving the room until the break between every ten auditions.

Katy stared straight ahead, barely listening. Instead she was seeing a hundred other auditions that had taken place in this room over the years. The breathtaking performance by Sarah Jo Stryker that won her the role as Becky in *Tom Sawyer* and the audition she gave for *Annie*, the same night she and Ben, another CKT boy, were killed when a drunk driver hit the van they were traveling in.

Katy recalled auditions by the Flanigan kids and dozens of others. Funny moments, like the boy who wore a swimming mask and sang "Rubber Duckie," and tender times when one of the older kids lost track of the words and quit midsong, only to be surrounded by a group of teens with one message—love and acceptance in CKT weren't based on performance.

There was the time one of the girls had worn a mermaid-style dress that made her miss the last step up to the stage and topple over, unable to get up. As awkward as the moment had been for the girl, she fought through and became one of CKT's stronger performers. Once shy, now the girl could laugh about the incident and how it helped her because nothing she would ever do onstage could be more embarrassing than that.

Katy could see it all, every performance replaying in her mind.

Rhonda clapped. "Okay, let's have the first ten in the chairs up front."

Tim Reed—always one of the first to show up for auditions—was in the group of kids who made their way down to the front. He was seventeen, so he had just a year left for CKT even if the theater wasn't being sold.

Dayne must've sensed what Katy was feeling, because he took hold of her hand and leaned in a little closer.

The first child onstage was an eight-year-old girl who didn't look a day over five. She wore a midcalf black velvet dress with her blonde hair piled high on her head.

As soon as she took her spot up front, the kids in the crowd let out a collective "Ahhh."

"Hi." She grinned. "My name is Tatum Selby."

Rhonda smiled and held up her hand, quieting the kids in the audience. "Okay, Tatum, what're you going to sing?"

"'Jesus Loves Me.'" The girl's face lit up with a smile like an angel's.

Her voice was clear and beautiful, and all Katy could think was, where would a child like her find a place to perform once CKT was gone? Tears filled her eyes, and she willed them to stay put. She'd promised herself she wouldn't cry today, that she would focus on the fun of the moment, the thrill of it.

But the question remained.

When Tatum finished, Tim Reed took the stage. He gave Katy a sad smile, a smile that told her he was feeling everything she was feeling. Not because he knew about the theater being sold, but because he had only a few more shows left before he'd be too old for CKT performances. Tim had been with CKT from the start, since Katy's beginning with the drama group. This would be his first show without Katy.

She returned the smile, and the pool of tears in her eyes grew. She gave him a nod, telling him that she believed in him completely. He could knock the song out of the park and be a leader among the cast whether she was here or not.

Tim sang a ballad from *Les Misérables*, and from the first words, the room was electrified with his presence. He had taken voice lessons for the past year, and when his instructor told him to practice keeping his vocal chords together, when she gave him a host of silly-sounding exercises to perform daily, Tim had clearly followed her instructions.

But it wasn't only his voice that made Katy hold her breath. It was something more, a depth in his eyes that couldn't be contrived. Bailey had complained that Tim wasn't paying much attention to her these days. But Katy had talked to his mother before auditions.

"Tim's taking his faith much more seriously," she'd said.

That had to be the difference now. When Tim finished singing and left the stage, Katy had no doubt. There could be no one better to play Jesus in CKT's *Godspell* than Tim Reed.

Rhonda looked over her shoulder at Katy and raised her brow. Clearly she and the other judges were feeling the same way.

Next to Katy, Dayne brought his head close to hers. "Jesus?" he whispered.

"Definitely."

They exchanged a smile, and Katy allowed herself to enjoy the moment. The future looked bleak for CKT, but for the next ten weeks, she had a strong feeling something special was going to happen for Rhonda and Chad and everyone involved in the production of *Godspell.*

She only wished she could be here to see it play out.

Bailey had goose bumps on her arms by the time Tim Reed wrapped up his audition. She and a few of the other teenage girls jumped to their feet with loud applause as he finished and took his seat.

She had a lot on her mind today. Her friend Marissa was still sleeping with her boyfriend, and something might be wrong with Ashley Blake's baby. All that and she wasn't sure what to do with her feelings for Cody. He was nicer than ever, still attending his alcohol classes and doing way better in school. And he had plans to leave for boot camp at the end of the summer. But something was happening between them, a connection that neither of them intended.

With those thoughts fighting for position and leaving her little room to concentrate on her audition song, Tim's performance brought everything into focus. He would get the part of Jesus, for sure. And how fitting, since he seemed a lot closer to God than before.

When she sat down, she caught Cody's look. He crossed his arms, and he seemed more distant.

Bailey nudged him and kept her voice quiet so only he could hear her. "What's wrong?"

"Nothing." He kept his attention on the front of the room, where another young girl was taking the stage.

"Yes, it is." She looked around. If Rhonda or Bethany heard her whispering, she could be kicked out. "Why'd you cross your arms?"

A long sigh came from Cody, and he met her eyes. His frustration seemed to melt away. "I just wish I could sing; that's all."

Bailey hesitated. "Oh." She straightened and watched the next audition. Cody wished he could sing? There it was again, a sign that he liked her, the same way she liked him. He must've been jealous about her reaction to Tim's song. Confident, cool, class charmer Cody Coleman, jealous. The thought stayed with her, and she made a mental note to talk to Cody about his feelings.

Lately her thoughts and interest were for Cody and no one else, but she'd done a good job of keeping them secret. Her parents still didn't want her dating Cody—especially not while he lived with them. And besides, he was headed off to the army. Even so, he didn't have to be jealous of Tim. Tim had never been interested in her anyway. Not really.

The next hour passed quickly, with lots of competitive auditions. At least four of the older girls already had a great shot at playing the woman caught in adultery—a part that would include two solos. Bailey checked her lyrics. She was singing "Once Upon a Time" from *Brooklyn the Musical.*

Before she went up with her group of ten, Cody squeezed her hand. "You'll do great."

"Thanks." She grinned at him. It felt like a flock of birds was trying to find its way out of her stomach. Her knees shook as she took a step back from him.

"Hey."

Bailey stopped.

"I'll be praying for you."

His words warmed her heart. "Thanks." She moved to the front, and when she was seated, she saw her parents and her brothers move up closer. Her mom gave her a little wave, and she re turned it.

When it was Bailey's turn to sing, every other thought left her head. The song was one she could've written—the idea that a fairy tale–type life must be waiting for her somewhere down the road. That one day all the confusion of today would clear, and she would have a life like her parents shared. Like Ashley and Landon Blake's and Katy and Dayne's.

As the song grew and built, Bailey could sense the audition was one of her best. When it ended, her friends roared their approval. The familiar faces before her were the safe kids, the ones she didn't have to worry about. They didn't party, and they shared her faith—not just as something they talked about but something they lived out every day.

For a moment she wondered where they might be if it weren't for CKT. The theater group gave them a place to connect, a way to know they weren't alone in their determination to make right choices. *Thank You, God*, she breathed as she grinned at Rhonda and Katy, then walked back to her seat. *Thank You for CKT. We need it here so badly.*

Before she reached her row, her eyes met Tim's. His smile told her he was proud of her, and she was glad. No matter what the coming months held for her and Cody, she wanted Tim's friendship. She looked up to him in every way that mattered.

When she made it to her seat, Cody leaned over and hugged her neck with one arm. "Way to go."

"Thanks."

Bailey was still relishing the success of her performance, grateful that she hadn't forgotten the words or cracked her voice, when she noticed a slight vibration coming from her purse. She reached in and pulled out her cell phone.

It was a text message from Marissa. *I took a test. It's positive. Please pray. I don't know what to do next.*

Bailey sucked in a quick breath. A test? She read the message again and then one more time. A pregnancy test? Was that what she was talking about? Bailey's stomach dropped, and she shut her phone. Marissa Young, her friend from Sunday school, was pregnant? At seventeen?

Cody gave her a strange look and nodded to her cell phone.

She shook her head and used her eyes to tell him she'd talk about it later. But even as she did, she could feel her heart breaking. If that's what Marissa meant, then life was about to change completely for her friend. Marissa's parents would be devastated, for sure.

Once, a few summers ago, Bailey and her mom had met up with Marissa and her mom for a day of back-to-school shopping. Over lunch, the four of them talked about the weddings that would be coming for the two girls someday. There was nothing serious or for sure about the talk, but it was fun to dream, fun to imagine the white flowing gowns and bridesmaids and flowers filling a church packed with family and friends.

Marissa admitted that she'd written a poem for her future husband, something about how her commitment to God would always be first and how she'd prayed for him since she was a little girl.

Bailey blinked, and the text message replayed in her mind. She tried to connect with the series of auditions, but her heart was a thousand miles away. Change wasn't something she did well. It was the worst part of getting older, the fact that nothing stayed the same.

When the auditions were over and the room grew loud with conversation and excitement, Cody shifted so he could see her. "What was the text?"

"Marissa." Bailey needed fresh air. "She thinks she's pregnant."

A groan came from Cody, and for a few seconds he said nothing. "She's the nice girl, right? The friend from church?"

"From school, too. She could've gotten a volleyball scholarship, but she dropped out of sports this year."

"For a guy."

"A college guy." Bailey could hear her mother telling her more times than she could count that relationships could wait, that these were the years to grow in faith and education and maturity. She grasped her knees. "Marissa wanted to wait until she was married."

Cody looked defeated. "Do you know the guy?"

"No." She shrugged. "He's at IU. Just another player."

The words seemed to hit Cody hard. He winced. "The way I used to be."

Bailey thought about all the girls who'd been connected to Cody over the years.

"Yeah, I guess." She stood, and before she could think of something else to say, Tim Reed came up and gave her a hug.

"Your song was amazing."

Tim sounded older, more mature or more confident. Whatever it was, Bailey felt her heart beat a little faster. "Thanks. You too." She caught Cody's expression as she pulled away. "Uh, Tim, you remember Cody, right? You met at my house."

"Yeah." Cody stuck out his hand. "Good to see you, man."

"You too." Tim turned his attention back to Bailey, and they talked for a few minutes about auditions and the callbacks scheduled for the next day. Tim knew Marissa, so Bailey purposefully kept that information to herself. People would find out soon enough.

When Tim was gone, and after Bailey's parents and her brother Connor had made a plan to meet back at the house for dinner, she and Cody walked out to the parking lot. It made her feel old, getting a ride home with Cody.

As they crossed the blacktop, he laughed in a quiet sort of way.

They reached his car, and she tilted her head. "What's so funny?"

"It would never work." His tone held a quiet defeat.

She thought she knew what he meant, but she wasn't going to guess. "What?"

Cody took a step closer and touched her shoulder. "Us." He smiled, but it was full of a sadness she hadn't seen in him before. He looked back at the entrance to the church. "Tim. He's your type. Not me. You deserve someone like him."

Bailey opened her mouth to say something, because a part of her wanted to tell him he was wrong. Anyone deserved a second chance at life, and just because Cody was an alcoholic and headed for the army didn't mean she couldn't fall for him. But she changed her mind.

How could she know any of the answers now? The only one that made sense was her mother's: Bailey was too young to worry about it. The way Marissa was too young. She shivered, thinking how much time she'd wasted thinking about guys. Look where that had gotten Marissa.

When they got in the car, she rolled her window down and let the night air in. She had friends and she had CKT. She had a

family who loved her and a faith that would
get her through the changes that were happening all around her.

For now, that was enough.

CHAPTER TEN

A WEEK HAD passed since the prayer meeting at her dad's house, and Kari still hadn't had a private conversation with Ashley. But Ashley wanted to keep up their walking at the high school—at least she'd said so when they were all together. Kari had called three times since, and Ashley was always preoccupied with volunteering in Cole's classroom, taking Devin in for a checkup, or cleaning the boys' bedrooms.

Kari felt terrible about her sister's situation, and there wasn't a thing she could do about it.

Jessie was at preschool, but RJ was

down for a nap, so she tiptoed across the kitchen and peered into the fridge. Brooke was coming over for lunch. Kari had made chicken salad, and she checked that it was covered, ready to go. The bread was baking, and she glanced at her timer. Another twenty minutes. She poured herself a cup of herbal tea and headed into the front room, where she could keep an eye on the driveway. She wanted to open the door before her sister had time to ring the bell and wake her son.

She sat down and cupped her tea with both hands. The warm mug felt good. Maybe it would stave off the cold, fearful feeling that had stayed in her heart since she heard the news. She wasn't a doctor like her sister, but by the time she and Ryan drove to her dad's house for the prayer meeting, she'd done enough Internet research to know the truth about anencephaly. The tests simply weren't wrong, and the birth defect was always fatal.

Always.

Kari took a sip of tea and felt the tears again. How could this be happening? And how could she convince herself to keep praying for a miracle when the situation looked so futile? She remembered the conversation she'd had with Ryan last night before they went to bed.

"You're feeling guilty." He'd taken her in his arms and run his hand along her back. For a long time he stayed that way, letting her lean into him.

She breathed in some of his strength and then stepped back so she could see his face. "You think so?"

"Yes." He had nothing but understanding and tenderness in his eyes. "You can't feel bad about having a healthy baby." He placed his fingertips beneath her chin. "Take everything inside you and put it into prayer. That's what Ashley asked you to do. Pray for a miracle."

The conversation faded from her mind, and Kari stared out the front window. She and Ashley had always been close, but they'd each had their days of grief. The time Kari lost Ryan during their college years, and then the roller coaster ride with her first husband, Tim. His affair and his murder—all in one year.

Ashley had been there during those hard times, usually with a strong opinion about what Kari should do next. But when Ashley gave her life to the Lord after working at Sunset Hills Adult Care Home, when she softened enough to let Landon catch her, it seemed like maybe Ashley was finished with her own rough times.

Kari held her mug to her cheek. The notion was ridiculous. None of them would ever be finished with the hard times until Christ called them home. As much as the Baxter family had survived over the years, they had much ahead. Times when one or another of them would doubt God or battle illness or injury. Times when their relationships would suffer because of one thing or another.

She exhaled, and the sound came from someplace deep in her soul. Today's lunch was for that very reason. Brooke and Ashley. The two of them hadn't talked since the meeting at their dad's house, and the one time Kari tried to bring it up to Brooke, she'd refused to discuss the matter.

"Ashley made herself very clear." Brooke's voice had been tense. "I was only giving my best advice, and she thinks I'm attacking her."

A van pulled into the driveway and parked. Brooke was still in her white coat from work. Her expression looked taut as she hurried up the steps, her body language saying much about her hurt.

Kari set her cup down and went to the door. *Let me be a peacemaker, God. Use me today, please. . . .* She opened the door. "Hi," she whispered. "RJ's sleeping."

Brooke nodded and stepped quietly into the house. "I could've brought lunch."

"That's okay. It wasn't any trouble."

They walked into the kitchen, and Brooke breathed in through her nose. "Smells good." She took off her white coat, set it on the back of one of the chairs, and smiled at Kari. "I haven't made fresh bread since I started med school."

Kari smiled. "We all have different gifts." She eased the door open with an oven mitt and pulled out the bread. She didn't want to waste time. "Any word from Ashley?"

"Not yet." She stood near the counter and motioned to the refrigerator. "Can I help?"

"No. I've got it." Kari brought the food to the table, poured Brooke a cup of tea, and added more to her own. When they were seated, facing each other, Kari prayed for the meal and then studied her sister. "I'm worried about you two."

"Ashley's overreacting." Brooke pulled

three brochures from her purse and set them on the table. "I'm leaving these with you. If more of us have a commonsense approach, maybe it'll help take the emotions out of the decisions ahead for Ashley and Landon."

Kari glanced at the brochures. She didn't need to open them to understand their message. Each of them had a title that dealt with abortions for medical reasons. Kari wanted to scream at her sister. It was one thing for an abortion to be Brooke's initial reaction to Ashley's ultrasound results. But now that Brooke knew Ashley's strong conviction, how could she still suggest such a thing?

"I know." Brooke waved her hand, slight disgust coloring her expression. "You think I'm terrible for saying it." She leaned forward, impassioned. "But this is not abortion for birth control's sake. The child has a fatal defect. The sooner Ashley can let this baby go, the sooner she and Landon could try again for a healthy child."

Kari was too shocked to speak. She sat back in her chair, her hands still wrapped tightly around her cup. "You're serious?"

"Of course." Brooke wasn't even a little

hesitant. "What's the point of letting a child like that live?"

"Brooke!" Kari released her cup and stood. She paced to the kitchen sink and stared out at the field behind their home. *God, give me the words. . . . Help me so I don't sound hateful.* She grabbed hold of the counter and spun around. "Do you hear yourself?"

"Of course I hear myself." Brooke clenched her jaw. "You and Ashley don't understand what will happen if she keeps this baby." She stood and marched over to Kari. When she was directly in front of her, she raked her fingers through her shoulder-length hair. "First off, the delivery is traumatic. A C-section is a must, and immediately the baby's head has to be covered to protect it." She paused. "And to hide the way its head is shaped. Then whatever few hours or days remain will be spent watching the child slowly die. It's a horrific experience, and it could traumatize Ashley and Landon for life."

Kari waited until her sister was finished. Brooke was wrong, but a screaming match would never win her over. She stood a little straighter and felt God's peace come over her. "At least they would have the chance to hold their baby, to say good-bye." Her voice was calm. "And they would know that their daughter's death didn't come at their hands but because God had called her home."

Brooke looked exasperated. "What about the trauma for Ashley and Landon?"

"What about the possibility that the test was wrong, and that even if it's right, God could still heal that baby?"

A sound like a frustrated laugh came from Brooke. "Never mind." She turned and walked back to her spot at the table. She gathered her brochures and stuffed them into her purse. "I have to go." She slipped her coat on, keeping her eyes from Kari's.

"You didn't eat." Kari hadn't wanted things to go this way. From the far bedroom, she could hear RJ starting to wake up.

"I'm not hungry." She took a few steps toward the door, stopped, and faced Kari once more. "Look, I'm not mad at you. Every-one wants this to be a moral issue, but in cases like this, it's a medical procedure. A difficult one, I agree. But I would advise it without hesitation if Ashley were my patient."

Kari moved closer to Brooke. Again she kept her tone calm. "The Bible tells us to choose life. Every time we have a choice, in every situation possible . . . choose life."

For an instant, vulnerability appeared in Brooke's eyes, as if she hadn't considered her suggestion in that light. "The child is going to die anyway." There was a cry in her voice, a pleading. "Life isn't an option for this baby."

Suddenly something occurred to Kari. "Remember what Pastor Mark said when Mom was dying?"

Brooke's expression lost any signs of a fight.

When she didn't say anything, Kari took a step closer and continued. "He said we should never be angry with God for the days we didn't get with Mom. We should be grateful for the ones we had." She blinked back tears. "Life is God's to give, God's to take. Whether that life lasts a few minutes or a few decades. Eight hours or eighty years." She put her hand on Brooke's shoulder. "Please think about that."

A long sigh came from Brooke. She looked tired of arguing. "I know you mean well."

Kari found a sad smile. "You too."

Brooke gave a final nod and then left.

When she'd closed the door behind her, Kari went to the window and watched her drive away. Ryan Junior was crying softly, and she needed to get to him. But before another minute passed, she had to pray. *God . . . don't let this come between us. Brooke's an intelligent woman, educated and up-to-date on the latest medical understanding. But Your Word says life isn't a matter of intellect or choice. It's Yours. Period.* She sighed, and the next part of her prayer came in an audible whisper. "Change her heart, Lord. Please."

She headed for RJ's room, still thinking about the exchange with Brooke. She placed her hand on her stomach, where her own little girl was growing healthy and sound. She and Ryan had come up with a name, though they hadn't told anyone yet. Anne Elizabeth—after Ryan's mother and her own. They would call her Annie.

Kari reached RJ's room and swept her little boy into her arms. Ashley's baby might end up being healthy too. The two cousins could become the best of friends, the way she and Ashley had dreamed they might be. Then the entire dialogue would wind up a waste of time. She kissed RJ's cheek. "Hungry?"

RJ stuck his fingers into his mouth and nodded.

As she carried him into the kitchen, she thought about Brooke's certainty. If the test showed anencephaly, then there was no mistake or getting around it. The possibility was a real one, of course. Either way, maybe the entire situation had come to them for one reason alone.

So that Brooke would never again recommend an abortion for one of her patients no matter what. And so that she would come to understand the truth about life—that it was God's to give and God's to take.

No matter how difficult the circumstances.

As she drove back to her office, Brooke gave an angry swipe at her cheeks and the tears that had fallen there. No one understood her. She wasn't advocating abortion for the sake of having a choice. She was offering the same medical advice she'd give any of her own patients. But Kari and Ashley were determined to make her the bad guy, the one Baxter sister who didn't understand God's plan for life or His truth.

She grabbed a tissue from the console of

her van and blew her nose. The worst part was that they were making her doubt her own advice.

Her eyes narrowed, and she focused on the green light just ahead. Many babies with such defects would naturally abort through a miscarriage. Undergoing an abortion for severe fatal defects, then, was like taking care of a pregnancy that the body should've eliminated but failed to do so.

Right? Wasn't that what she'd always told herself?

The light ahead of her turned red, and she slowed to a stop. *God, I'm not trying to go against Your truth. Surely You know that.*

Daughter, all life is Mine. . . .

The words rang loud and clear in her heart, in a way they rarely had before. Her sisters had talked about hearing God, and in the days after Hayley's near drowning, Brooke had on occasion heard what she thought was the Lord's response. But over time she'd doubted that, because lately when she prayed the conversation seemed to be one-sided.

Still, there was no denying the words that had echoed in her heart just now. Were they Kari's words lingering? Or was God Himself trying to speak to her? Of course life was His, and of course He was capable of miracles. Her little Hayley was living proof. But anencephaly? Babies simply didn't get healed from that. Other situations played in her mind, times when a patient would start bleeding and be sent to the hospital for a procedure that would in effect complete the miscarriage, ridding the woman's body of any remaining tissue from the pregnancy.

Wasn't that all an abortion would do at this point? Remove from Ashley the life that was already dying inside her?

Brooke returned to work, but her heart wasn't in it. Two of her nurses asked her if she was okay.

"I'm fine," she told them. "Just distracted."

She needed to talk to Peter. He'd been a doctor longer than she had, and in the past year or so he'd spent far more time reading the Bible each morning than she did. He could shed light on the subject, especially since they'd talked about it that night after the prayer meeting at her father's house. Peter had been noncommittal then, but he'd promised her he would think more about it, pray about it. Maybe now he'd have an answer.

That night after dinner, when the girls

were sitting at the table in the playroom coloring in their new Easter coloring books, Brooke found Peter parked in front of the television. She came up and stood a few feet from him. "Can we talk?"

Peter hesitated, then took the remote and flicked off the TV. "Sounds serious."

"It is." She sat down on the other end of the sofa, leaving enough space between them so she could read his expression. "I tried to have lunch with Kari today."

"Tried?" Peter shifted so he was facing her.

Brooke launched into the story of how she'd gone to Kari's house hoping to convince her about Ashley's need for an abortion. "Kari talks to Ashley more than I do." She sat cross-legged, her back to the arm of the sofa. "I figured she might have more influence."

Peter frowned. "What happened?"

She told him how quickly things had escalated and how she'd left without eating. "It's like everyone in my family has a one-track mind when it comes to abortion. Even when it's medically the best option, like it is for Ashley."

Brooke expected Peter to nod in agreement and spout off a list of statistics as to why she was right. All day she'd known that if she could only have his validation, she wouldn't have to doubt herself. But instead he rubbed the back of his neck, stood, and took slow steps toward the window. The sun had already set, but it was dusky outside, the silhouette of tree branches sharp against the not-quite-dark sky. He raised his arm and rested it on the glass.

"Peter?" She pulled her legs up and hugged her knees to her chest.

After several seconds, he turned, and his face showed the brokenness he must've been feeling inside. She'd seen him look this way only one other time. After Hayley's accident, he'd allowed himself to get hooked on pain pills. The quick and certain addiction nearly split them apart, but at the last moment he arranged to meet her at a spot where they'd hiked over the years. There he confessed that he was sorry and that he wanted to work on their marriage. His expression then was the same as it was now— all confidence and self-assuredness gone.

Peter shrugged, and it was clear that his answers were still taking shape. "I've thought about this every day since that night at your dad's house." He leaned on the windowsill and rubbed his neck again. "I've always seen things the way you're seeing them. That sometimes abortion is the most necessary and smartest choice to make."

"That's changed?" Alarm filled her heart.

"Maybe." He sighed. "I've recommended abortion several times. This week I thought about those cases and whether the abortion actually served its purpose to help the mother." He gave a slow shake of his head. "I'm not sure it ever really did. I'm not sure they had closure."

Closure? Brooke's head was spinning. She eased her legs over the side of the couch, her eyes locked onto her husband's.

"But more than that, there's the Bible." Peter walked back to her and sat on the edge of the sofa. "Life is a blessing and a gift from the Lord. Not once does Scripture show an example of eliminating a life out of convenience or for medical reasons." He took hold of her hand, his voice tender. "I've looked, Brooke."

She thought about that, and inside she felt her convictions begin to crumble. But at the same time she realized something. If she were to allow Peter and Kari and Ashley to change her mind now, then what did that say

about the abortions she'd already recommended, the ones that had already taken
place? She shuddered at the ramifications,
and her resolve doubled.

Her eyes held his, and she hoped her
smile was enough to hide her fear. "We
might have to agree to disagree about this
one." It was what they'd been told when
they'd gone for counseling after Peter's treat-
ment for the pain medication addiction.
Sometimes in a marriage it was better to
agree to disagree on the things that didn't
matter specifically to the marriage. This was
one of those things. At least it seemed that
way at the moment.

Peter gave her hand a soft squeeze. "God
speaks to us all at different times, in different
ways. I'm only telling you how He's been
speaking to me."

The alarm in Brooke's heart returned with
a vengeance. God had been speaking to Peter? The way He'd spoken to her in the van
on the way back to the office earlier today?
She brushed her hair away from her face
and stood. "Okay, well . . . thanks for understanding. I'll go check on the girls."

She was glad Peter didn't chide her or
ridicule her, glad he didn't ask her to change

her way of thinking. She'd spent years in med school, years developing the standards by which she practiced medicine, the advice she gave her patients. The things Peter had decided were good for him didn't always apply to her. He must've thought the same thing, because he didn't try to change her mind, didn't condemn her.

Before she left the room, a realization struck. Their differences in the area of medical abortions must've been harder on Peter than she first thought. Because as she left the room, she looked back at him one more time. He wasn't reaching for the remote or getting comfortable on the sofa again.

His eyes were closed, his head bowed in silent, unmistakable prayer.

CHAPTER ELEVEN

LUKE WAS STILL thinking about the office and several complications with a handful of Dayne's contracts when he walked through the door of the rental house they were living in for a few more months until their new home was ready. The moment he stepped inside, he tripped on a toy truck. He bit his lip and stopped just inside the entryway. Plastic dinosaurs were lined up along the hallway with an occasional toy Jeep or race car.

In a room at the other end of the house, he could hear Malin crying. She had another ear infection, and Reagan seemed overwhelmed most of the time. He gave the toy truck a light kick and dodged the dinosaurs on his way into the living room. There was a load of unfolded laundry on one chair and a dirty plate on the arm of the sofa. The place was a mess. Again.

"Reagan?" He could hear the frustration in his voice as he set down his briefcase. It wasn't like she had a job outside the home. She only needed to deal with the kids and keep the house clean. He stretched his neck one way and then the other. *Calm*, he told himself. *A sick kid makes for a tough day*. Especially with Malin, who cried more than any baby he'd ever known.

"Back here." Reagan's voice rose above the sound of the crying.

At that moment, Tommy came running from the back hallway, a T. rex in his hands. "Rooooaaaar!" he growled and raised the dinosaur toward Luke. "I'm a T. rex, Daddy!"

"Yes." Luke bent down and kissed the boy on his head. There was a bandage on his pointer finger. Luke caught his hand and studied it. "What happened here?"

"Malin's door got me."

Luke straightened. "Oh, boy," he muttered. "Come on—let's go find Mommy." He took hold of Tommy's good hand, and the two padded down the hallway to Malin's room.

Reagan was sitting in the rocking chair, patting their daughter on the back. "She's got a fever."

Luke leaned against the doorframe. "What did the doctor say?"

"He gave us more antibiotics and told me to take her to a specialist. She probably needs tubes in her ears."

"They've said that before." Luke felt worn-out. He'd battled with studio executives and flawed contracts all day, and every hour he'd looked forward to this moment. Now he almost wished he'd stayed late at the office.

"They're serious this time." Reagan whispered a hushing sound into Malin's ears, but the child was still whimpering. "This is her third ear infection this year."

"It feels like the tenth." He gave her a weak smile.

"Tell me about it." She set the rocker in motion again. "It's not her fault, though."

"And Tommy?"

The boy was on the floor now, moving the dinosaur through the plush carpet, making growling sounds.

"Well, this morning when I was putting drops in Malin's ears, he got into the freezer and pulled out a box of frozen sausage. The cooked kind, thankfully. He was on his sixth sausage by the time I found him."

"He ate frozen sausage?" Luke looked down at his son.

Tommy cast him an impish grin. "I like sausage."

Reagan raised her brow. "Yes, and then he found the crayons in the kitchen drawer and drew a large, expressive picture of a T. rex on his bedroom wall."

"I'm a painter." Tommy was still on his hands and knees, and he turned in a tight circle, the dinosaur sounds louder than before. "T. rex looks very mean."

Luke felt his frustration rising. The house wasn't theirs. Whatever damage they did would be deducted from their deposit. "Did you punish him?"

"Sure; I gave him a time-out." She leaned her head back against the chair. "But before his time was up, he went to Malin's room and started playing with her door."

"Where were you?"

For the first time, Reagan's expression grew angry. "Doing my nails, Luke." She sighed. "What do you think? I was making lunch. I can't follow him around every minute of the day."

"So he slammed his finger?"

"Of course, it's not enough for him to open and shut the door like a regular person." Reagan gave their son a stern look. "He had to hold it with both hands spread wide apart."

"'Cause I'm a dinosaur, Daddy." Tommy looked as innocent as an angel.

"Yes, and then our little dinosaur pinched his finger near the hinge so hard I thought we were going to need a trip to the emergency room."

Luke knelt next to Tommy. He took hold of the boy's hand but kept his eyes on Reagan's. "Was it bad?"

"It split the skin on either side of his fingernail. It bled a lot, but I don't think it'll need stitches."

"Band-Aids are good dinosaur claws!" Tommy waved his bandaged finger around and made another roaring sound.

Malin's crying grew loud again, and Reagan raised her voice so she could be heard. "On that note, how was your day?"

Every phone call and legal document he'd

taken care of today came to mind, and he opened his mouth to share some of it. But at the same time, he thought about the day Reagan had just painted and started to chuckle. He rose and took slow steps toward his wife. "It doesn't matter."

Reagan looked slightly confused by his laughter. "It does." Her voice was softer than before, barely understandable against the backdrop of a wailing Malin. "Just because my day was crazy doesn't mean I don't want to know about yours."

"Let's just say this." He leaned in and kissed her on the lips. "It was a whole lot easier than yours."

He took Malin from her and rocked his daughter until she calmed down. By then Reagan had made Tommy clean up his mess, and she had ground beef cooking on the stove. Sanity of the bedtime hours was within reach, and even over dinner Tommy was quiet enough that they were able to talk.

"I've been thinking about Ashley." Reagan's concern showed in her eyes. "We're supposed to pray for a miracle. But what if God doesn't want a miracle for this baby?"

"All babies are a miracle." It was something Luke's father had said over the years, and the words came easily off his tongue. "No matter what condition they come in."

Reagan thought about that. "I guess so."

"But I know what you mean." Luke put his fork down. "I've been thinking about her too. She's been quiet."

"She has. I talked to Kari this morning. She says no one's seen Ashley since the meeting at your dad's house."

Luke's heart ached at the thought. "I need to call her."

"Kari says that Brooke's sure about the test. If the ultrasound showed that kind of birth defect, then Ashley's baby has it. No doubt."

Luke remembered something his mother had said back when he was sure he would never find Reagan again, never make things work with her. *God loves to spoil the understanding of mere mortals.*" He smiled and reached for his fork. "God has a plan for this child, same as any other. That's the part I'm going to hang on to."

The conversation shifted, and after dinner the nighttime routine began. There were baths for both kids, with Reagan taking special care to make sure no water got into Malin's ears.

Tommy took his T. rex into the tub with him, and Luke sat on the edge holding the dinosaur. As he did, he silently thanked God for the chaos of his home and the life that they were living. Malin might need tubes in her ears, but overall his family was healthy and happy. He couldn't imagine what Ashley must be feeling and how she would handle the coming months if indeed her baby lived only a few days. He would call her tomorrow to encourage her.

As for his reaction when he came home from work, he was sorry and told Reagan so when they finally fell into bed that night. He had no right to be angry or frustrated with the bedlam that sometimes marked his home. This was the life of having young children. Someday they would look back and smile at this time, wondering at how fast the years had disappeared and wishing for the sound of a crying child or the parade of dinosaurs across the kitchen floor.

And the growl of a blond, blue-eyed T. rex who would only be little for so long.

It was Saturday, the middle of April, and the warm weather had given way to a few days of thunderstorms. John didn't mind. He loved Indiana's thunder and lightning, as long as the storms didn't spin off tornadoes. And there were none in the forecast.

Now it was late afternoon, and the sun was out again. He and Elaine were walking on the path that wound around the downtown park, the place where their friendship had first taken root. He preferred the park to the path behind his house. Especially now that things were moving forward with Elaine. Since he'd made his feelings known, it didn't feel right walking with her on the same path he'd once walked with Elizabeth.

The conversation today was about Ashley, a subject they'd tried to avoid in the past week. Every time it came up, one of them would respond in the same way. There was nothing to talk about, no sick baby to cause worry. Never mind the medical statistics. God was in control. Ashley had asked them to pray for a miracle, to believe that the test was wrong or that her baby would be healed. It seemed wrong to do anything else.

But now, John wasn't so sure. He'd talked to Ashley's doctor and asked about the test. Making the call was tricky, since the doctor was bound to keep details to herself because of the patient privacy rules. John was careful about his questions.

"My daughter's ultrasound," he began. "Are you sure about the results?"

"I've looked at them a dozen times since then." The woman sounded defeated. "There's no doubt in my mind."

John hadn't pushed for more details. What more could there be?

Now his pace was slow, the path still damp from rain this morning. Next to him, Elaine was quiet, thoughtful. A blue jay dipped low over the path in front of them and soared to one of the low branches of a nearby maple tree.

"The thing is . . ." John took a deep breath. The air smelled of rain and damp grass. "I understand where Brooke's coming from."

Elaine raised her eyebrow. "You do?"

"She's a product of her education, her generation. Abortions are fast and easy and legal. She doesn't see it any other way."

"But you do, right?" Elaine slowed her steps.

"Of course." His heart went out to his oldest daughter. Each of his kids had talked about how off she was on this, how she couldn't have a very strong faith if she could recommend an abortion. "Brooke's wrong, but we're all wrong if we can't find a way to love her despite her opinions."

Elaine angled her head. "True."

They walked a little farther. At the playground, they spotted Jim Flanigan with his four youngest boys. They were playing a game of flag football, the boys laughing out loud. John and Elaine stopped and watched for a few minutes. Three of the boys were black, and Ricky—the youngest—was white. But as the kids ran and played and yelled for the ball, there wasn't a difference between any of them.

They were kids, all of them. Created by God and perfect in His sight.

John waved, and they continued on their walk. "I've been thinking about Ashley's baby."

"Mmm." She wove her fingers between his. "I'm praying for a miracle, the way Ashley asked."

"Me too. But what if God is asking Ashley and Landon to take this journey—the journey of having a child with a fatal birth defect?"

Elaine gave him a sad look. "I've thought about that."

"It'd be like walking through fire. But if God asks that of Ash, then He'll ask it of the whole family. We would need to walk right alongside them because she and Landon would need all the support they could get."

"Yes." She stared straight ahead. "My daughter miscarried her first child. She mourned that baby the way a mother would mourn the death of any child."

John lifted his eyes to the heavens. "So there's a fine line here between doing as Ashley's asking us to do, praying for a miracle—" he paused—"and helping her handle what might be the reality of her situation."

Elaine was quiet for nearly a minute. "God always makes the lines clear just when we need to see them."

John felt her response straight to his soul. He stopped and turned so he was facing her. He took hold of her other hand and tenderly kissed her. His feelings for her had grown stronger since he'd made his intentions clear. She was more than his friend and companion. She was stirring inside him feelings of love he hadn't known he'd ever feel again. This was one of those moments.

He searched her kind, gentle eyes. "Thank you . . . for pointing that out."

"You're welcome." She leaned her head on his chest. "Thanks for understanding."

John took a few steps back and released one of Elaine's hands. This wasn't the place for long face-to-face conversations, not out in public this way. Especially when he hadn't told his kids yet that things between him and Elaine had intensified.

They started walking again, and John watched another blue jay work to dig up a worm. When the bird had the worm firmly in its beak, it flew off toward a distant tree. Somewhere in a nest on a branch, a baby bird was about to get fed. It was a mother's instinct to care for her child. Ashley was only doing what any mother would do, praying for the diagnosis to disappear.

And maybe it would. A resolve came over John, and he swallowed back a lump in his throat. If not, he would pray that he and Elaine and his other kids could support Ashley and Landon like never before. In the meantime, he would do what Elaine suggested.

Pray that God would make clear the lines between wanting a miracle and walking through fire.

CHAPTER TWELVE

JENNY HAD NEVER imagined the conversation she was about to have. The boys were outside with Jim so she and Bailey could be alone in the living room. Marissa Young was on her way over. This would be Jenny's and Bailey's attempt to talk Marissa into telling her mother immediately and, even more importantly, keeping her baby.

She looked at Bailey and tried to remember everything her daughter had said. "She's still coming, right?"

"That's what she told me. She's afraid to talk to anyone but me." Bailey made a skeptical face. "She was really mad I shared it with you, but I told her I tell you everything. She doesn't want her mom finding out from anyone but her, no matter what."

Jenny looked out the window at Jim and the boys. Their newest thing was flag football. Jim and one of the boys would form a team, and the rest of the boys would make up the other. Even Connor was getting in on the action—though he was more comfortable onstage. She watched her boys, young and innocent, laughing with their father without a care in the world. *God, please make them young men of virtue, boys who are willing to wait until they're married*. She couldn't imagine one of them coming home with the news that his girlfriend was pregnant.

But even if one did, she and Jim would love that son and hold him, cry with him, and do whatever they could to help him be a father or to support a decision of adoption. They would get through the ordeal with Christ leading the way, and they would come out on the other side with their family still intact.

Which was more than she could say for Marissa.

"What're you going to tell her?" Bailey sat cross-legged on the chair near the piano.

The sun streamed through the window and splashed gold on her natural highlights. But she looked tense.

"First she has to tell her mother. Absolutely. And next she needs to know that the baby inside her is a human life." Jenny looked out the window again, and a slow sigh slipped between her lips. "I want her to know her options, that she can connect with our crisis pregnancy center and get a free ultrasound. That way she can hear the baby's heartbeat, probably even see the baby's spine at this point."

"Really?" Bailey's mouth hung open. Her face looked pale. "It's so weird to think there's really a baby growing inside her."

Jenny wanted to say that it was more sad than weird. "Is her boyfriend still pushing for an abortion?"

"Yeah. Last time I heard." Bailey ran her tongue along her lower lip. "It's going to be awkward. This talk."

"Difficult situations make for awkward moments." As discouraged as Jenny was about Marissa, she couldn't have been prouder of Bailey. She'd admitted her feelings for Cody, but since the situation with Marissa, her take on life was black-and-white. This wasn't the time for a boyfriend. "You hear from Tim?"

"I see him at rehearsal. The other day I told him about my plan. No boyfriends until college." She giggled. "He said he thought Cody and I were going out. I set him straight."

"Is Tim seeing anyone?"

"No. He feels the same way. Dating too young just gets you in trouble." The doorbell rang, and Bailey raised her eyebrows. "Speaking of trouble . . ." She hopped up, and after a quick hello, both Bailey and Marissa returned to the living room.

Marissa looked like she'd been crying. "Hello, Mrs. Flanigan."

"Hi, Marissa." Jenny stood and hugged her, then returned to her seat.

Marissa took the spot on the sofa next to Bailey's chair. "Wow." She blew out hard through pursed lips. "I can't believe I'm here."

"It's okay, honey." Jenny leaned forward and clasped her hands. "No one's going to judge you. What's done is done."

"My whole life's about to change." Marissa didn't whine or let out any dramatic sobs. But tears trickled down her cheeks. "Why didn't I think about this before?"

It was the question thousands of teenage girls asked themselves every year. Jenny allowed some time to pass before she started in. "The question, Marissa, is what to do next."

Bailey was quiet, her gaze downcast. Something about having her friend here and discussing the baby must've made Marissa's pregnancy seem more real than before.

"Yes." Marissa sniffed. "That's all I can think about. Bailey probably told you that my boyfriend wants me to have an abortion."

Jenny wished the young man were here in her living room. She'd tell him exactly what she thought of his decision to sleep with a high school girl and then order her to get rid of the baby. "I'm going to say something that won't make you very happy."

Marissa looked at Jenny. She seemed to have more resolve than before.

"You need to talk to your mother, Marissa. Before another day goes by."

Fear filled Marissa's eyes. She swallowed hard, looked down at her lap, and gave a slight nod. "I know. I'm planning on it."

"Marissa, look at me." Jenny prayed her tone sounded as kind as she intended. When Bailey's friend lifted her eyes, Jenny continued. "If you don't tell your mom, I'll call her. She has to know."

The girl's eyes grew wider. "I'll tell her, Mrs. Flanigan. I will."

"Good." Compassion made Jenny's throat thick. Marissa was so young, so afraid. Jenny waited until she found her voice. "Next, you must understand that your boyfriend doesn't love you, sweetheart. If he loved you, he would've respected you. He would've wanted whatever was best for you. Instead he pushed you to have sex with him, and now he's pushing you to do something that'll make *his* life easy." Jenny's voice was soft, full of concern. "But having an abortion could never make *your* life easy. The rest of your days you'll know when that baby's birth date would've been, and you'll count off the milestones that never occurred. When the baby should've walked and talked and headed off to kindergarten. You'll carry that child in your heart as long as you live. I promise you, Marissa."

More tears filled the girl's eyes, and she nodded. "I've been thinking about that."

"There's a bumper sticker that says, 'Abortion doesn't destroy one life. It destroys two.'" Jenny's heart went out to Marissa. The issues at hand were too great for a girl so young. "I've talked with friends who've had abortions. They agree with that bumper sticker completely. They tell me even though Jesus forgives them, they'll struggle forever with forgiving themselves."

Bailey took a breath and looked at Marissa. "What'd you tell your boyfriend?"

"I told him I couldn't decide yet."

"There's something else to consider." Jenny tried not to let her alarm show. With all Marissa had been taught in church and by her parents over the years, how was it even possible that she was considering abortion? Jenny clenched her fists, begging God for the right words. "None of this is the baby's fault."

"I know." Marissa put her hand over her midsection. "I keep thinking if only I could be brave enough, I'd have the baby and give it up for adoption. My parents know people who are desperate for a baby. I heard them talking last week at church."

Jenny remembered something. "There's a couple at CKT trying to adopt also." She tried to keep her enthusiasm at bay. Adoption might be the perfect option for Marissa.

"The thing is, if I tell my parents, they might want me to keep the baby." She dabbed her fingers beneath her eyes.

"They're always talking about how someday me and my brother will give them half a dozen grandbabies. That sort of thing. I'm afraid my mom would rather raise the baby than let me give it up for adoption."

Jenny leaned back in her seat. No wonder Marissa hadn't said anything to her parents. She bit her lip. "I think your mom would be more understanding than that. Adoption is a wonderful choice for a lot of girls. If you were honest with how you feel, I'm sure they'd stand by you and support an adoption."

Marissa twisted her face and shook her head. "Do you know how disappointed they're going to be?"

"They'll still love you." Bailey reached over and put her hand on Marissa's shoulder. "They'll get over the shock—you know they will."

"Maybe."

"We could be with you." Jenny had thought about the idea before, but she hadn't remembered it until now. "If you want, Bailey and I could be there when you tell them."

Marissa shook her head. "That'd only make my mom madder. Because you two knew before she did."

Jenny could understand that. She stood and moved to the spot on the sofa next to Marissa. "I know you're scared. But please . . . don't have an abortion. Your baby deserves to have a life; don't you think?"

Marissa was crying harder now, and she hung her head. Even still, she managed to mumble, "Yes."

"Okay, let's take it to God." Jenny held Marissa's hand, and Bailey took her other one. Jenny led the prayer, asking God to give Marissa courage and a clear, honest picture of the life growing inside her. "Give Marissa the courage to talk to her parents today, Lord. Protect Marissa from the devil's lies and help her to hear Your voice above that of her boyfriend or anyone else."

When they finished praying, Jenny gave Marissa the information on the Bloomington Crisis Pregnancy Center. "They have counselors who'll talk to you and your mom." She allowed the hint of a smile. "And they'll give you an ultrasound so you can see live pictures of your baby."

Marissa nodded. She wiped her eyes and stood. "Thanks for talking to me." She hugged Jenny, then Bailey. "It helps. Talking to my boyfriend is so . . . I don't know, so confusing."

Jenny wanted to tell her to break up with the guy. He was obviously no good for her. But she couldn't throw too much information Marissa's way. If Marissa went against the boyfriend's wishes, his personality was bound to get ugly. The breakup could come then.

For now Jenny only nodded. "I'm sure it's very confusing. That's why we're here." She patted the girl's arm. "After you talk to your mom, let Bailey know. Otherwise . . ." She hesitated, making sure Marissa understood. "I'll have to call her."

"I understand." Marissa thanked them both.

When Marissa was gone, Bailey dropped back to her seat. "I can't believe it."

"Which part?" Jenny sat next to her daughter. She too was drained. Watching Marissa grow up, she never could've imagined that the girl's life would take this turn.

"That she's still staying with the guy, even after all this." Bailey stared out the window at Jim and the boys. "Daddy always told me there was a sure way to know if a boy really loved you." She turned her attention back to her mother. "If he talks you into doing physical stuff, then he doesn't love you. Period. Because that means he's just in it for himself."

"That's not what he'll say in the moment."

Jenny gave her a sad smile. "He'll make it sound like it's the best thing for both of you."

Bailey was quiet. "I guess I found that out with Bryan."

"Exactly." Jenny put her arm around Bailey's shoulders. "It's very easy to fall into temptation."

"But it helps if you know what to look for." Bailey smiled and patted Jenny's hand. As she did, she stood and took a step toward the doorway. "I have math homework due Monday." She took another few steps and stopped. "Hey, thanks, Mom. I don't know what I'd do if I couldn't talk to you about stuff, you know?"

Jenny felt her daughter's words all the way to the center of her soul. "I feel the same way."

As Bailey jogged off, Jenny couldn't help but thank God. Because in a different set of circumstances, the girl in trouble could be Bailey. Even with great communication and even with her convictions in place, the wrong sort of guy could turn her head, and her life could change in a single hour. It was one more reason Jenny was glad for CKT. The drama group gave Bailey an outlet where, for the most part, dating was discouraged.

Kids had too much fun in groups to need the one-on-one feeling of dating.

Jenny went outside and sat on the picnic table.

"Throw it this way, Dad!" Justin was on Jim's team. Jim winged the ball at him, and Justin jumped to catch it. Then he was off, headed for the far side of the yard.

"He could . . . go . . . all . . . the . . . way!" Jim held up both hands. "Touchdown!"

Ricky plopped down on the grass and lay sprawled on his back. "I think it's halftime."

"Yeah." Shawn dropped down beside him. "We're getting killed."

Jim spotted Jenny. "Okay, guys. It's half-time. Go in and get a drink."

The boys scrambled for the house, laughing and teasing each other. Connor was the last to file in, and he stopped near Jenny. "Is Bailey okay?" Concern flashed in his eyes.

Jenny loved this about her oldest son, the way he cared so much for his sister. Connor didn't know about Marissa, but he could sense something was wrong. That much was obvious. Jenny took his hand. "She's fine. The talk was for Marissa, not Bailey."

"Is Marissa in trouble?"

Jenny didn't want to lie, but she didn't

want to shatter Connor's innocence either. It was too soon for him to know the details of Marissa's situation. "She's got some things she needs to tell her parents. That's all."

"Oh." Relief showed on Connor's face. "I hope she figures it out."

"Me too."

Connor went in and Jim jogged up. "Hey, gorgeous."

"Hi." He still had a way of making her insides turn to mush, the way he'd done since the first day she met him. She patted the spot beside her on the picnic table. "We had a good talk with Marissa."

"I was praying for you."

She smiled. "I could tell." The late-afternoon air held a chill. She slid closer to him. "I told her she had to tell her parents, and we talked about the pregnancy clinic in town, how abortion wasn't fair to her baby."

"Did she hear you?"

"I don't know." Jenny looked past their back field to the trees at the edge of their property. A hawk circled high overhead, probably the same one that always hung around out back. She took a long breath. "She's confused. Her boyfriend's filling her head with trash."

Jim clenched his jaw. "Our boys better not do that."

"They won't." She put her hand on his knee. "At least I hope they won't."

He leaned into her, and the two of them were quiet for a few minutes. Jenny loved times like this, when they were so close they could practically read each other's minds. When the Lord said, "The two will become one flesh," He must've been thinking about couples like her and Jim.

The dogs spotted them at the same time, and both of them came running up. Reggie and Mandy were yellow Labs, one twelve years old and fit, the other three and endearing but strangely lazy. From a distance they could easily tell which one was Mandy because of the way she waddled along at her own pace. Jim held out his hand and patted both their heads. "Hey, puppies. How's it going?" He grinned. "They get credit for at least one lost touchdown."

Jenny laughed. "Let me guess . . . a tackle?"

"Definitely." Jim rubbed beneath their chins next. "Connor was in a full run for the end zone, no one in his way, when the dogs galloped up and cut him off." He laughed.

"Connor hesitated, and Reggie jumped up and licked his face. That tripped him and the touchdown was gone."

"I'll bet Connor loved that." She petted Mandy.

"Okay . . ." Jim clapped and pointed. The dogs took the cue and ran off together toward the far reaches of the field. "They're such good dogs."

"You're a good trainer." Jenny snuggled close to him again. "By the way, did Justin tell you what they'll be studying in school next week?"

"Slavery." Jim leaned his elbow on one knee and looked at her. "Makes me wish we could keep them young forever."

"I was thinking that too."

"I mean, they need to know." Jim put his hands behind him on the picnic table and leaned back. "Slavery was part of our country's heritage, an awful part. They need to understand that. But right now they see it the way we've taught them. God has a different color for every person. People will hate you because you're black, and they'll hate you because you're white. Each time the problem is with the person who's hating, because God made each person the exact right color."

Jenny smiled. "Maybe you should teach the unit."

He stared into the distance. "I think we need to have a family meeting tonight. Talk about racism so they'll hear it from us first."

"Hmmm." Jenny liked the idea. "Because it works a lot of different ways."

"Exactly."

"Not just your skin color. They'll hate you for being a Christian or a Jew."

"For being uncoordinated or having red hair." Jim was quiet again. "The fact is, our country messed up badly back in the days of slavery. And if we don't fight for all people to be free, it could happen again—with some other people group."

"Yep." Jenny patted her knees. "Sounds like a family meeting to me."

Jim turned to her, and with one hand he framed her face. "These are the easy years—you know that, right?"

Jenny thought about the struggle earlier with Marissa. "It could certainly be a lot worse."

"Bailey is navigating the waters of being a teenager with all the grace and maturity I've always expected from her." Jim sucked in a quick breath. "But the boys are next. Soon they'll all be driving and wanting to date and trying to figure out what's important."

When he put it that way, Jenny couldn't help but agree. "So we enjoy these years while we can."

"Exactly." Jim kissed her, slow enough that it made her remember how it felt to be young and in love.

She drew back and smiled at him. "We need to pray."

"Every day."

And with that, they went inside to gather up the kids for the family meeting. As they did, Jenny was grateful that this time the topic was something they could all agree on, something straightforward with obvious truths they could stand on. The meeting reminded her to pray for Marissa, who should that very evening be asking her parents to have a meeting.

One that would be more difficult than any other in all her life.

CHAPTER THIRTEEN

Ashley was cutting Devin's peanut-butter sandwich into bite-size pieces when Landon walked into the kitchen.

"Cole caught another frog."

She glanced out the open back window. "There must be a hundred of them in the bushes out back."

"Sounds more like a thousand." Landon kissed her. "That kid loves frogs. I can't get him inside."

"He can play a little longer." She checked the clock on the microwave. "After church, Sundays should be for catching frogs. If you're a little boy, anyway."

Landon gave her a sheepish look. "Or even a big boy." He tousled Devin's hair.

Devin had jelly on his cheeks and on most of his fingers. He reached up to Landon. "Kisses, Daddy!"

"Sure, buddy." Landon kissed a clean spot on their son's cheek. Then he moved to the refrigerator. "Leftover chicken tonight?"

"That or nut-nut butter." Ashley sat down in the chair closest to Devin's high chair. She felt wonderful, and the mood in their home had lightened over the weekend. Despite a few thunderstorms, the sun was back, and her baby girl was more active than ever. Ashley had no doubt about the miracle God was working in her. Everything was going to be just fine.

Landon opened the fridge and lifted the tinfoil from the leftover chicken, snagging a piece. He popped it in his mouth, covered the chicken, and pushed it back into place. "I had to test it."

"And?" Ashley could feel the sparkle in her eyes.

"It'll be a great dinner." He leaned on the fridge. "Our frog hunter's bound to be hungry. What about you?"

"Chicken sounds great. In an hour maybe,

okay?" She focused on Devin. "Want some milk?"

"Milk, milk, milk!" Devin banged his hands on his high chair tray. Then he laughed as if that were the funniest thing he'd ever said or done.

Landon opened the fridge again, pulled out the milk, and handed it to Ashley.

Ashley poured Devin some milk in a sippy cup, then set it down on his tray. She looked at Landon.

The smile and easy way he'd had a few minutes earlier was gone. Instead he looked pensive as he studied her.

"What's on your mind?"

Landon opened his mouth to say something, but then he pressed his lips together. He shook his head and leaned back against the fridge once more. "I've wanted to talk to you all weekend, but . . . I don't know. There didn't seem to be a right time."

"Talk about what?" Ashley steeled herself.

"The baby, Ashley." Landon crossed his arms. "We've been walking around like nothing's wrong, like we never got the diagnosis."

Ashley felt the walls of normalcy she was living within begin to crumble. "The baby's moving." She made a sound that was part laugh, part desperation. "She feels healthier than either of the boys ever did."

"That's good. But . . ." Landon was struggling. He hung his head for a moment, and when he looked up, she could tell he didn't want to say whatever was next. "I guess I think it'd still be smart to have a plan."

Shock blew its acid breath straight into her face. "A plan?" She felt dizzy. Was he saying what she thought he was? "You mean like Brooke's plan?"

"No!" Landon let his hands fall to his sides. He looked angry and misunderstood. "Not that sort of plan. Let me finish."

"Fine." Ashley didn't want to fight, not after such a great weekend.

"I'm only thinking that maybe we need to think things through, in case the baby really has this . . . this problem."

She put her hands on her hips. "How can we ask God for a miracle if we're doubting His abilities?"

"I'm not doubting Him, Ashley." Outside they could hear Cole singing something about chickens and roosters and long-legged frogs. "I'm on your side, remember?"

Ashley was shaking, but she ordered herself to calm down. "I want to enjoy my pregnancy, my baby moving and kicking inside me." She lowered her voice. "I believe God's going to give us a miracle. Our baby's going to be fine."

"I want to believe that too. But maybe we should see a specialist. Maybe someone can help us."

"There you go." Ashley began to shake harder. Why couldn't he understand? "I tell you I believe our baby's fine, and you say we should see a specialist? Why, Landon? Can't you trust me?" She put her hands over her midsection. "If something was wrong, I would know it. I would feel it. But she's moving around like any other healthy child."

He sighed and his shoulders sank. "You have to face the possibilities."

Devin banged on his high chair tray again. "All done. . . . All done."

Ashley turned away from her husband and tended to their son. The whole time her hands trembled and her heart raced. If Landon wouldn't believe with her, then no one would.

When Devin was cleaned up, she glanced at Landon. Suddenly the look on his face, the fear and doubt about their unborn baby, told her she had just one choice. She had to get out of the house or she'd scream.

"Ashley . . . I mean, think about it." Her husband's tone said he thought she was a lunatic grasping at straws in a situation where there was nothing left to grasp at.

She grabbed her purse and dug around for her keys. "I'm going for a drive."

"Ashley, don't. . . ." Landon came to her. "I want the best for you, for our little girl. That's all."

"Then why can't you believe God'll give her a miracle?"

"God's still God even if things don't go your way." His words were slow and profound.

Ashley hated the way that made sense. "Miracles, Landon. We're talking miracles. You of all people should know about miracles." Her voice broke and she moved closer to him, aiming her words straight at his heart. "You should've died rescuing the little boy in that apartment fire. But God had other plans for you. He gave you a miracle, and He'll give our daughter one too."

Any trace of anger left Landon's face. These were familiar roles for them, roles they hadn't played in a long time. Ashley threatening to run and Landon trying to think of some way to make her stay. "I believe in miracles, Ash." He touched his fingers to her face. "I have you, don't I?"

His touch melted her. She took his hand and kissed it. "Then how could you want me to see a specialist? I don't want doctors or tests or a diagnosis." She could feel her old self stepping in, the one that was wildly independent. "All I want is to feel my little girl moving and growing inside me and to believe—" she closed her eyes—"with everything I am that when she's born she'll be healthy and whole."

She opened her eyes and pulled her keys from her purse. No matter what he said, she needed time alone. "Can you watch the boys?"

Landon looked hurt. "Where are you going?"

"I'm not sure." She took a few steps back. "I need to think."

"What about dinner?"

"I'm not hungry." She nodded toward the backyard. "I'll be back by the time you both eat."

"Ash—" Landon's eyes pleaded with her—"don't get crazy on me, okay?"

She hesitated. "I won't. I love you."

"Love you too."

Ashley went to the garage and her van waiting inside. She was halfway down the street before she knew where she was headed. Because if her mother were here, she'd have at least one person who wouldn't doubt. Her mother would stroke her hair and give that look of quiet certainty that yes, of course everything was going to be okay. Her mother would've been telling the rest of the family how important it was to believe, how doubt wouldn't get them anywhere.

And so there was really only one place she could go. The cemetery on the edge of town, the one where the grass had long since grown back over the place where her mother was buried.

Ashley drove slowly, carefully. This wasn't a fit of rage; it was a quest to hold on to whatever lifeline of hope God might give her. As she neared the cemetery, she felt her baby daughter move inside her. A smile tugged at her lips. "I feel you, little one. You're going to be perfect and whole and healthy. I know it."

The cemetery was empty except for a few cars. She had maybe fifteen minutes of sunlight left. Ashley climbed out of her van and walked past the other markers, through a grove of bushes, and on toward her mother's tombstone. She would've known the way blindfolded. Because this was the place where she sometimes had to go, the only place besides the old Baxter house where she could still feel like her mother was with her.

As she walked, she thought about Landon. He didn't understand her occasional trips to the cemetery. "Your mom isn't there, Ash. You know that."

"The part I used to love is there." Ashley would feel her throat choke up at the thought. "The part I would hug when my world was crashing in is there beneath that stone."

Landon would give up at that point. He had told her a number of times that everyone was entitled to grieve in their own way. But for himself, he wanted to think of her mother happy and healthy in heaven, more alive than ever. Well, fine. Ashley wanted to think of her that way too. But the fact remained that her body was buried at the cemetery.

And now—like other times before—Ashley wanted only to be with her.

She came to the small stone bench by her mother's grave and sat down. For a while she kept her eyes on the sky, the fading light. But then she lowered them to the words etched in the marble. Like always it took a few minutes for it to all soak in again, for Ashley to accept once more that her vibrant, loving mother was really gone.

Shadows fell over the grave site, and Ashley bowed her head. "Please, God, tell my mom how much I need her." She whispered the words and waited. She expected to feel a reassurance, the sense that her mother's endless hope might somehow join her own, solidifying the feeling of an impending miracle.

Ashley waited and waited. But all she could hear were the words of her husband, her best friend. *"God's still God even when things don't go your way."* She looked up at the gathering storm clouds in the northern sky. A chill came across her arms, and she hugged herself. Her mother would've believed for Ashley, but Landon believed too.

Then in a rush, it hit her.

Landon believed not just that God could give them a miracle but that God might not. And that even then, He was still God, still sovereign. The way He'd been when her mother wasn't healed from cancer. Landon was right, but she hadn't been willing to see that until now.

Ashley needed to hope, to expect a miracle where her baby girl was concerned. But the miracle might not come. An ache sliced through her heart and settled deep inside her. The child was God's, not hers or Landon's. Whatever happened, God would use it in His perfect plan. She felt her throat tighten, and her vision blurred. Had God brought her all the way out here so she could see the obvious? If it only took belief for miracles to happen, her mother would still be alive.

God loved her mother, and still her mother had died. Exactly like Landon had said. The ache inside Ashley became a great sense of remorse. Landon was so good to her, letting her impulsively leave him and the boys. He had always given her the space she needed, and this evening was no exception.

She took another look at her mother's tombstone and then hurried back to her van. The miles couldn't pass fast enough as she drove home, and when she pulled into the driveway, she could hardly wait to get inside.

Landon was sitting next to Cole, the two of them eating chicken and buttered bread when she burst through the garage door and into the kitchen.

Landon turned, and his expression told her he wasn't angry. "Hi."

"Where'd you go, Mom?" Cole had a bite of chicken in his mouth. Devin was playing with his Elmo doll. Cole wrinkled his brow. "Dad said you took a drive."

"I did." Her eyes never left her husband's. "Can I talk to you for a minute?"

He pushed back from the table and patted Cole's shoulder. "Be right back, buddy."

Landon followed her around the corner into the family room. When they were barely out of Cole's sight, Ashley pulled him into her arms. "I'm sorry. Landon, I'm so sorry."

She felt the tears, but she didn't want to cry. She still wanted to believe there was nothing to be sad about, no reason to doubt. But when she drew back, she met Landon's concerned eyes, and she had to tell him. "I'll see a specialist if you want me to."

"Honey . . ." He stroked her hair and studied her. "You don't have to. I just thought maybe . . ."

"No, you're right. That's the responsible

thing to do." She clung to his shoulders. "I shouldn't have walked out."

"Sometimes we need that, Ash. I understand." He kissed her again, and when he caught her eyes, she could see all the way to his soul. "But next time you walk out, take me with you. Okay?"

She laughed, but it was wrapped around a cry. "I love you, Landon."

"Everything's going to be okay." His expression told her he meant what he was saying but not necessarily because their baby was going to be healthy. Because with God and each other, they would find a way through. He pressed his fingers to her abdomen. As he did, their baby kicked his hand. "Hey! I felt that."

"See? She'll probably be a soccer player and prove the whole medical field wrong."

"She can kick. I'll say that for her." Landon wrapped his arms around Ashley again. "Thanks for coming back."

Ashley smiled, and together they returned to the kitchen. Devin had joined Cole. He was sitting on the floor beside his big brother, his Elmo doll on his lap. She stopped and held on to the image, her boys young and healthy.

Cole lifted his eyes to them. He seemed to register that whatever might've been wrong, things were okay now. He grinned and gave his brother a wary look. "Devin thinks Elmo's real."

Ashley linked her arm through Landon's. In his eyes, all signs of doubt were gone. They would see a specialist, and they would do whatever was necessary to help their unborn daughter. But they would hang on to their hope, their beliefs that God would give them a miracle. And they would enjoy this pregnancy.

Ashley looked back at Cole. "Elmo might not be real to you, but he's real to Devin." She put her free hand over her stomach. "Sometimes it makes us happy to think something. Even if the whole world thinks something else."

CHAPTER FOURTEEN

DAYNE STOOD AT the sink in his Malibu home and stared out the window at the Pacific Ocean. He had no reason to be upset. He and Katy had moved into the beach house, and for two entire days they'd escaped the glare of the press. Dressing in sweats and baseball caps, they took walks along the shore and came and left through the house's private beach entrance.

The first sign of photographers had come this morning. Two cars were parked outside on Pacific Coast Highway, and three guys sat together on the beach a dozen yards away from their private entrance to the sand.

They had neither swim trunks nor beach towels, and each of them sat next to a big black camera bag. Paparazzi, of course.

Dayne poured himself a glass of water and watched one of the guys look over his shoulder. "We're not coming out," he wanted to shout. But the guy wouldn't hear him anyway. And if he opened the window, he'd only cause all three to aim their high-powered lenses straight at him. Dayne Matthews takes a drink of water! News at eleven!

He turned around just as Katy came hurrying into the kitchen. A wisp of her blonde hair was pulled back on either side, making her look wide-eyed and innocent. Her hair was longer than it had been in a while. She wore jeans and a peach lace shirt over a longer white one. The combination made her look irresistible.

She smiled at him. "You ready?"

"Yeah." He studied her. "You look pretty happy for someone about to face an onslaught."

"An onslaught?" She peered out the kitchen window. "Of blue skies and sunshine?" A laugh spilled from her. "I think I can handle it."

Dayne tried not to feel frustrated. "An onslaught of photographers." He stood beside her and looked out. "They've found us."

She put her hands on his shoulders and turned him so he was facing her. "That's part of the deal, remember? We promised we wouldn't let it bring us down." She lowered her chin, her eyes dancing. "Otherwise we should take the next flight home to Bloomington and forget the whole thing."

"Let's go." He looped his hands around her waist. "We can be in Indiana by dinner."

"Very funny." Katy stood on her tiptoes and kissed him. Her voice softened. "Come on, Dayne. We've made a commitment. Let's face it head-on and make the best of it."

He wanted more than anything to share her confidence, to believe that the adventure they were about to take would pacify the tabloids and bring the two of them closer than ever before. But his doubts were as vast as the blue water that made up his backyard. He brought his lips to hers and wished for the fifth time that the day were already behind them. He nuzzled his cheek against hers. "Thanks."

"For what?" Her voice was lighthearted and full of optimism.

"For believing that we're doing the right

thing." He took a long, exaggerated breath. "Maybe if I stay close to you I can catch your enthusiasm."

She tilted her head. "We're doing the best we can. You have a contract to fulfill; having me in the movie with you takes away your concerns about doing love scenes with other actresses. Meeting today with the folks from *For Real* gives the press a legitimate way to capture us on camera." She held up both hands and smiled. "Everything works out fine. End of story."

He raised one eyebrow. "I hope so."

Katy let her hands fall to her sides. Her eyes were still full of laughter, but she pretended to be exasperated. "Come on, grumpy. We have an appointment."

Dayne couldn't help but smile. She had that effect on him. And she was right about every aspect of why they were taking the course ahead of them. Today was the big meeting with the producers of *For Real*, a chance to find out exactly what they'd gotten themselves into by agreeing to the reality show.

Katy led the way toward the garage door, with Dayne a few feet behind. But before they reached it, he stopped. "Katy."

She turned around.

"Let's pray first." Dayne felt a sense of peace with even the mention of prayer. Last night he'd talked to his missionary friend Bob Asher. Bob had warned him that there was no way to take on the things that Dayne and Katy were about to take on without constant, fervent prayer. Yet all morning Dayne had done nothing but worry about the paparazzi, wishing them away from his home and dreading what was coming.

Katy held out her hands. "Good idea."

"Yeah." He made a face. "I should've thought of it before." He took hold of her fingers and closed his eyes. The anxiety he'd wrestled with all morning crept back into the shadows. "God, we're not really sure what we're getting ourselves into. But You know our reasons, our motives." He still didn't feel altogether confident when he prayed. The words weren't pretty and eloquent like when Katy talked to God. But he meant every word. He gritted his teeth. "What I'm trying to say is, God . . . please protect us. Help us grow closer in the coming months, and don't let anything get between us. Not ever. Help me to have the joy that Katy has, since You tell us to be joyful. Thanks, God. In Jesus' name, amen."

When he opened his eyes, Katy was staring at him. Her eyes shone from a private place inside her, one only he was allowed to see. "That's exactly what we needed."

He glanced out the window. There were four cars now, and he gathered his determination. "We'll need it often."

They went to the garage, climbed into his BMW, and popped the garage door. "Here we go." Dayne looked over his shoulder and started to back out. As he did, three cameramen jumped in his way. He was tempted to rev his engine, give them a scare.

But Katy put her hand on his. "Take it slow." She sounded calm, confident.

When his car was completely out of the garage and the photographers had backed up enough so he could lower his garage door, Katy opened her window.

The paparazzi sensed a photo opportunity, and they hurried out of the driveway and onto the small piece of grass that made up Dayne's yard.

Katy smiled and waved at them. "Go on, Dayne," she said through her smile. "They're out of the way."

The men raised their cameras and began rapid-fire shooting, moving in as close as they could to the car without getting their toes run over.

"Katy, how long are you back in Los Angeles?"

"How's married life?"

"Is it true you'll be starring in a movie with Dayne, and what can you tell us about it?"

Dayne focused on the traffic on PCH. With Katy distracting the press, he was able to look for an opening and back out when the highway was clear.

The entire time, Katy laughed and smiled, never giving them anything but a happy picture of the two of them. "Everything's fantastic!" she told them. "And, yes, I'll be in the movie with Dayne."

For her benefit, Dayne kept his expression pleasant. But once he slammed the car into drive and took off, he turned angry eyes toward her. "What was that?"

Shock and hurt filled Katy's face. "I was helping you get out of there."

"They don't need to know about the movie." He glared at the road ahead of him. "Not yet, anyway."

"If they don't know, they'll hunt us down until they find out." Her voice was louder than before, indignant. "I thought that was the plan, Dayne. Give them what they want so they don't have a reason to chase us."

Dayne looked in his rearview mirror. All four cars were in hot pursuit behind them. "Take a look, Katy."

She glanced over her shoulder, then slumped in her seat. "Okay, so they're not used to the idea yet. Even so, we don't have to run or race through traffic." She tossed her hands. "So what if they chase us? They can come up behind us and on either side if they want to. They can take a thousand pictures of us driving on PCH. Big deal."

"It *is* a big deal." Dayne felt a layer of sweat on his forehead and upper lip. This was the same road where they'd chased him and Randi Wells, the same highway where he'd nearly been killed. "I can drive the speed limit and stay in my lane, but that doesn't mean they won't cause an accident." He was shouting, and he made an effort to lower his voice. "Can't you understand that?"

Katy was quiet. She turned her attention to the road. After a while she looked over her shoulder again and spoke in a voice that was calmer than before. "It's dangerous for them, too. This chasing routine." She looked at him. "I have to believe that eventually—if we give them the smiling photos and we answer their questions—they'll stop chasing."

Dayne was driving with one hand. He looked in his rearview mirror one more time. "Good luck." As soon as the words were out of his mouth, he was hit with regret. If he was letting the press get to him already, how were they ever going to make it through the movie? He gave her a sheepish look. "I sounded like a jerk just then."

Her expression softened. "I was going to say so."

The rest of the drive, Dayne tried not to notice the cars chasing them, the photographers snapping photos of the back of his car at every stoplight. Katy was right. Let them take a thousand pictures. Rags didn't run photos of the backs of celebrities' cars. It was a waste of their time, and maybe they really would grow tired of the chase. Dayne and Katy had banked their next few months on the possibility.

The offices for the producers of *For Real* were in Santa Monica on the Third Street Promenade—a renovated section of town with lots of movie industry office suites. They parked out front, and the paparazzi screeched to a halt. One of the drivers pulled a U-turn and grabbed a spot across the street, and the other three found legal and illegal parking spots not far from Dayne's car.

Dayne opened Katy's door for her, and as they headed through the front doors of the building, he heard one of the photographers shouting at the others, "I told you! They're working with *For Real!*"

Once they were inside and on the elevator, Katy gave Dayne a lopsided grin. "See? Now that they know we're working with a reality show, they'll have lots of opportunities."

"And you really think that'll dim their interest?"

"No." Katy seemed to be careful with her response. "But it should take away their need to chase us."

"We'll see." They stepped off the elevator and walked through a door down the hall that took them into the offices of *For Real.*

A receptionist blushed beet red. "Uh, hello, Mr. Matthews." She looked at Katy. "Ms. Hart. I'll let them know you're here." She disappeared down a hallway, the click of her heels filling the office space.

Dayne made a funny face. "Ms. Hart, huh?" For the sake of the movie, Katy was still going by her maiden name. It was a de-

cision made by the film's director and producers. Having a different name from Dayne
would give Katy her own identity. He gave
her a grin, trying to ease the tension he was
still feeling. "As long as you're Katy
Matthews back in Indiana."

She pressed her fingers to her heart. "I'm
Katy Matthews in here, where it matters.
Whether I'm in Bloomington or Los Angeles."

Before he had time to respond, two men
appeared in slick Hollywood attire—tight
black shirts and jeans. Each had neatly
styled hair. One wore a pair of diamond stud
earrings, and the other had small silver
hoops. Both grinned and welcomed them.

Once they were situated in the office, the
man with the hoop earrings took the lead.
His name was Hans something, and he had
an accent Dayne couldn't identify. "Let's start
with some background information." He nodded to his partner and then looked at Dayne.
"For each episode, we'll include as much
backstory information as possible."

"Right, and we understand you were
adopted and you've reconnected with your
birth family." Ken, the one with diamond stud
earrings, crossed his legs and moved his
hands in front of him. "That's simply a fabu-

lous detail for the show." He had a pad of paper and a pen. "Go ahead and give me the names and phone numbers of—I don't know—let's say at least three of your family members. The ones you've found."

Katy sucked in a quick breath, but before she could say anything, Dayne sat up straight in his chair. "There won't be any information about my birth family. None at all."

The faces of the men across from him went blank. Ken uttered a quick laugh. "You're kidding, right?"

Dayne pictured his family and thought about the latest Baxter information, the details about the possible trouble with Ashley's pregnancy. He had to resist the urge to grab the guys by their collars.

Katy gave him a look, begging him not to lose control.

Deep breaths, Dayne told himself. *Deep breaths.* He tried to sound casual. "The contract we signed gives you and the photographers associated with your company permission to film and shoot us during the movie only. The subject—according to the contract—is our married life and the logistics of honeymooners filming a movie together."

He paused and settled back into his seat. "Period."

"Right." Hans gave a nervous laugh. "But the audience will want more than that."

Dayne stood. "Well, gentlemen, if our deal goes beyond the scope of our contract—" he reached for Katy's hand—"then I guess we have nothing else to talk about."

"Wait!" Ken was on his feet too. "Sit down, Mr. Matthews. If you're not comfortable discussing your birth family—" he gave a severe look to his partner—"then we won't talk about that."

Hans smoothed the wrinkles in his shirt. "I will say, though, that as long as you're Dayne Matthews, people will be digging. If you don't want to talk about your birth family, I'm sure there are plenty of people in Indiana who will."

Dayne gritted his teeth. Of course they knew what state his birth family lived in—the story had been in the press. But it still made him angry that they would bring it up now. "We'll stick to the contract or we'll walk."

"Very good." Ken smiled. He looked highly nervous, as if later he might give his partner a long lecture for nearly losing the deal with Dayne Matthews.

Half an hour later, Dayne and Katy had given Hans and Ken the details about their wedding—how they'd been able to pull off a secret ceremony—and the honeymoon they'd been on ever since.

The men took copious notes, nodding and smiling and making dramatic gestures when the story seemed almost too good to be true.

When Dayne was satisfied that the men had all the information they needed, the four of them shook hands, and Dayne led Katy to the car.

In the elevator, he fell against the back wall and groaned. "This is going to be a nightmare. I can feel it."

"Dayne . . ." Katy's tone begged him to have a better attitude.

"Did you hear them?" He stood straighter. "They're already looking for dirt, and we haven't even started."

"What dirt?" She clasped her hands, and she looked prettier than she had all day. "They won't talk about your family. You already told them you'll pull the plug on the show the moment they do."

"So they'll have their photographers working on it in the background. They might not break the news on the show, but they'll break it one way or another. The story of Ashley's pregnancy, my dad's relationship with Elaine . . . something."

"Dayne, come on." She took a step closer, just as the elevator door opened.

They walked out, and Dayne stopped near the tinted glass and peered through. The paparazzi cars weren't where they had been. "They're really gone?"

"See!" Katy smiled and took his hand. She opened the door and led the way to his car. No one jumped out and took their picture; no cars screeched up with the drivers spouting questions at them.

Once they were on their way back to the Malibu house, Katy gave him a knowing look. "Didn't you say a lot of the photographers work for the same company that produces *For Real*?"

"Yes." Dayne had been certain the photographers would be outside waiting for them. So maybe the plan might work after all.

They stopped at a market in Malibu and bought salmon and wild rice for dinner. Not once the rest of the day did they talk about the press. Instead they dreamed about the movie and how they would bring their characters to life.

Before they turned in for the night, Dayne opened the patio door and let the ocean breeze fill the room. "I feel a lot better." He climbed into bed beside Katy and lay on his side, facing her. "Sorry about earlier."

The moon shone in through the open door and made Katy's eyes sparkle. She eased closer to him. "That's what the nights are for." She turned onto her side and kissed him. "So we can forget about whatever trouble the day might've turned up."

Dayne loved her, loved being married to her. She was everything he'd ever hoped to find, and nothing—not a movie and not the press—was ever going to come between them.

But that night as he slept, he was restless. Sometime before sunrise he had the sense that he was outside on the beach with Katy. It was the middle of the night and there wasn't a light in the sky, not the moon or stars, nothing.

"It's dangerous," he told her. "Take me with you."

Katy only smiled, waved, and ran out into

the surf. He watched her dive into the water and swim out to sea. At that moment, she went under and didn't come back up.

He jumped to his feet. "Katy! Katy, come back!"

He raced into the water and started swimming, swimming for his life and for her life and for everything that ever mattered to him. There was no sign of her. He thrashed at the water, but just when he was going to take another breath of air, just when he was about to scream for help from someone—anyone—he began gulping in huge mouthfuls of water.

Breathing was impossible, the water filling his lungs and making him desperate for a single breath. *Katy, where are you? Where'd you go?* His words were a silent scream, and from underwater he could suddenly see straight ahead as far as the ocean went. The water was clear and blue, even though it was the darkest of nights. But there was no sign of Katy. She was gone, and he couldn't hold his breath another minute.

"No!" Dayne sat straight up, gasping, grabbing at his throat.

"Dayne!" Katy sat up next to him and put her hand on his shoulder. "What is it? What's wrong?"

He must've shouted, because she looked terrified. He was panting, still trying to catch his breath. Then he realized what had happened. He'd been dreaming. He hadn't gone down to the beach with Katy in the dead of night, and certainly neither of them had gone swimming. She was here beside him, in bed, where she'd been when they fell asleep.

"I'm sorry." Dayne breathed out long and slow. He put his arm around her and held her close. "I had . . . I had a nightmare."

She was pale, but calm had returned to her face. "About what?"

He eased her back and searched her eyes. "I dreamed I lost you."

"Dayne . . . honey. That's terrible." She pressed her face against his chest and stroked his back.

"It was so real." He could feel his heart rate returning to normal.

"Never." She held him tighter than before. "You'll never lose me."

"Promise me, Katy." He met her eyes again. The feeling of desperation was still there, and he couldn't get enough of her. "Don't ever leave me. Don't let this movie get in the way of what we have. Please . . ."

The look in her eyes told him she thought the idea was absurd. "Nothing could ever come between us. You know that."

But Hollywood was his world, and he'd seen it happen. Even to couples with the best intentions. They held on to each other for another few minutes, and when they lay back down, they didn't let go.

Long after Katy had fallen asleep again, Dayne watched the open patio door and the sheer curtains dancing softly in the ocean breeze. She was right; she had to be. She wouldn't leave him, and he wouldn't leave her. Nothing would change.

No matter how crazy the next few months became.

CHAPTER FIFTEEN

A DAY ON the lake was Ryan's idea, and Landon was grateful. It was Memorial Day, and for more than a month, he and Ashley had found one reason after another to postpone the appointment with a specialist. For now it was enough that they were praying and believing and asking their family to do the same. Today was mild and sunny, and a day on the water with their families was just what Ashley and Kari needed.

The rest of the Baxters planned to meet them later in the afternoon at their picnic spot. Only Brooke and Peter wouldn't join them. The strain between the sisters was worse than ever. Ashley and Kari were trusting the evidence of their eyes—the way Ashley appeared to be healthy, her baby growing and kicking like any other unborn child. Landon had to admit that everything certainly seemed fine.

But Brooke continued to feel strongly that the baby was indeed going to be born with a fatal defect. When peace efforts were made by John or Luke or one of the others not directly involved the way Landon and Ashley or even Kari was, Brooke's answer was always the same. "I'm the only one who's thinking about Ashley in all this."

Brooke had told John last night that she wouldn't come to the picnic. She felt misunderstood and unwanted. Peter would've come, John said, but he wanted to support his wife. And so no one from their family would attend.

Landon sat at the back of the boat with Devin on his lap. Ryan was at the wheel, taking them at a leisurely pace around the perimeter of the lake. Cole and Jessie were side by side on their knees, looking down at the white water churning up in the boat's wake.

"Sometimes you can see big fish behind a

boat, right, Dad?" Cole turned and looked at Landon over the bulky shoulder of his life vest. "Really big fish, right?"

"Sometimes."

"Wow!" Jessie's eyes opened wide, and she studied the white water. "You're smart, Cole."

Jessie was several years younger than Cole, so the two didn't share the one-upmanship that existed between Cole and his rival cousin, Maddie. With Jessie, Cole always took on the role of big brother, passing on bits of information and patting her on the arm occasionally, looking out for her.

Ryan couldn't hear the exchange, but Kari was sitting opposite Landon. She had RJ in her arms. "Cole knows a lot about fish. Some fish like the movement of water and the bubbles."

Cole patted Jessie on her life jacket. "Ask me anything you want, okay?"

She smiled, satisfied with his offer.

Ashley had been talking to Ryan, but now she slid closer to her sister. She studied their two oldest children. "I love their relationship. It's so easy."

"It is."

The friendships between siblings and

cousins were much simpler at Cole's age. Landon ran his hand over Devin's arm. "You doing good, buddy?"

Devin pointed at the water. "Fish!"

Landon laughed. "Cole's gonna catch you the biggest fish of all; right, Cole?"

Cole gave him a thumbs-up. "Right, Dad."

He turned his attention to Ashley. She was watching him from the other side of the boat.

"Love you," she mouthed.

He returned the words her way, but he wanted to tell her he wasn't the only one. Brooke loved her too. But now wasn't the time. Instead he smiled and let the sunshine warm his face and his heart.

From the driver's seat, Ryan looked back at the group. "Everyone having fun?"

"Yes, Daddy." Jessie looked at Cole and waved her fingers a few times. "Me and Cole are friends. Right, Coley?"

Cole broke into a smile. "Yeah, we're best friends."

Landon took a deep breath. Everything was good and right, an hour of boating still ahead of them, the lake calm and blue and dotted with other boaters getting in on the first part of summer's action. He savored the feeling. There was no reason to feel uptight or worried.

He'd been finding more truth in the Bible lately, and yesterday he was struck by a verse he stumbled across. It wasn't something new or words he hadn't read before. The Scripture came from the Sermon on the Mount, when Jesus was telling the people not to worry. One verse in particular stood out: *"Who of you by worrying can add a single hour to his life?"*

Landon closed his eyes and leaned his head back. Since worrying couldn't add an hour to his life or to his baby daughter's, what was the point? What was Brooke gaining by sticking to her determination to help Ashley grasp the reality of anencephaly? Ashley wasn't having an abortion; that much was decided.

Why not take a deep breath and enjoy the days spread out before them? The way they were doing today. Landon stretched his hand over the water. The cool mist sprayed his arm and felt wonderful. *God . . . we're doing the right thing, aren't we? Enjoying Ashley's pregnancy?*

There was no loud or audible response,

nothing that even echoed in his heart. But the verse filled his mind again. *"Who of you by worrying . . ."*

Ashley's approach to her pregnancy was as good as any. Landon had talked to John about the need for a specialist, and at this point it didn't really exist. If the baby had the neural tube defect, they would know soon enough, and good-byes would come shortly after the baby was born. If not, then there was no point ruining the next three months by fretting and being sad.

Ashley had canceled two appointments for ultrasounds. "I don't want to know," she'd told Landon after pulling out of the second one. "Whatever's going to happen, an ultrasound won't change anything. Right now I feel fantastic, and our little girl seems perfectly fine." She looked at him with eyes full of love. "Isn't that enough?"

It was for Landon, and it seemed to be more than enough for Kari and Ryan because neither of them was pressuring Ashley to get to a doctor. He looked at Cole and Jessie, side by side. They were laughing at a barking dog running along the shore.

Cole had his arm flung around his cousin's shoulder. "I think he's trying to race us."

Jessie grinned at him. "Yeah, I think so."

Landon shared a smile with Ashley. Yes, life was good for now. He could only pray that when they reached the other end of whatever lay ahead, Ashley and Brooke would have the ability to smile and put their arms around each other. That they'd find themselves side by side once again, sharing the love that came with being family, and they'd remember how to spend a day together. The way Cole and Jessie did.

Ashley tilted her head back and breathed in the lake air. Nothing like a day on a boat, the rolling feel of the water, and the warm breeze in her face. She smiled at Landon, grateful that he was entertaining the boys.

Then she turned to Kari. "I'm glad baseball season's almost over."

"I know." Kari shifted RJ onto the bench seat between them. She shaded his face with a towel. "Little League's pretty intense."

"Cole had a great coach, but still every game felt like the World Series to those little guys."

They talked about one of the games when a set of parents from the opposing team had clung to the fence screaming at their son to

make a play at first base. The scene reminded Ashley of Cole's basketball season
and the father who wouldn't let his son run
down the court without yelling at him about
one error or another. The difference was that
the Little League parents alternated between clinging to the fence and yelling at
their son and walking off and hiding behind
the snack stand.

"I asked Jenny Flanigan what was going
on. She's been doing kids' sports longer
than I have." Ashley raised her eyebrows.
"She told me she'd talked to those parents
before. Apparently they get so nervous when
their son's up to bat that they have to leave
the area."

Kari laughed. "That's ridiculous." She was
quiet for a moment, watching the lake ahead
of them. Then she turned to Ashley. "Have
you heard from Katy or Dayne?"

"Last week." Ashley felt her baby move,
and she smiled. "Katy called. She said this
weekend they were moving to New Mexico
for the location scenes."

"How's it going?" Kari looked concerned.

"It's tougher than she thought." Ashley remembered her sister-in-law's tone. "I think

she's worried about how much worse it could get."

"The press?"

"Katy thought a reality show would ease the pressure."

"Nothing close?"

Ashley thought about the recent headlines. "I guess it's worse than ever." For the past several weeks, Katy and Dayne had made the cover of nearly every tabloid, with headlines questioning whether a new marriage could survive the pressure of making a movie together and doubting their motives for doing the reality show. Some magazines even questioned Katy's ego, asking if maybe she was falling for fame, craving the attention.

The situation was difficult, but Ashley knew Dayne and Katy and their love for each other. No matter what the press said, their marriage could stand a few months of scrutiny. She drew another long breath. "I told her she and Dayne should come home for a couple days, drop what they're doing, and find their sanity again."

"Good idea."

"She said it might not happen for a while.

Their schedule's pretty intense between now and then."

"Must be crazy, having cameras in their face every time they turn around." Kari stretched out her legs. "The reality show airs when? First of the year?"

"Yes, sometime in January."

The conversation shifted to their dad and Elaine. "I think he's falling for her." Kari kept her tone light, but there was a seriousness in her face.

Ashley hadn't thought much about her father's friend, but the idea no longer threatened her. "You might be right." She remembered a conversation she'd had with Jenny. "Jim Flanigan saw Dad and Elaine walking at the park. They were holding hands."

Kari winced. "Hard to picture."

"I still feel that way sometimes." She slipped her long-sleeve shirt on so she wouldn't get too much sun. "Landon's helped me see things differently. Dad shouldn't have to be alone just so we can keep our memories intact."

"True."

RJ cuddled up between Kari and Ashley. "Tired?"

"Just till the fish come." He grinned at Kari,

but his eyes were heavy. He was asleep before the conversation shifted back to baseball and how next year there wouldn't be only the regular season but all-star games.

"I don't want to think about it yet." Ashley stroked RJ's blond hair. "It makes me glad for summer. No sports or practices or reasons to hurry."

"Mmmm." Kari tilted her face toward the sun. "We should do this again next weekend."

"We used to get out here more."

"Before we had so many kids." Kari patted her stomach and then Ashley's. "After this summer, it'll be a few more years before we can make a habit of boating."

Warmth spread from Ashley's heart. She could've hugged her sister, talking with her about her baby as if everything was going to be okay. The awkwardness that had been between them after Ashley's ultrasound was gone now. She and Kari were walking four times a week again, dreaming about the future.

She and Kari would dress their daughters alike and take them to baby classes together. They would learn to walk and talk and play together, and some far-off day they'd be in the same class at school.

All of it was possible when Ashley was with Kari, and she loved her sister more than anything because of it. She was at peace in Kari's presence, believing as she'd believed from the beginning. That she was going to enjoy her pregnancy and that at the end of August, God wasn't only going to give her a baby girl.

He was going to give her a miracle.

CHAPTER SIXTEEN

THE SENSATION THAT someone was always watching her, always taking her picture, was a constant feeling, one Katy was getting used to. Even now, when Dayne was nowhere near and she was working closely with the horse trainer—the one hired by the production company.

Rick Elliott was the trainer, a local guy in his early twenties who seemed more comfortable on a horse than anywhere else. He'd worked with Dayne earlier in the week, and now, on the first day of June, it was Katy's turn.

She was in a dusty arena on the horse

they were going to use in most of the scenes, a sorrel with a beautiful coat and mane.

Rick was facing her on a horse a few feet away. "The goal here is that the horse'll sense your body, your movement. On screen we don't want you to look like you're working hard to make the horse respond." He grinned at her. "Horse and rider should move like one. Remember that."

Katy wiped her brow and tossed her ponytail over her shoulder. "You mean by leaning forward?"

"The movement is more subtle than that." Rick climbed down off his horse. He put one hand on her lower back, the other on her knee.

She could feel the cameramen moving in, could sense them recognizing a photo opportunity. She wanted to pull away, but that would only make the moment more awkward.

Rick applied a slight amount of pressure to her lower back. "Press in like this."

The guy wasn't suggestive or flirty, but the connection between them felt more intimate than Katy liked. She did as he asked, shifting her pelvis. At almost the same time, the horse began walking forward.

"There!" Rick stood back. "That's what I'm talking about."

The lesson continued, the cloudless sky offering no protection from the sizzling Santa Fe sun. She wished Dayne were going through the training with her, but he was in meetings with the producers, and this afternoon he was flying to Los Angeles for a meeting with the financial backers of the film.

They'd been working on the movie for less than a week, and she felt like she hardly saw Dayne. So far the experience was fun and even exhilarating—as an actress, anyway. But it wasn't at all what she'd pictured. She and Dayne were exhausted by the end of the day when they dropped into bed at the suite the studio had rented for them. It was part of a hotel complex that the production company had reserved entirely for the cast and crew. That gave them some time without the paparazzi, but it didn't matter. Cameras were aimed at them every hour they were on the set, and what was left was barely enough time to sleep.

For the next twenty minutes, Rick led Katy through a series of exercises until she had the hang of making the horse move with little work on the reins. The horse had obviously done this sort of training before, which made it easier for Katy.

When Katy was finished, Rick came to her side and slipped his hands around her waist. He helped her down and gave her a crooked grin. "You know this picture'll be on the covers of every tabloid next week."

Katy laughed. "They can print what they want." She used her eyes to tell Rick she wasn't interested—whether he was or not. "It won't change the truth."

"That's what your man said too. One of the stable girls was talking to him, and he told me later that it didn't matter what pictures the press took." Rick tipped his hat to her. "See you after the break."

Familiar feelings of love and assurance wrapped their arms around her. Dayne was missing her as much as she was missing him. The news was good to know. She headed across the arena to the buffet spread out on three different tables. The cameras stayed on her as she walked, and she turned and smiled at them. "Anyone seen Dayne?"

"He's in his trailer talking to Randi Wells," one of them called back.

A round of laughter came from the group of photographers.

Very funny, Katy thought. Dayne was meeting with the producer. But the paparazzi loved a conflict. First they snapped a hundred pictures of her in the arms of Rick, and then they suggested Dayne had his attention somewhere else.

She shook her head, her smile still in place. "Always full of good news, right, guys?" She waved and then turned her back. At the first table, she found a paper plate and piled it high with fruit salad and a few chicken wings.

"They were telling the truth." One of the bit-part actors approached her and filled his own plate. "Dayne's been talking to Randi for the last hour."

Katy didn't let her surprise show. Was Dayne really in his trailer talking to Randi Wells? And why now, just hours before he was scheduled to board a plane for Los Angeles? "Amazing how news travels around a location shoot." She tried to look unconcerned.

"This ain't nothing." The guy was a ranch hand from Santa Fe, a local who would be one of the cowboys working the livestock in a few of the horse scenes. He took a napkin and grinned at her. "I've been on movie shoots where couples got divorced then and there. You never know what's going to happen." He wandered off and joined a group of extras.

Katy found a chair by herself and kept her back to the paparazzi. As much as the reality show gave them open season to take pictures and video footage during the filming, they couldn't get to this part of the set. She stared at her fruit, and suddenly she wasn't hungry. Every photographer was still watching, waiting. Looking for a sign that something wasn't right.

Dayne and Katy had separate trailers for the location filming, and Katy hated that too. It had made sense at first. They would each need a place where makeup artists could do their work and where changes of clothing would be readily available. Katy assumed that when they weren't getting ready for a scene, they'd spend time together in one trailer or the other. But it hadn't worked out that way. Their schedules were different almost every day.

Katy wanted to talk to Dayne right now, but she had the feeling that by knocking on his trailer door, the paparazzi would smell a problem. Why else would she be checking in on her husband only minutes after learning that he was on the phone with one of America's favorite actresses?

She picked up her fork and stirred the fruit. The entire notion was ridiculous, a waste of time. If Dayne was talking to Randi, then he must've had a good reason. She was his friend, after all. Back when he was in the hospital, Randi had admitted her feelings about Dayne to Katy. But she had also admitted that she wanted to buy a Bible because she admired Dayne's faith.

Maybe that's what the call was about.

Katy would eat her lunch and then find her husband. Never mind what the paparazzi thought. If she had the right look on her face, they couldn't dream up more than a midafternoon rendezvous. She and Dayne had nothing to hide. No, they weren't spending as much time together as she wished. But their feelings for each other were stronger every day.

No horse trainer or lonely starlet was going to change that.

Katy waited an hour before heading to Dayne's trailer. She followed her plan and gave the paparazzi who trailed her a sly smile as she knocked on the door and proceeded up the two steps and inside. When the door was closed behind her, she turned, and there at the back of the trailer, she saw Dayne.

He had the phone pinned between his ear and his shoulder, and he was packing a small suitcase. He smiled at her and motioned for her to sit down.

She did as he asked, but her heartbeat felt erratic and unsteady. She gripped the arms of the chair and watched him.

If he was talking to Randi, the conversation wasn't a private one. He was laughing and saying something about the film, about the craziness of the press and how he was glad it wouldn't last much longer without a break. Another month, maybe. The conversation ended, and he snapped his phone shut.

"Hi." He pulled her to her feet. "Is it my imagination, or do we hardly see each other?"

"It's not your imagination." Katy didn't want to be angry or short with him. Still, she wanted to know, and there was only one way to find out. "Who was that?"

"One of the backers. He's got dinner planned for seven tonight." Dayne kissed her and then studied her eyes. "Something wrong?"

Here it was, her chance to let it go or

make herself look like she was doubting him. She took a steadying breath and made her decision. "I wish you weren't leaving."

Relief seemed to come over him. He smiled at her before he turned back to his packing. "I wish you were coming with me."

Katy watched him. Funny how their roles had changed. When they first returned to the house in Malibu, Katy had been the calm one, the one ready to take on the press and make the best of the situation. But now that they were on location, the cameras were wearing on her.

"You seem better about the paparazzi."

"They can't chase us." Dayne shrugged. The sun had been good to him. He looked tanned and relaxed, more handsome than ever. "That's the only thing I worry about, Katy. They can take all the pictures they want, but when they put our lives at risk . . . that's when I draw the line."

"Oh." She angled her head. Hopefully Dayne would have an equally relaxed atti-tude when the tabloids ran pictures of Rick helping her off the horse.

Dayne asked her about the horse training, but before their conversation really had a chance to take off, he looked at his watch, then zipped his bag shut and picked it up. "I've gotta run." He gave her a quick kiss. "Call you tonight, okay?"

"Dayne . . ."

He already had his hand on the trailer door, but he stopped and looked at her. "Yeah, baby?"

"Why am I feeling scared about us?"

"Katy . . ." His tone softened, and he set his suitcase down. He held his arms out to her, and she went to him, slipping into the familiar feel of his embrace. "This is what it's like on a movie set. Crazy busy, rushing every which way."

"I don't like it." Her voice was a whimper against his chest. "I miss you."

"The best part's just ahead." He crooked his finger and lifted her chin so he was looking straight into her eyes. "Everything's been building up to the scenes between you and me." He hesitated. "Hey, I hate it too. I could drop it all and fly home to Bloomington tomorrow."

"But we have a promise to keep." Katy knew the right answer, and now, lost in his eyes, safe in his embrace, she felt her world straighten once more on its axis. "Thanks." She touched her lips to his. "I needed this."

Dayne held her eyes a few seconds longer. "I'll call you tonight." He grabbed his bag and stepped outside.

She waited a few beats, then chided herself. The press would see them leaving separately and wonder if trouble was brewing. She hurried out the door behind him, the familiar smile plastered on her face. "Love you," she called after Dayne.

He was already climbing into the limo, but he turned around and waved. "Love you too."

The cameramen caught every moment, and the video crew that was almost always running film captured it too. As Katy headed back to the arena for her next horse lesson, she heard two of them talking.

"No trouble in paradise," one called out.

"Not yet, anyway."

Laughter came from the group, but Katy didn't turn, didn't let them see her reaction. By now she was getting good at hiding her real feelings, but if she turned around, she had no doubt they'd see the truth. She was furious. Was this what the reality show was all about? Staying on the lookout for trouble between her and Dayne? She should've expected that they'd want conflict, but she never imagined this. Almost as if the cameramen were taking bets on when the first cracks would appear.

For Real had a reputation for giving viewers a behind-the-scenes look at a work situation. A husband and wife starring opposite each other in an upcoming blockbuster movie was just the sort of show they were known for. So why the push for some kind of rift in her marriage?

Katy was glad she had the next two hours scheduled with Rick. Otherwise she'd be tempted to march over to the photographers and ask them what they were trying to pull off.

Everything feels out of control, God. She kicked at the dirt as she walked into the arena. It was soft and fine, and a cloud rose as she shut the gate behind her.

"Whoa there." Rick held the reins of her horse even as the stallion jumped. "Save that for the movie, okay?"

"I tripped." Katy grinned at her trainer. She didn't need two hours of Rick asking questions. She kept her smile in place as she approached him. "Sorry."

"Hey, Katy." He kept his voice low so he couldn't be heard by the paparazzi gathering outside the arena fence. "I know things are rough for you." He seemed to look straight to her core. "I'm here if you wanna talk. I don't have anything going on tonight."

She looked away. "Thanks, Rick." She wasn't about to open up to the horse trainer about her insecurities and doubts. That was a conversation for Dayne alone. "The only thing I'm struggling with is this horse. We start filming live-action scenes in a week." She slipped her foot into the stirrup and eased herself into the saddle without his help. "Now where were we?"

He shrugged. "Okay. Offer stands."

Rick didn't bring up anything personal for the next two hours. But there was no mistaking the fact that he seemed to enjoy the moments when they were close, when he was showing her what to do with her legs or when he had to hold her hand with the reins so he could demonstrate the slight movements she was expected to produce on camera.

Before they were finished, he tied his horse up to the closest fence post. "We need a few minutes of bareback riding."

Katy had read the script. Rick was right; she and Dayne had a scene next week in which Katy would be on the horse bareback, and Dayne would jump up behind her. The scene involved an argument that culminated in an angry ride together across the pasture.

Rick took the saddle off the horse, then helped her back on.

Again cameras clicked behind her. Katy didn't pay much attention. The idea of riding without a saddle was the scariest part of her horse training.

"This is where your body'll come into play. Remember what I told you." Rick walked in front of the horse, and the animal followed without any further command. They made a loop around the arena, and Rick nodded to Katy. "Ease back in your seat."

Katy did as he asked, and the horse came to a gentle stop. "Like magic."

"Exactly." Rick grinned. "Okay, now hold on to his mane. I'm going to get on behind you, and we'll bring him up to a trot, nothing faster."

She wanted to slide forward, but she was up as far as she could get without sitting on the horse's neck.

"Ready?"

"Ready." She braced herself in case the horse took off.

Rick was very athletic. He made an agile

move of getting up behind her, and with only the slightest sound from him, the horse moved forward. Rick eased his hands around her waist and spoke near her ear. "Very nice. You're a natural."

Katy almost asked him if he'd ridden double with Dayne, or if she was the only one who needed the benefit of his training. But the sun was setting in the western sky, and the training was almost over for the day. Besides, it felt good trotting around the arena with someone as skilled as Rick. She could imagine taking this ride at a faster pace with Dayne.

The scene was bound to be a strong one.

Two video cams and half a dozen still cameras captured every minute of her ride with Rick, and now as he brought the horse to a stop, they seemed to zoom in even closer.

Rick didn't appear to be in a hurry to get off. He leaned into her and laughed. "You're gonna show up your husband if you're not careful."

"Get down, Rick." Katy kept her tone reserved and cautious, the way she'd talk to one of her drama students.

"You're welcome." He swung himself off

and helped her down. His eyes held hers a few seconds longer than necessary. "I gave you a compliment."

"Thank you." She smiled, then brushed the dirt and horse hair off her hands and jeans.

She was on her way back to her trailer when she spotted the director headed her way.

"Katy, I've been looking for you."

Her smile was genuine this time. "I've been bouncing around on that horse all afternoon."

Stephen laughed and put his arm around her shoulders.

The cameras were capturing every move, but Katy didn't care. The director was a Christian, a man of virtue. He was also very warm and almost fatherly with his cast. Let them take their pictures. She grinned at him. "What's up?"

"I've looked at the dailies from the past week." He whistled low and his eyes lit up. "The camera loves you. You're brilliant on-screen. Absolutely brilliant."

"Thanks." His compliment was one of the first good things that had happened today. Because when it was all said and done, when the filming stopped and she and

Dayne found their way home and back to how things had been before, a movie would be all they had to show for this time. Two hours of footage. From the beginning she'd been afraid that she would be the weak link in a cast with Dayne and a handful of other stars with far more experience than her.

Stephen walked slowly beside her. "It's true." He looked at his watch. "Hey, have dinner with me tonight. Dayne's gone, and I've got something I want to talk to you about."

In any other setting, Stephen's offer would have made her suspicious. But this was the movie industry, and they were on location. Nothing was the way it normally might be. Stephen certainly wasn't interested in her; he only had something on his mind he wanted to talk about. She felt herself nodding, and the plan was set.

Just before seven, Stephen knocked on her suite door. He was dressed nicer than usual. Katy hesitated. *Don't make too much of it*, she told herself. *He's an important man in the industry; of course he dresses nice for dinner*. Stephen was a father figure, nothing more.

He gave her an approving look as they

walked to his car. "Your beauty is that rare kind, Katy Hart. It comes from inside you first."

She allowed a nervous laugh, one that dismissed the compliment. She shifted the conversation to her horse training session.

"Rick has a crush on you. He's telling everyone." Stephen opened the car door for her.

She rolled her eyes. "Rick's had a few too many hours in the sun."

Her comment made him chuckle, and the atmosphere between them remained relaxed and casual through the ride to the restaurant and on into dinner.

Three photographers arrived a few minutes after Katy and Stephen were seated. They took a booth across the restaurant, one with a full view of Katy and Stephen.

It doesn't matter, she told herself. *I'm allowed to have dinner with my director.*

They'd talked about every aspect of the film, and now Stephen anchored his elbows on the table. "Okay, this is why I wanted to talk to you."

She held her breath. Whatever was coming, Stephen was treating it like a big deal.

"When we're done shooting this film, I'll be working with a very talented cast on another picture. It's a drama about a young

woman with a beautiful family and everything going for her, but she has a secret. And
that secret drives her to depression and the
brink of despair." He leaned closer and took
hold of her hands. "You'd be perfect for the
part, Katy."

The cameramen at the far table were forgotten. Katy's head began to spin, and a
dozen different thoughts swirled about,
none of them making sense. The idea struck
a nerve and challenged her. She felt her
eyes get big. "Really? You want me as the
lead?"

Stephen released her hands and leaned
back in the booth. "Katy Hart, my dear, you
are a star. You just haven't figured it out yet."
He cocked his head. "And maybe that's part
of your charm. You don't know how good you
really are."

A light-headed feeling came over her.
Was this really happening? Why wasn't
Dayne here to help her make sense of this
offer? One of the best directors in the movie
business wanted her to star in his film. She
swallowed hard. "Dayne's not in the movie?"

"It doesn't need a big name for the male
lead. The character is married, but the
strength of the film comes from the female

part." He smiled bigger than he had all night. "The part that belongs to you."

Katy grabbed at the only thought that made sense. "I'm flattered, Stephen. Truly." She thought about the upcoming year. CKT was closing down, and Dayne had three more movies left on his contract. Why couldn't she take the offer? Being in movies was what she'd dreamed about when she was in college.

"So . . . can I tell the team you're interested?" Stephen was beaming like a proud parent.

"It sounds wonderful." She set her fork down and tried to focus. "I need to talk to Dayne, of course." Questions flooded her mind. "Where will it be filmed?"

"England. The budget's big enough to give us location shots where we want them. We'll be there maybe six or seven weeks."

The news was like a glass of cold water straight in her face. Six or seven weeks in England, away from Dayne? Tabloid headlines filled her mind about actors married to each other and trying to carry on separate careers in different parts of the world. Almost always the strain became too much. She started to shake her head, because if this next film came between her and Dayne, then the answer was no.

But she hesitated. This was only one film. She tried to focus on the director sitting opposite her.

"You and Dayne talk it over." Stephen slid his plate back and stood up. "Where's his next movie taking him?"

"I'm not sure." Katy stared at her plate. Why hadn't she and Dayne talked about that? "I guess we have a lot to catch up on."

"Don't worry." Stephen chuckled. "Being on a set together can still feel like you're on opposite continents."

"Yes." She stood.

Stephen put his hands on her shoulders. "I hope you say yes, Katy. The film would definitely take your career to the next level."

"Thank you, Stephen."

He grinned at her. "I had a wonderful time tonight." Then without warning, he leaned in and kissed her on the lips. Not the sort of kiss meant for a lover but the kind common to Europeans, the sort she'd seen passed around like handshakes in her short time in the movie business.

In the distance, there was the rapid sound of every cameraman capturing the moment.

Katy felt sick, and she refused to look at the far table, where the paparazzi sat. "It was very nice. Thank you." She smiled at Stephen.

He looped his arm through hers. "Now let's get you home. You have more horse training in the morning."

Stephen meant nothing by the kiss; Katy was certain. His tone, his expression, all of it told her he saw her as a special daughter, someone he wanted to take under his wing and help along in her acting career. As they left the restaurant, Katy wasn't worried about Stephen's intentions or what he thought of the kiss they'd just shared.

She was worried about the cameramen.

CHAPTER SEVENTEEN

THE HOURS COULDN'T pass fast enough for Dayne. Being in Los Angeles without Katy made him miss her more than he had imagined. Going to dinners with financial backers, meeting with studio executives at swanky nightclubs . . . this was his old life, the one he'd walked away from.

His earlier meetings had gone well, but he was frustrated at the outcome of a talk with his agent an hour ago. The director of Dayne's next film was looking at Randi Wells as the lead, since their first romantic comedy had done so well.

"What about Katy?" Dayne had no intention

of doing another film with Randi. "We're doing great with this picture. Why not another?"

"It won't work, Matthews." His agent was a good guy, but he knew the business better than anyone. "People will be intrigued by one film with you and your wife, but more than that and they'll think you're limiting yourself. If you can't star with anyone but Katy Hart, then your acting career isn't long for this world."

Now Dayne was sitting in one of the largest booths at the current Santa Monica hot spot, with four of the producers of his next film, the primary director and casting director, and Randi Wells.

If Dayne didn't know better, he'd feel the whole thing had been set up. Randi had called him three times in the last few days. Nothing felt right about her life. Her divorce was nearly final, and the kids seemed torn between her and her ex-husband. On top of that, she hadn't found anyone who could bring perspective to her life the way Dayne had.

"I'm not asking for anything more than friendship, Dayne," she'd said. "I know you're happy with Katy."

Randi didn't have any idea just how happy. He tried to keep their conversations short, but now here they were, in a dimly lit nightclub at midnight, where everyone was drinking but him. He swirled what was left of his sparkling water and tried to keep his attention on the director.

"We're shooting in Mexico, and my vision for this film is that it'll take romantic comedy to the next level." He turned to Dayne. "The way your last film with Randi did."

"Mexico?" This was the first Dayne had heard about the location. "How many weeks?"

"Six or eight at least." The director looked proud of himself. "Cabo is perfect for the script."

Dayne felt beyond defeated. Six or eight weeks in Mexico? When would he have time for the lake house and Bloomington and the life he dreamed of having with Katy?

"Cabo, Dayne . . . sounds perfect." Randi gave him a look from across the table. She wore a skintight shirt and tight black pants. Her hair was a lighter shade of blonde, and she had turned heads all night. Rumor around the industry had it that Randi was running more and in better shape now that she was single.

There was no denying the fact that Randi looked great. But her looks had no effect on Dayne but one—she made him miss Katy even more. He didn't belong here, as the shoulder for a crying woman who had long ago made it clear how she felt about him.

The producer was sharing his vision with the director, practically shouting over the pulsing music. It was a private club, so there were no paparazzi lurking in the corners. Still, Dayne's meeting with Randi was bound to make it into a headline one way or another.

And Katy needed to know about it from him, not the tabloids. Because she had nothing to worry about. He'd tried to call her before dinner, but there was no answer. She was probably out with some of the cast— something they hadn't had much time to do with the intense schedule they'd all been following.

Two starlets in their early twenties moved off the dance floor, breathless and adjusting their skimpy shirts. They spotted him and weaved their way over, paying no attention to the meeting in progress.

"Dayne, where've you been?" The red-head was definitely drunk. She laughed as if she'd told a funny joke, and her friend steadied her so she wouldn't fall. "I've been looking for you all my life."

Her friend had straight blonde hair. Both

of them were frequently on the covers of the tabloids. "What she means is, we both have." The actress tossed her hair over her shoulder and gave Randi a rude look.

The studio guys were caught up in their own conversation, and Dayne was grateful. He gave the young women a guarded smile. "Maybe you didn't hear. I got married."

The blonde sized up Randi. "Doesn't look like it."

"Get lost." Randi flashed haughty eyes at them. The buzz around town was that the blonde had clashed with Randi a time or two before.

"You don't own him." The blonde found Dayne again, and her look couldn't have been more suggestive. "When you're tired of the action at this table—" she pointed across the dance floor—"we'll be over there."

The redhead laughed again. "You're mine first—don't forget!"

"Stop." Her blonde friend pretended to be angry. "Dayne's a married man. Whatever that means."

They walked off, still laughing, holding each other up as they went.

As Dayne watched them, a series of memories came rushing back. This was how it happened back then. One of the hot young actresses would come up and tell him hello, and by the end of the night he'd take her home. The reality suffocated him. How could he ever have lived like that?

Beneath the table, he felt a tapping against his foot. He looked at Randi.

She motioned to the men at the table and then mouthed, "Wanna dance?"

Was she kidding? Dayne was starting to feel himself sweat. What was he doing here? He nodded to the glass of gin and tonic in her hands. "No more."

Randi pouted at him. "I'm not driving."

His look was intended to put an end to the subject. But instead, she lifted her glass and gave him a defiant look. She tossed her head back, and in a few quick gulps, she finished the drink. She held up her hand, and a waiter was at her side in an instant. She kept her eyes on Dayne. "Another one. Make it a double."

Dayne felt the situation spinning wildly out of control. Randi was drinking, and when that happened, sometimes she wouldn't be able to leave the place without help. But who would help her?

The studio executives were winding up

their conversation, and one of the producers reached out and shook Dayne's hand. "I think we have another winner on our hands."

"Randi's committed to the film." The director winked at her. "I think we'll bow out and let you two brush up on your chemistry."

Disgust came over Dayne and rushed through his veins. He wanted to be angry at the studio guys, tell them that they had a lot of nerve trying to start something between him and Randi. But the music was too loud to say much. Dayne leaned close. "My wife's doing great."

The director's expression went blank. "Your wife?"

"Yeah." Dayne put his arms up along the back of the booth and nodded. "You didn't ask about her."

"Oh." The man laughed and looked at the others. They wore expressions of mild confusion. "Your wife. You mean Katy Hart."

"Yes, her." Dayne had to yell to make himself heard. "We're doing really well."

The director hesitated. Then he gave a single clap. "That's wonderful." He nodded to his partners for approval, and they exchanged a round of equally sincere nods. "Marriage is a great thing."

The waiter brought Randi her drink, and she downed it almost immediately. Every time Dayne looked at her, she was watching him, doing her best to flirt with him.

After a minute's conversation on the virtues of marriage, the men stood and left. On the way out, one of the younger producers stopped by the table with the blonde and the redhead. He slipped the blonde a piece of paper, leaned close, and kissed her cheek. The two exchanged an intimate smile, and the group was on its way.

The light from the disco ball at the center of the ceiling caught the producer's wedding ring as he walked out of the club.

Yeah, Dayne thought. *Marriage is a great thing.* Especially in Hollywood, where it meant almost nothing. It was as if Dayne was seeing all of it for the first time, this slice of the movie industry and its social scene. No wonder so many of his friends had opted to forgo marriage. Living together created much less paperwork when the end came— as it most always did.

He crossed his arms and tried to stop the ache in his gut. The dream flashed again in his mind, the one where Katy had disappeared in the ocean. He wanted to rush out of the club and call her, tell her that maybe he was wrong about doing this film or any other one after it.

This atmosphere was crazy.

Before he could make a decision about what to do next, Randi slid around the booth to the spot next to him.

"Listen—" he leaned close so she could hear him—"I think it's time to go."

Randi's eyes were only half open, and she looked unsteady. "You smell nice."

A frustrated breath came from Dayne, but it was lost in the noise of pounding music and conversation. "Randi, how many drinks did you have?"

"These?" She held up her empty glass, and her hand swayed a few inches in either direction. "Three or four." She set the glass down and giggled. "Or five or six."

The blonde and the redhead across the dance floor waved at Dayne, but he looked away. He had to get out of here. He turned to Randi, intent on getting her out of the booth somehow. "Time to go," he shouted. He didn't want to sound angry, but he couldn't take another minute.

Randi only giggled again. She reached up and put her hand on his face. "Kiss me,

Dayne." Her words were less slurred. "Kiss me like we do in the movies."

Panic seared through him. "Randi!" He took her hand from his face. "You're drunk. You need to get home."

Dayne had a car waiting for him outside, but what about Randi? And what about the paparazzi who were bound to be out on the street? He gritted his teeth. This wasn't fair. He couldn't leave Randi, but he didn't want to share space with her in a tabloid photo either. He looked around the room. There had to be someone else here, someone who could take care of her.

The young women across the way were sliding out of their booth. Their attention was still on him, and suddenly Dayne knew. He had no choice but to get Randi out of here as quickly and carefully as possible.

Randi was laughing, and once more she tried to touch his face. "You're a kidder, Dayne Matthews. You know you love kissing me."

"Come on." He took hold of her arm and gently pushed her toward the edge of the booth. He helped her to her feet, and she lurched badly.

A slight cry came from her, but it mingled with her constant string of giggles. "Oops. I almost fell." She covered her mouth and made her eyes big. "Don't let me fall, Dayne boy."

The starlets realized he was leaving. The redhead blew him a kiss and gave him a sad look, as if to say maybe next time.

Dayne could barely draw a breath. He linked arms with Randi. "Let's go."

She stumbled alongside him.

As they reached the door, the bouncer nodded at him. "She's been like this a lot lately."

"Wonderful." Dayne rolled his eyes. Why was it his responsibility? "Can I leave her with you?"

The bouncer held up his hand. "Not here, man. Sorry." He glanced down a hallway. "The boss don't like drunk celebrities hanging around the front door."

The noise from the club was only a distant hum here by the front desk.

Randi gave him a sad pout. "Don't leave me, Dayne." Her eyes pooled with tears. "You're my only friend."

"Oh, brother," Dayne mumbled under his breath. He nodded to the bouncer and moved to the front door. He would've paid a thousand dollars for a baseball cap and a hooded sweatshirt, anything to hide his identity. For certain the paparazzi would be waiting outside. This was a spot where they were sure to get a dozen great shots every hour.

He opened his cell phone and called his driver. "Pull up. I need a quick exit."

"Will do." The guy was older, one of the best in the business. Dayne had ridden with him before.

Through a tinted window, he watched the limo pull up right in front of the doors of the club. "Randi." He gave her a light shake. "Can you walk on your own? Just for a few steps?"

"Sure." Her tears were gone, and she looked happier. "Whatever you want."

"Okay." He carefully released his hold on her arm. "Go on, Randi. Walk toward the door."

She took three wobbly steps and then fell to one knee. "Ah!" She cried out, and the cry became another bout of laughter. She struggled to get up. "Dayne! Help!"

The bouncer raised one eyebrow, and his message was clear. Get her out—now.

Dayne took hold of Randi's arm, put it over his shoulders, and helped her to her feet. Fine. The photographers could take whatever pictures they wanted. The only person he needed to explain things to was Katy.

And she would understand completely. With the condition Randi was in, he had to help her. What choice did he have?

He walked her to the door, pushed it open with his foot, and stepped outside. Sure enough, a blast of lights hit him square on, and a dozen cameras began firing.

At the same time, Randi seemed to catch a second wind. She balanced better than before and threw her arms around Dayne's neck. She rubbed her nose against his. "Love you, Daynie."

"Nice work, Matthews," one of the cameramen yelled. "How long you been married? Two months?"

Dayne pushed Randi back as gently as he could. The driver was out, opening the back door of the limo, and Dayne guided her inside. Then without looking back, he slipped inside next to her.

She put her hand on his knee and tried to flirt with him, but her eyes never quite made contact with his. "Know what I miss?"

Dayne ignored the question. He leaned back on the headrest and shaded his eyes with his hand.

"Where to?" The voice came over the intercom at the back of the limo.

Dayne pushed a button and gave the driver the cross streets near Randi's home. She lived half an hour away. Now if he could only get her to lean against the far door and fall asleep.

Instead she rested her head against his shoulder. "You didn't answer me."

"Randi . . . you're drunk." He pushed her a few inches away. "Go to sleep."

"I miss kissing you, Dayne. You and me . . ." She smiled and swayed a little. "You and me were the best."

Dayne was certain she would regret this in the morning. But still he had to get through the next half hour. He wasn't worried about getting seduced. He had no interest in Randi Wells. But she was determined. He looked at her, hoping she could understand what he was about to say. "Slide over, Randi. You're going to hate yourself for how you're acting."

"It's not an act. You're the only one who cares about me."

Dayne let the comment pass. He stared out the tinted window and wondered if maybe she was right. Maybe he was the only one who cared about her. The magazines said that her ex-husband had moved on to his much younger costar, and her kids spent a lot of time with their nanny. Her father was dead, and she wasn't speaking to her mother.

So who really cared about Randi Wells? Who cared about a lot of those in the circle of Hollywood's elite? Ten million fans would jump at the chance for a night with Randi, a night with any of them for that matter. But who really cared?

A shudder passed over Dayne, and he silently thanked God for placing Katy in his life. Katy and Bob Asher and the Baxters. Otherwise he'd probably welcome the chance for a night with his friend, his former costar. And he'd be just as lonely and lost as her.

A few minutes into the ride, Dayne saw the cars behind them. The paparazzi stationed at the club had caught up to them, staying dangerously close and weaving in and out of traffic so they wouldn't lose his limo.

Dayne felt his heart fall to his knees. He should've expected this, the paparazzi following them. And why not? A photo of him helping Randi into her house well after midnight would probably run on the front page of every magazine in a couple of weeks.

Randi had fallen asleep, and he nudged her. "Hey . . . you're home. Wake up."

She straightened slowly and blinked a few times. For a moment she looked confused, but then she must've recognized him because a suggestive smile lifted the corners of her lips. "Mmmm, c'mere." She lifted her arms and was about to put them around his neck when he took hold of her wrists.

"No, Randi." He dug around the inside of her small purse and found her keys. Then he opened the door and stepped out. "It's time to go in."

"You're comin' home with me?" She set her legs out and onto the ground. She remained motionless for a few seconds.

"Randi!"

"Okay . . . okay." She held her hand out to him.

He took it and pulled her to her feet. He could hear the car doors opening behind him, feel the cameramen rushing up to him. "Go ahead!" he shouted. "Take your pictures. And tell me you've never tried to help a friend."

"Some friend, Matthews!" It was the same smart mouth who'd said something back at the nightclub.

Dayne hesitated. He clenched his fist. He could imagine the pleasure of shoving it deep into the guy's face.

"Go ahead, Dayne." The guy obviously understood what was about to happen. "I've got the camera right on you. Take your best shot. Let it fly."

Dayne narrowed his eyes and looked away. A fight would prove nothing. It would only look worse in a headline: "Dayne Matthews Punches Photographer while Helping Randi Wells into Her House." No, he couldn't have that in print. He stared at the front door and kept walking.

Behind him, his driver was waiting. "How long, sir?"

"Not long."

"Yeah." One of the photographers laughed. "Fifteen, twenty minutes tops."

Dayne's rage was getting the best of him. Their comments made him furious and sick at the same time. He moved faster, and Randi did her best to keep up.

"Wow . . . it's a race!" She was still laughing, but her eyes were wide, slightly fearful. "Don't let me fall."

They reached her door, and he found the right key. The entire time, he could feel the paparazzi just a few feet behind them. What right did they have to do this? They were trespassing, harassing him. He could call the police and report them. But what would it prove? A slap on the wrist and they'd be back again.

Dayne opened the door and helped Randi inside. As soon as he could, he slammed the door. *Go ahead*, he thought. *Write your stories.* He'd been here a few times before, and now he couldn't get out of her house fast enough.

She clung to his waist as they walked down the hallway to her bedroom. He flipped on lights as they went.

"You love me, right?" She squinted up at him. The lights were brighter than anything in the club or limo.

"Oh, sure, Randi." He didn't slow his pace. "This is just how I wanted my night to go."

Once he got her into her room, he set her on the bed. He was looking for a light switch when she started to take off her top.

"No!" He held up his hand. She could figure out how to get into bed by herself. "Good night, Randi."

She let her top fall back into place and held her hand out to him. "Help me. I need you."

Her voice was whiny, and even though he wasn't tempted by her, he could feel the

Holy Spirit urging him to leave. He took another few steps back. "Talk to you later, friend."

She was still calling after him as he jogged back down the hallway and through her front door. He stopped, surprised. The paparazzi had disappeared. "Of course," he muttered. "Who wants a picture of a guy keeping his word?"

On his way back to his Malibu house, he tried calling Katy a few times. She had to know about the events of the night. What if some gossip columnist blasted the news on the Internet or on one of the entertainment cable channels? Katy could be flipping the channels, wishing he would hurry and come home, and she could see the pictures of him and Randi.

"Come on, Katy. . . . Answer the phone."

Finally he tried one of the other actors, a guy he'd worked with a few times before.

"Yeah?" He sounded distracted.

"Hey, man, I'm looking for Katy."

"Katy? Yeah, she's getting a late-night lesson from old Rick, the horse trainer." The guy laughed.

"Listen, man, this isn't funny." Dayne

hated being so far away. Whatever was happening on the set, he needed Katy. Now. "Where is she?"

"Just kidding, Matthews." His voice grew more serious. "I think she's having dinner with the director. Just the two of them."

Dayne thanked his friend and snapped his phone shut. His heart raced, and he squeezed his eyes shut. What was happening? Katy had gone to dinner with Stephen? Alone? He raked his fingers through his hair and opened his eyes. He had no reason to doubt her, no reason to suspect anything was wrong.

But all he could think about was something Katy had said one night last week. They'd been talking about the dailies from their shooting in Los Angeles, and Katy had smiled. "Stephen is incredible. Sometimes I'd like to get inside his head and see things the way he sees them."

Was that why they'd gone out to dinner the same night Dayne left for Los Angeles? He stopped himself and stared at the floor of the limo. Nothing was wrong, nothing a little time together wouldn't fix. But one thing was certain. Letting a reality show invade the set was not working out the way he and Katy had planned.

The press weren't chasing Dayne and Katy through town, because they didn't have to. That part was going according to their intentions. And they had known the reality show would place interest in their marriage at an all-time high. He tried not to notice, but there was no escaping the recent headlines about Katy and him being the perfect couple with the perfect marriage. He thought about the photos with Randi probably being sent across some e-mail even at that moment.

The problem with being America's favorite couple hadn't been obvious when they agreed to the reality show. But now Dayne could see exactly how the paparazzi were thinking. Because the magazines would build them up for only one reason.

To watch them fall.

CHAPTER EIGHTEEN

JENNY FLANIGAN TOOK her seat next to Jim and glanced at her program. The weeks of rehearsal had flown by, and now it was opening night for *Godspell.*

"It was a good idea, this play." Jim leaned into her. "Bailey and Connor seem a lot closer to God."

"Maybe He's preparing them." She looked at her husband. "Katy said this is it. The theater's definitely being sold."

Jim had reason to celebrate the closing of CKT. Without the theater group, there was nothing holding the Flanigan family here, no reason he couldn't walk away from the problems on his high school team and take a position with one of the interested NFL teams this summer. But his expression held nothing but sorrow. "I don't know what these kids'll do without it."

"I've thought about starting my own group, finding a theater at the university, something." Jenny felt the familiar frustration. "But Bethany Allen, the coordinator, says they've already tried everything."

The conversation dropped off, and Jenny watched people filling the seats. Most of the regulars were here, the families who'd been with CKT since its beginning and supportive community members like the Baxters. Jenny turned in her seat and watched John and his friend Elaine file in. Behind them were four of John's kids and their spouses and children.

Ashley was walking with Kari—both of them very clearly pregnant. Ashley scanned the audience and spotted Jenny. The two exchanged a smile.

Jenny faced the stage again. Bailey was nervous about tonight. She had a couple of solos and a scene where her character was caught in adultery. Cody was coming in his own car straight from work. His job at the batting cages didn't give him enough hours, so Jim had gotten him a position at the school working in the weight room. That way he'd leave town with a little money when it came time to head out for boot camp.

The commotion and excitement around the theater grew, and Jenny savored it. She looked up to the box, the seat where Katy usually sat on opening night. It was sad that she and Dayne weren't here. Katy would've been impressed with the job Rhonda and Chad had pulled off. Jenny had attended three of the dress rehearsals last week, and each one was better than the last. The power of the parables shone through in each scene, and by the end of the last rehearsal, Jenny had noticed several parents wiping their eyes during the crucifixion scene.

She nudged Jim. "The boys seem excited."

Jim looked down the row at their four youngest, dressed in button-down shirts and their best church pants. He chuckled and shook his head. "They're way more cultured than I was at that age."

"I like it, how they're equally comfortable in a theater or tearing up the soccer field."

"The football field, you mean." Jim grinned at her.

It was an ongoing joke between them,

whether their three Haitian sons would ever really love football as much as they loved soccer. Jenny had no doubts. With a talented football coach for a father, the boys would gravitate toward the gridiron one way or another. It was destiny.

Something caught her eye and she looked up. Dotty Young, Marissa's mother, was walking over. Jenny felt a wave of anxiety. She hadn't talked to Dotty since Marissa told her about being pregnant. As far as Jenny understood, Dotty didn't know that anyone outside her family was aware of her daughter's situation.

Jenny kept her smile in place. "This is awkward," she whispered to Jim. "What am I supposed to say?"

There was no time for Jim to answer her.

"Hello!" Dotty stopped at their row and slid past Jim.

Jenny stood and hugged the woman. "It's good to see you!"

"I thought I'd find you here. Opening night and all." Dotty looked happy and carefree, as if she didn't have a worry in the world.

Jenny felt her suspicions rise. Either Marissa hadn't really told her mother after all or the woman was determined to put on a good face. Before she could say anything, she spotted Marissa near the back of the theater. The girl had on a baggy sweatshirt. She looked slightly heavier, but she was doing a good job of hiding her pregnancy.

Jenny blinked and focused on Dotty. She had to clear the air, had to let Dotty know that she already knew about Marissa's trouble. Jenny leaned closer so no one else around them could hear. "I understand Marissa told you about—"

"The show?" Dotty waved her hand dramatically. "Oh yes. Marissa wouldn't miss Bailey's opening night for anything."

A silence fell between them, and Jenny felt Jim elbow her. "So . . . how're things at home?"

"Great." Dotty lifted her hands. "No complaints. Marissa pulled off a 3.8 on her last report card. We're still hoping she'll get a scholarship to the University of Michigan. Her dad and I are both alums, you know."

"That's right." Jenny wanted to scream. Was the woman serious? Did she not see what was happening with her own daughter? "Is Marissa still dating that boy, the one in college?" Another elbow from Jim, and Jenny allowed a lighthearted laugh. "Just wondering."

Dotty frowned. "We didn't care for him. He's out of the picture. Just as well. Marissa has too much ahead of her to worry about a boyfriend right now."

"Exactly." Jim spoke before Jenny had the chance. "That's what Bailey's been saying too."

Jenny found her resolve. Jim's warnings were most likely a reminder that this wasn't the time or place, and he was right. But she couldn't stay completely silent. Jenny touched Dotty's elbow. Her tone grew more serious. "We need to talk, okay? Tomorrow morning, maybe?"

Dotty's expression changed, and she blinked twice. "Is something wrong?"

"Yes. But we can't talk about it now." Jenny managed a sad smile. "What time can I call tomorrow?"

"Uh . . ." Dotty bit her lip. Worry flashed in her eyes. "Say around ten?"

"Perfect." The small talk continued for another minute, and then Dotty hurried off to join her daughter in one of the rows near the back.

"Unbelievable." Jenny watched her go. "That woman doesn't have a clue about Marissa."

"Marissa lied?"

"Apparently." She returned to her seat. "I'll have to tell her tomorrow morning. I told Marissa I would."

"You have to. . . . I guess I can't believe she lied to Bailey."

"Yep, the very next day after our talk. Called Bailey and said she'd told her mother, just like I'd asked her to."

The music started, and the houselights went down. Cody came rushing down the aisle and maneuvered his way into the seat at the end of the row, the one they'd saved for him. He gave Jenny and Jim a smile and pretended to wipe the sweat from his brow. He'd made it just in time.

CKT's interpretation of *Godspell* was completely glorifying to God. It began with a heartrending version of "Prepare Ye the Way of the Lord," performed by one of the older boys who played John the Baptist. The message was clear. Something big was about to happen; someone big was about to come into their lives.

The pace of the music changed, and the stage filled with kids—all of them dressed in street clothes, the way they'd look if John the Baptist came walking into their greenroom downstairs. Bailey had a spot near the front, and Connor was close to her. Both of them were featured in the number—probably because of their dancing ability.

Jenny snuck a look at Cody. As he watched Bailey, a sweet, shining sadness filled his eyes—something Jenny hadn't seen before. A longing, maybe, or a regret. She wasn't sure, but she couldn't mistake how much he cared for her. Anyone could've seen that much.

One of Bailey's scenes was after the opening number, and she pulled it off beautifully. She and Jenny had prayed in her room every night for the last week, and Bailey had asked each time for the same thing. That her part might touch the hearts of people who came to the show.

Now, as Bailey fell to a heap before her accusers, as she allowed Jesus, played by Tim Reed, to take her by the hand and help her to her feet, Jenny could only imagine how Marissa Young was feeling. How badly she needed the touch of the Master's hand. How wonderful it would feel to have Him help her to her feet and lead her away from the life she'd stumbled into. And Jenny wondered something else. Whether all the pray-

ing they'd done was less for an entire audience and more for one specific person.

The frightened, pregnant girl sitting at the
back of the theater.

As with every CKT performance, John Baxter bought opening night tickets for his entire
family. It was a tradition now, something the
whole group looked forward to. John loved
everything about CKT's version of *Godspell*.
He loved the feel of Elaine sitting beside him
and the way the kids onstage brought humor
to certain parables and emotion to others.

When the lights lifted for intermission, he
looked at his family spread out over a three-
row section of seats. The tension between
Brooke and Ashley finally seemed to have
eased. They weren't sharing the same row,
but at least they'd both come. That was a
start, anyway. Brooke had promised him that
she wouldn't bring up Ashley's pregnancy
again, no matter what she personally
thought. The idea of an abortion now wasn't
something even Brooke recommended. Ashley's baby was far too developed to do anything but carry her to term.

"No one wanted to listen to me," Brooke
had told John last night. "So I'll drop it. But

when that baby's born and the family's not ready for a fatally ill child, don't forget I was the one who tried to help."

John had to agree with Brooke on one point at least. By now Ashley should've gone back to Dr. McDaniel for another test. Her baby was due in two months, and she and Landon didn't have any idea what to expect. They were still praying for a miracle, expecting one. John was praying too. He'd learned with Hayley that all things were possible with God. But if God had a different plan this time, Ashley needed to be ready. He let the thought pass.

"You're thinking of Ashley." Elaine smiled at him. "Right?"

"Yes." He looked at her and had to fight the impulse to kiss her. Whatever else happened, he could only imagine his feelings for Elaine getting stronger. There would be long walks and longer days and nights on her front porch, their latest favorite spot. "She needs to see her doctor."

"She does."

John turned so he could see Ashley, smiling and talking to Landon, Kari, and Ryan. One of them must've said something funny, because Ashley tipped her head back and laughed out loud.

Elaine took a slow breath. "I have to admit, though, that no news seems to have been good for her." She narrowed her eyes, thoughtful. "Does it really hurt if they don't find out until a few weeks before the delivery?"

John ran the idea through his mind. If Ashley and Landon's baby had anencephaly, they would need to schedule a C-section and prepare for their daughter's death. He studied Ashley, the way she looked happy and trusting, as if everything was going to go exactly as she wanted it to. He shook his head. "I guess it wouldn't hurt. As long as they see the doctor in the next month or so."

"Good." Elaine smiled. "Maybe God'll give them a miracle after all. She looks rested and beautiful."

"And the baby's more active than either Devin or Cole." John settled back in his seat. "At least that's what Ashley says."

The lights dimmed, and the second act began. Halfway through, during one of the scene changes, John felt a tap on his shoulder. He turned around and found Cole's face only inches from his.

"Papa, next time . . . me and Maddie wanna try out for the show." He was whispering a little too loud. "Okay?"

"Okay." He patted Cole's hand. "You'll have to talk about it with your mom."

John turned his attention back to the stage, but his heart went out to Cole and Maddie and any other child interested in CKT. According to Ashley, the theater was in big trouble. CKT might be shutting down. If that happened, his grandkids might never know the wonder of being part of a group as good for them as CKT.

The end of the show was far more powerful than John expected. Tim Reed did a fantastic job playing Jesus, and as he walked among his friends at the Last Supper, he looked deeply troubled over what was about to happen. As the crucifixion took place, John heard sniffling coming from several of his kids and grandkids. Elaine too was dabbing her eyes.

Knowing that Jesus had died for their sins was a truth all of them lived with, sometimes too easily. But watching Jesus' death take place through a live drama brought the reality home. The play ended with a glorious resurrection scene, the victory of Christ sure and complete.

John blinked back his own tears as he watched the Jesus character delight in seeing his friends again, shaking hands and hugging those who crowded around him.

Much was in store for the Baxter family. He would need to decide how and when his relationship with Elaine would go to the next level, and they would experience the births of the two newest grandchildren. CKT might be packing up and leaving town, and besides that there was the drama playing out with Katy and Dayne. The tabloids were looking for any crack in their happy marriage.

All that, and the part that really mattered was this: the things they would go through soon and in the years ahead were only the starting line. The real story—the hope they all had—lay in what they'd just been reminded of onstage. Not the devastation of the Crucifixion or any other trial that might come their way.

But the reality of the Resurrection.

CHAPTER NINETEEN

THE FAMILIAR WAS all around her, like old friends gathered for a final farewell, and Katy couldn't stop crying.

For the first time in what felt like a month, she was sitting next to Dayne without a single camera trained on her. The lights were dim and the show was coming to a close; the final performance of *Godspell* was under way. The final CKT show in Bloomington, Indiana.

It felt wonderful to be off the movie set, even for a few days. A week had passed since her dinner with the director and Dayne's trip to Los Angeles. They'd talked about their experiences, how the cameras had caught things that were bound to give the wrong impression. Not just to the world but to each other. But no amount of talking seemed to ease the doubt caused by their time away from each other.

The horse training had wrapped up early that past week, and Rick was no longer making eyes at Katy across the arena. Even so, the work was long and draining. Katy and Dayne still hadn't shot their scenes together. Stephen kept telling her how wonderful she was and that she lit up the camera.

Katy had no idea how. All she could think about was the very real strain between her and Dayne. She felt her marriage being pulled at from every side, and she seemed helpless to change that fact. She and Dayne had talked a few nights ago about Stephen's offer for Katy to star in his upcoming film when *But Then Again No* was finished.

Dayne had looked at her as if she were crazy. "Are you kidding?"

"Of course not." Anger poked pins at her. "What're you saying, Dayne?" She was in his trailer, and the air was stuffy. "You think they gave me the part opposite you as a *favor*?"

"Of course not." He threw his hands up and spun around, turning his back to her.

"I'm trying to get us *out* of Hollywood—" he let loose a sarcastic laugh—"not start up a whole new career for my wife."

"It's not like I came looking for a career." She took two steps and reached him. "Look at me, Dayne."

He turned around, his eyes blazing. "But that's what's happening." He shook his head, and this time his laugh sounded bitter. "I can't believe you're falling for this."

"I'm not falling for it." Her voice was raised, but she didn't care. "CKT is closing down, so what am I supposed to do? Sit around the lake house waiting for you to shoot a movie in—where is it? Mexico?—with Randi Wells?"

He held his hands up. "I'll pull out tomorrow, Katy. If that'll make you happy, I'm done."

"I'm not asking you to pull out. It's just . . ." She clenched her teeth. "Why shouldn't I make another movie as long as you are?"

"Because." His face was red, his anger as strong as anything she'd seen from him. "This business will swallow us whole and spit us into the gutter, hating each other. I've seen it. Don't kid yourself. It could happen." He stormed past her toward the trailer door. As he reached for the door, he turned and looked at her, and his anger fell away. In its place was a fear Katy hadn't seen before. "It's already happening." He hesitated. Then he pushed his way through the door before she could respond.

Though they'd had several chances since then, the topic hadn't come up again. Without a resolution to the argument, the tension between them was nearly constant. Even if they had faked their way through a dinner at the Baxter house and an afternoon picnic at the lake with Kari's and Ashley's families.

Katy dabbed a tissue beneath one eye and then the other. The tension between Dayne and her, and now this—the finality surrounding her.

The last scene in *Godspell* was winding down, and Katy's throat was thick with emotion. Here, in the theater where she'd first seen Dayne Matthews, she'd have to tell the kids and parents that it was all over; the whole wonderful ride had come to an end. But her tears weren't for the kids of CKT only—they were for her marriage, her relationship with Dayne.

Doing the reality show had been a mistake. She knew that now. But there was no turning back, no changing the way things had become complicated and strained. Her shoulders shook a little, and she could feel Dayne watching her. So why didn't he reach out and take her hand? Was he that upset with her, that angry over her desire to do another movie? If so, then she'd drop the idea. She could stay at home and stare at the walls if it meant finding their way back to how things used to be.

Onstage, a coffin was surrounded by weeping kids, their acting at an all-time professional level. Then, suddenly, the box collapsed, showing the entire theater that there was nothing inside. The coffin was empty.

A gasp came from the actors, and then Tim Reed came running down the aisle to the stage. He held out his hands, and the kids who had been crying only moments earlier started laughing, exclaiming over the goodness of God.

God . . . we need that here today. Please give me the strength to say what has to be said. But more than that, fix whatever's wrong with me and Dayne. Katy dried her cheeks with the backs of her hands and reached into her purse for another tissue. Fear took over where sorrow had just resided. In its wake, her tears stopped suddenly. In fifteen minutes she would be making an announcement she'd never planned to make.

And why wouldn't Dayne take her hand?

The show ended and the houselights came up. Everyone in attendance was on their feet, giving the kids and Rhonda and Chad the ovation they deserved.

Katy looked around, and the memories surrounded her. The faces in the crowd had shared with her in so many productions, so many parent committees and opening nights. So many lasts, like this one.

I want this, Lord . . . not another movie. Not the tension between me and Dayne. How did everything get so bad? She wanted an answer, wanted the Lord to appear before her and tell her what to do. Should Dayne pull out of his contract? Were the next few months going to destroy the love they'd worked so hard to find?

An hour passed while Rhonda and Chad handed out awards to the cast. The top honor—the Rose Award—went to Tim Reed. The trophy was given to the student actor who most exemplified Christ during the run of the show.

"In this case," Rhonda told them, "Tim not only exemplified Christ; he played Him. Tim took everything we asked him to do and added something extra every time."

The kids—who were easily excited anyway—stood up to honor Tim.

The winner of the Rose Award was always allowed to say a few words. Tim kept his message short and to the point. "Without CKT—" he looked straight at Katy—"I'd be some lost kid wondering what to do next. CKT has given me a place to use my gifts and shine for God at the same time." His smile was for her alone. "If I had my way, I would never be too old for CKT."

Katy could hardly draw a breath. Did he know what was coming? Or was he only feeling nostalgic about the fact that according to CKT guidelines, he had just one more year with the group?

The award ceremony wrapped up, and the kids presented Rhonda and Chad with a gift certificate for dinner and tickets to a musical in Indianapolis. As sad as the situation was, Katy smiled at her friend, silently wishing her all the happiness possible. Chad was returning to Cleveland later this summer, when the CKT camps were finished.

Rhonda had talked to Katy last night after the show. "I'm going with him." She was beaming, her eyes full of the sort of love and hope that Katy had seen somewhere before. "I'll live with the area coordinator in Cleveland, and Chad and I will codirect next year's shows."

Katy already knew the answer, so what she said next was more a statement than a question. "You're in love with him."

"I am." She smiled, then lowered her voice. "He's the one I've been praying for all my life. I can sense it."

Katy hugged her friend. No matter what trouble her own relationship was in, she was consumed with joy for Rhonda. "I'm so glad. You deserve this."

Rhonda asked her about the movie. "I mean, it must be wonderful, being married to Dayne and working with him on the set." Her eyes shone, more because she kept glancing at Chad across the room. She focused on Katy. "Is it just the best?"

The moment wasn't right for true confessions. Katy smiled and hid her breaking heart. "It's great."

One of the kids had called Rhonda, and she gave Katy a hasty good-bye.

Now—watching Rhonda and Chad onstage together—Katy quietly celebrated for her friend. She hadn't only found love; she'd found a normal love. Regular love. The beautiful kind of love that didn't draw attention from the tabloids. A love where no one on earth would ever wish it to fail. Chad took Rhonda's hand, and as they returned to their seats, the kids cheered again.

Bethany was taking the stage, and already she had tears in her eyes.

Here we go, Katy thought. Next to her, Dayne finally worked his fingers between hers. He kissed the top of her head and gave her hand a squeeze. He whispered, "You can do this."

She studied his eyes. *Do what?* she wanted to ask. Tell the CKT families that the drama company was closing down? Or move on to a movie career without him? Somehow she had a feeling his words held a greater meaning.

"Most of you know that Katy and Dayne are with us this afternoon." Bethany glanced in their direction.

Katy found a subdued smile, and Dayne did the same.

The kids went crazy, cheering and clapping and grinning at the two of them.

When the noise died down, Bethany continued. Her voice was choked by sorrow.

"Katy has some news for us. She wanted to tell you herself."

Katy released Dayne's hand and stood. It occurred to her that half the people in the audience probably thought her news had something to do with her coming back to direct the next show. Little did they know. She took a breath and walked up the stairs toward Bethany.

They hugged each other, and Bethany whispered, "I'm sorry. I wish there were another way." She handed the microphone to Katy.

"I know." Katy smiled at the woman she'd learned so much from, the woman without whom CKT never would've come to the area in the first place. She watched Bethany return to the audience. Then, for the first time since the news had been final, she looked into the faces of her three hundred friends, people who had been like family to her since she moved to Bloomington. "First, a huge congratulations to Rhonda and Chad and all the kids. *Godspell* was fantastic."

The kids erupted into more applause and cheers. Katy didn't cut them short. After this there would be few opportunities for the kids of CKT to celebrate. She kept her eyes away from Dayne. *One problem at a time, God. . . . That's all I can handle.* Her knees felt weak, and she gripped the microphone a little more tightly.

When the enthusiasm died down, Katy scanned the audience. "I'm afraid the news isn't good."

A few whispers rose from the crowd, but then a hush fell over the kids and their families.

Katy had rehearsed this talk on the private jet the entire flight from Santa Fe to Bloomington. The only way that made any sense was to tell them quickly, in as straightforward a manner as possible.

She looked at Rhonda. "For some time now, the owners of the theater have been thinking about selling. Apparently there's interest from a number of developers who want to . . . build high-rise condos here instead."

Shock filled the faces of a number of people. A quiet gasp worked its way around the theater.

Katy caught Tim Reed's eyes. They screamed sorrow and anger and maybe even betrayal. Not toward her but toward whoever might dare sell their theater out from beneath them. She held his eyes. "We found out that the owners of the theater have made up their mind. Tomorrow they're putting up a For Sale sign."

The entire room reacted. Some of them put their hands over their mouths and others covered their faces. Bailey and a few of the older girls sitting up front put their arms around one another. They had tears in their eyes.

Katy turned her attention to Bethany, and a sad smile tugged at her lips. "Bethany and the other CKT board members have done everything possible to find a new theater for you. Anything available would only lease us space for a night or a weekend and so—" Her voice cracked.

Everything was wrong with the scene playing out. This was where someone was supposed to yell, "Cut!" and they'd regroup and think how they could write a different ending. The kind of ending that made people want to stay and watch the show again. Only this time it wasn't an act or a movie; it was real. After investing so much of her life, her soul, in the kids and families before her, Katy had no choice but to tell them it was over.

Tears blurred her vision, and she looked down. For a moment, she lowered the microphone. She was still gathering her strength, trying to imagine how she might say the next bit, when she heard footsteps and felt Dayne beside her. He put his arm around her shoulders and steadied her. He reached for the microphone, and the gesture touched her deeply. He still cared about her. No matter what tension the movie had caused between them, she could never doubt his feelings for her.

But these were her kids; the program and families had looked to her and no one else. She was the only one who could deliver this message. She leaned into Dayne and held the microphone up again.

Everyone in the audience looked frozen, bracing themselves for whatever was coming.

"Without a theater, we can't have CKT in Bloomington." Katy wondered if they could hear her heart pounding over the PA system. She had taught her kids not to break the fourth wall, a way of looking out across the audience without actually seeing them. She used the technique now as she finished. "And so we've made a decision we never wanted to make. After the summer camp program, CKT will close down in this area." She paused. "Rhonda will be moving to Cleveland to help with CKT there."

Tears spilled onto her cheeks. She allowed herself to focus on the faces once more, and again her gaze fell on Tim Reed. "I'm sorry." Her words were a tortured whisper. "I'm so sorry."

The microphone fell to her side, and she hung her head. As many times as she'd thought about making this speech, she'd never once imagined the reaction she might get. And now she wondered if they'd quietly leave the building or demand for something to be done.

She buried her face in Dayne's chest and fell against him. How could it be over? And how come she and Dayne were letting it happen? There had to be something they could do for their marriage and for the kids before them. She heard the sound of people moving, heard the families and kids standing. *They're leaving*, she told herself. *They blame me for not fighting harder to keep CKT, for selling out to Hollywood. And now they have nothing left to say.*

Her thoughts were all but strangling her when she felt the first hand on her shoulder. Then another and another. She opened her eyes and turned out of Dayne's embrace. Quietly and with tears on many of their faces, the men and women and kids of the CKT family were making their way up to the stage, surrounding her and Dayne.

They weren't going to abandon her, not now and not ever. She felt the sobs gather in her heart, where she could do nothing to hold them back. And still her friends kept coming.

When the stage was full, they gathered just below it, and when everyone was close, when they were all holding hands or reaching out to Katy and Dayne, Tim Reed began to pray. "God, we shouldn't really be surprised. Nothing worthwhile comes without a fight." His voice was clear and strong, but Katy looked at him. His cheeks were as wet as most of the other kids'. "We've been through hard times before, and we'll get through this." His voice grew tight. "We need a theater, God. Please . . . find us a place where we can act. We need CKT in this community."

A few other kids prayed. One girl spoke through a series of sobs. "I was the kid everyone picked on at school. I had made up my mind that life wasn't worth living." She took a few quick breaths. "I wanted to end it all." She sniffed. "I even had a plan . . . and then someone invited me . . . here."

Katy's eyes were still open. Her heart ached for the girl. She had known CKT was important to the young actress, but none of them had known that God had used the drama group to save her life.

One after another kids prayed, begging God for another chance, a way to keep the program going.

When finally there was only the sound of sniffling and quiet, stifled sobs, a few of the kids began to sing. "'Great is Thy faithfulness, O God my Father, there is no shadow of turning with Thee. . . .'"

This was where the victory lay; Katy could feel it deep inside her. They could tear down the theater and stop them from having productions, but no one could take away the hope they had in Christ, the bond they shared.

Dayne tightened his hold on Katy, and he added his voice.

Others joined in, all of them stubbornly clinging to faith in a God who would provide for all their needs, a God whose mercies were new every morning—every single morning.

No matter how dark the night before them.

CHAPTER TWENTY

SUMMER ARRIVED EARLY in Bloomington and never let up. Ashley thrived in the warmer weather, holding close the feeling of newness all around her. The blue skies and fresh-cut grass and life bloomed bold and vibrant everywhere she looked. Even in the mirror. She was carrying this baby lower than her other two, and despite lingering shadows of doubt, the child was constantly active. Ashley was more in tune with this baby, more aware of when she napped and when she was active.

Sometimes she and Landon would sit next to each other on the sofa long after the boys were in bed, a warm breeze drifting through the open window, and they'd take turns placing their hands on her swollen stomach, knowing for sure that their baby daughter would find the pressure point and kick it for all she was worth.

They'd named her, and now they didn't refer to her as the baby or their little girl. They called her Sarah Marie. Sarah was Landon's mother's name, and Marie was Ashley's mother's middle name. When the two cousins were born, their names would represent much of the history and heritage that would help to make them who they would eventually become.

Landon was particularly happy that his firstborn daughter would have his mother's name. His parents had moved to Phoenix, but they still came to Bloomington twice a year to visit with the kids.

"My mom taught me how to love," Landon had confided in Ashley on one of their lazy walks through the neighborhood. "Having one name from my mother and one from yours is the perfect way to honor the love that's brought us to this point."

Ashley only smiled and played her baby's name over and over in her mind. *Sarah.* The name meant princess, which was even more fitting. Because Landon had said from the beginning that he already had one princess by marrying her. Having two would be a precious gift from God.

With summer in the air everywhere around Bloomington, Ashley couldn't get enough of being outside. Landon would come home from a day at the firehouse, and she'd already have Devin in his stroller. There was a small park six blocks from their house, and they began making the trek there every evening. Cole would skip ahead, stopping once in a while to examine a worm or point straight up at a bird's nest.

The park had a small stream, and they typically spent the first half hour pushing Devin on his favorite swing while Cole hunted for baby frogs.

"Baby frogs are the best thing about June," he had said more than once. He would hold his arms out as wide as he could. "In just a few months, they'll be huge! But in June you can still catch 'em and put 'em in a jar."

Several times Cole brought along his favorite jar and captured a pair of baby frogs, which he transplanted to their own backyard.

"Just to make sure we have lots here, too. They eat flies, you know." He was back to being a carefree child now that baseball was almost over. He hadn't mentioned sports lately, and Ashley was grateful. This was what summer was about—endless days of make-believe and magical expeditions through backyard bushes and streams and along lakeshores, looking for snakes and frogs and baby birds.

Cole still held out hope that the baby growing inside Ashley wouldn't be Sarah but Steve. Once in a while, his eyes twinkling, Cole would come running in from outside, place his grubby hand on Ashley's belly, and lean real close. "Hi, Steve! Hurry up and grow big so you can come out."

In the past month he'd perfected winking, and after having a one-sided conversation with "Steve," he'd wink at Ashley, flash his ear-to-ear grin, and race back outside. Devin was more active than before, so Ashley spent many afternoons out back, holding his hand and helping him keep up with Cole.

Now it was the second Monday in June, and Ashley had a different route mapped out for their early evening walk. Landon came through the door a few minutes earlier than usual, and their eyes met. Her breath caught in her throat, the way it still did when Landon walked in. She could hardly believe she'd almost walked away from him, almost let him go.

"Hi." She smiled. "How was work?" She hooked her fingers through the belt loops of his uniform pants.

His eyes were full of light and love and a depth she'd never seen in any other man. He framed her face with his hand and eased his fingers into her hair. "Has anyone ever told you—" a smile played on his lips—"you have the most beautiful hair?"

Ashley gave him a look that was part teasing, part endless, limitless love. She took a step closer and brushed her cheek against his. "Not today. Not until now."

The comment about her hair always made Ashley smile. It was what dear old Irvel had told her time and time and time again back in the days when Ashley worked at Sunset Hills Adult Care Home. The woman had Alzheimer's, and every time she saw Ashley, she was struck by her hair. Landon had noticed the pattern once when he came to visit Ashley at work. He used the line every now and then ever since.

"Mmm." Landon nuzzled his face along hers. "You smell good."

"You too." Ashley linked her hands at the base of his neck and leaned back so she could see his eyes. "I like when you smell like you did when you left home." She wrinkled her nose. "The smoke thing makes me a little nervous."

He chuckled. "No fires. Washed and detailed the rig and cleaned the firehouse. That's about it."

She swayed with him, hearing the music of the years in her soul. "My kind of day." She savored the feel of his heartbeat. "I made chicken salad for later."

"Again?" Landon lightly touched her shoulders, his eyes bright with a familiar teasing. He raised his eyebrows. "Not that I'm complaining. I like chicken salad." He grinned. "Even if I don't have a choice."

"What can I say?" She giggled. "It's the only thing that tastes good. At least I'm not craving sauerkraut, like Kari."

In the other room, Cole was helping Devin with his shoes. He came bounding into the living room, his brother on his heels. "Did Mom tell you?"

Landon held out his hands, swept Cole up

into a hug, and swung him around. "Hey, how was your day?"

"Great." He winked at Ashley. "Mom wants to walk to the store for rocky road ice cream."

"Is that right?" Landon glanced at Ashley. "Pickles too?"

Ashley laughed as she pulled the stroller from the front closet. "Actually, Katy told me that the tabloids hit the shelves today. I'm more interested in the magazines than the ice cream."

Cole pointed to himself. "Me and Devin are more interested in the ice cream."

"After another night of chicken salad, I'll be more excited about the ice cream too." Landon rubbed Cole's blond head. He gave Ashley an easy smile and nodded toward their bedroom. "I'll change real quick."

Ten minutes later they were on their way, Landon pushing Devin's stroller. "Have I mentioned lately that I love living here?"

Ashley tilted her head back. The sun warmed her to her core. "It's beautiful, isn't it?"

"Best June I can remember."

Cole had been bopping along ahead of them, but he stopped, his face serious. "Maddie says July and August are supposed to be really hot."

"Good." Ashley didn't care how hot it was. She felt better than ever, and if it hit a hundred, they'd simply hang out at the lake. "Maybe we'll get one of those blow-up rafts this year and spend our afternoons on the water."

"Or at the Flanigans'!" Cole's eyes lit up. "Ricky said we can come every day if we want to."

"There you go." Ashley smiled at her oldest son. "We'll have the best time ever."

"Yep!" Cole skipped ahead again and found a broken piece of a tree branch on the side of the road. He tapped it along the sidewalk as they went.

Landon took a deep breath and turned to her. He looked relaxed and happy, but his expression told her he had something on his mind. "So tell me about the tabloids."

She looked straight ahead, remembering her recent conversation with Katy. "The photos from earlier this month will probably hit today. Katy's worried about it."

"Oh." A light dawned in Landon's eyes. "The weekend they were apart?"

"Right. She had dinner with her director, and Dayne went to LA for business meetings."

"That's right. . . . He ended up giving

Randi Wells a ride home." Landon winced. "Yeah, I guess that could get ugly."

"It wouldn't be so bad if Katy wasn't already feeling tension between them. They hardly have any time together, and everywhere they turn, people point a camera at them." Ashley felt her lower abdomen tense up. She put her hand on her swollen belly and slowed her pace. She sucked in a breath through her teeth. "Oooh."

"Baby . . ." Landon's eyes filled with concern. "What is it?"

Her middle was hard and tight, and she stopped completely. "It's okay. False contractions." She waited a few more seconds, and her muscles began to relax. She took a long breath and started walking again. "I've had a few of them this afternoon." She didn't want Landon to be concerned, so she smiled. "Nothing to worry about."

Cole stopped up ahead. He banged his stick against a tree trunk, then stooped down. "Red ants! The whole tree's covered with red ants."

"Don't stand there, buddy." Landon gestured for him to move back. "They'll be up your leg in a minute."

"Yikes!" Cole brushed at his shoes and

ankles. "Two were already on me!" He danced away from the spot and kept going, staying in the middle of the sidewalk.

Landon turned his attention back to Ashley. "You sure they're false?"

"Definitely." Ashley found the same pace as before. "I'm only seven months along."

He was quiet for a few minutes. They crossed a busy street and headed for the market. Before they reached it, Landon put his arm around her. "I love the way you've handled this."

If Ashley had it her way, they'd go right up to Sarah's birth without mentioning the possibility of a problem. That way, she and Landon could spend the days dreaming about Sarah's life and the plans God might have for her, remarking about how walking lulled her to sleep and how she was most active just before bedtime. But every now and then they had to talk about the possibility. Ashley was seven months pregnant, after all, and she still hadn't been back for another test.

She slowed her pace and looked straight to his heart. "I couldn't have handled it at all without you."

"The Bible tells us not to worry about tomorrow." His smile was as warm and genuine as the sun. But his voice held a warning as well. "As much as possible, I think we've done that."

Ashley hesitated. "But . . ."

His smile fell off a little. "But I think it's time you get back to Dr. McDaniel."

"I know." Ashley refused to let her fear get the upper hand. "I'll make an appointment for the end of the month."

Landon gave her shoulders a gentle squeeze. "That'll be good. We'll still have time before she comes."

"Right." Ashley's mouth felt suddenly dry. She wanted to talk about something else, anything but what another ultrasound might turn up. "She'll probably be fine. More active than Cole, if this pregnancy is any indication."

"I wouldn't be surprised."

Ashley felt the dark clouds of fear lift once more. She couldn't have gotten through the last few months without Landon. He'd gone along with her every wish, dreaming beside her and talking about little Sarah as if neither of them had a single reason to be concerned. Together they prayed for a miracle but never with the sort of hushed tones and panicked words that marked hospital vigils. Rather with hope and certainty that something wonderful was going to come of their daughter's birth.

They headed into the store, and Ashley led the way to the nearest checkout. Before she picked up the first tabloid, the trouble Katy was worried about screamed at her from at least three covers. One showed a split image, where the photo on the right was Dayne face-to-face with Randi, their noses touching. It was hard to see Dayne's full expression, but Randi was grinning, flirty eyes focused straight at him. On the other side was Katy appearing to be in the arms of her director. Their lips were touching, a full-fledged kiss apparently in progress. The bold headline over the two images read, "Trouble in Paradise?"

"Oh no." Ashley reached for the magazine. But next to it was another and beside that two more. All of them had some form of the unflattering photos with equally dismal headlines. She held one out to Landon. "This is terrible!"

Landon looked more sad than shocked. He knew Katy and Dayne weren't interested in other people. He gave the magazine back to Ashley. "What'll this do to them?"

An urgency filled Ashley. "It'll hurt; that's what."

"But nothing's happening. I mean, not really."

Landon didn't follow the headlines on the tabloids. He didn't spend as much time at the grocery store as she did. Ashley gritted her teeth. "It works this way every time. They focus on a couple and talk about how they might be getting together and wouldn't it be great if they got together. Then they fight to be the first one to break the news that yes, in fact the couple did get together! Hooray!" She kept her voice low, but she was getting worked up. "They don't give the couple a month before the headlines start hinting about whether the couple's work schedule or differences or family issues might be putting strain on the marriage."

"Really?" Landon made a face. "That's crazy."

"I know, but people buy it. They eat it up." Ashley nodded to the rack of magazines, feeling her anger rising. "They move quickly from hinting about a problem to finding one. Anything. One of them has a drinking problem, or the other is too driven to make movies. If there isn't a problem, they'll create one." She held up the magazine again. "Like this. And then . . . it can ruin a couple."

Landon looked worried. "Katy's not like that, though. Dayne either. They won't let this garbage bring them down."

"How can they not?" She had to call Katy. She pulled her cell phone from her purse. "From where they're living, it probably feels like the whole world's pulling them apart."

"Are you calling her?"

"Yes." Ashley held up her finger to her husband. "I'll be right back." She hurried just outside the sliding doors, where the cell reception was better, and dialed Katy's number. No wonder Katy had seemed distant when she was home. She'd been worried about the photos, and now the pieces were all coming together. Dayne and Katy hadn't been married three months, and already they were in trouble.

Dear God, give me the right words. This is too serious to ignore. They needed to cut their ties with the reality show, finish the movie, and take a year off. Both of them. No one could stand this kind of scrutiny.

On the fourth ring it went to Katy's voice mail. Ashley wasn't surprised. Katy had said she was busy every day from morning until night.

Her message played out, and at the beep, Ashley took a deep breath. "Katy, it's Ashley. I saw the tabloids." She hesitated. Most of what she wanted to say was too much to leave on a message. "I'm worried about you, friend. Maybe you and Dayne need to drop the reality show before you both pay the price. Call me, okay?"

She returned to Landon and the boys and gave him a nervous look. "I left a message."

"I don't know." He glanced at the row of magazines again. "It'll be rough for a while, but I think they're pretty stable."

Ashley ran her fingers through her hair. "Weird things happen in that business." She turned away from the tabloids. "I just hope she calls back."

Three hours later, after they'd walked home with their ice cream and a bag of magazines, after they'd eaten another dinner of chicken salad and finished off half the ice cream, while Ashley and Landon were giving Devin a bath, Katy tried to reach her. Ashley didn't see the missed call until she was turning in for the night. She listened to the message, but there wasn't much to hear.

Katy sounded like she was crying. "Thanks for caring, Ashley. . . . We can't get out of the show, and as for me and Dayne . . . it's not good. Talk to you later."

As Ashley closed her phone, her stomach tightened again like it had earlier. The pressure took her breath, and for fifteen seconds it made her forget about Katy and Dayne. As it eased up, she felt a sense of reassurance. False contractions were normal, another sign that this was like any other pregnancy, free of complications.

Which was more than could be said for Katy and Dayne's marriage. Ashley closed her eyes and prayed for her brother and his wife, for the love they'd worked so hard to find and the marriage they desperately needed to protect. Then she made a plan to call Dayne in the morning and pray with him. Whatever she could do to offset the damage spread across the tabloids.

Before it really was too late.

CHAPTER TWENTY-ONE

DAYNE COULD TELL something was wrong the minute he walked into the location dining hall. The studio had rented an entire ranch for the shoot, and meals were held in a lodge with twenty cafeteria tables.

For the most part, lunch was over. Katy was shooting an indoor scene with the character playing her mother. She'd be lucky if they finished up in the next hour. Only a half dozen extras and gofers were scattered at a couple of the tables. As Dayne walked in with a few other actors, the action at both tables stopped. Two of the guys whispered to each other, and one of the tables cleared.

Dayne kept walking, but as he passed their tables, he spotted a smattering of tabloids spread out across both. "Great," he muttered.

"They're relentless lately." The actor beside him was older, a veteran. He gave Dayne a friendly punch on the arm. "They'll get tired of you eventually."

"Doesn't feel like it." Dayne grabbed a turkey sandwich and an apple and headed for the table where the extras had been sitting a minute earlier. He wasn't even situated before he saw the cover of the closest magazine. "What?" He dropped to the bench and pulled the rag closer. An angry groan came from the base of his throat. "I knew it."

The cover had a photo of him and Randi and another of Katy and Stephen. The smaller headline beneath Katy's photo said, "Oops! Wrong Romance on the Set!"

He hung his head for a moment. His actor friend was caught up in a conversation near the food line, and Dayne was glad. He didn't need an audience now. His heart slammed around like an errant pinball, but he had to face whatever the magazines held. He looked at the cover again and quickly opened it to the centerfold section. Sure enough, there he was in half a dozen photos with Randi Wells. A picture of the two of them leaving the nightclub arm in arm, one of them rubbing noses, and another of him helping her into his limo. The most damaging picture was the biggest, a shot of Randi leaning on him as he used her keys to help her into her house.

Below the photos and a heading that read, "Second Time Around?" was a short story saying that Randi was considering the role starring opposite Dayne in his next film—the one scheduled to shoot in Mexico this fall. "The world already loves the on-screen chemistry between these two. Now that Randi's single and Dayne's new marriage is on the rocks, maybe these stars will find real love the second time around."

Anger raced through Dayne's veins, consuming him. They didn't know a thing about real love. He should call his attorney and file a suit against the rag. Never mind that the magazine was owned by the same company that produced *For Real*. Celebrities had sued tabloids in the past and come out victorious. Not that it would stop them. Tabs could pay out hefty settlement fees and still keep printing dirt on celebrities. Gossip was lucrative.

He scanned the next few pages and read a quote from a "source close to Katy Hart" that she had been impressed with her director from the beginning. "Rumor is he wants Katy in his next film too. Insiders think he's interested in more than Katy's acting ability."

Dayne shoved the magazine aside and glanced at the others scattered on the table. The news was the same in each—positioned differently and with headlines that varied by a few words. It didn't matter which tabloid a person picked up; the message was clear. Katy and Dayne's new marriage was on the rocks. Big-time.

His appetite was gone, his rage too great to allow room for anything else. He picked up his plate and tossed it in the trash. Then, without turning back to check on his friend, he left through the side door. He didn't quit walking until he was past the arena and halfway across the thirty-acre field behind the ranch.

Dayne was supposed to film another scene in half an hour, but that could wait. For now he needed space and perspective before he stormed up to the director and quit. He stopped and put his hands on his hips, his back to the ranch and its outbuildings. Amazing that a camera crew hadn't followed him out here. This was newsworthy, after all. The day the tabloids hit the stands, loaded with the most dirt on his marriage so far. Certainly the viewing audience would want Dayne's reaction.

The hot sun baked his shoulders, but he didn't care. Within an hour Katy would finish her scene, and then what? Since they'd been back from Bloomington, they were constantly at odds. He'd disregarded rumors that she'd been too friendly with the horse trainer, Rick, while he was in Los Angeles, but when they talked about it, her reaction was defensive.

"Give me a break." She'd rolled her eyes and then waved toward the arena. "I did everything I could to stay away from the guy. I treated him like he was twelve."

Clearly the magazines were trying to create conflict. But he and Katy couldn't simply ignore the stories in the tabloids. Like any marriage, they needed to communicate. The trouble was, if they talked about the stories in the rags, there was a sense that maybe they were believing them.

It was a no-win situation.

And most of the time they didn't have the chance to talk anyway. Katy was busy all the time, giving an interview to this or that magazine and doing prepublicity radio spots for the movie. If that wasn't enough, they'd made their decision. Since Dayne would be busy in Mexico, Katy could take the role in their director's next film, the one shooting in England. Which meant once this film wrapped up, they'd have hardly any time before they were separated for as much as two months.

Dayne rubbed the back of his neck and stared as far into the sky as he could. A pair of hawks made lazy circles against the blue. What was he doing here in New Mexico? He should be home in Bloomington. He'd never planned to marry an actress. If this was the life he wanted, he could've stayed with any of the dozen women he'd dated over the last ten years. Katy was different; that was what made her attractive. She was honest and genuine and devoted to God.

He paced a few steps in either direction and pulled his cell phone from his jeans pocket. He flipped it open and dialed his dad's number. Five seconds passed and then ten. He studied the phone, trying to make out the signal indicator in the glare of the sunlight. *Come on . . . connect. Please, God . . .* But after twenty seconds, a series of beeps sounded and a message appeared. No signal available.

His dad would've had something to say to him, some bit of wisdom or advice. He'd stayed in a happy marriage right up until the day Elizabeth died. Dayne crossed his arms and looked at the ground between his feet. Was he jealous of Katy? He let the question hang around his heart for half a minute. No, he wasn't jealous. She could have a career in the movies if she wanted.

He slipped his hands in his pockets and looked past the split-rail fence that bordered the ranch to the highway beyond. A part of him wanted to keep walking, head down to the blacktop road, and figure a way out of the madness. He closed his eyes and exhaled. But he needed to get back before Stephen sent a search party for him. When he returned, he couldn't allow anything but his usual relaxed demeanor, the easy grin. When all he wanted to do was find Katy and run for their lives, for the life he wanted to share with her. Yes, the next few hours would test his acting.

A deep breath filled his lungs, and he found his resolve. Maybe he could check in on Katy before he started filming and let her know he loved her. No matter what the paparazzi were trying to do. If he hurried, he might find her before the reality show people shoved a camera in his face again. He turned around and took the first steps back to the set, and he heard someone yell, "Roll it! Get his reaction!"

The *For Real* camera crew was set up at the edge of the ranch, a video camera aimed straight at him. Even as his heart was breaking for Katy, and as his earlier rage once again consumed him, Dayne did the only thing he could do.

He smiled.

The hours became days, and the days became two fast and harried weeks. It was the last Monday in June, time to start shooting the intimate scenes between Katy and Dayne. The love scenes.

Dayne was in his trailer, pacing and staring out the tinted windows every few seconds, looking for Katy. What was taking her so long? Why wasn't she more anxious to meet with him? Didn't she feel things going sideways? Couldn't she see that the stories in the tabloids were the work of *For Real*?

There was a knock at the door, and Dayne felt himself exhale. Finally. He took long strides and opened it. "Katy, I—" He stopped cold.

"Uh, yeah . . . sorry, Dayne." It was one of the other actors. "Katy asked me to tell you she can't make it. She's busy in wardrobe." The guy shrugged and shifted his eyes downward for a few seconds. When he looked up again, there was an awkwardness in his body language. No question the actor felt bad for bearing this news. "She said to tell you she'll see you on the set in an hour."

"Thanks." Dayne forced himself to appear casual, confident, easygoing. The way Dayne Matthews was expected to react. He smiled. "Tell her I'll see her there."

But when he closed the door behind him, he leaned against it. She wasn't coming. Whatever the problems between them, they were bad and getting worse all the time.

He didn't have to guess what was waiting

for him outside the trailer door. The crew of *For Real* was closing in, capturing their story. *Look*, their actions shouted. *America's golden couple is struggling! The strain of working on a movie together is ripping them apart! Everyone tune in and see for yourself!*

Dayne straightened, reeled back, and drove his fist hard into the hollow door, shattering the first layer of wood. His knuckles started bleeding, but he didn't care. He was breathing hard, and he stepped back, furious with himself and even angrier with the camera crew outside.

How could he have agreed to the reality show? The problem wasn't Katy, of course. Her ignorance of the business had convinced her that having a reality show on the set was a good thing, that they wouldn't have to run from the press if they gave interviews and allowed pictures all day long. Even after everything that had gone wrong by having the press on the movie set, Dayne could understand what Katy was thinking. How would she have known any different?

But what was his excuse? He should've said something that morning on their honeymoon when he took the call from his agent. Some nights he went to sleep dreaming about how different life might be if he'd only said no. No, they wouldn't parade around for any camera crew, because their story simply wasn't sensational enough. Dayne and Katy were already married. Any good storyteller knew that once the conflict was resolved, it was time to pull out.

Unless more conflict could be created.

How had he missed that? How could he have put their marriage on the line for a chance to avoid being chased by the paparazzi?

He dropped to the nearest chair, anchored his elbows on the table, and covered his face with his hands. His leg ached, the one he almost lost in the car accident. He rubbed it and clenched his jaw. The accident had nearly killed him. Of course he would've been open to an idea that might avoid another wreck. He replayed in his mind Katy's reaction to the first batch of cover stories two weeks ago.

After taking a few minutes alone in the field behind the ranch, he'd found Katy in the dining area surrounded by a couple of the producers and film editors. The magazines were piled at the end of her table.

His heart beating in his throat, he motioned for her to step away for a minute. She did as he asked and followed him out the side door to a quiet spot. The *For Real* crews were somewhere nearby, but for a few minutes, they were alone.

Dayne took her hands in his. "I'm sorry." His fingers shook and he swallowed, trying to find his voice. "Nothing happened with me and Randi. I want you to know that."

"I trust you." Katy smiled, but it didn't come close to reaching her eyes. "I just wish there would've been someone else at the club who could've driven her home." She angled her head. "You know?"

"I tried that." He didn't want to mention the young starlets who'd been bothering him. "I wanted out of there. . . . I didn't know what else to do with her. She was too drunk to walk."

Katy pulled her hands from Dayne's and folded her arms. "I could tell by the way she was leaning on you."

A frustrated sigh came from him. "See . . ." He turned away and then quickly faced her again. "I knew you'd be mad." He hadn't wanted to bring up the shots of her, but now he did so without holding back. "Not like you turned in early that weekend." He waved his hand back at the lodge, working to keep his voice low. "Everyone on the set's talking about whether you and Stephen really have a thing."

"That's ridiculous." She was angry for the first time since they'd stepped outside. "Stephen kisses everyone like that. He wanted to talk about his next movie. Nothing more."

"To the average grocery shopper walking through the checkout, it looks like more." He threw his hands up. Nothing was working with her. "Both our pictures look like more. That's why I'm sorry."

Katy steeled herself, the same way she had a number of times when they said goodbye over the past few years. The look in her eyes was something he hadn't seen since then, and he couldn't figure out what she was feeling. "Forget about it." She looked past him. "I'm in a meeting. I need to get back."

He wanted to scream at her. What meeting could possibly be more important than working this out? "Are we okay, then? You and me?"

"Sure." She shrugged, and something cold flashed in her eyes. "We're like every other Hollywood couple, Dayne. I go my way and you go yours, and the press captures every moment for the whole world to see." She managed another halfhearted smile. "I guess we both knew what we were getting ourselves into that night."

And with that, Katy was gone. Her comment was fired at him, not herself. Dayne knew she felt no sense of guilt for having dinner with the movie's director. Every time they'd discussed the photos from that night her attitude was the same. She was innocent, carrying out business. And he was careless, allowing a movie meeting with Randi to drift late into the night, placing him in the position to look to the world like his marriage meant nothing.

"I know you're not a playboy," she'd told him, "but your fans don't know it."

Last week's magazines hadn't helped the situation. There were no more shots of Katy with Stephen, but the press had found batches of unused pictures of Dayne and Randi. The headlines continued to sound the alarm. Could it really last? Could the top celebrity of the day marry a small-town girl and really have it work out? Or would Dayne find himself unable to resist the glamorous women who had always pursued him?

As for Katy, the take by the press was slightly different by the second week. Headlines said things like "Katy Hart Turns Cold Shoulder to Cameras" and "Katy Questioning Her Role as Dayne Matthews' Wife." The stories made her look embarrassed and heartsick, not speaking to Dayne and quietly nursing her wounds from her husband's tryst with Randi Wells.

The memories of the past few weeks lifted. Dayne lowered his hands and stared out the window of his trailer. He couldn't do anything about the slant of the tabloid stories, but he could do something for his wife. He could demand a break in the schedule and take her back to Bloomington. He could walk with her around Lake Monroe and sit with her on their deck at the lake house. His love for her had ignited in that world, not this one. So going back even for a week might change everything. He could hold her hands and pray with her and promise he'd be more careful in the future.

But first she had to agree to meet with him. The last two weeks she'd stayed up late in the living room of their rented suite, and most mornings he'd find her curled up on the pullout couch. That's how bad things had gotten. This morning, she was gone before he stepped out of the shower. When he analyzed the situation, he couldn't make any sense of it. She knew him better than anyone ever had. She couldn't possibly doubt his loyalty.

So then what was the problem?

He ordered his anger back into the shadows of his heart and studied his knuckles. Something else had to be going on. If only they could find thirty minutes alone to figure it out, to work through it.

Dayne went to his closet, grabbed a denim shirt, and slipped it on over his white T-shirt. He'd been hitting the gym for an hour each morning just to work through his frustration. Every minute of his workout, he'd wrestle with God, asking for wisdom and trying to understand how everything wonderful had gotten so bad.

But for now they had a movie to film.

He buttoned up the lower half of the shirt and glanced in the mirror. The worn-in Wrangler jeans and boots made him look like he belonged on a ranch. As he was leaving his trailer, he stopped at the door and ran his fingers over the splintered hole. *I'm sorry, God. I'm all out of answers. Please show us the way.*

Dayne hesitated, waiting for a response. But none came. He drew a long breath and stepped out of his trailer.

He worked with makeup for half an hour and met with one of the editors. When it was finally time for the scene, he walked out of the lodge and stared at the arena. From where he stood he could see Katy standing next to Stephen and three of his assistants. She was nodding, smiling.

In that instant he had to wonder if there was more at stake than her anger at him, her doubt. Maybe being in a movie, being the subject of so much attention, was changing her. He shuddered, and a sick feeling choked him. Katy was much too genuine for something like that to happen. His mouth felt dry, and as he headed toward the set, he reassured himself over and over again.

But his doubts remained.

One of the assistant directors spotted him first. "Dayne!" The man waved at him to follow. "We need to get you on the horse."

"Right." He smiled, because now that they'd heard his name, the *For Real* cameras were once again following him. Happy Dayne Matthews, unaware of the world falling apart around him. That's all he was going to let them see today.

The scenes they were about to shoot would have to carry the emotion of the film. The first was maybe the most pivotal of all. After more than a decade apart, Katy's character had finally found Dayne's character— though he didn't know this. By this point in the film, viewers would know both Katy and Dayne, and they'd understand that her search for Dayne had led to this point: the culmination of Katy's search and, for Dayne, a shocking visit from a past love he thought he'd never see again.

A shiny silver sedan had been moved onto the set, and one of the production assistants was helping Katy into the driver's seat. Across the way, another assistant had Dayne's horse saddled and ready to go. Dayne had ridden a friend's horse off and on while he lived in Malibu, but working with Rick had helped him feel more comfortable. He had no trouble mounting the horse and getting set in his saddle.

"Okay, Dayne, why don't you trot him around a few times, get him worked in a little."

Dayne clucked his tongue twice, and the horse responded immediately. How strange this was going to be, having Katy come to him for the cameras when she hadn't made a point of coming to him in real life. He wasn't sure what sort of emotions the director would get today. They were barely speaking to each other. Even so, his heart beat faster at the thought of seeing Katy face-to-face. Even if it was all an act.

"All right, let's have quiet on the set!" Stephen took charge.

Around the set, people stilled and watched the action in the arena.

"Signal the car . . . and . . . roll it!"

Katy pulled the sedan into view and parked in the spot closest to the arena. She stepped out, and Dayne could feel her watching him, feel her eyes on him the same as they'd been on him when he showed up at the Bloomington Community Theater closing night a lifetime ago. He slowed his horse and watched her.

Dayne had been acting in movies half his life. He knew that here and now he should've been in character, living life through the eyes of the man he was playing in the movie. A slow recognition needed to take place, then shock and a sad longing that the years could never erase.

Those emotions were there, every one of them. But his character was forgotten. His eyes locked onto Katy's, and he squinted. He didn't have to imagine what it would feel like to be seeing the only woman he'd ever loved for the first time in ages. It was happening.

Katy walked closer, her gaze never veering from him. She reached the edge of the arena and slipped in through the gate. As she did, he eased himself off the horse. The scene called for tears. Not dramatic weeping or wailing, not even crying. Just watery eyes and a few lone tears on each of their cheeks. Katy took a few steps toward him and stopped. And suddenly she wasn't standing before him in the middle of a movie set with fifty people watching.

All in a rush, Katy was standing on a simple stage in Bloomington, congratulating the cast and crew of *Charlie Brown*, and he was lurking in the back row, knowing that he'd never seen a woman as beautiful and transparent. She was sitting next to him on a bench at Pepperdine University, and he was falling a little more for her with every passing hour. And she was running with him in the pouring rain trying to escape a wicked thunderstorm, and he was talking to her that night in the pitch-dark, telling her about his child and how the baby had been aborted without his say. She was holding his hand and trying not to fall in love with him.

She was lying beneath a dusty old Christmas tree on the Bloomington stage, shocked as he walked up and helped her to her feet, and she was crying, holding the ring he'd brought for her, and he knew—absolutely knew—that somehow they could work through their very different lives. And she was standing in front of him in the most stunning wedding dress, and he was promising her forever with the ocean breeze in their hair.

The images flashed in his mind as he dropped the horse's reins and took slow steps toward her. She did the same, and he could see all the way to her soul. Her expression told him she wasn't acting either. They were letting the world have its way with them, and both of them were sorry. Dayne's eyes silently screamed the message, and so did hers.

No makeup artist ran out with glycerin drops, not for either of them. Because the emotions they were feeling were real and deep and greater than anything they could've conjured up in a moment of brilliant acting. As they reached each other, as Dayne took Katy into his arms and held her, he knew this much. They weren't even halfway through the fire with the reality show, and the tabloids were bound to bring more of the tension that marked the last two weeks. But the feelings here were beyond acting.

Because the tears on both their cheeks were real.

CHAPTER TWENTY-TWO

TROUBLE LAY AROUND every corner as far as Jenny could see. Marissa and her mother were no longer speaking to each other or to Jenny and Bailey, and Jenny wasn't sure whether the teenage girl had chosen to keep her baby or not. Katy and Dayne were in a fight for their marriage, and CKT was closing down.

But somehow, set against the backdrop of summer, all of it felt manageable. If there was a predominant season in heaven, Jenny Flanigan believed it would be summer. The long days and warm nights felt endless no matter how rushed the rest of the year was.

With summer came the sense that all of life slowed to smell the deep green grass, to watch fireflies dance on an evening breeze, or to hear the gentle lap of lake water against the sandy shore.

Summer was barbecues and quiet conversation in the fading light of a nine o'clock sunset. It was cutoffs and flip-flops and afternoons on Lake Monroe. Despite the concerns in Jenny's heart, the sun soaked into her bones, refreshing her and making her feel close to God.

All these thoughts filled Jenny's mind as Jim pulled their boat away from the dock and set out across the lake. Today held no soccer or baseball or football. Cody was with them, and for the next four hours, they would pull the kids around on the inner tube and let the braver ones try water-skiing or wakeboarding. Their boat was equipped with everything they needed, and the sunny sky promised that the fun could last until dusk.

She stretched her legs out and rubbed her bare feet against Jim's. "It's a perfect day."

"Makes me glad we're not moving to Denver or Green Bay." He grinned at her. "Not that I don't think about it."

Relief filled her heart again. They'd had

the big talk earlier this month. The front offices of five NFL teams had asked Jim for interviews. This time it had been Jim's decision completely. No cajoling or convincing on her part.

"Bailey will be a senior in the fall," he'd told her the night he made his decision. "Whether we have CKT or not, she needs to be here."

Jenny had felt as though she'd been holding her breath for days leading up to that moment. "Thank you, Jim." She wrapped her arms around his waist and hugged him. "I know this isn't easy for you."

"Coaching jobs will always be there." He had smiled at her. "The kids won't."

And so there was no rush, no need to call a Realtor and put the house on the market. But with CKT leaving town, this was bound to be their last year in Bloomington. Jenny faced the sun and closed her eyes. She was going to enjoy every minute. And maybe—if Jim felt God leading him back into coaching for the pros—a job would open up in Indianapolis and they could still stay.

She felt a damp hand on her bare shoulder. "Mom, can I go first in the tube?"

Her eyes opened, and she looked into the

earnest face of her youngest, Ricky. "The first three in the boat get the first ride." She shrugged. "Rules are rules."

"But I was last because I ran back to get Dad's sunglasses." He wasn't whining, but he was coming close. "Please, Mom. . . . Please!"

Connor had been one of the first three in the boat. He was sitting across from Jenny, and at the sight of his brother—his life jacket bunched around his neck—Connor grinned. "Take my spot, buddy. No big deal." He elbowed Bailey, who was sitting beside him. "I'd rather ride with Bailey. She's a riot on the tube."

Cody was sitting on Bailey's other side. He looked around her and gave Connor a high five. "Let's try to dump her!"

"Great." Bailey pretended to be put out. "Thanks, guys."

Jenny took in the scene, studying the way Bailey's eyes lit up when she turned toward Cody, how she lowered her chin and laughed more easily than usual. She'd been smart so far, but in the last few weeks Jenny had had a feeling her daughter was falling for Cody again.

Of course, Cody's plans were set. He was scheduled to leave for boot camp earlier than before, on July 9, less than two weeks from now. Whatever else the future had in store for Cody and Bailey, it most certainly held heartache.

Last night Jenny had been working on a magazine article when Bailey found her.

"I'm worried." She took the chair next to Jenny's. Her eyes were shadowed with a fear that was uncommon for her. Bailey had always been a little more serious than Connor. But usually that seriousness presented itself in maturity and determination, not fear.

Jenny pushed back from her keyboard and studied her. "What about?"

"Cody." She bit her lip. "He told me he could be in Iraq before the end of the year."

"That's true." Jenny and Jim had talked about the possibility. The president was sending more troops, trying to finish the job. Cody was bound to see action soon.

Bailey folded her hands. For a moment she seemed too overcome to speak. Then she swallowed hard and looked at Jenny. "That last soldier? The one who died when the roadside bomb exploded? He was only two years older than me, Mom. I checked my yearbook, and we were in leadership the same semester."

"It's close to home." Jenny put her hand on Bailey's knee. "Have you heard how the other guy from Clear Creek's doing? The one who lost his leg?"

"He came by school the other day and talked to the coaches." She shrugged. "I guess he's going to Indiana University to be a teacher." She narrowed her eyes. "He told Dad he doesn't want anyone feeling sorry for him. He made the decision to fight for the United States, and he took the risk. Now he'll make the best of it."

Jenny was quiet for a moment. "That's the way Cody feels too."

"I know." Bailey's smile was soaked in sorrow. "It's just . . . every time I picture him in an army uniform, I see him fighting some battle I'm not sure he can win. It keeps me up at night."

"I heard something once." Jenny stroked her daughter's light brown hair. "Whenever you can't sleep, it's God's way of telling you to pray. That there's someone who needs your prayers."

Bailey nodded slowly. "I like that."

"So when you're worried about Cody and you can't sleep, use that time to pray for him." Jenny wanted to probe deeper, ask Bailey if her feelings for Cody had gotten stronger. But she wanted Bailey to take the lead.

Instead Bailey stood, and an anxious sigh filtered past her lips. "I'll still be worried. Until I get the call that he's home safe."

"That could take years."

"I know." Her eyes danced. "We're going to write to each other."

Jenny raised one eyebrow. "Really?"

"Just as friends." Bailey's answer had been quick. "He said it'll make him feel like he's back home. Even for just a few minutes."

Jenny blinked, and thoughts of that conversation faded.

Jim stopped the boat and directed Connor to make sure the knot was tight on the tube, the rope secure off the back hitch.

Jenny raised the orange flag, alerting other boaters that they had swimmers in the water. "Okay . . . you can jump!"

It was Flanigan tradition that whenever they boated, if Jim stopped the boat and cut the engine, the kids would jump off the sides and cool off. Justin and Shawn started a splashing match, and the others joined in.

But after a few minutes they all scrambled back into the boat except Ricky, BJ, and Justin—the three with first-ride honors in the tube.

As the last of the kids were pulling themselves onto the swim board and back into the boat, Jenny caught something that didn't surprise or alarm her. Cody was at the back of the boat helping Connor out of the water and then Bailey. But as Bailey climbed onto the swim board, she held on to Cody's hand a little longer than necessary.

Jenny felt an ache in her heart. Today might feel endless and carefree—while they still had all afternoon to enjoy the water. But not too far down the road they would all say good-bye to the young man who had become part of their family. His leaving would be hard on all of them, but for Bailey, it would be one of her greatest losses ever.

They could only pray that the good-bye would be temporary and that when the soldiers finally came home from Iraq, Cody would be one of them.

Bailey didn't want to catch her parents' attention, but the feeling of Cody's hand in hers sent heat and shivers through her like nothing ever had. He helped her back into the boat, and then—almost as if he didn't want to—he released her fingers. But their eyes stayed connected.

The truth—the thing she hadn't wanted to admit even to herself—was that she'd fallen for Cody. Even though she didn't want a boyfriend, and even when she'd been convinced by the actions of her friends that relationships at her age too often led only to heartache, she'd still fallen for him.

Bailey grabbed a towel and wrapped it around her waist. She sat next to her mom, across from Cody. He was talking to Connor, but she couldn't help but catch a glance or two of him. Since he'd stopped drinking, he'd put in a lot more time in their home gym, and it showed. He looked healthy, strong, and tanned, and Bailey remembered all the reasons she'd had a crush on him back when she was just a freshman.

Lately they'd gone on bike rides through the neighborhood and taken long walks down to the frog pond at the end of the street. Sometimes her brothers would tag along, but that was okay. She and Cody weren't admitting anything to each other. They'd never even held hands until today, and that was really only so he could help her into the boat.

She was still talking to Tim Reed, but the only thing on his mind was college and where he'd been accepted and how he'd have to make a decision about which school he'd attend come fall. Bailey could feel him pulling away, accepting the fact—the way they'd all had to accept it—that CKT was closing down. The members of the group were bound to go their own ways.

Twice since the For Sale sign went up in front of the theater, she and Tim had held meetings with some of the longtime CKT kids and a few of their parents, trying to think of a way to keep the drama group going. But no one had any answers. Bethany Allen, the CKT coordinator, truly had checked every-where. No place but the community theater could house their plays three times a year, and the theater was going to be torn down for condominiums.

An article had run in the paper last week stating that there was a bidding war going on for the building. From all accounts, city offi-cials expected the theater to be sold by the end of summer, with building plans going into effect some six or eight months later.

Bailey had already cried buckets of tears over the loss, but now the battle and every wonderful thing about CKT seemed like something from her past.

She caught Cody's eye and grinned. Then she looked out at the water. They'd talked about Cody's dream of going to college after he served in the army and his hope to one day settle down in Bloomington.

"Maybe I'll coach like your dad," he'd told her.

Sometimes Bailey thought he wanted to say something else, something more. Like maybe that she was part of his future plans too. He could come back from fighting the war and get his teaching degree, and the two of them would get married. It was possible—if God allowed it.

But those were the thoughts she didn't tell anyone, not even her mother.

"Okay—" her dad looked over his shoulder at her brothers in the tube behind the boat—"ready?"

All three of them gave the thumbs-up sign. "Ready!"

Her father gave the boat a burst of gas and began doing big S-turns. This part of the lake was empty, so he could take wider turns than usual, pulling the tube over his wake and then cutting into smooth water again. The boys laughed and barely held on, and on one of the turns, Bailey's feet touched Cody's.

He smiled at her, but he shifted and created space between them.

Bailey was glad. His actions were different from what they'd been with other girls in his life. Even if he didn't feel the same way about her as she was starting to feel about him, he respected her. And that made her feel beyond special.

She and Cody and Connor took the next ride, and her dad kicked his speed up a notch. She sat in the middle, so when the tube hit a high part of the wake, instead of bouncing her out of the tube, the jolt bounced out both Cody and Connor. The three of them laughed so hard they could barely breathe.

The day felt as though it would never end. Cody wakeboarded, something they'd seen him do before. But he was stronger now, and when he jumped the wake, he grabbed the board and spun it before landing on the water again.

The boys gathered at the back of the

boat, hollering their approval and shouting for more.

Bailey smiled at her mother. "He's good."

"Very good." Something in her eyes said that she understood what Bailey was feeling, and that she was okay with it on this level. Dreams were free, and they were part of what summer was about.

When the sun started to set, her father brought the boat to shore. They all helped dry down the hull, and then her dad pulled the fishing poles from the back of his SUV. "Nothing like a little night fishing." He smiled and handed a pole to each of the boys.

When he came to Bailey, she shook her head. "Cody and I are taking a walk." She gave Cody a crooked smile and nudged him with her elbow. "Right?"

Cody gave her dad an innocent look. "Uh, right. . . . I guess we're taking a walk."

Her mother was loading the wet towels in the back of their Suburban, and now she came up and stood by Dad. "What's happening?"

"Bailey and Cody are taking a walk." He gave a look that said he didn't mind.

"Don't be long." Her mom's voice was pleasant. "We're leaving in twenty minutes."

Bailey shouted at her brothers, "Catch a big one!" as she and Cody walked toward the trail that wound around the lake.

They were well out of earshot of her family when Cody laughed. "At least give me a warning."

"What?" She loved the way she felt, fresh from a day in the sun, only a few boats still churning up the nearby lake. A giggle tickled her throat. "They know we're friends, Cody. It's not like it's a secret."

"True." He sounded doubtful. "It's just . . . they don't want anything . . . you know . . ."

"What could happen?" She turned and took a few steps backward. "You're leaving." She spread out her arms and ran a few yards in front of him. "Not like you'll fall in love with me in ten days."

"Bailey . . ." He stopped, his head cocked. His tone told her he didn't know what to make of this . . . whatever she was doing.

She faced him again, laughing harder than before. "What?"

"Come back here."

"No." She turned and ran a few more steps. "Catch me!"

At first she heard him groan, but then he

muttered something about how she'd be sorry and took off in her direction.

She ran as fast as she could, loving the chase, breathing the warm wind in her face and the smell of grass and moss and damp earth. He was closing in on her, of course. He was much faster than her, and after another five yards, she felt both his hands on her waist—but only for a second.

She stopped, and her laughter made it hard to breathe. A few more steps and she bent over, her elbows on her knees. "I didn't think . . . you could catch me."

He was barely out of breath. "Please." He seemed to make sure there was distance between them. He leaned against the closest tree and brought one foot up onto the trunk. For a long time he just looked at her, a slight smile pulling at his lips.

She thought he might ask what she'd meant about falling in love, but he didn't. Instead he nodded to the trail. "Ready to walk?"

The laughter was still fading from her voice. "Okay . . . unless you wanna chase me again." She grinned at him. "It was pretty fun *letting* you catch me."

"Oh . . . okay." The sarcasm in his voice was fun and light, like everything else about the early evening.

They started walking, and once in a while their arms or elbows brushed against each other.

Cody was the first one to move the conversation toward something more serious. "I'm ready to leave . . . I think."

Bailey kicked at a loose rock. "How can anyone be ready for war?"

"I don't know. It isn't the war part. It's the whole commitment, the sacrifice." He glanced at her. "You know, the time and everything."

"Yeah." She didn't want to look at him, didn't want to think about him leaving in ten days, having his hair buzzed short and showing up at boot camp. She lifted her chin and stared at the darkening sky. Should she say something? Should she let him know a hint of what was in her heart?

Cody shoved his hands into the pockets of his shorts. "I couldn't have done it without your parents. Your dad, especially." His cheeks were red. "He's like the greatest guy ever."

Tell him, she thought. "You know what I think?"

"What?" His pace was slower than before.

"I think—when you're older and finished with the army—you'll be a lot like him."

A shy kind of laugh came from him. "Yeah?"

"Yeah." She kicked a couple of smaller rocks in his direction.

Cody took a step to the side and kicked them back toward her. He started to speak and then stopped. A long sigh came from him, and he faced her. "I have to say something."

Bailey's heart thudded in her throat. Darkness was falling over the path, and soon it would be time to head back to her family. So what was this? Her voice dropped. "Okay."

"I never . . ." He gritted his teeth and looked away for a moment. Whatever he was trying to say, it wasn't easy for him. "Bailey, I never meant to be anything more than your big brother." He looked defeated. "You know?"

She wasn't quite sure she understood. An awkward laugh came from her. "What do you mean?"

The muscles in his jaw flexed, and he looked around, as if he were hoping the words might be hanging in the air. "I feel like things are . . . like maybe you think it's . . ."

Gradually she understood. He was giving her the biggest shutdown of her life. She took a step back, but she smiled. She held up her hands. "Me?" She laughed and hoped it didn't sound too fake. "Cody, you are like a big brother." Another laugh. "Nothing more. Promise."

He studied her. "Really?"

"Definitely." Bailey nodded to him to start walking again, and he did. She elbowed him. "Can't believe you thought I . . ." She was playing the part, saying the only thing she could to save face.

"Yeah, well . . ." He laughed, but he still seemed a little nervous. "I just wanted to make sure . . . I mean, you know . . . before I leave."

"Of course." Her heart was wounded, but she couldn't let him see it. How crazy she was, thinking a guy like Cody—who'd dated so many girls—might fall for an innocent girl like her. "You're my brother and my best friend all rolled into one." Tears stung her eyes. She couldn't let him see her cry. She spun around and began running back the way they'd come. "You can't catch me twice."

She began running, but tears blurred her eyes. *God, why did I even say anything?*

Now I've made a fool of myself. He probably thinks I'm ridiculous. She could hear him calling after her, chasing her again though not with the same energy. Her vision was more blurred than before, and she didn't see the tree root sticking up out of the ground across the path just ahead. Her foot hit it wrong, and her ankle turned beneath her. She fell onto her side, halfway into the brush that ran along the path.

"Bailey!" Cody reached her and immediately crouched on the ground next to her. "You okay?"

"My ankle." It was killing her, the pain throbbing through her foot and up her leg. "I turned it."

"Here." He climbed over her good leg and knelt in the thick grass. He took her foot gently in his hands. "Can you move it?"

The pain was bad but not as bad as her hurt pride. Bailey lay flat on the dusty path, crooked her arm, and raised it over her eyes. She groaned. If she could've dug a tunnel and crawled away, she would've.

"Hey." Cody set her ankle down on the ground. He moved up near her face. "Bailey, look at me."

She didn't want to. But she was stuck. She couldn't even get up without his help at this point. Moving slowly, she brought her arm back down and squinted at him. "That was graceful, huh?"

"Well—" his eyes sparkled just a little— "you *are* a dancer." He gestured toward the path. "And that move was, well, you know, really unique."

"Great." Bailey squeezed her eyes shut. Maybe the twisted ankle would make him forget the conversation earlier.

"Hey, open your eyes." Cody's tone lost the humor from before.

She blinked and propped herself up on her elbows. A few pebbles dug into her forearms. "I think I can stand up."

"Wait." His face was only a few inches from hers, and for a few seconds it seemed like he might kiss her. The nervousness from before was back. "You know what I was trying to say earlier . . . right?"

Bailey didn't want to answer him. So she raised her eyebrows and gave him a painful grin. Her ankle was throbbing. She tried to move it and winced. "Help me up, big brother."

Cody linked his arm beneath hers and gradually helped her up. "It's a little swollen."

"I can move it." She hobbled a few steps. "It's just sprained."

They walked back together, and when they reached her family, Bailey could walk on her own with just a limp. Her parents looked at her, but before they could ask, she held up her hand. "I'm fine. Just a sprain."

Cody smiled at the rest of her family. "I told her it looked great as a dance move."

Everyone hesitated, and then Connor laughed.

By the time they were all in the Suburban, the whole group was laughing. Bailey was glad. Her fall took their attention off her walk with Cody. And it allowed the tears that had been gathering in her heart since Cody's statement to fill her eyes once more. Her family wouldn't know. It was dark in the SUV, and besides, half her brothers were laughing so hard about their fishing adventure that they had tears in their eyes too.

Bailey ran her hand along her shin. Her ankle would be fine in a few days, but her heart might take weeks. At least now she knew the truth. Cody would never see her as more than a little sister. What she'd been feeling between the two of them wasn't the beginning of love or even an attraction.

It was nothing more than her overactive imagination.

CHAPTER TWENTY-THREE

ASHLEY'S ULTRASOUND WAS later that morning, and Landon was up earlier than usual. It was the last day of June, and so far he'd done exactly what Ashley asked. He'd enjoyed this pregnancy as much as he'd enjoyed her last one. Maybe more.

Their little girl was very active, and Landon and Ashley agreed that she'd develop a spunky personality. Ashley would sing to her, hymns that her mother used to sing to Cole when he was a baby. "The Old Rugged Cross" and "There Is a Redeemer." Those times, Cole and Devin would cuddle up next to them, and Cole would lay his hand on Ashley's stomach.

"She's moving really quiet now." Cole's eyes would grow wide. "She likes when you sing, Mom."

The last few weeks had been filled with one delightful moment after another. Only a couple of dark clouds hung on the horizon. First, that Ashley and Brooke still weren't speaking any more than they had to at family dinners. And second . . . well, second they would find out about today. At the ultrasound.

John had warned Landon that with anencephaly, ultrasounds were rarely wrong. They might've all wanted to believe a wrong test was possible or that God would give them a miracle, but today's news could confirm the worst.

Landon poured himself a glass of orange juice and leaned against the counter with his back to the kitchen window. Ashley was still sleeping. Last night in bed she'd been more tense than she'd been since the first ultrasound. She kept her hand on her stomach, and when Sarah would kick, she'd smile and stroke the area, communicating with their daughter the only way she could.

"Nervous?" He'd been stretched out on his side, watching her. "About tomorrow?"

"There is no tomorrow." Ashley smiled, but her eyes were deep and afraid. "As long as we have right now, tomorrow's a million hours away."

Landon drank down half the cup of juice. Now it was only three hours away. Then there'd be no more walking around the topic, no more believing the best or refusing the truth.

He'd talked briefly with Ashley about that last night. Just so she was clear on what today might hold.

"We've prayed about the results of this next test." Landon ran his fingers softly through her hair. His words were tentative, careful. "Whatever they are, we'll believe them." He paused. "Right?"

She met his eyes, and they begged him not to talk about this, not until maybe minutes before the test. "Yes, Landon. We'll believe the tests. Whatever they are."

Landon had to be sure. Because if the results were more of the same, if Dr. McDaniel still saw a fatal birth defect on their baby daughter, it was time to form a plan, time to acknowledge their loss and prepare for it. If not, then today would be a great day of celebration. Believing the test results was important because having faith that God would grant them a miracle was one thing. But if they received bad news today and chose to look the other way, that wouldn't be faith.

It would be denial.

And Landon couldn't live that way, no matter how difficult the truth might be.

He was about to check on Devin when the phone rang. He looked at the time on the microwave. Just after seven o'clock. Too early for most people. He answered it before the next ring so Ashley wouldn't need to get it.

"Hello?"

"Landon, it's Brooke." She sounded exhausted. Like maybe she'd been crying. "I had to call before work. I didn't wake you, did I?"

"No, not at all." For an instant, Landon wondered if something else was wrong with Brooke or Peter or one of their girls. "What's up?"

"I've been awake since three. Couldn't sleep." She sniffed. "This whole thing with Ashley and me is tearing me up. I hate it."

A heaviness surrounded his heart. "Ash hates it too." He tried to find the right words.

"She's doing everything she can to protect her baby. To protect herself. That's how she sees it, I think."

"Which is exactly the problem." She sounded upset. "Your test later this morning is going to confirm everything Dr. McDaniel told you the first time. And since Ashley hasn't allowed that possibility, today's going to devastate her, Landon. It is. I don't know how she'll handle it."

Landon felt his defenses rising. Brooke was a pediatrician, but she didn't know everything. "The stages of her pregnancy have gone perfectly normal. The baby moves and kicks and sleeps." He didn't want this conversation with Brooke. Not while hope still lingered. "Ashley looks great; she feels great. I think it's normal for her to believe everything's going to be okay. Once in a rare while a mistake is made on an ultrasound. I researched it."

"Not after sixteen weeks gestation." Brooke allowed all her breath to leave her at once. "Seriously, that just doesn't happen. I can't find a case on the books where an ultrasound misdiagnoses anencephaly after sixteen weeks."

A knot formed in Landon's gut. "Maybe the

ultrasound machine had a problem." He tried to sound casual, friendly. But the call was shaking him to the core. "Like I said, her pregnancy's going along perfectly."

"It's always like that with anencephalic babies." She groaned. "Look, I don't want to ruin your morning. That's not why I called."

"Why did you call?" Landon's tone was a little short, and he regretted it. "What if Ashley would've answered the phone?"

"She wouldn't have picked up, not with my number on caller ID." Brooke sniffed again. "I called so you'd listen. So you'll be ready to help Ashley later today when she gets the news. Please . . . believe me. Today's going to be so hard for my sister." Her voice broke and she hesitated. "I love her, Landon. I'm afraid for how she'll be once she accepts the truth."

Mixed emotions assaulted him. Brooke meant well by her call, even if he didn't want to hear this negative reminder hours before Ashley's test.

Landon steadied himself and closed his eyes. "Thank you, Brooke. I know you love her." He blinked and turned so he could see out the window. The sky was cloudless, the sun already warming up the start of another day. He squinted against the bright light.

"Whatever happens this morning, God will get us all through it."

He thanked her again for calling, and they hung up. He wanted to find his way back to the place where he'd been before the phone rang. Drinking his juice and remembering all the wonderful moments he and Ashley had shared with their unborn baby in the last few weeks, believing that today's results could go one way or the other.

But all he could think about as he set his glass down and padded into the hallway toward their bedroom was a fire he and his station had fought when he lived in New York City. It was a warehouse, fully involved, and he and a group of guys were needed on the roof. One of the captains had found him before he headed up. "Stay to the edges. Don't let the men get near the middle."

Landon had tried to tell his guys, but several of them didn't listen. Guys who lost their lives that afternoon. Even still Landon wondered if he could've been more ready in that situation. Whether he might've done something to save the men, something to help them face the dangers of the fire.

The memory lifted, and Landon felt a chill run down his spine. Brooke hadn't called because she knew it all or because she wanted to put herself into a situation where she didn't belong. Her call had been a warning that landing in the middle of a fatal diagnosis without his help might destroy Ashley.

For that reason, Brooke had been right to call. Landon would be ready this morning, ready to support Ashley no matter what the news. Never mind that he wanted to cling to his wife's optimism; he would be strong for Ashley and go into the appointment heeding Brooke's advice.

Expecting the worst.

Ashley heard the phone ring, and at the same time she realized Landon was up. *He'll answer it*, she told herself. She spread her arms out and felt the weight of her baby.

"Morning, Sarah." She ran her fingers over her tight abdomen. There was a shift inside her, and Ashley watched her unborn baby move from one side to the other. "You're more squirmy than either of your brothers, little one." She patted the firm side of her stomach, where her daughter now lay, and a quiet laugh played on her lips.

The other day Cole had seen Sarah shift like that, and his eyes had gotten so big they looked perfectly round. "Mom, that's like an alien movie or something."

"It looks funny," she'd admitted. "It just means Sarah's getting ready to join us out here."

Cole wrinkled his nose. "Did I do that when I was inside you?"

"Yep. Not as much as Sarah though." She tickled his tummy. "You were sleepier."

"Not much else to do in there." Cole patted her round stomach. "You know what, Mom?"

"What?"

"I'm sort of getting used to the idea of a sister." He shrugged. "Girls need big brothers to keep 'em safe. And maybe one day she'll be going to her first day of kindergarten, and I can walk her to school. So none of the third graders call her a kindergarten baby." He stuck out his chest. "I'd be good at that."

"Yes, Coley." She kissed the top of his head. "You'd be very good at that."

He flashed her a grin, then ran to find Devin.

Those were the sorts of moments she was enjoying most about her pregnancy, the way Cole was old enough to ask questions about the miracle of life and the private times she and Landon shared with their un-born daughter.

Ashley shifted, and from the other room she heard Devin's soft little voice. "Mommy . . . Mommy . . ."

She smiled and pushed herself out of bed. It was more of a struggle these days. Sometimes she wondered if her due date was wrong and maybe little Sarah was going to come early. She couldn't remember being this big this early with the boys. She pressed her hand to the small of her back and went to find Devin.

He was standing in his crib, pacifier in his mouth, blanket in his hand, blond hair stick-ing out in a classic bed-head look. He kept the pacifier in place with his teeth and sang out one more time, a precious melody with a simple lyric. "Mo-mmy . . . Mo-mmy . . . Mo-mmy!" Then he smiled and laughed.

"Come here, sweet boy." She bent her knees a little as she swept him into her arms. He could only fit on her hip now, but he didn't seem to mind. Devin was so sweet na-tured. He didn't have half the mischievous-ness of Cole—at least not so far.

He laid his head on her shoulder and pat-ted her stomach. "Hi, baby."

"That's a nice boy, Devin." Joy filled her and warmed her despite the slight chill in the house. She wasn't in a rush to start the day. She had three hours until her test, so she eased herself into the rocking chair. She whispered in Devin's ear, "Wanna rock with Mommy for a little bit?"

"Mmm-hmm." He kept his head on her shoulder. Then he started to hum.

When Devin hummed, Ashley knew exactly what was supposed to come next. "Want Mommy to sing?"

Devin nodded and pressed his head closer against her. He pulled his blanket up to his face and snuggled into it.

Ashley added a hum of her own, because that's what she always did when Devin wanted a song. These were the simple rhythms that came with motherhood, the ability to read a child, to know a child's needs before they could even be voiced. She took a long breath and smoothed Devin's soft cotton pajama top. "'Jesus loves me! this I know, for the Bible tells me so. . . .'"

By the time she reached the line in the song that talked about Jesus being strong, Devin gave three little grunts for emphasis.

Then he lifted his head, looked straight into her eyes, and giggled. Cole was that way too. Loving the "He is strong" part most of all.

She could hear Landon across the hall waking up Cole. He had a spelling test at summer school today—a review of all the words they'd learned that year. Classes lasted for three weeks from eight to noon. Lots of Cole's friends were going, and with Ashley's pregnancy, they'd decided to let him attend again this year.

But summer school didn't mean Cole was less nervous about his test. Last night they'd all prayed that he would stay calm and re-member all the words they'd worked on since September. They randomly tested him from the review sheet, but with two hundred words on the list, they could only go over a tenth of them.

Then after prayers, Landon had figured out a way to take Cole's mind off the spelling words. "Mommy has an important test tomor-row too." He sat on the edge of Cole's bed. "So we'll pray for your spelling test, and you pray for Mommy's test at the doctor's office."

For a heartbeat, Cole looked concerned. "Is something wrong with Mommy?" He looked from Landon up to Ashley.

Her answer was quick. "No, Coley. Mommy's fine. The test is for baby Sarah."

"Oh." Calm had returned to his features instantly. Cole had no reason to worry. In his limited experience, babies never had any trouble.

Now she could hear him talking about the spelling test in the next room. "Try me on *attitude*, Dad. I sometimes get *attitude* wrong."

"Okay, spell *attitude*." There was a smile in Landon's voice.

"A-t-t-i-t-u-d-e." Cole rattled the letters off, no problem. "Attitude."

"You know what I think, buddy?"

"What?"

"I think you're worried about nothing." Landon laughed. "Now how about you get out of bed and hit the shower. We need to leave in forty minutes."

Ashley leaned back in the rocking chair and allowed herself to be fully aware of her happiness. Devin's warm little chest against her own. Her husband, so kind and compassionate, loving Cole as if the boy were his very flesh and blood. A baby daughter on the way, one who would be doted on by her two big brothers every day of her life. All that and she'd never felt healthier. This pregnancy—

more than her others—truly made her glow from the inside out.

She started in once more with the song. "'Jesus loves me! this I know. . . .'"

And the message hit her all over again. Jesus loved her; that's why life was so wonderful. There was no reason to think all that would change in a few hours at the doctor's office.

Ashley held on to that thought as she dressed Devin and made breakfast for her family. They ate together, and Cole entertained them with stories about pet day coming up and how last year Bobby Weinstein and his dad had brought their pet boa constrictor and a live mouse, which he fed to the snake, and how two of the girls and one of the boys had to be helped into the hall because they started screaming that someone needed to save the mouse.

The story was wonderfully distracting, and Ashley savored it, as she savored every moment that morning. Landon drove Cole to school at eight, and the next hour flew by. On the way to the doctor's office, they dropped Devin off at Kari's house.

On her way back out to the van, Kari stopped her. Their eyes held for a few seconds, and Kari pulled her into a long embrace. "I'll be praying."

Ashley pulled away before her sister did. She smiled and nodded. "Thanks." The facade of confidence she'd kept up for so long began to crumble. There was no hiding from the facts. She was on her way to find out if her baby was deathly ill after all. Her smile faded, and this time she moved into her sister's arms willingly. "Pray hard, Kari. Please."

Then, so she wouldn't start crying with Devin a few feet away watching, she hurried down the steps and into the van.

Landon hesitated before backing down the driveway. "Ashley . . . you all right?"

Her hands were suddenly cold and clammy, and she felt sick to her stomach. She lifted her eyes to his. "I'm scared."

He leaned over and hugged her. "God knows what's coming. He won't take us anywhere we aren't capable of going."

In His strength, Ashley wanted to say. But what if the test results were horrible and she couldn't remember how to find Christ's strength? What if she collapsed or couldn't breathe?

She folded her hands and willed herself to stay calm. "I'm okay." She looked down at her belly. As she did, Sarah kicked at her hand, and despite Ashley's fears, she managed to smile. *Everything's okay. It has to be okay.*

The drive to Dr. McDaniel's office and the ten minutes in the waiting room blended together, and in no time Ashley was dressed in a cotton gown, waiting for the doctor. She looked at the clock. Across town, Cole was probably just starting his spelling test. *Help him, God. . . . Help him remember.*

"God's with us, Ash." Landon stood next to her, his hand on her shoulder. "I can feel Him here." He paused. "It's okay."

A part of her wanted to scream, what if it wasn't okay? But she smiled at him. "I was praying for Cole."

Landon was starting to say something about Cole's spelling test when Dr. McDaniel walked in. The woman looked somber from the moment she came into view. "Ashley, Landon . . . it's good to see you."

For the first time, Ashley felt slightly guilty. She'd canceled three appointments and avoided returning the doctor's phone calls. No one could force her to see a doctor. Not when she was enjoying her pregnancy so much.

"We're sorry it took so long to get in." Landon must've felt awkward too. He hesitated, as if he was trying to think of the right excuse. But instead he simply let his apology stand on its own.

Dr. McDaniel slipped her hands into her pockets and smiled, but her expression remained serious. "It's okay. I understand." She turned to the ultrasound machine and flipped a few switches. "I'm glad you came in now." She adjusted the screen and reached for the tube of gel on her counter. "How're you feeling, Ashley?"

"Perfect." Ashley's answer was fast, as if by saying so she could stave off any doubts about the health of her baby. "The baby's moving a lot. I can track her sleep patterns and when she's more active."

Dr. McDaniel's back was to them, but she nodded. "I always loved that about my pregnancies."

Ashley felt herself relax. The woman couldn't be expecting the absolute worst. Not if she was making small talk like this. Landon was still beside her, his hand still on her shoulder, but she wasn't sure what to do next. "Want me to lie down?"

"Not yet." Dr. McDaniel faced them and leaned against the counter. She seemed to be warming the tube of gel with her hands. "Are you ready for this test?"

And there it was—the doubt that had obviously been there all along.

Ashley's throat was dry, and she couldn't find the words. She reached up and covered Landon's hand with her own.

Landon caught her silent signal. "We're as ready as we can be." His voice was thick, full of emotion. "We understand that whatever the results are today, we'll have to deal with them."

"That's what I was hoping you'd say." Dr. McDaniel directed her attention to Ashley. "I've been praying for you, just like you asked. But sometimes with God we have to look a little harder for the miracle." She touched Ashley's other shoulder. "Understand?"

Ashley didn't want to understand. She looked at the door, and for a minute she considered running. She could race down the hallway and back to the van, and they could pick up Devin and take him to the park. That way her baby would be safe from any test results or terrible diagnosis.

But none of that was possible, because it wouldn't change the fact that she needed this test. That's why she was here. So that she and Landon could figure out a way to live with the results.

Ashley exhaled and looked at Dr. Mc-Daniel. "I understand."

"All right then." She patted the table. "Stretch out right here and we'll take a look."

Ashley eased back on the crinkly paper. She wondered if Dr. McDaniel would be able to hear the baby's heartbeat over her own. Each hard, fast beat seemed to come with a message. *Please, God . . . please, God . . . please, God . . .*

Landon stayed at her side, his hand on her shoulder again.

Please, God . . . please, God . . . please, God . . .

The doctor moved Ashley's gown aside and squirted the cool gel onto her belly.

Ashley closed her eyes. *It's okay, Sarah. . . . It's just a test. Don't be afraid, baby girl. Don't be afraid.* The weight of her baby made it hard to draw a breath, so she pursed her lips and forced herself to exhale. Anything to create room in her lungs for a little oxygen.

She could hear Landon breathing harder than before, but neither of them dared say a word.

Dr. McDaniel spread the gel across Ashley's abdomen and pressed the round tip of the wand against her skin. Instantly Sarah's heartbeat echoed through the room.

Please, God . . . please, God . . . please, God . . .

This was Sarah's active hour, and today was no different. She kicked at the ultrasound device, and Ashley wasn't sure whether to laugh or cry. *See*, she wanted to say, *my baby girl's always active like that.*

Ashley opened her eyes because even if the test results were bad, she wouldn't be able to tell. And this was her chance to see the baby she'd been singing to and communicating with. The screen held the image of the baby's legs. They looked long, like a dancer's legs. Yes, maybe Sarah would be a dancer.

She placed her hand over Landon's and gave it a squeeze.

He did the same, and she could tell he was thinking similar thoughts. "She's beautiful."

Ashley nodded, her eyes glued to the screen.

"Definitely a girl." Dr. McDaniel kept her voice even.

The image changed, and their daughter's arms and hands came into view. Pretty hands, hands that would maybe one day hold a paintbrush or a stethoscope or a basketball. Her little girl's hands. Tears filled Ashley's eyes because this was amazing, this view of their daughter.

Again the doctor moved the tool, and now Sarah's profile came clearly into focus. Tiny nose and high cheekbones, a face Ashley would kiss and clean, the face that would be in their family photos, gracing the walls of their house as she grew older. One that would get made up for her high school prom, the face that would be surrounded by soft hair the same color as Cole's and Devin's.

Sarah, baby, I can see you! You're perfect, honey. Don't be afraid, little girl. I'll keep you safe.

The doctor was looking at her baby's head, at her skull. She was taking measurements, typing something into the computer, freezing the image, and then letting it go live again. More measurements, more typing.

Ashley closed her eyes again and held

her breath. *Please, God . . . please, God . . . please, God . . .*

Dr. McDaniel was saying something about Sarah's head, about an opening near the base of her neck.

Ashley opened her eyes, confused. Everything looked fine, didn't it?

The doctor froze the image. "Ashley and Landon, I need you both to look very closely."

She could feel Landon nodding, and she did the same. All the while her heart thudded out the message. *Please, God . . .* She swallowed and forced herself to grab a quick breath. Everything was going to be okay. That's what Landon told her. . . . That's what she'd been telling baby Sarah. Everything was going to be—

"The neural tube defect is clear in this area right here." Dr. McDaniel pushed a button, and the image became live again. She shifted the tool and pointed to a blurred section near the back and top of Sarah's head. "Can you see that?"

Just then, Ashley felt her baby move. Sarah's hand came into view, and she stuck her thumb into her mouth. Ashley wanted to shout at the doctor. How could her daughter have a brain defect if she was able to suck her thumb? Anyone knew that was the sign of a healthy baby, right?

"She's . . . she's sucking her thumb." Landon's voice still held hope. "Could she do that? If she has a neural tube defect?"

"Yes." Dr. McDaniel's voice was kind but firm. "In the womb, babies with anencephaly respond very much like a normal, healthy child." She pointed to the image on the screen again. "But what we see here is classic of a neural tube defect." She froze the image again and turned so she was facing them. "Your baby has anencephaly. There's no doubt whatsoever."

Her words were like so many arrows through Ashley's heart. She brought her free hand to her face and covered her eyes. What had she told Landon last night? That she would accept the test results. But what about the miracle? What about all their prayers and dreams for this little girl?

She felt a drop of wetness hit her cheek, and then she felt it again on the palm of her hand, the one covering her eyes. She lowered her arm and looked at Landon. He was pinching the bridge of his nose, his face contorted. And he was crying.

Her heartbeat wasn't screaming out a

message anymore. Ashley couldn't hear it or even feel it, as if in a moment's time a part of her had died right along with the diagnosis. If her baby wasn't going to live, maybe she wasn't going to live either. And the possibility made her angry.

"I'm sorry." Dr. McDaniel cleared her throat. "I'm so sorry." She turned off the machine and handed Ashley a few paper towels so she could clean the gel off her stomach. "I'll give you a few minutes. Then I need to see you in my office."

It was a nightmare; it had to be. How could this happen? Had she done something wrong? Brooke had said something once about anencephaly happening when a woman didn't get enough folic acid. So was that the problem? Had she missed a dose of vitamins that would've saved her daughter's life?

Ashley wiped at her stomach, and a numbness came over her, almost as if she were watching the scene happen to someone else. She closed her gown, and Landon helped her sit up.

"Baby . . . I'm sorry." He wrapped his arms around her and pressed his face against hers. "I can't believe this."

Ashley rested her hand against his back and felt him shaking, felt the sobs having their way with him. But all of it seemed like some kind of strange dream.

By the time she dressed and they went to Dr. McDaniel's office, Landon had regained control. He held her hand and talked to the doctor about a C-section versus a traditional delivery and about planning for their baby's death—whatever that meant for them.

The one thing that resonated with Ashley was the delivery part. "If I have a C-section, the baby has a better chance of living?"

Dr. McDaniel's face fell, and she looked as if she might cry too. "A better chance that your baby will live *longer*, Ashley. There's nothing we can do that will allow your baby to live."

"Longer, like . . . like years longer?" Her anger was stronger than before, because she wouldn't give up on Sarah without a fight, not without demanding her daughter get the best possible chance at life.

"No." Frustration colored the woman's expression. She looked like she might say something about how Ashley should've come in sooner or how accepting the truth earlier might've helped them get through this ordeal. But instead she studied Ashley's chart and gave a sad shake of her head. "A C-section might help your baby live longer. A few hours, maybe a day at the most."

"Fine." Ashley sat up straighter. "Then let's schedule the C-section."

Dr. McDaniel looked at her computer screen. "Your due date's roughly the third week of August. I'd like to deliver you earlier than that. So we don't run into any issues with labor. Labor can be very hard on a baby with anencephaly." She paused. "How about Wednesday, August 9?"

"Fine." Ashley couldn't wait to get out of the office. Every minute here was a minute wasted, a minute when she and Landon and Cole and Devin and Sarah were robbed of being the family they were today. While Sarah was still active and alive.

The meeting wrapped up, and Ashley stopped listening to the details. Landon was listening. That was enough.

They were halfway to the van when it all hit her. She stopped and turned to Landon. She felt dizzy and breathless, black spots circling in front of her eyes. She couldn't do this, couldn't move forward another step.

Landon must've known she was going to

pass out, because he put his arm around her and helped her to a grove of trees at the middle of the parking lot.

A bench sat between the trees, and Landon carefully lowered her there. "We'll get through this, Ash. We will." He stroked her hair and kissed her face.

There, with the sun streaming through the trees and the fresh air filling her lungs, Ashley let the realization sink in. As it did, her tears came all at once, rivers of them. She couldn't get the date out of her mind—Wednesday, August 9. If this were any other pregnancy, she'd be counting down the days and hours, waiting for her due date. A little more than a month.

"Landon . . . I need more time."

"I know, baby."

This wouldn't be a countdown to her baby's new life, and that was what seized her with fear and anger and outrage. It would be a countdown to her baby's death. The sobs ripped at her, shook her to her core, and she placed her hands on either side of Landon's face. "How?" She felt her face twist into a mass of grief. "How could God let this happen?"

She hoped Landon might have an answer. He always had an answer. When she was running from him all those years ago, when the questions were too great for her to deal with, he had sought her out and told her the truth. One answer after another. But here, there was only the sound of the distant traffic and the breeze in the trees above them. The question hung there, screaming at them. Why would God allow it? Why give them a little girl who would die almost as soon as she was born? And Ashley understood the silence between them.

Because for the first time, even Landon couldn't think of an answer.

CHAPTER TWENTY-FOUR

LANDON BECAME THE front man. He broke the news to Kari when they picked up Devin, leaving Ashley to sit in the van.

Kari put her fingers to her mouth, and tears filled her eyes. "No . . . Landon, no. It can't be."

Landon was in a hurry to leave. "We'll need some time." He hugged Kari and hoisted Devin onto his hip. He grabbed the diaper bag on the floor near the door. He felt nauseous, unable to make any sort of small talk.

"Landon, I'm so sorry." Kari's hand went to her own round belly, and she shook her head. "Tell Ashley I'll be praying."

Landon nodded, but deep inside he wanted to say not to bother. It was too late for prayers. His faith—the faith that had stayed strong through nearly losing Ashley and through his ordeal at Ground Zero— was suddenly very tired. His knees shook as he stopped in the doorway. "Thanks, Kari. We'll be in touch."

That afternoon, when Ashley was cuddled up with Devin watching SpongeBob SquarePants and waiting for Cole to come home, Landon made the only call he had the energy to make. The call to Ashley's father.

"The baby has anencephaly." Landon sat at the kitchen table and massaged his temples with his free hand. "The tests are conclusive."

"I talked to Kari." John sounded weary too. Beaten down by the impossibility of anything good coming from this situation. "I'll tell the others."

"Thanks." His chest hurt from the sadness inside him. "If you could, ask everyone to give us a few days. I think we're going to need it. We still have to tell Cole."

John agreed, and before they hung up, he hesitated. "God's still in control."

A long breath filtered through Landon's

lips. "In my head I know that. But . . . I don't know. I'm struggling with this one."

Silence filled the phone line. "I'll be honest with you, Landon." John's voice was thick with sorrow. "I am too."

Landon had barely ended the call when he heard Cole walk through the front door. Their neighbor had two kids at Cole's elementary school, and earlier that year they'd worked out a deal for summer school. Every other week they took turns bringing all the kids home. Landon was glad this wasn't their week.

Cole's backpack hit the floor. "I aced it! I really aced it!"

Ashley didn't want to tell Cole about the baby, not yet. Landon didn't blame her. What would it hurt going through a few more days pretending everything was fine?

Landon pulled himself up from the table and moved into the family room.

Cole was dancing around in front of Ashley, grinning. "Dad!" He raced over to him and waved a piece of paper in the air. "A hundred percent! Can you believe it? I only missed one out of fifty words."

Landon smiled and held out his arms.

This wasn't the time to correct him about his percentages. "Come here." He swung him up and around a few times and then set him back down. "I knew you could do it!" Sadness didn't stand a chance in the sunlight of Cole's smile.

"You must've prayed for me." He studied his test and pointed at a word halfway down the list. "See that? I even got *attitude* right!" He looked from Landon to Ashley. "So did ya? Did ya pray for me?"

"Yes, Coley." Ashley set Devin down on the floor. He propped himself up on the edge of the sofa and toddled a few steps closer. She patted the spot next to her. "Let's take a look at all those words."

The afternoon passed in a blur of Cole's excitement. In the celebration of all he'd accomplished in his spelling test, he seemed to forget entirely that Ashley had even gone in for a doctor's appointment. Twice Landon exchanged a look with Ashley, silently asking her whether it was time.

But the look in her eyes said the same thing both times. Why tell Cole now? Instead Ashley spent every possible moment that afternoon with the boys, holding Devin's hand in the backyard while Cole hunted for his favorite frog. As the day wore on, Landon began to worry about her. Was she still in denial, even now, after the diagnosis was so clear? If so, he wasn't sure how he'd get through the next month.

After dinner they walked to the park, and only then, when Cole was skipping ahead and Devin was sleepy in the stroller, did Landon realize how quiet Ashley was being. He glanced at her and there, for the first time since her breakdown in the parking lot, he saw tears in her eyes. He slipped his arm around her shoulders, and a sense of relief came over him. She wasn't in denial. Just doing her best to enjoy what little time they had left with their daughter.

That night and through the next day, Ashley resisted Landon's subtle suggestions that they needed to tell Cole. Instead she and Cole found time to sing to Sarah, marveling over her movements.

Not until Friday night, after she'd read to the boys and the four of them had prayed, not until the lights were out in the boys' rooms and the doors were shut did Ashley turn and fall into Landon's embrace.

He could tell she was crying, not because she was sobbing or out of control. But because her hot tears soaked through his shirt and onto his chest. "Baby . . ."

"You're right." She wiped her nose and looked at him. "If we wait any longer it's like . . . it's like we're lying to him."

It was exactly what Landon was feeling. Cole was eight years old. He would need time to prepare for the loss of his little sister, same as they needed time to prepare. Landon held her, slowly swaying with her. "Do you want to tell him?"

"No." She grabbed at his shirt and held on. "I can't do it, Landon. I don't want to see his heart break."

"Shhh." He steadied her, understanding her. "I'll take him fishing tomorrow morning. I can tell him then."

"Okay." She took a few quick breaths and continued to cling to him. "Why us? Why?"

Landon hated seeing her this way, hated that there was nothing he could do to make her feel the hope she'd felt just a few days ago. But he was grateful, too. Ashley needed to grieve. They both did. Because every day brought them closer to the inevitable. They still needed to talk about the impossible—a funeral for their daughter.

But that could wait.

For now it was all either of them could do to think about breaking the news to Cole.

Landon crept into Cole's room just before sunup. "Hey . . . wake up." He sat on the edge of his son's bed and rubbed the boy's back. "Wake up, sleepyhead."

Cole opened his eyes and looked around, confused. "I thought . . . I thought it was Saturday."

"It is." Landon smiled. "I have a surprise for you."

"You do?" Cole sat up partway. "Right now?"

"Yep." Landon pointed across the room. Two fishing poles were leaning against the doorway. "You and I are going fishing!"

"Really!" Cole was up and out of bed like someone had thrown a glass of cold water at him. "Before the fish are even awake?"

"Exactly." Over the last few years, this had become their favorite time to fish. Right around sunup when the fish were still waking up. "Come on. I made you scrambled eggs."

"Wow, Dad . . . you won't believe this." Cole rushed to his dresser drawers and pulled out his favorite faded khakis, the ones with lots of pockets for fishing lures. "I dreamed we were fishing, and we caught the biggest fish of the summer!" A silly grin lit up his face. "And now we're going fishing for real. I have a feeling it'll be a trip we remember."

Landon loved the boy's attitude. A nervous knot formed in his stomach. Whether they caught any fish or not, they were bound to remember this fishing trip. Probably forever. He waited while Cole slipped into a red shirt and pulled on yesterday's socks. When his shoes were on and tied, he stood up and held his hands out to his sides. "How's that for record time?"

"Perfect. Your eggs'll still be hot."

Since Ashley and Devin were still sleeping, Landon and Cole shared a quiet breakfast, then loaded the fishing poles and red cooler into the Durango. Landon had made a couple of ham sandwiches and grabbed several water bottles for later. But the cooler also held a few small containers of worms, which were always the best bait this time of day.

Cole chattered all the way to the lake, telling about how Jimmy Jones had failed his spelling test. "'Cause he was cheating, Dad. Isn't that bad?" He swung his feet, which didn't quite touch the floor of Landon's SUV, his excitement tangible. "He was looking on Mary Jo's paper, and the teacher caught him. Got sent to the principal and everything."

Landon kept his eyes on the road ahead. "Makes you glad you studied."

"Yeah, but even if I didn't, I wouldn't cheat. Not ever." Cole tapped his fingers on his knees. "Know why?"

"Why?" Landon wasn't paying close attention to Cole. He was trying to imagine how he'd break the news to him and whether he would ever be the same again afterward.

"Because God wouldn't like that." Cole shrugged. "You can't pray to God for help and then cheat your way through a test. God might never answer any other prayer ever again."

"Hmmm." Landon glanced at him. "I don't think God works like that." The message was necessary. Especially in light of what was to come.

"Really?"

"Definitely. If Jimmy Jones tells his parents the truth, and if he tells Jesus he's sorry for cheating, God'll forgive him. He can still pray all he wants."

"And God will hear him?"

Landon narrowed his eyes and looked

straight ahead again. He needed to say something that would act as a transition for the conversation yet to come. "God doesn't answer our prayers just because we're good. Sometimes He doesn't answer them the way we want and—" A rush of emotion caught him off guard. He swallowed, trying to find his voice. "And sometimes we don't understand why."

"Oh." Cole's enthusiasm dimmed. "You mean like . . . I could've prayed for my spelling test and still done real bad?"

"Yes. You might not have studied enough, or you might've been distracted." Landon clenched his jaw. The next part was for himself as much as Cole. "No matter how you did on your test, God would've been with you. It's just . . . prayers don't always get answered the way we want." He gave Cole a quick look. "Understand?"

Cole's face fell. "Sort of." He was quiet for a minute. Then they passed another pickup loaded with fishing gear. Instantly Cole's mood lifted. "We're gonna beat them there, huh, Dad? We'll have a spot before they do, and that means we'll get the bigger fish."

"Maybe, buddy. We'll see."

They found a close parking spot and

lugged the cooler down to their favorite place along the shore.

Cole craned his neck in either direction. "I think we're first out."

Landon wasn't about to point out the ten or twelve fishing boats anchored in the lake. Those fishermen had probably been at work for hours already. Instead he patted Cole's head. "You might be right."

They took a container of worms from the cooler and peeled the plastic lid off.

"I like the fat ones." Cole dug his finger around the dirt until he found a worm that suited him. "There. This one's perfect." He winked at Landon. "I say crappie and shiner minnows are for the birds. Fat worms are the best."

"Fat and squirmy." Landon pressed a wiggly worm firmly onto his hook. Then together they moved to the water's edge. Landon had chairs in his Durango, but he and Cole rarely used them. If they needed to sit, they could balance on the edge of the cooler. For now they would stand at the shore and see if the fish were interested.

"Watch, Dad!" Cole had been fishing with Landon since he was in kindergarten. He moved his rod back and cast out into the lake with the same grace as most adults. He grinned at Landon. "That's farther than last year, huh?"

Landon chuckled. "Probably ten feet farther." Even on a day that would be marked with sorrow, Cole could make him laugh. The boy was so competitive. If they could survive the insanity of youth sports, Landon had a feeling Cole would become a very good athlete. Competition was simply in his blood— even when his only opponent was himself.

"I don't know." Cole studied his bobber. "Maybe twenty feet more."

Again Landon laughed. "Okay, twenty."

Then, the way it often did when they first started out, their conversation dropped off. Landon cast out, and for half an hour they reeled in a little and then a little more and then all the way so they could check their bait and cast out again. Cole was like a little pro, and Landon hoped the boy might catch something early. Before the mood was ruined.

Landon reeled his hook out of the water and moved back to the cooler. His worm was gone, and by this time Cole's probably was too. He was about to suggest they take a break and pop open a couple water bottles when he noticed a jerk on Cole's line.

"I got one!" Cole braced his legs and held tight to his rod. The cuffs of his khakis got wet as he moved a few steps closer to the water. "It's a big one; I can feel it!"

Landon hoped so. He leaned his pole against the cooler and hurried to Cole's side. "Reel it in!"

"I am!" He fought against the pull on his line, his body angled sharply back. "Here it comes!"

Right then, a fish surfaced and began flopping hard, fighting the hook. Landon moved behind his son and helped him steady the pole. "Don't lose him."

"He's huge, Dad! Super huge."

Closer and closer the fish came, splashing and thrashing in the water. Finally the fishing line was short enough that Cole hauled the catch out of the water.

Landon let out a loud hoot. "Cole . . . you did it! The biggest fish in a long time!"

"It's a bass, right, Dad? Isn't it a bass?"

"A ten-pound bass by the looks of it."

Cole would've fallen down in his fight with the fish, but he leaned hard into Landon's arms until the fish was on the ground at their feet. "Look at that guy." Cole bent over, staring at the fish. "Let's measure him!"

"Let's get him on the chain first." Landon hurried to the tackle box and pulled out the catch chain. He ran back and crouched over the bass. "You wanna get the hook?"

"Sure." Cole stooped down, grabbed the fish by the mouth, and removed the hook like an expert.

As he did, Landon slid one of the catch chain hooks into the fish's mouth and around its gills. "There. We got him."

Cole stood up and pumped his fist in the air. "He's perfect!" He bent over, studying the fish again. "More than ten pounds; don't you think?"

Landon lifted the chain a few times. The fish thrashed against the hook. "Twelve pounds, maybe thirteen."

"Yahoo!" Cole took the chain and heaved it over his shoulder. "I'll set it in the water." He flopped the chained fish into the water and then pressed the spike on the other end deep into the grassy shore. "There." He stood up and brushed the sand off his hands. "That'll hold him."

"Let's have some water."

"Good idea." Cole ran up the slope to the cooler. "A catch like that can make you thirsty."

They shared a bottle of water and talked about what Ashley would say when she saw the fish. "She'll think it's the best one since summer started, right?"

"We haven't caught anything close." Landon was glad about Cole's fish, but he wasn't sure how to transition the conversation to the baby. "How about we try again? So I can catch one?"

"Yeah! Or maybe I'll catch another one, and you can have it!"

They baited their hooks and stood side by side. The shore was thick with tall grass on this part of the lake, the area best known for catching bass near the surface. They returned to their favorite spot, and after a while, Cole moved closer. He slipped his arm around Landon's legs and leaned against him. "Thanks, Dad. For taking me fishing."

Landon's heart melted. He put his arm around Cole's slim shoulders. "This is the best part of summer."

"Yep."

For a long time they stayed that way, until finally Landon couldn't wait another minute. Cole needed to know the truth. Then they could deal with wherever that led them.

"Hey . . ." Landon slowly reeled his line in. "Let's take a little rest, okay?"

Cole yawned. "Okay." He brought his line in and secured his hook. He set his pole against the closest tree and checked on his fish. "I think he's scaring all the other bass away. He was probably the leader."

"Probably."

Cole trudged back up to the cooler and sat on one corner.

Landon took the other and handed him his own water bottle this time. "You hungry?"

"Not yet." He rubbed his flat stomach. "Those eggs are still filling me up."

Landon nodded. The knot in his gut was back, and he lifted his eyes to the sky. *You didn't give us a miracle, God . . . but give me the words for Cole. Please . . .* He realized as the silent prayer filled his heart that his faith was still not what it had been before. But at least it was still there, and he was grateful. He would need it to get through what was coming next.

"Cole . . . remember the day you did your spelling test, how Mom was getting a test that same day?"

Cole pulled up one leg and hugged it. He cocked his head. "Oh yeah. I forgot about that. The test wasn't for Mom; it was for baby Sarah, right?"

"Mmm-hmm." Landon's heart was tripping along at double speed. He ran his tongue over his lower lip. "Anyway . . . well, the test didn't turn out so good."

A curious look came over Cole. He lowered his leg and turned so he could see Landon better. "What d'ya mean?"

If there was a way around what needed to be said, Landon would've found it. Instead he took a long breath. Then, very slowly, he released it. "Baby Sarah is sick. Really sick."

Cole stood, his arms limp at his sides. "But she isn't even born yet." He blinked twice. "How can she be sick?"

This was the hardest part. Landon raked his fingers through his hair. "She's not sick like we get sick, with a cold or a sore throat. Inside Mom, her head didn't grow right. It's a bad problem." He looked deep into Cole's eyes. "We found out that she isn't going to live very long."

Death was something Cole understood. He'd watched his grandma get sick and die from cancer, and now his big blue eyes pooled with tears. "How long?"

"Maybe only a few hours or a day or two."

"You mean . . ." His lip and chin quivered, and he rubbed his eyes. He was trying to stay tough, but it wasn't working. "You mean, she's going to die right after she's born?"

"Yes." Landon ached to pull Cole into his arms, but he wanted to make sure his son understood first. "Her life will be very, very short."

"So . . ." A tear slid onto his cheek, and he wiped it with his fist. The move left a smudge of dirt beneath his eye. "She won't get to walk or talk or . . . or go to kindergarten?"

"No, buddy."

"That isn't fair." Anger flashed in Cole's eyes, and it was clear he was fighting with everything he had not to break down completely. "Every baby should have the chance to grow up. Plus, God could make her better, right?"

There it was, the question Landon had been dreading. "Yes. God could do that, but so far He hasn't. And, well—" tears stung at his own eyes—"the doctor wants us to be ready because it looks like Sarah will die very soon."

Something changed in Cole's face, and his uncertainty and anger were replaced with fear and then a sudden, intense rage.

"No, Dad! No! She can't die!" He spun around and ran to the edge of the water. A big rock sat there, and he dropped down on it and covered his face. "No! It's my fault!"

Landon had expected Cole to struggle with the news. But those last muffled words lifted him from the cooler and sent him hurrying down the embankment. "Cole . . . come here."

He shook his head hard. "I did this; it's all my fault!"

"That's the craziest thing you've ever said. Come on." Landon walked closer and stood in front of his son. He placed his hands on the boy's shoulders. "Look at me, Cole."

When Cole moved his hands, his fear and grief were almost more than Landon could take. Sobs came over Cole and shook his shoulders. "I . . . I was supposed to pray for the test, remember?"

Suddenly Landon had an idea where Cole was headed with this.

Before he could say anything, Cole was on his feet, wide, fearful eyes trained straight at his own. "I was supposed to pray. We made a deal. You and Mom pray for my spelling test, and I'd pray for her test. Only I didn't pray, Dad. I forgot. So it's my fault."

Landon pulled Cole close and held him. "Never would God work that way. Never ever."

Cole was sobbing too hard to say anything.

"Remember our talk on the way here?" Landon kept his hands on Cole's shoulders and took a step back. He waited until the boy looked at him. "Remember I told you that God doesn't always answer our prayers the way we want?"

"Yeah, but . . . I told you I'd pray."

"We were praying. Mom and I were praying the whole time, ever since we found out she was pregnant."

Amazement came over Cole. In another switch of emotions, he seemed to let go of the possibility that Sarah was sick because of something he'd done, and he caught on to something even more difficult. "You were praying . . . and it didn't work?"

Landon lowered himself to Cole's level and looked straight into his eyes. "It did work, Cole. Baby Sarah could've died a long time ago. Even before we knew who she was." He wasn't sure where the words were coming from, but he didn't stop to think about it. "Instead look at all the fun we've had singing to her and feeling her kick and move in Mom's stomach."

"But you asked God to make her healthy." Cole's expression was softer, wounded. "You didn't just want her healthy for a little while."

"No, but think about this. Every single person will die one day. Every one of us. Me and Mom and even you. Living here—" Landon waved toward the shore and the lake and the homes beyond it—"it's just for a little while, Cole. For all of us." He brushed his knuckles against his son's cheeks. "Our home is in heaven, where we'll all be together forever."

For the first time since Cole understood about Sarah, a sense of peace seemed to come over him and mix with his sadness and fear. "Where Grandma Baxter lives?"

"Right."

"So Sarah's going to live—" Cole angled his head, like he was putting the pieces together—"but she'll just live in heaven."

"Exactly."

Cole nodded. He was quiet for a while, staring out at the lake. When he spoke again, there were tears in his voice once more. "I'll miss that little sister."

"I'll miss her too."

They held on to each other again for a long, long time. And as the minutes passed, Landon realized that something remarkable had happened. He hadn't known how to explain the situation to Cole, how to reason that even after praying for Sarah's health, she was going to die anyway. But instead of confusing Cole, the boy had understood it better than he or Ashley. If that wasn't proof of God's mercy and grace, nothing was. Because their little girl was indeed going to live. She'd live and run and talk and sing in heaven, where she'd wait with Grandma Baxter until they could all be together.

Now they only had to figure out how to say good-bye until then.

Before they left, Cole walked over to the chain and bent down near his big fish. He fiddled with the clasp that secured the bass to the chain, and with a sudden burst, the bass swam away. Cole stood and watched him go. A sad smile pulled at the corners of his mouth.

"Buddy . . ." Landon went to him, his voice gentle. "What'd you do?"

Cole turned. "I let him go."

"How come?" None of them much liked

the taste of bass, but the fish truly was the biggest catch of the season. Normally Cole would've been bursting at the seams waiting to show Ashley his prize.

The innocence in Cole's expression was as sweet and simple as his faith. He shrugged, his eyes glistening. "I didn't want him to die."

With that, Landon nodded and patted Cole's shoulder. They packed up their gear in solemn silence, thoughts of life and death heavy on their minds. And of heaven, too.

Because of that, somehow they would survive the loss of little Sarah.

Even if it took all their faith to do it.

CHAPTER TWENTY-FIVE

THE FAMILIAR TENSION was there between Katy and Dayne as they walked from the SUV to the Baxter picnic spot on Lake Monroe. Katy had explained to the director how important the Fourth of July was to Dayne's family and how badly they needed the break. The man agreed. Katy had agreed to work on his next film, and he would pretty much do whatever she asked to keep her involved.

Katy had hoped the time away would ease the strain, but they'd been home since Sunday afternoon, and so far it had netted nothing but a lot of silence.

Dayne shaded his eyes so he could see down the bank. "Ashley's here."

"Good." Katy hoped to see her sister-in-law. Everyone in the family knew the bad news by now, but Katy hadn't talked to her yet. She wasn't sure what to say when she did, but she didn't want to miss the chance to spend time with her. Especially when she and Dayne needed to be back on the set by tomorrow afternoon.

They trudged a little farther down the hill, and Dayne stopped and faced her. He had a bag of food in his arms and a couple of collapsible chairs slung over his back. "I know things aren't great right now." He looked like he might take her into his arms, but he held back. "I wish I could blink and everything would be okay." His struggle was obvious in his features. He nodded toward where the rest of his family was already set up and starting the day. "But for their sake, let's fake it today. Okay?"

His request cut her deep. Wouldn't it have been just as easy for him to tell her maybe this was the time to start over? to take her in his arms and kiss her and beg her to give their marriage a fresh start?

Katy stared at her husband. "Fine." Anger

steeled her heart and made her feel cold even with the warm breeze off the water. "I'm getting pretty good at that act."

"Katy . . ."

She started down the hill and threw a forced smile back in his direction. "Come on, Dayne. We wouldn't want anyone to think we're fighting."

He made an exaggerated sigh and caught up to her. "I didn't mean it like that. It's just . . . they have enough to worry about."

"Whatever."

Dayne was starting to say something else when John Baxter turned and waved them over to his table. "Over here, guys. . . . There's lots of room."

Katy smiled and approached him. "Hi!" She leaned in and kissed John's cheek. "Looks like everyone's here."

Dayne hugged his father and set his bag of food on the table. He looked out over the lake. "I've missed this."

"You two need a break." John studied Dayne, then Katy. "How are you . . . really?"

For a moment, Katy's facade almost cracked. She wanted to collapse there on the picnic bench and admit that things were terrible. Rumor on the set was that Randi was calling Dayne every day, anxious to work with him on another film and needing his friendship while she tried to survive being a single mom. Gossip was flying across the set and in all the tabloids, and the only time she felt connected to Dayne was during their scenes together—which still hadn't even involved so much as a kiss. But Dayne's request echoed in her heart, and she lifted her chin. "It's good to get away."

"Yes." Dayne looked relieved, and he seemed to send her a silent thank-you. "The set's a little hectic right now."

"How's it going with the reality show?"

Katy almost laughed, but she realized John honestly didn't know. The show wasn't running until after the first of the year, and for now the only way a person would know how bad life on the set had gotten was by reading the tabloids. John Baxter probably hadn't done that in all his life.

"It's not like we thought." Dayne sat on the table next to his father and rested his feet on the bench. They were both facing the water. "They want more than what they're getting during the shoot." He frowned. "They're always looking for a conflict."

Katy unpacked the bag of food, her attention completely on John and Dayne's conversation.

John was quiet for a few seconds. Then he turned to Dayne. "I saw a few of the magazine covers at the market." His look held a gentle warning. "I know you love Katy, Son . . . but be careful."

Katy wanted to second the motion. Didn't Dayne see what a woman like Randi Wells could do to their marriage? She was forcing herself on Dayne, and he was too nice to see it. How could he talk to her every day, and how come he hadn't told Katy about the phone calls? She was hearing about them from the other actors and even the assistant director. "Oh," someone would say, "Dayne's on the phone with Randi Wells again."

But never, not once, had the news come from her husband. So what was Katy supposed to believe? If something wasn't starting up between them, then what did he have to hide? He had to know how she was feeling about Randi, how it was easy to believe the tabloids were right when they said Dayne was contemplating an affair.

Katy took the spot next to Dayne just as Kari and Luke headed up the hill toward them. That's when Katy noticed Ashley and

Landon. Their picnic was set up with their boys quite a ways from the rest of the Baxter family.

Dayne must've noticed it at the same time. "How's Ashley?"

"Keeping to herself." John looked more upset than he'd admitted so far. "There's a struggle between her and Brooke. They're keeping their distance."

Kari and Luke reached them and said their hellos, joining the others at the table, their conversations quiet and ripe with discouragement. Ashley and Brooke weren't talking, and Kari was feeling guilty about her healthy baby in light of all Ashley and Landon faced with their little girl.

At some point, Katy forced herself to tune out. The heartache around her was more than she could bear, more than she could process. She directed her thoughts to the complications the future might hold when she starred in another movie. Dayne would be busy filming with Randi, so it couldn't possibly matter. No sense in her staying home in the big lake house by herself, waiting to get the latest news about her husband from the tabloids.

Katy let herself get lost in the blue of the

lake and the sky beyond it. Wasn't it only yesterday when everything felt right? when Ashley and Landon were two of the happiest people she'd ever met, and John didn't look scathed by any sort of worry? It felt like moments since Dayne had brought her to this same picnic last year, her new engagement ring shining in the sun.

Nothing could go so bad so fast and still be real. She breathed in slow through her nose. There was only one answer for how things were now. Maybe none of it had been real in the first place. Maybe the Baxters were like any other family, putting on a good front and trying to present a unified image when in fact their conflicts ran just as deep as anyone else's. And as for Dayne . . . maybe the only happy endings in his world didn't happen in real life but in the movies.

Where faking happiness wasn't only expected—it was applauded.

Kari was grateful Ashley had showed up at the picnic, but even so, the situation was dire for all of them.

Kari had called her last night and begged her to come. "You'll feel better if you get out." She tried to keep her tone light. "Besides, you can't miss the Baxter family picnic. It wouldn't be the same without you."

"Brooke'll be there," Ashley said. "She's probably hoping for a way to tell me she told me so."

"Ashley!" Kari couldn't believe such a mean thing had come from her sister. "You don't believe that."

Ashley had hesitated. "No—" she released what sounded like a frustrated breath—"but it feels like that. She tried to tell me a dozen times, and I wouldn't listen. Now she's right and I'm wrong."

"What would it have mattered?" Kari hated the conflict in her family. If God would use her as a peacemaker, she was more than willing. "Even if you'd believed her, you wouldn't have had an abortion. And you would've lost those months where everything seemed wonderful."

"True. But she's still right. And I hate that, Kari. I just hate it. I wanted God to heal this baby so badly." Her voice broke. "Whatever happened to God being bigger than medical technology? bigger than a diagnosis?"

Kari had wanted to tell her sister that God was infinitely bigger, no matter how their situation played out. But this wasn't the time.

She let a few seconds pass. "Just come to-morrow. Please, Ash. We all want you there."

Ashley made no promises, but she and Landon and the boys had shown up anyway. Kari figured their presence had more to do with Landon than last night's phone call. But either way, they were here. Now if she could just get her sisters to talk.

Before Ashley's arrival, Kari had joined Brooke at a table on the far side of their picnic area. "Hey . . . can I sit here?"

"Sure." Brooke's tone and expression were aloof, but they did little to hide her pain. She wasn't the most emotional of the Baxter sisters, but when she was feeling something, she'd never been able to hide it. Today was no exception. She kept her attention on Maddie and Hayley, both in life jackets and splashing at the water's edge. "I wish Erin were here."

"Me too." Kari didn't want to rush into a conversation about Ashley. Brooke needed to know that Kari was interested in her and not just in a peace treaty. "I talked to her yesterday." She'd made the call right after talking to Ashley. Sometimes she wondered if God hadn't planned for her to be the one keeping all of them together, the sister who refused to be too busy to call and keep everyone in touch.

Brooke looked at her. "Is she coming out in August?"

"Yes. She wants to be here when Ashley's baby is born. She has tickets for the weekend before."

A smile softened Brooke's eyes. She touched Kari's blossoming stomach. "By then this little one might be here."

"I can't wait." She stretched her back and moaned. "This little one's riding right up between my ribs. Sometimes I can barely catch a breath."

"That's how Maddie was." Brooke laughed. "Feels like a lifetime ago."

Kari looked down the beach at the girls. Cole was racing Maddie along the sand, and right then the two of them stopped and joined Jessie and Hayley a little ways up on the grass. The cousins were getting along well today—a relief in light of the other struggles in play. She focused on Brooke's youngest. "I still can't believe how well Hayley's doing."

"Me either." Brooke's eyes narrowed. "I'm tempted to think she'll always struggle with learning, but I can't even say that. She shouldn't be here, and she certainly shouldn't be walking and talking and playing with her cousin. There are no can'ts with that little girl. Only God knows how far she'll go from here."

Kari wanted to ask why Brooke hadn't felt the same way about Ashley's baby, but that would only make the tension worse. Instead she waited a few beats. "Ashley's not sure what to say to you, how to approach you now that she knows you're right . . . about her baby."

"That's ridiculous." Brooke's voice told just how much the situation was hurting her. "I've always been here for her. She thinks I'm the enemy, but it's not me." She spread her hands across her chest. "I'm a doctor, and I know how impossible it is to have a faulty ul-trasound reading with a diagnosis of anen-cephaly. And that makes me the bad guy somehow."

"It's not that." Kari chose her words care-fully. "I think she's still remembering your ini-tial suggestion. About the abortion."

"Look—" Brooke faced Kari—"that doesn't make me the bad guy either. An abortion is the preferred way of handling anencephaly because it spares the family the incredible grief of having a birth overshadowed by an almost simultaneous death." Her tone was heavy with sadness. "Do you have any idea how hard that's going to be on them? It could change them forever."

Kari thought about that. She'd done online research on neural tube defects over the past few days. The baby could be born with a disfigured face, her forehead and eyes compromised because of the missing sections of skull. All told, Brooke was right about the trauma. The experience would be devastating. Ashley would welcome her daughter and bid her a gut-wrenching good-bye at the same time.

"But, Brooke—" Kari turned compassionate eyes to her sister—"all of life changes us. We go through the birth of a child, and we're changed forever. The death of a mother—" she smiled even as tears welled in her eyes—"and we're never the same again. We can't run from the things in life that change us. Maybe we have to embrace them."

Brooke's expression closed off some. She nodded and gave Kari a guarded smile. "Thanks. I'll keep that in mind." She stood. "I told the girls I'd build a sand castle with them." And with that she took a few steps, smiled again, and jogged down the beach.

Kari wasn't sure if the conversation had helped, but it was the best she could do. Now, though, sitting at the picnic table with Luke, her father, Katy, and Dayne, nothing seemed to be going right. She could sense the tension between Dayne and his wife, but she didn't feel like it was her place to ask them about it. The tabloids told the story, really. There were problems—mostly concocted, clearly, but problems all the same. She was praying for them. She wasn't sure what else to do.

Her father was deep in conversation with Dayne, and at the far end of the table, Katy seemed lost in her own world.

"Do you see it?" Luke leaned close to Kari. Reagan was in a blowup raft with Tommy and Malin. Every now and then Tommy would wave at them and shout about finding big water. Luke would wave and smile, but he seemed as distracted as the rest of them.

"What?" Kari couldn't get comfortable. She put her hands behind her on the table and tried to lean back.

"Ashley. She's hurting so bad, it kills me."

Luke's voice was low enough that the others couldn't hear him. "I don't know what to do."

"Hmmm." Kari loved being around Luke, loved that he and his family had moved closer. His own marriage still had its rocky times, but at least he was willing to talk about his struggles. Kari stared across the picnic area. Ashley was sitting at the same type of table by herself. Landon and the boys were twenty yards away, working on a sand castle not far from the one Brooke was building with her girls.

"I mean, look at her." Luke sounded beyond frustrated. "I hate seeing her like this." He leaned forward and dug his elbows into his knees. "I tried talking to her earlier, but she gave me one-word answers. It's like no one can get through to her."

"What would Mom do?"

Luke cocked his head and thought for a minute. "She'd sit next to her and hold her hand. Or give her a hug."

"Right." Kari smiled at the memory. "Mom knew that sometimes words weren't needed."

He stood up and took a deep breath. "Then that's what I'm going to do."

As Luke left their table and headed

toward Ashley, Kari felt the most brilliant ray of hope shining across her heart. Yes, these were troubled times. But they would find their way through them, and they would do so with faith and love, and sometimes—when words weren't needed—they would do so with a hug.

Because that's what Baxters did.

With every step Luke remembered different times when Ashley had helped him. When he was little and fell off his two-wheel bike, and Ashley had run inside to get a washcloth and a few minutes later gently rubbed the rocks off his scraped knee. And when he was older, before she left for Paris, when she took a walk with him and told him to stay in school, to never give up on his dreams.

But the most vivid memory was the time when she'd sat him down on a bench on the campus of Indiana University. It was there, when Luke had been making some of the worst decisions of his life, that Ashley told him the truth about Reagan. She'd had a baby, and the baby was his. Luke's child.

At that time, Luke had been living with a wacky woman he'd met in one of his communications classes. He'd thrown his beliefs to the wind and was openly living a life contrary to the one his parents had raised him to believe in. Then and there, with other students coming and going all around them, Ashley had called him on every wrong thing he was doing.

Because she loved him.

The memories flashed through his mind in a few seconds, and as he reached her, he could only hope that now—when she needed his support—he would know how to give it. Mom wouldn't have needed a conversation or a solution to the problems Ashley faced. She would've simply been there. Breathing the same air. And that would be enough.

Luke reached Ashley, and this time he didn't ask how she was or if she wanted to talk. He just took the seat beside her and sat close enough that their shoulders were touching. Together they stared straight ahead at the lake and at the kids building their sand castles.

Ten minutes passed before Ashley turned to him. "Thanks."

"For what?" He grinned, trying to find that place with his sister where the two of them always connected, where the friendship they'd started back as little kids still grew strong.

"For being you." She faced the water again. "For just being."

Luke's heart felt lighter than it had all day. This was what he'd been looking for, a chance to reach out to Ashley and let her know she was loved. No matter how dark the days ahead looked. If he were in her place, he wouldn't want his family lined up with sad faces and apologies. He'd just want to know that somewhere down the road, when the sadness lifted and it was okay to laugh again, his family would still be there for him.

The way all of them would be there for Ashley. Even Brooke.

It took another few minutes, but Ashley began talking about past Independence Days. Before long they were both smiling, remembering last year, when Landon lost a bet and had to jump in the lake with his clothes on, and other times, a decade ago, when Ashley and Luke had built a homemade canoe in their garage and used the Fourth of July to test it.

"I think we lasted maybe ten seconds before it sank." Luke laughed. "It was the world's worst sailing effort."

"For sure." She wasn't quite laughing, but her tone was lighter than it had been earlier. "You were always up for my crazy ideas."

"What was I supposed to do? You were the great Ashley Baxter, and I was just your kid brother. I would've built a rocket and tried to launch it to the moon if you'd asked me to."

They were quiet again for a few minutes.

"Hey, Ash . . . all those years of you asking me for things . . . ?"

"Yes?" There was a tenderness in her expression, a vulnerability.

"Can I ask something of you?"

She put her hand on his knee and smiled. "Sure, little brother. Want me to build a sand castle with you? shape it like a canoe or a rocket poised for the moon?"

"No." He looked deep into her eyes, beyond her fear to the place where her sadness knew no bounds. "Can we all be there? When your baby's born?"

She hesitated, and then her eyes flooded with tears. "Oh, Luke . . ." She wrapped her arms around his neck and held on to him for a long time. Finally she gave him the answer he was waiting for. "Yes . . . yes, you can all be there."

"Love you, Ashley." He ran his hand along

her back, willing her to feel his strength. "You can do this."

"I know." She sniffed.

For a long time they stayed that way. A brother and sister who through the years had ridden out life's storms together. This time there was nothing either of them could do to change the outcome, but Luke would do what he could. He would be there.

And they would say their good-byes to little Sarah together.

CHAPTER TWENTY-SIX

CODY'S FINAL TEN days flew by the way Bailey had known they would. After his talk that day on their walk around the lake, she didn't let herself daydream about the future. Instead she and Cody simply spent the days like a couple of kids—boating, tossing a football, and playing Ping-Pong late into the night.

But now it was Sunday morning, and Cody was downstairs getting ready to leave. Bailey washed her face and slipped into a T-shirt and shorts. She was terrified about what the future held for Cody, but she no longer wondered whether he'd come back for her. He didn't think of her that way, and that was okay. The truth had sunk in, and Bailey didn't care.

As long as Cody came back alive.

Bailey hurried downstairs, and all through her mom's pancake breakfast she couldn't find the appetite to take more than a couple bites. She wanted a few minutes alone with Cody, and she wasn't sure she was going to get them. They needed more time, another week or another day. She still had more to tell him.

The idea was still consuming her when Cody finished eating, rinsed his plate, and stuck it in the dishwasher. Then he turned to Bailey and nodded toward the back door. "Take a walk with me?"

Bailey was afraid she'd start crying right then, but she held back. "Sure."

The boys—who were at the age when everything Bailey did usually caused a burst of laughter—stayed unusually quiet. *They understand,* she thought. This was their last day with Cody. There was nothing funny about that.

Cody opened the door, and she followed him outside. He motioned to the path that led along the side of the house and through the backyards of two of their neighbors and on into a wooded area.

He didn't say anything until they were almost to the trees. "You're thinking the worst again." He stuck his hands in his pockets and gave her a crooked grin. "Aren't you?"

She wanted to laugh, but she couldn't find the strength. Her knees shook as she walked. "I'm trying not to."

"I'll be safe, Bailey. I told you." His tone was lighthearted, easygoing, the way it was so often. "God's got my back, and besides, I'll have your letters to look forward to."

"Yeah." She willed her tears to stay put. Cody wouldn't want her to cry. Not now.

"What?" Cody took a few steps in front of her and turned, walking backward so he could face her. "The ever-faithful Bailey Flanigan has doubts?" He made a funny face.

"Not really." She laughed, even though she didn't want to. "I know God'll be with you, and of course I'll write. I promised." She felt her smile fade. "It's just that . . ."

"I know." He turned again and fell in beside her. "You're not sure how you'll go on without my charming presence around to bug you all the time."

Bailey liked the way he was keeping things light. She didn't want a dramatic talk right now. They'd had enough of those in the nights leading up to this moment, conversations about the war and whether it was necessary and talks about his anger toward his mother for never being there for him. But here, so close to good-bye, she preferred this Cody—the one who made her laugh. She kicked at his foot. "Yeah, Cody. . . . I won't know what to do with myself."

"You'll find something. Tim Reed's around this summer, right?" He lifted his chin. "You deserve a guy like him."

Bailey laughed but only because she didn't know what to say. Tim Reed was too busy for her, even if he was the greatest guy ever. And as for Cody, he'd made his feelings clear. He thought of her as a sister. But sometimes—in moments like this—she wondered if he was only lying to himself and to her. Because everything inside her told her that he had feelings for her. But maybe that was just because he was leaving today.

They walked for ten minutes, talking about her mother's pancakes and how he probably wouldn't have a meal like that again until he came back to visit on leave.

After a while, he stopped and faced her. She had the same feeling she'd had that day on the path near the lake. That maybe, in some crazy moment of reckless abandon, he might actually kiss her.

"I'll miss you, Bailey." It was his first attempt at being serious this morning.

She didn't want a good-bye scene, but they had no choice. This was why she'd wanted to have some alone time with him, after all. So she could tell him good-bye her own way, without everyone watching. She put her arms around him.

Cody had been very careful not to be physical with her. Though she'd seen him hand out hugs to his friends without a second thought, this was only the third time he'd hugged her.

And he did hug her. He put his arms around her shoulders and held her for a long time. As he released her, he kissed her on the cheek. "Stay the same, okay?"

Bailey allowed herself to get lost in his eyes. This wasn't love, but it was the closest thing to it she'd ever felt. "You know I will." The feel of his kiss on her cheek was making its way down her arms and legs. She wanted him to kiss her again, but she knew he wouldn't. He had already told her how he felt, and he would stick to that. She was sure.

"And don't get a boyfriend." He released her shoulders and took hold of her hand. "You'll be too busy with school and Bible studies for any of that."

"Oh, really?" Bailey grinned at him.

"Yeah." Cody started walking again, still holding her hand. "My good girl doesn't have time for boys."

He was teasing her, and after a few steps he released her hand. They were quiet until just before they left the woods. "I want you to know something." He looked at her, his pace slower than before.

"What?" She could tell from his tone that whatever was coming next, he wasn't joking anymore.

"If anyone could make me change my mind about enlisting, it'd be you. Being with you lately has been . . ." He looked up through the trees to the sliver of sunlight beyond. "It's been different from anything else in my life, different from any friendship ever."

There it was again. *Friendship.* Bailey refused to let herself be discouraged by the word. She smiled at him. "I'm honored."

"I mean it. You and your family are what I'll

miss the most." He looked at his watch. "Come on, Bailey. Your ankle's fine, right?"

"Right." She loved this, that he was closing their time together with the silliness and laughter that had marked most of the last few weeks.

"Okay, then race me back to the house."

She didn't give him time to signal a start. Instead she set out as fast as she could, as if by running like the wind she could escape the painful good-bye. He wasn't giving it his best effort, because he lagged a few feet behind and never once sounded out of breath.

At the end, when she touched the back door first, Cody only shrugged. "See? I always knew you were better than me." He was joking with her; he had to be. But his eyes looked deeper than they had all morning.

That look was all Bailey could think about as they went inside and the series of good-byes began. Cody started with the boys. They gathered around him, giving him hugs and high fives.

"Get the bad guys, Cody!" Ricky saluted him, and then he ran and grabbed Cody's duffel bag.

Shawn and BJ and Justin kept their words quiet. Even Connor—usually the life of any

Flanigan moment—only hugged Cody and then uttered a soft-spoken good-bye.

Her parents were next.

Bailey had thought she could get through this moment, but that idea went out the window when her mother came into the room with Cody's pillow beneath her arm and tears in her eyes. "You almost forgot this."

Dad had been watching from a few feet away, but now he came up beside Mom and pulled Cody into a long hug.

Bailey felt the first tears then.

"You'll always be a son to me," she heard her dad whisper. "Watch yourself. Stay safe."

As he pulled back, there was the sound of a car horn from the circle out front. Cody's ride was here.

Bailey crossed her arms and willed herself to be strong. But her tears came regardless. She rocked onto her toes and tried to believe that in just a few minutes they wouldn't see Cody again for a year or more. Maybe not ever.

God, keep him safe. Hold him in Your arms. She sniffed, and Ricky noticed her tears. He looped his arm around her waist.

Her mother hugged Cody next. The tears had already choked out her voice, so she gripped his shoulders as she pulled away. "Come back, okay?" The whisper was all she could manage.

Cody didn't face Bailey all this time, and she wasn't sure what he was thinking. This had to be hard on him too, but he was staying strong so far.

Before they walked him to the door, her dad held his hands out. "Come on, everyone. Circle up. Let's pray for Cody."

In that moment, Bailey saw the truth. Cody wasn't as strong as he pretended to be. His face was scrunched up in knots, his eyes squeezed shut against the sadness.

Her dad was the only one who could talk, so he led the prayer. "Dear Lord, we release Cody into Your care. You brought him here for a reason, and You take him from us now for an even greater one. Please let him know that, like all soldiers who serve the United States, his sacrifice of time and energy and service will not be in vain. Let him know that Americans everywhere live in debt to him and those like him." His voice was heavy with sadness. "We ask that You keep Your angels around him and keep him safe. And we pray that he would feel Your love and ours every step of the journey ahead of him.

Thank You for Cody, Lord. We won't forget the time he's had with us, and we pray for many visits in the future. In Jesus' name, amen."

Cody seemed more in control now. As the group moved toward the front door, he put his arm around Bailey's dad's shoulders. "Thanks for everything." He stopped and looked her dad in the eyes. "I don't know what to say."

"You'll do the same thing someday for someone the Lord puts in your life." Her dad patted his shoulder. "Now go get the job done."

The last thing Cody did before he walked through the door was come to Bailey. He hugged her once more, and this time he almost seemed to cling to her. The feelings his embrace released in her were more than she could understand, more than she could describe.

He took a step back and locked eyes with her. "Bye, Bailey. . . ."

"Bye." She held up her hand and watched as he grabbed his things and hurried down the walkway to the waiting car. Two guys sat in the front, and the driver popped the trunk and motioned for Cody to toss his bag in.

Cody did, then climbed into the backseat. He gave one last look in the Flanigans' direction, one final wave. And in that moment, as his eyes locked onto Bailey's one last time, and as the car he was riding in pulled down her driveway, turned right, and disappeared up over the hill, Bailey understood the strange and overwhelming feeling.

Her heart was breaking because Cody Coleman was gone, and nothing between them would ever be the same again.

Cody watched the Flanigan house until he couldn't see it anymore.

"You okay, Coleman?" The guy driving let out a loud chuckle. "Old Buck here had a meltdown when he said good-bye."

Cody wasn't about to admit to anything. He yawned. "I'm fine. Hey, guys, I'm getting some shut-eye before we hit the airport."

"Okay." The driver chuckled again. "We'll leave you alone."

He wanted to tell the guy to quit being a jerk, but he couldn't. The three of them would be together on the plane ride and all through boot camp out in Washington State, where they'd been assigned. He might as well try to get along with them.

Besides, the guy probably figured that Cody wasn't really tired. He needed an excuse to close his eyes so the others wouldn't see his tears. The Flanigans were the first family he'd ever really had, so maybe he shouldn't have enlisted. Maybe he should've taken Jim's advice and gone to community college. He could've played another couple years of football and stayed with them.

For a minute Cody thought about telling the driver to turn the car around and let him off. He didn't want a stint in the army or boot camp or anything that would take him away from the love he'd found here.

He took a long breath and held it. What was he thinking? He'd gone round and round with himself, and he always came back to the same thing. He'd made a mess of himself in high school, drinking all the time and using one girl after another. This was his chance to become a man, to do something worthwhile and earn a college education in the process. He loved being an American, and fighting for his country seemed like the right thing to do. Even if it practically killed him to leave.

Besides, if he was honest with himself, it

wasn't the whole Flanigan family that was hardest to walk away from.

It was Bailey.

Cody hated lying to her, but he could feel her falling for him, and the last thing he'd wanted in the days before he left was for her to see the truth. That he'd fallen for her first. He thought about her constantly, dreaming of what life might be like if he were one of the good guys, a Tim Reed or one of the guys at CKT who never struggled with drinking or sex or anything more than getting a passing grade in chemistry.

That was the sort of guy Bailey deserved, and he had no doubts that one day that was the sort of guy she'd fall in love with. Her feelings for him weren't love—they were a crush. A crush that had come from laughing together and talking late into the night. Bailey was good for him; he'd figured that out early on after his brush with death. But he wasn't good for her—him with his ugly past and laundry list of troubles.

Once in a while he would catch a look from Jenny or Jim, and he could almost read their minds. *Be our daughter's friend*, they seemed to tell him, *but don't ever let it be-*

come something more. They'd brought him in as a project—not as a young man suitable for dating their daughter. Cody exhaled hard and squeezed his eyes more tightly closed. But all he could see was Bailey. In the last ten days, things had been especially difficult. He'd convinced her that his feelings for her were only those of a brother, a friend. Nothing more. And he applauded himself on the effort. But the lie had done nothing to change his feelings. If anything, they'd gotten stronger as his last day drew near.

Now and then he'd even find himself daydreaming about the future, how he would put in a few years with the army and maybe become an officer. He'd make something of himself and then come back and tell Bailey how he felt. How he'd felt since that first night when she cried on his shoulder about her troubles with Bryan Smythe.

In his imagination, Bailey would feel the same way, and they'd get married and raise a family like hers, full of kids and love and laughter.

Right now though, with boot camp starting on Monday and every mile taking him farther from the Flanigans, his dreams didn't feel romantic or inspiring or even the least bit like they might come true. They felt impossible.

But impossible or not, if God would let him hold on to one thought in the months ahead, one that that would push him to stay safe and do his best, it would be this:

The way he felt with Bailey Flanigan in his arms.

CHAPTER TWENTY-SEVEN

IT WOULDN'T BE long now. Landon was aware of that fact more with every passing hour. It was the fourth Sunday in July, and Ashley preferred to stay close to home. Tonight the dinner dishes had been cleaned up for an hour, and country music played softly in the background.

Once in a while they watched a movie together, but mostly Ashley wanted to play Yahtzee or Scrabble or checkers. She could beat Landon pretty handily, but Cole almost always gave her a fight.

Tonight it was Pictionary, and they all sat around the kitchen table watching Cole. He was lost in concentration, his tongue curled up around his lip as he tried to draw for them. It wasn't a conventional game in the sense that Devin didn't really count and they needed four people to have two teams. They were playing their own version where if the person drawing could get someone to guess his picture before the sand in the minute-long timer ran out, then both the drawer and the correct guesser would move ahead three spaces. If not, no one moved until the next round.

"Come on." Cole turned his pencil upside down and tapped the eraser on his picture. "Don't you see it, guys? It's right there."

The picture was of two soft-looking, roundish objects with spots on them.

"Potatoes!" Ashley jumped in her seat, clearly certain she had the right answer.

Cole smacked his forehead. "Ugh!"

"Not potatoes?" Ashley sat back in her seat, perplexed. "Swiss cheese?"

"Come on, Mom. That's the best you can do?"

"At least she's guessing." Landon rested his forearms on the table and studied the drawing. "I don't know . . . planets?"

The sand ran out, and Cole gave the picture a few quick taps with his pencil. "High-heeled shoes. They're right there, plain as sight."

Cole was learning about clichés and metaphors. But often he didn't get them right. Landon didn't bother to correct him. *Plain as sight* worked maybe even better than *plain as day*, anyway.

Devin toddled around the table, his pacifier in his mouth. He looked sleepy, and when he grew bored of the action in the game, he sat down a few feet away, where Ashley had spread a bin of Mega Bloks for him.

The game continued until eight o'clock. At that point they declared Ashley the winner, and they packed the game back into the box.

"Let's read down here tonight." Ashley stood and stretched. Her face looked thin, but her stomach was bigger than Landon could remember it being with either of the boys. She waddled over to the sofa and dropped to the middle seat. "Get *Horton Hears a Who!* okay, Landon?"

They kept a bookcase of their favorite stories downstairs for moments like this. Landon found the book and handed it to her. He stood behind her and massaged her shoulders. "Want a cup of tea?"

"Mmmm. That'd be perfect."

Landon enjoyed waiting on her. She didn't ask for much, and she never complained. But he knew she was suffering inside. However great the loss of little Sarah was, Ashley would feel it more than any of them because she was closest to their baby, feeling her every move and kick and sleep cycle.

He made her a cup of chamomile tea and brought it to her, setting it carefully near the middle of the coffee table so Devin couldn't reach it. The boys were already cuddled next to her, one on each side. He took the spot next to Cole and nodded to Ashley.

"Horton Hears a Who!" She smiled at the boys. "'On the fifteenth of May, in the Jungle of Nool, in the heat of the day, in the cool of the pool . . .'"

Landon could recite the book by heart. Ashley had read it to Cole a hundred times when he was younger. But then the book got put away for a few years. Only in the past weeks had Landon found it up in Cole's room, dusted it off, and brought it downstairs, where they'd read it more often.

Ashley went on about Horton hearing a noise and the noise coming from a dust speck and how Horton was the only one who heard anything at all.

"The people were too small to see, right?" Cole liked to ask questions.

"Yes, Cole. That's right." She put her arm around him and kept reading.

Landon watched, amazed. Before this pregnancy, Ashley would sometimes get the slightest bit frustrated with Cole's interruptions. But now her patience seemed limitless, and Landon wondered if that was because of little Sarah. Every day felt more precious because of her.

Conflict entered the story when the Wickersham Brothers made a pact to get the dust speck and destroy it. But Horton remained faithful, determined to save the Whos and reiterating to anyone who would listen that a person was indeed a person, no matter how small.

Devin plucked his pacifier from his mouth and pointed at the picture of the Whos. "Baby!"

He was talking a little more each day, and now his exclamation was more fitting than he could've possibly known.

Cole leaned around Ashley and patted

Devin's hand. "That's right, Devin. The Whos are like babies. Too small to see, but they're still people. Just like you and me."

Ashley exchanged a look with Landon, one that seemed to express her gratitude for Cole, whose compassionate heart was a reflection of the best in both of them. She took a breath and finished the story. After she closed the book, none of them got up.

Cole put his fingers on Ashley's abdomen and patted it. He leaned close. "Hi, baby Sarah. Whatcha doing in there?"

Ashley hadn't said much about the baby moving that evening.

Landon put his hand on her shoulder. "Is she awake?"

"A little." Ashley put her hands on either side of her swollen stomach, and after a few seconds she smiled. "I felt something. Maybe she heard Cole's voice."

"Little Sarah, did you like the story about Horton?" Cole used his best singsong tone, talking to her the way he'd talked to Devin when they first brought him home from the hospital.

Landon tried not to think about the obvious. That the conversations between Cole and this special daughter would for the most part be limited to whatever happened in moments like this.

"Know what I think, Sarah?" Cole laid his hand flat over Ashley's stomach. "I think you're like the Whos, and maybe, if we keep you very, very safe, you'll live a really long time. Like me."

Ashley was still smiling, but her eyes were wet.

Cole sat up a little, still watching Ashley's stomach, waiting for a response.

Then, as if the baby was listening to every word and anxious for more, Ashley's belly shifted.

Cole gasped. "She's snuggling against me, Mom!" His eyes were full of shock and wonder. He moved close again. "Hi, baby Sarah. I'm your big brother Cole. I love you, baby."

Devin watched, curious. He had his pacifier back in his mouth and was happy simply to cuddle up against Ashley.

Landon put his hand alongside Cole's. It was just like Cole said. Little Sarah was pressing against their hands, as if she was trying to get closer to wherever the voices were coming from.

After a while, she stopped moving, and

Cole turned to Landon. "Is it too late for God to fix her?"

"No." Landon's tone was tentative. Cole asked these sorts of questions often, and Landon had done nothing to discourage him. Children processed tough situations differently than adults. If Cole was curious, they would give him the freedom to say what was on his mind.

"Really? So it's not too late?" Cole's eyes lit up.

Landon tried to think of the right way to expand on his answer. "It's not too late, but right now it seems like that isn't God's plan for Sarah. Maybe He wants her to live in heaven instead. The way we talked about at the lake that day."

"Yeah." His shoulders slumped a little, but there were no tears. "I guess."

Devin's eyelids were getting heavy, and Landon could sense that Ashley was tired too. "Okay, boys. Time to brush your teeth."

Cole stood and wrapped his arms around Ashley's neck. "Night, Mom."

"Night, Coley." She kissed him and he did the same to her.

Then he stooped down and kissed her

belly. "Night, Sarah." He patted her. "Sleep good."

Landon lifted Devin into his arms, and with Cole at his side, they headed upstairs. When teeth were brushed and flossed and prayers were said, Landon hit the lights in both rooms and came back downstairs. He found Ashley still sitting where she'd been earlier, only now she was sipping her tea.

"It's good, honey." She smiled at him. "Thanks."

"Did you hear from Kari?" Landon took his spot beside her. "Last I heard she was having contractions."

"That was this morning. I need to call her before I go to bed. Kari always has long labors, but you never know."

Landon loved this, the intimacy of being close to Ashley without anything but the thoughts in their hearts to keep them busy. "How are you?"

"Good." She met his eyes. "Sad."

"Hmmm." He put his arm around her shoulders and leaned his head against hers.

"We only have a little more than two weeks left." Ashley sighed. "I keep wishing I could stay pregnant forever, that Sarah might never have to come out. She's fine as long as she's inside me."

They hadn't yet talked about a funeral or burial. Neither of them could bring themselves to broach the subject. But Landon had a plan—in case Ashley was too overwhelmed to help him come up with one after Sarah was born. There were several open plots in the cemetery near where Elizabeth Baxter was buried. A number of them belonged to John, so Landon was sure he could purchase one for Sarah. Maybe one near the end of the row by the trees that ran along the edge of the cemetery.

Landon shivered. It was wrong, completely wrong, to be thinking about cemetery plots as part of getting ready for the birth of a child. The very idea turned his stomach.

"What's the matter?" Ashley craned her neck and studied him.

He was thinking of an answer when the phone rang. "Hold that thought." He bounded into the kitchen and grabbed the receiver. "Hello?"

"Landon, it's Ryan. We have a baby daughter. Anne Elizabeth." There were tears in his voice. "She's beautiful. Kari wanted me to call you."

As painful as the path ahead of them would be, Landon felt nothing but pure joy for his brother-in-law. He grinned, and as the baby's healthy cry filled the phone line, Landon felt the sting of tears. "Hey, friend . . . congratulations! What're the statistics? Ashley'll want to know."

"She's twenty inches long, six pounds, three ounces. Checked in just after six o'clock. She came earlier than we thought, but she's perfect."

Another surge of joy filled Landon's heart. "We couldn't be happier for you." He got a few more details, like the fact that Kari was going home tomorrow morning, so if they wanted to visit, they should stop by the house and not the hospital.

When the call ended and Landon returned to the living room, he looked at Ashley and his heart felt ripped in half. She had her hands over her face, her shoulders shaking. He took his place by her side. "Ashley, honey?"

She dropped her hands, and even through her tears, she allowed a short laugh. "I'm so happy for them. Tell me about her."

Landon gave all the details he knew. At the same time, he stroked her hair, letting her cry.

"She sounds beautiful. She would've been . . . the perfect cousin for Sarah."

Landon understood her tears then. She wasn't crying because she was jealous or because the situation at hand wasn't fair. She was crying for the precious little Anne Elizabeth, who would never know her cousin, never share adventures to the park or the first day of school with her. Never go to dances with her or find a best friend in her.

"They were supposed to be closer than sisters." Ashley covered her face again and let her tears come.

"I know, baby." He thought about the two girls—one so healthy and whole, her life just begun, the other with only days left to live. "I know."

The loss was vast and great, and maybe worst of all was this: every time Landon and Ashley looked at Anne, they would see their precious daughter. When she played in the nursery, they would see Sarah in the empty spot beside her. And on the first day of kindergarten, they would see their daughter in the seat next to Anne—no matter who occupied the chair. At the Baxter reunions, there would always be an emptiness next to Anne Elizabeth. It was inevitable, really.

The gift of Anne's life would be celebrated and prized in a way that left no room for sorrow over what might've been. But she would also be a reminder of all they'd lost with Sarah. Even if they admitted that to no one but each other.

Ashley spent an hour the next day with Kari. Annie—as they were already calling her—was beautiful, and Ashley couldn't help but notice the resemblance between the infant's profile and the one they'd seen on the ultrasound of their own daughter. She held the baby, and she ached for the chance to hold Sarah.

Then, just as quickly, she chided herself. When they placed Sarah in her arms, she would have almost no time left with her. And so there was no rush, no rush at all.

The guys left Ashley and Kari alone to coo at baby Annie and marvel at her. Also to cry, the way they did after only a few minutes.

"Ashley, you're so strong." Kari held Annie close to her chest and rocked her. "I can't believe you came."

"Of course." Ashley swallowed back the ocean of sorrow welling inside her. "Every time I see Annie, I'll think of Sarah. And that's okay. It's a good thing. A blessing from God."

Ashley wasn't sure how she'd stayed so positive during the visit, but when she and Landon reached the van, when they buckled Devin into his car seat and headed off to pick up Cole at the neighbor's house, she felt the darkness all but consume her. For a long time she was silent, staring out the window.

Landon gave her space, keeping quiet and leaving the radio off.

Before they got home, Ashley looked at him. "I want her buried near Mom."

"Okay." Landon glanced at her and then back at the road. "I'll talk to your dad."

Ashley nodded and fell silent again. There was no way now to view her pregnancy as anything other than what it was—the last few weeks with a daughter they would never know, never have the chance to raise. The most certain thing about her birth was her death, so Ashley was glad they at least had a plan.

The rest of the afternoon, Ashley stayed to herself, and before dinner she found Landon out back with the boys. She motioned for him, and when he jogged over, she bit her lip. "Would you care if I went to the cemetery? Just for half an hour?"

He hesitated. "I'll go with you."

"Next time." She made a hopeful face. "Okay?"

His expression told her this was different from the last time she'd gone, when she'd left the house in a rush without telling him where she was going. He took a step back, his eyes confident. "Be careful."

"I will."

Ashley was in the van and out of the garage in a couple of minutes. Once she was on the road, she rolled down the window and let the air wash over her face. She had a few questions for God, and she wasn't sure if there was any place she'd rather ask them than at the cemetery. The place where all of life had a way of coming into focus.

On the way she kept one hand over her baby. She left the radio off and sang one of her mother's favorite hymns. "'O Lord my God! When I in awesome wonder consider all the worlds Thy hands have made . . .'"

As the song grew and built, Ashley's voice didn't waver. She'd never been much of a singer, and during her rebellion against God for so many years, she hadn't sung at all. She never had a reason in France or after she came home single and pregnant and ashamed.

She could argue that she didn't have a reason to sing now, but what choice did she have? These were her baby's last days. She wanted Sarah to hear her voice, hear her praising God even in the darkest of days. And she wanted to see her daughter's burial place firsthand, picture how it would look and how close it would be to her mother's.

The song lasted until she parked the van, and as she walked between the tombstones, she kept humming. This was a cemetery, but she wouldn't let the song die. Sarah would be frightened if she stopped singing, if she sensed the way Ashley was more tense, more heartbroken with the reality of death surrounding her.

When Ashley reached her mother's stone, she stopped and looked around. Her dad owned several plots, right? Wasn't that what he'd told them when they buried her mother? She tried to remember what he'd bought. Certainly the spot next to her mother would belong to him one day.

A thought caught her off guard.

Or would it? He'd been spending most of his free time with Elaine, and neither Ashley nor any of her siblings would be surprised if he remarried. But what would happen to the plots at that point? Would her dad want to be buried near Elaine or near their mother? She felt her stomach twisting and turning, and she forced the thought from her mind. Cemetery plots weren't for the dead; they were for the living. So of course Dad would be buried near Mom.

Ashley dismissed the idea and took a few steps closer to the bench—the one where she'd come from time to time when she needed to think, when she needed to remember her mother's voice and wisdom and gentle touch. Now she looked to the side of the bench where the land was open. If her father owned that area, the spot would be perfect for Sarah. That way Ashley could sit on the bench and be close to both of them. Even though she knew they wouldn't be here.

She dropped down onto the bench and exhaled. She was more tired than before, her body preparing itself for the coming birth. At the same time, she was getting her heart ready for the greater inevitability.

Her daughter's death.

The back of the bench was hard on her spine, but she leaned against it anyway. Clouds gathered in the sky, and thunderstorms were in the forecast. She rested her hands on her stomach, and the questions that had been plaguing her came to the surface once more.

"All along I've prayed for a miracle." Ashley narrowed her eyes and stared at the building clouds on the horizon. "I understand, Lord . . . that my baby won't live long. And I understand that almost certainly her organs won't be used to save the life of another baby. She'll be too sick for that." Her whispered prayer was tinged with just a little anger. "Your Word tells me that in all things You work for the good of those who love You."

She hadn't wanted to cry, but suddenly the desperation of the situation was more than she could take. "All things, God!" Her whisper became a cry, and she clenched her fists. "But where's the good in this?" She was angry, but she didn't care. The cemetery was empty except for her and God and little Sarah. The thought of her daughter made her bring her voice down. She didn't want to scare her baby, not ever.

"What I'm asking, Lord, is where's the miracle?" Tears choked her voice, and she massaged her throat. "And why this baby?" She looked at her mother's tombstone. As she did, a quiet answer seemed to stir in her soul.

Daughter, My promises are faithful and true . . . but you must look for Me in the gentle whisper.

The gentle whisper? Ashley sat up straighter, struck by the certainty of the still, small voice inside her. She'd read something a few months ago about the gentle whisper. Something from First Kings. She made a note to check it later. Was the miracle of Sarah's life going to come in the gentle whispers?

She couldn't imagine what that could mean, but at least she'd done what she'd come to do. She looked one last time at her mother's stone, then walked back to her van.

On the way home Ashley hummed the hymn one more time through. "'How great Thou art! . . . How great Thou art! . . .'"

Sarah liked when she sang, so Ashley did it as often as she could. Also it felt good to praise God—even when the answers were slow in coming.

When Ashley got home, she found Landon barbecuing hamburgers, and she slipped her arms around his waist. She wanted to tell him about the gentle whisper, but she had to check her Bible first, needed to read the story one more time for herself.

"I did it." Her eyes were dry as she looked at him. "I asked God my questions." She leaned close and rested her forehead on his chest.

Now it was up to God to show her the answer.

The way maybe He'd already done.

CHAPTER TWENTY-EIGHT

JOHN WASN'T SURE he'd ever felt this discouraged. He wanted to be strong. He was the patriarch, the father of all the adult kids looking to him for some kind of sign, some superhuman strength. But the impending loss of Ashley's first daughter was weighing on him more than he wanted to admit.

It was two days before the scheduled delivery of Ashley's baby. In a few minutes John would leave for Elaine's house so the two of them could go shopping. The trip had been her idea.

"Regardless of the outcome, we should celebrate this baby's birth the same as any other." Elaine's voice had held a level of emotion that was uncommon for her. "We didn't have a shower for Ashley. But I want to buy something special, something pink and satiny and soft and pretty. Her baby deserves that sort of welcome, don't you think?"

Actually, John hadn't thought about it until Erin arrived from Texas. She was downstairs now, she and her girls inside making breakfast. Sam had stayed behind, busy with work. But Erin had brought a gift. A pink and white handmade blanket crocheted with lamb's wool. Erin had tears in her eyes when she lifted it from her suitcase. "I hope . . ." She bit her lip, clearly struggling. "I hope she lives long enough to use it. Even once."

Now that the birth was forty-eight hours away, John had never felt more right about anything. Of course they needed to get Sarah a gift. Her birth was a celebration, and it would be one they would remember forever. Even if John would have to work to hide his discouragement.

He told Erin good-bye and drove to Elaine's. She was waiting for him, her smile lighting up her eyes as much as her face. When she climbed in the car, she leaned over and kissed him. "I'm glad we're doing this."

"Me too."

Most of the way to the mall they talked about Katy and Dayne. "I can't seem to shake the feeling, this discouragement deep inside me. Maybe it's more about Dayne and Katy than Ashley's baby."

"They're dodging a lot of dirt. That's for sure." Elaine folded her arms and leaned against the door so she could face him. "How long have they been back in town?"

"Since Saturday. The director let them have a few extra days in light of the situation." He paused. "They're coming for dinner tonight, same as everyone else."

"Even Brooke?"

"She says she'll try." John gripped the steering wheel and shook his head. "Maybe that's what has me down. Brooke and Ashley."

"Added up, there's a lot to be down about." She reached for his hand. "But out of everything ahead of us, I think the situation with Katy and Dayne is the most frightening."

"Me too." The traffic was sparse, the way John expected it to be on a weekday morning. He turned the car into the local mall and found a parking space near the entrance to Macy's. "I'm afraid for their marriage."

"And they're both doing films after this?"

Elaine took off her sunglasses and slid them into her purse. They climbed out and headed for the door.

"Different films, different continents." John stopped once they were inside. "Any idea where the baby stuff is?"

"Come on." She smiled and looped her arm through his.

They went down a series of aisles, and sure enough, Elaine knew where she was going. The pale pinks and blues of the baby department lay spread out before them. They moved into a small alcove beneath a sign that read Newborn.

Sorting through the soft pink gowns and receiving clothes stirred hope in John's soul. Ashley's baby would look beautiful in any of these outfits. They spent nearly half an hour looking before John spotted one that was far more special than the others. It was a gown in the softest pale pink cotton he had ever run his fingers across. It was trimmed with white and pink satin, and it came with a matching hat and booties. Best of all, it matched the blanket Erin had made for the baby.

Elaine touched it and studied it closely, both inside and out. "It's absolutely gorgeous."

A lump formed in John's throat, and he

swallowed so he could find his voice. "Then it's perfect for little Sarah."

"I found this, too." She held up a sterling silver frame. *Our Precious Baby Girl* was engraved across the bottom. Elaine blinked back tears, but her smile remained. "I thought this could be from me."

It was something John hadn't thought about. Photos. Someone would need to be in the delivery room, capturing the moment, taking pictures so Ashley and Landon would have something to remember Sarah by. Something to prove that her brief life had counted. "Yes." He gave a little cough to help clear his throat so he could speak. "They'll love that."

They were in line paying for the gifts, asking that the outfit and the frame be wrapped so they could give the presents to Ashley and Landon tonight after dinner, when John's cell phone rang. He was distracted, searching his wallet for his debit card.

He opened the phone with one hand and held it to his ear with his shoulder. "Hi . . . just a minute." He finally found the card and slid it across the counter. Then he repositioned the phone. "Hello? This is Dr. Baxter."

"John, it's Landon." There was panic in the

young man's voice. John pressed his finger to his other ear so he could hear better. "Ashley's in labor. We're at the hospital right now. They gave her something to stop the contractions, but Dr. McDaniel wants to take the baby in a few hours. As soon as everyone can get here."

"Okay." John felt his heart skip a beat. "I'll call the others. Don't worry about a thing, Landon. Just be there for Ashley."

"I will." He hesitated. "And pray, will you? There're still so many things that could go wrong."

"I'm with Elaine. We'll both be praying. And we'll see you soon."

He closed the phone and stared at Elaine.

The cashier was finishing the transaction. She grinned at them, and in a cutesy voice she said, "Sounds like someone's in labor!"

John found a smile for the woman. "Yes." He looked at Elaine again. "My daughter."

The woman beamed. How could she know that the celebration of this baby's birth would be short-lived?

With his eyes he told Elaine there was trouble. "You stay here while they gift wrap, okay? I need to call the others."

Elaine's face was tight with fear. John had already shared with her why the baby wasn't supposed to come early, the dangers of contractions on a baby with anencephaly. If the doctor didn't stop the labor, the baby could be stillborn.

John hurried outside and began with Kari, who offered to call Erin and Luke. Next John called Dayne, but there was no answer. Finally he dialed Brooke.

"Listen, could you or Peter bring a camera?" He could hear the urgency in his voice.

"Video or still?" Brooke sounded as desperate to help as any of the others, and John wondered if a breakthrough might yet lie ahead for his two daughters today.

"Both if you have them."

"Okay. I'm at work, but I'll run home. I know where Ashley is. We'll see you there."

Elaine hurried out the door just then, the packages in a bag. "I have an idea. I'll watch the kids in the waiting room. That way you won't be distracted when you get to meet Sarah."

John froze, and for a moment he could only stare at the woman he'd come to care so much about. "You would do that?"

"Of course." She looked for traffic and stepped out toward his car. "Let's hurry. We'll go to my house and get my car; then we'll go to yours. I'll follow you and Erin and the girls over to the hospital."

John was amazed. He wasn't sure he would've thought of that—the fact that Erin and the girls needed a ride. His mind was racing in circles with only one thought shouting any sense at him. Ashley was about to give birth to her daughter, and then they might have only minutes to tell her hello. And minutes more to tell her good-bye.

Elaine was a gift from God, and after today he was certain he couldn't imagine his life without her. His cell phone rang again as he backed out of his parking space.

"Dad, it's me, Luke. I'm at work, but I'm leaving right now. I'll get Reagan and the kids, and we'll be at the hospital in a little more than an hour. Please . . . make them wait if it's possible."

"I will. Drive safely."

Other calls came streaming in. Kari hadn't been able to reach Ryan, probably because he was on the football field doing conditioning with his team.

"That's okay." John kept his voice calm. This was when his family needed him. He didn't have time to feel discouraged now. "I'll swing by the field and see if he's there. You get the kids ready. That way you'll be able to leave as soon as Ryan gets home."

"Thanks, Dad." There was a cry in Kari's voice. "I have to be there. I just have to be."

Elaine nodded at the slight change in plans. "It's on the way. Take me with you. We can go by my house afterwards." She had the bag of gifts on the floor near her feet. "What about Dayne?"

Dayne! John still hadn't gotten ahold of him. "They hardly ever answer their phones."

"Try." Elaine opened his cell phone and handed it to him. "If they don't answer, I'll find them myself."

John's heart raced, and he made a conscious effort to keep from speeding. He had Dayne on speed dial, so once more he punched in the number seven and hit Send. On the other end a phone began to ring.

Come on, Dayne. . . . Pick it up. We need you there. The phone kept ringing. After the fourth one, Dayne's voice mail came on.

At the beep, John left another urgent message. "Ashley's in labor. It's eleven-fifteen in the morning, Monday. The doctor will be taking the baby by C-section sometime around one o'clock. Please, Dayne . . . you and Katy need to be there. Hurry."

He hung up and tapped the phone on his leg. What were Katy and Dayne doing, anyway? They'd been home since Saturday, but neither of them had talked to him or anyone else in the family. Were things worse than he thought? worse than even the tabloids knew about?

John pushed the thoughts from his crowded mind. Ashley needed his prayers right now. Ashley and her baby daughter. He was a doctor, but there was nothing he could do to help them. And the fact that he couldn't really help was maybe what had him more discouraged than all the rest combined. So while he hurried to the high school, and as he walked out onto the football field and found Ryan and told him the news, and as he drove Elaine home, and on the solitary trip back to the Baxter house with Elaine driving behind him, he did the only thing he could do. The thing that took no medical training but more faith than he had felt in weeks.

He prayed.

Dayne was out back on the deck overlooking the lake when he heard his cell phone ring inside the house. He made no move to answer it. Katy was at the store, but as the ringing stopped, he heard her pull up.

Never mind the call. He could call the person back. Right now he didn't want to talk to anyone but Katy. And since they'd come home, she'd had little to say. He'd asked her more times than he could remember exactly what was keeping her so quiet.

Now, inside the house, he could hear her putting away the groceries. *God . . . Katy and I need to figure things out before we lose it all.* It could happen; he was convinced. Somewhere along the way she'd started to believe what she was reading. Or maybe what she was hearing on the set.

This morning before she left for the store, she'd found him and looked at her watch. "I'll be gone an hour. If you have any phone calls to make."

She was gone before he could stop her. He called her cell, but she didn't answer, so he did the thing he'd been wanting to do since the trouble on the set began. He called his friend Bob Asher.

It was earlier in Mexico City, but Bob had time for him, the way he always did. After their initial small talk, Bob cut to the chase.

"I've been watching the tabloids online. Your marriage is in trouble, friend."

"It is." For the first time Dayne had to admit what was obvious to everyone else. He and Katy were in real trouble. At a time when most couples would be figuring out how to share a bathroom, he and Katy had unwittingly welcomed the world to take shots at their marriage.

Bob talked to him for half an hour, and before they hung up, he prayed. "I'll tell you this—" his voice held a warning that wasn't often there—"do whatever it takes, Dayne. Your marriage is more important than all of it."

The words had stayed with Dayne ever since.

He'd walked outside to the deck and studied the gathering clouds beyond the far shore of the lake. He would wait here, begging God for the right words, and when Katy got home, he would tell her he was finished, through with movies. He'd relocate to a deserted island and throw it all away if only she'd believe him. And he'd have to talk about Randi Wells too. He'd left the topic alone, because why would Katy want to hear about Randi's problems?

But her comment on the way out told him

she wasn't only thinking about Randi; she was believing the rumors. Anger swelled within him every time he thought about it, but anger wouldn't help him now. Punching doors or shouting would get him nowhere. He needed to heed Bob's wisdom, the Bible's wisdom, if he and Katy were going to find a path back to the way it had been.

Katy was still putting away groceries. He could hear the click of her wooden sandals, sense the tension in her quick steps. She came to the door. "You have a message." Her tone told him she thought it was Randi.

Fine. Dayne resisted his anger one more time. "Check it for me, will you?"

"Oh, sure. What's the password?"

He rattled it off. "I ignored it on purpose. I don't want to talk to anyone but you."

She gave him a look that said she wanted to believe him. But then she turned back into the house.

A moment later, Katy opened the patio door and stepped out. Her face was pale, her lips slightly open. "Dayne, Ashley's having her baby today." She looked back inside and then at Dayne again. "Your dad wants us at the hospital right away."

"Is she okay?" He was on his feet, the silliness of Hollywood gossip reduced to meaningless drivel in as much time as it took for him to picture his sister about to give birth to a baby who wouldn't live through the week.

"I don't know, but your dad sounded worried."

He met Katy in the doorway and framed her face with his hand. "I'm sorry for everything that's happened. It's not like it looks; you should know that."

The softness he'd fallen in love with appeared in her eyes, the way it hadn't for months. "I miss you. Even when you're here, I miss you."

Dayne searched her eyes and felt himself falling in love with her all over again. Whatever it took, they had to fight for their marriage. Especially with the schedules they would face in the months ahead. Otherwise the world would gladly tear it to pieces. "I love you, Katy Matthews. Please . . . don't ever let go."

She touched her finger to his lips. "Come on. We can talk about it later."

And with that, they rushed through the house and out to the 4Runner. As they left, Dayne had one sign that Katy was ready to find her way back to the beginning, back to the happiest days of their lives. For the first time since they'd been home, the tension was gone. That and something else.

She was holding his hand.

CHAPTER TWENTY-NINE

ASHLEY WAS LYING in the hospital bed when she found the Bible story. She was right; it was in First Kings. Somehow reading the story would bring her peace; she was convinced. Not so much because of the specific details but because of the gentle whisper.

The hospital room smelled of antiseptic, and the whir and steady beeps of her monitors reminded her constantly about the event at hand. Her baby was about to be born.

But even so, she wanted to read the story. She smoothed the open pages. Landon was in the hallway with the boys, keeping them entertained and watching for the others.

She looked at the page and started at the beginning. The story involved the prophet Elijah, who by chapter 19 had gotten into pretty deep trouble. A verse early in the chapter showed Elijah begging God, "I have had enough, Lord. . . . Take my life."

The circumstances were different, of course, but wasn't that how she'd felt a time or two? When she came home from Paris or when she thought she might have AIDS. Even now, with the diagnosis of her baby's neural tube defect, Ashley had at times felt beside herself.

Eventually, Elijah's journey led him to the mountain of God. And there, finally, the word of the Lord came to him. "What are you doing here, Elijah?"

Elijah responded, and God did a strange thing, an act that Ashley related to most of all. He told Elijah to stand on the mountain because the Lord was about to pass by.

Elijah did as he was told, and he became witness to a number of great and dramatic displays of power. First a powerful wind shattered rocks and tore at the mountains. "But the Lord was not in the wind," the Scripture read. Next there was an earthquake, but the

Lord wasn't there, either. Then came a fire, but the Lord wasn't in the fire.

When Elijah must've thought God wasn't going to pass by at all, he heard a gentle whisper. Elijah did not need to ask. He knew deep in his heart that here was God in the gentle whisper. The encounter strengthened Elijah, and he was able to return the way he'd come and carry out God's work.

All because he was patient enough to hear the Lord in the gentle whisper.

Ashley closed the Bible and set it back on the nightstand. So what was the message? Part of it seemed obvious. She had asked for a dramatic miracle, proof that God was here with her, caring for her, loving her. But she had asked for an earthquake or a fire. Only when she fully admitted to herself that her baby wasn't going to live had she found the courage to ask God about her prayers, why they hadn't been answered.

And that's when He'd told her about the gentle whisper.

She felt her baby move, and she sheltered her abdomen with her hands. She wasn't afraid. Dr. McDaniel said they'd been able to stop the contractions. Her baby would most likely live through the delivery. Even though birth would be the beginning of the end for Sarah, a part of Ashley was thrilled because in a few hours she would meet this daughter of hers, the little girl she'd come to love so much.

She was about to take a drink of water when there was a knock at her door.

Her dad walked in holding a bag. "Ashley . . . I have something for you and Sarah."

Hearing her daughter's name spoken out loud made her heart ache, but at the same time it made the situation more real than ever before. She was about to have a daughter, a girl she could hold and love for however long God lent her to them. In that way, Sarah wasn't so different from any other baby.

Her father came to the side of her bed and set the bag on the floor. He hugged her, studying her. "They stopped the contractions?"

"Yes. I'm fine now. . . . Sarah too. Her heartbeat's perfect." Again it seemed a cruel truth that in the womb, her daughter's health and behavior were healthy and normal, in stark contrast to what lay ahead.

"You're feeling okay?" He leaned on the bed rail and looked beyond her calm exterior.

"I'm sad. Otherwise, I'm fine."

Her dad brought his lips together in a thin line, as if there was more he wanted to say, more about the unfairness of the situation or maybe how he wished he could do something to help. But instead he reached down and pulled out a box wrapped in shiny silver paper with a single pink bow. He handed it to her. "This is for Sarah."

Ashley took it, her fingers trembling. "A baby gift?" Why hadn't she thought about this part before? In her determination to enjoy her pregnancy, she hadn't planned for the victory of her baby's birth.

"I can't believe you thought of this, Dad." Ashley removed the bow and set it on the side table, then carefully ripped the paper off. Beneath the lid lay the most precious pink receiving gown. She ran her fingers over it. Tears blurred her eyes. "Sarah will look perfect in it."

"I have to confess." Her dad's eyes were damp too, but he smiled anyway. "It was Elaine's idea."

It took a few seconds for this truth to sink in. Elaine, whom Ashley had struggled with from the beginning, the woman who at times almost seemed to be forcing her way into their family. Ashley's mother would've done this if she were here, because there was a level of thoughtfulness that only a mother could have. But instead it was Elaine who had remembered little Sarah. Elaine who understood that the days ahead weren't only about death but about life. A precious, brand-new life.

"Tell her . . ." Ashley blinked, and two tears slid down her cheeks. She wiped at them with her fingertips. "Tell her thank you for me."

Her dad was clearly choked up. He nodded and reached into the bag one more time. A smaller box was wrapped in a similar way. "This one's from her."

Ashley opened it, and her hands shook as she removed the silver frame from its box. She ran her fingers over the words along the bottom. *Our Precious Baby Girl.*

Even when she acknowledged that her father had a right to his friendship with Elaine, she'd never had any intention of actually relating to the woman. Ashley could be cordial, even friendly. But only as a way of accepting the inevitable. Not because she wanted a connection with Elaine.

Because a connection of any sort would feel like she was betraying her mother.

But Ashley didn't feel that way now. Elaine had done what only her mother would've done. She had acknowledged Sarah's birth as an event significant in its own right, and for that Ashley would always be grateful. She held the frame to her heart and squeezed her eyes shut. "Is she here?"

"She'll be here later." John's voice was strained. "She's offered to watch the kids when Sarah's born, so we can all be together."

Hot tears coursed down Ashley's cheeks. Here was one thing, then. One good thing that had come from the tragedy of Sarah's birth defect. She would see Elaine in a different light from now on, and Ashley had no doubt they would become friends. Elaine loved Sarah. That was all that mattered.

The door opened again, and Ashley opened her eyes. Landon stepped in. He looked harried and frantic. "Everyone's here except Luke and Reagan. But he called. They're fifteen minutes away." He was breathless. "Katy and Dayne just got here. Elaine brought craft paper and crayons. She's got the kids drawing pictures for Sarah."

Her father smiled. "I'll let you two be." He hugged her one more time. "We'll be waiting down the hall. The whole group of us." He grinned at Landon. "What are there? Twenty?"

"Twenty-one." A short laugh came from him. "Counting me."

Her father left the room, and Landon walked to the bed. He saw the wrapping paper, and he lowered his eyebrows. "What's this?"

"My father." Ashley made a sound that was more cry than amazement. "He brought Sarah an outfit."

Guilt and regret came over Landon in a hurry. "I should've thought of that."

"It's okay. Neither of us did." She dabbed at her cheeks again. Then she handed the silky gown to Landon. "Isn't it perfect?"

"Yes." Landon looked like he'd had the wind knocked from him. "Your dad thought of this?"

"Actually, no. It was Elaine." Ashley's heart overflowed with gratitude toward the woman. "She didn't want us to lose the celebration of Sarah's life." Ashley blinked so she could see clearly. "Isn't that the sweetest thing?"

Landon picked up the silver frame and

then, for the first time since the second ultra-sound, he broke down. Tears filled his eyes, and he leaned over Ashley, taking her in his arms. "I can't believe . . . the love out in that hallway. No baby will ever have a more loving life."

The door opened a few inches. "Ashley? It's Erin. Can I come in?"

Erin! She was back from Texas, and now she too would share in Sarah's life. Ashley sat up a little. "Definitely."

Landon stood back and leaned against the wall. "Welcome home."

"Thanks." Erin had a wrapped box beneath her arm. She looked from Landon to Ashley. "How are you, Ash?"

"I'm not sure." Ashley held out her arms. All her sisters had daughters, and they all loved their children very much. But Erin—who had struggled so long to have babies of her own—understood maybe a little more than the others what Ashley was going through.

Erin hugged her for a long time. Then she handed Ashley the wrapped gift. "I made this for Sarah."

The realization of what her sister was saying took a few beats to sink in. Ashley opened the box and found a soft pink and white crocheted blanket. "You—" she looked up at Erin—"made this?"

"Yes." Erin's eyes were dry, but her face shone with love. "I wanted you to know how much we're looking forward to meeting her."

Ashley held the blanket in her hands and brought it to her face. It was soft and warm and cuddly. Erin had four little girls and a husband who was rarely home. "How in the world did you find time to make this?"

"I worked on it at night." Her eyes glistened. "I'd sit in one of the girls' rooms and pray. For all our kids, one at a time. And especially for Sarah." Her chin quivered. "Sam calls it my prayer blanket."

Ashley was overwhelmed. Her family's love was like a safety net, created by God Himself. Like Landon said, love would reign today—no matter how quickly good-byes came. And suddenly she wondered if Brooke was here, Brooke who had been so sure that an abortion was the answer for Ashley's baby. The two of them had said very little to each other, and Ashley wasn't sure their relationship would ever be the same.

She lowered the blanket and looked at Erin. "Is Brooke out there?"

"Yes." Erin's expression changed. "She and Peter are both here."

Ashley tried to picture them mingling with the others, and her defenses went up. What was her sister doing? Defending herself? Trying to explain that Sarah's birth and death would be unbearably hard and letting anyone who would listen know that Ashley and Landon were crazy to put the family through this?

"Is . . . she saying anything negative, anything about Sarah?"

"No." Erin reached out and took Ashley's hand. "She and Peter are sitting by themselves. Brooke won't talk to anyone. She's been crying since she got here."

Ashley hesitated. She wasn't sure what to make of that. Was she crying because she felt guilty for her attitude? Or was her heart breaking because of the strain between the two of them? Ashley would have to talk to her later.

In the movies, Brooke would've already been in to see her. She would've apologized and begged Ashley's forgiveness. But this was real life, and in real life, people did things to hurt each other. And the right person wasn't always the first one to make a move toward healing, because life wasn't fair. But life was short, and there wasn't time to worry about who should make the first move or who should say sorry first.

Ashley had learned that much.

She exhaled, weary of the conflict between her and Brooke. She squeezed Erin's hand. "Do me a favor?"

"Anything."

"Tell Brooke I'm glad she's here." She could feel God with her, giving her the words and the strength to say them. "Tell her I'm sorry we haven't talked sooner."

Her dad popped his head in. "Everyone's here. Luke and Reagan and the kids just walked off the elevator."

"Thanks, Dad."

Erin bent down and kissed Ashley's cheek. "You're amazing; you know that?"

"No. This family's amazing." She looked long into her sister's eyes. "All I can do is try to keep up."

With promises to talk to Brooke, Erin left the room, and Landon stepped up to the bed rail again. "Forgiving Brooke?" He placed his hand gently alongside her face. "There's your miracle, Ash."

She nodded, overcome.

Before Landon could say anything else, Dr. McDaniel walked in. "Looks like we're ready." Victory shone in her smile, victory and determination. "Let's make this happen."

"I can stay, right?" Landon looked more nervous than he had all morning.

"The whole time. I'll get ready and meet you in the delivery room." Dr. McDaniel put her hand on the door, then looked at Ashley. "They'll be in to get you and give you the epidural in a few minutes."

When the doctor was gone, Landon bent over Ashley and kissed her on the lips. "You're the bravest woman I know, Ashley Baxter Blake. I won't leave your side."

She wrapped her arms around him and held him. "I'm not brave." She sniffed a few times.

"Yes, you are." He kissed her again and stood up just as two nurses and the anesthesiologist entered the room. "You can do this." He backed up, leaving room for them to work on her. "We both can."

CHAPTER THIRTY

A STREAM OF people came and left from Ashley's room, and in a blur of activity she had to lie on her side and bring her knees toward her chest. The epidural needle hurt but only for a minute. She kept her hands on her abdomen. "It's okay, Sarah," she whispered. "It won't be long now, baby. Mommy's waiting for you."

Please, God, let her live. Let us have this day. . . .

The prayer came as easily as breathing, even here, where God had allowed her the greatest heartache of her life. A story in the Bible showed the friends of Jesus staying with Him even after nearly everyone else had fled. What about you? Jesus asked them. The friends said simply that there was nowhere else to go, because Jesus was the Son of God.

And so it was for Ashley. There would be no turning her back on the God who had given her Landon and Cole and Devin, the God who had given her a family whose love knew no bounds. The Lord alone had forgiven her and made her capable of forgiving. And He had given her Sarah. She needed Him now more than ever.

Landon kept his word. Even when it felt like a dozen people were working on her, wheeling her into the delivery room, talking in hurried, clipped voices, he was always beside her, his hand on her shoulder or at the base of her neck.

"The delivery won't take long," Dr. McDaniel told her.

Normally, the doctor explained, the father would be allowed to watch a C-section. But this time—since they weren't sure exactly what condition Sarah would be in when she was born—they wanted Landon to stand near the head of the bed. He did as he was told, holding tight to Ashley's hand as the surgery got under way.

Ashley felt a series of tugs and stretches but no pain. No one had told her what to expect at this point, whether her baby would cry or whether the birth defect made crying impossible. Those were details they might've learned if they'd visited Dr. McDaniel more often, but Ashley wouldn't have changed a thing. There was no way to prepare for the birth of a baby with anencephaly. It was a road they could only walk together and with God leading the way. Whatever happened next.

There was a flurry of activity, and Dr. McDaniel grinned. "Oh, Ashley . . . your daughter's beautiful."

As soon as she got out the last word, an infant's cry pierced the room.

Ashley couldn't move or breathe or speak. She had cried more today than she had in a long time, but still the tears came. Rivers of them. The beautiful sound was coming from her daughter, from the baby she already knew so well. As long as Ashley lived she would remember the sound of that cry; it resonated deep inside her, creating a bond between her and her little girl that nothing could ever break.

Landon leaned over her, and his tears mixed with hers. They said nothing, because there were no words for a moment like this.

Again there was a rush of activity as their baby was whisked to the far end of the room.

Dr. McDaniel was still working on Ashley, stitching her up. She peered over the curtain. "Your little girl is very strong." Tears glistened in the doctor's eyes. "They'll clean her up, and you can hold her. It could take a few minutes."

Ashley didn't want to ask any questions. Instead she held on to the sound of Sarah's cry, even as her baby was moved from that room and into another. For a moment, panic seized her. She tensed up and looked at the doctor. "Where're they taking her?"

"Your husband gave us her new clothes. The nurses want to dress her so she's ready to see you."

This part wasn't normal, but it made sense. The back of Sarah's head would be covered only by a thin membrane of skin and hair. Great care would be needed to dress her. The minutes passed slowly. Ashley wanted to push the screen off her stomach and climb down from the table so she could find Sarah.

But Landon was here, helping her survive the wait, whispering quiet prayers and telling her again and again that she could get through this.

Finally, Dr. McDaniel was finished with her. Nurses stepped in and covered her with fresh, warm blankets, and Ashley was wheeled into the biggest labor room she had ever seen.

"We understand you'll have a few visitors." The nurse smiled.

"Yes. Quite a few." Ashley was grateful that so far no one was showing her pity. She didn't want pity and sadness and sorrow. She wanted a celebration.

The nurses were still getting her situated when Dr. McDaniel walked in carrying a small pink bundle. The woman was far more mother than doctor in this moment. She handed the baby to Ashley. "I'd like to introduce you to your daughter."

As soon as Ashley had the baby in her arms, their eyes connected. A quiet gasp filled Ashley's heart and soul. "Landon . . . look at her!" She brought her fingers to her daughter's soft cheeks. "She's perfect."

And she was. Dr. McDaniel had warned them—in one of the moments when Ashley was barely able to hear the details—that their daughter could be partly or grossly deformed. But that wasn't the case at all. Sarah was dressed in the outfit her father had picked out, the matching hat covering her head. Her eyes were open, and her hands moved gracefully near her chin. It was impossible to tell there was a thing wrong with her, and for a minute, Ashley wondered if she'd been healed, if maybe she didn't have a neural tube defect after all.

She lifted questioning eyes to the doctor. "She's . . . is her head . . . ?"

"Yes, Ashley." A sad certainty colored the woman's expression. "You don't have long."

Ashley nodded slowly, accepting the reality at hand. She looked down at her daughter again. "Hi, Sarah. . . ." She held her up enough so they were facing each other. "Remember my voice? I'm your mommy."

Sarah's eyes looked straight into Ashley's. The eyes that would never have the chance to look at her across the dinner table. Eyes that were deep blue, like her own. Ashley memorized the look of them, because some far-off day in heaven, she would look into them again. And when she did, she wanted the two of them to recognize each other.

Landon leaned in closer, the three of them in their own private world. "She looks like you, Ashley. Just like you."

"Here." She carefully handed the baby to him.

He nuzzled her close and whispered, "Hi, princess. . . . Your daddy loves you, Sarah."

Twice more they passed her back and forth, marveling at her tiny nose and delicate features, amazed at her alertness.

Then it was time to let the rest of the family meet her. As per the plan Landon had created, Dr. McDaniel let Cole in the room first. He came in looking small and scared, his eyes wide. Almost immediately he fixed his attention on the pink bundle in Ashley's arms.

"Is that her?" He walked closer, and when he reached her side, he stood on his tiptoes.

"Yes, this is your sister, Sarah." Landon stepped back so Cole could be closer.

"Isn't she pretty?" Ashley's heart was beating harder than before. She didn't want Cole to be afraid of the baby, but he was acting stiff, uncomfortable.

"She doesn't look sick." Confusion filled his voice. "I thought you said she was sick."

"She is." Landon put his arm around Cole's shoulders. "She won't be with us very long."

"Maybe the doctor's wrong." Cole looked at Landon. "Can I hold her?"

Ashley felt herself relax. This was what she expected of Cole, the strong determination. If he wanted to hold her, then his time with Sarah would be all Ashley had hoped it would be.

Cole sat on the chair next to the bed, and Landon gently lifted Sarah from Ashley's arms.

"Be real careful, okay?" Landon tenderly placed the baby in Cole's arms. The nurses had bundled her in the blanket in such a way that it would protect her head for this type of handling. Landon stooped down so his face was next to Cole's as they studied Sarah.

"She's so light." He grinned at Landon and then at Ashley. "She's the lightest little sister ever."

"Devin was that light when he was little." Ashley leaned onto her side so she could see. "You can sing to her, if you want."

Cole thought about that. "Okay. I'll sing the one you always sing, Mom." He looked at Sarah and hummed a few notes. Then in the softest voice, he began to sing. 'Jesus loves you! this I know—' he leaned closer and rubbed the tip of his nose against hers—'for the Bible tells me so; little ones to Him belong . . .'"

Ashley didn't dare blink. In the short list of memories that would make up Sarah's place in their family, this would be among her favorites. And when Cole reached "They are weak but He is strong," Ashley felt a rush of truth in her heart. She'd been singing the song ever since she found out she was pregnant, singing it to Cole and Devin and knowing that her unborn baby could hear every word.

But now the song held so much more significance. Because no baby was weaker than their little Sarah, but that was okay. No one was stronger than her God.

Cole sang the song once more, and then he handed the baby back to Landon.

"Cole, would you ask everyone else to come in?" Landon took a deep breath. As Cole left, Landon looked at Ashley. "I could stay like this for hours, just the three of us."

"Me too." She held out her hands and brought Sarah close to her chest. "But I want her to meet everyone who loves her."

They didn't need to remind each other that time was short. The doctor had already told them. There was the sound of footsteps in the hallway outside the room, and when the door opened, the entire Baxter family filed in. Her father was at the front of the line, and he came up first.

"Look at her, Dad." Only a handful of times had Ashley felt so much joy, so much love. She breathed in deep, keeping the tears at bay. This was the celebration of Sarah's life, and Ashley wanted it to be marked with smiles. "Isn't she pretty?"

Her dad took the baby, and for an instant she saw on his face the same emotions she had felt earlier. But he had probably talked to Dr. McDaniel in the hall. He knew the truth, even if the evidence in his arms told him otherwise. John brought the baby close and kissed her cheek. "She looks like you, Ashley. The way you did as a baby."

"Really?"

"Same nose, same cheeks . . ."

From the back of the room, something caught Ashley's attention and she looked up. There, with a camera slung over one shoulder and a video camera over the other, was Brooke. Her eyes were red and swollen, but she smiled at Ashley. "Your baby is beautiful." She worked her way past the others. "Dad thought maybe you'd like me to take pictures."

And like that, the ice between them melted.

Brooke passed the cameras to Peter, then came closer. "I'm sorry, Ashley." She bent over her, and the two embraced. "I was wrong." Brooke pulled back and searched Ashley's eyes. "This has changed me. Forever."

"She's so precious, Brooke." Happy tears choked Ashley's voice. Love was providing a backdrop for this day, breaking down walls and bringing victory, just like she'd prayed. "Wait till you hold her."

Brooke looked at their father. "Can I?"

"Of course." He handed Sarah to Brooke.

For a long time Brooke simply stared at the baby, her face washed in wonder. "Hi, Sarah. I'm your aunt Brooke, and I love you. I love you very much."

Ashley couldn't fight the tears any longer. She let them come, but she never stopped smiling. Because this was another of those moments, the memories of Sarah's life that she would never, ever forget.

Each of them had a chance to hold Sarah.

Some of them whispered private things to her, and others cooed and smiled at her, the way they might with any baby.

An hour into their time together, a nurse came in and took Sarah for a quick checkup. Ashley didn't ask what they were checking. It didn't matter.

But when they brought her back, the nurse's expression was grave. "You don't have long. An hour, maybe two." She handed Sarah to Ashley. "I'm sorry."

"Don't be." Ashley gazed into her daughter's eyes. "She's the most loved little baby ever."

The nurse smiled and excused herself, and the outpouring of affection and attention continued.

Ashley watched as Sarah was passed to Dayne and Katy hovered next to him. She wasn't sure, but Ashley sensed that her daughter's life might be causing a breakthrough for her brother and his wife. That here—in a hospital room marked by life and death—Hollywood and its gossip maybe seemed ridiculously unimportant.

When they passed the baby on to Kari and Ryan, Ashley noticed something encouraging. Dayne put his arms around Katy and held her. Like a drowning man holds tight to a lifeline, he held her. They whispered to each other and Katy smiled, her eyes bright the way they used to be.

So maybe this was the miracle of Sarah's life. That she was able to bring Katy and Dayne back together before they might've walked away from everything good and right and true.

Ashley watched as Maddie and Hayley and Jessie took turns cooing at Sarah. Cole kept pace with them, moving from one of his cousins to the next and commenting each time about how pretty Sarah was. "She likes you, Maddie. See? She's smiling at you," he said. And then when Hayley held her with the help of Peter, Cole said it again. "She likes you too, Hayley. See that look on her face? That means she likes you."

Ryan had Devin on his hip. He brought the child to Landon, who was again holding Sarah. Devin had his pacifier in his mouth, but as he stared at Sarah, he pulled it out and pointed. "Baby!"

"Yes." Landon kissed Devin's cheek. "That's your baby sister."

Cole stood on his tiptoes again and peeked at Sarah. "She likes you, Devin. See that look in her eyes? She likes you a lot."

Ashley realized she was crying but only from a place of joy that knew no limit.

And through all of it, every precious minute, Brooke kept the video camera aimed at baby Sarah. When she had footage of each person holding her, whispering to her, and praying over her, she switched cameras and took dozens of still shots. No question they would have much to remember this time by.

As the second hour passed, Landon brought Sarah back to Ashley. His look was solemn. "I don't think she's doing well."

Ashley looked at her daughter, and she could see the difference. Sarah's face had gone from pink to a washed-out gray. Her eyes were still open, but she was blinking them more than before, the way Devin did when he was fighting sleep. Only Sarah wasn't fighting sleep.

She was fighting death.

And Ashley knew that this too was a miracle. Because she felt inside her the strength to help Sarah let go. She looked up and met the eyes of each person in the room, and only then did she realize that Elaine hadn't yet been in. "Dad, could you tell Elaine I'd like to see her?"

Her father left, and when he returned, he had Elaine at his side. A picture that looked right to Ashley, more right than she could've ever imagined.

Ashley held out her hand. "Elaine . . ."

The woman came, and though she was not Ashley's mother and could never take that place, she had brought a sort of love to the day that only a mother could bring. Elaine took her hand and smiled first at her, then at Sarah. "Your baby's beautiful, Ashley."

"Thank you." Ashley couldn't say much. Her emotions were almost more than she could handle. But as her eyes met Elaine's, she hoped Elaine might understand what she was trying to say, the words filling her heart. The thanks for loving her father when he was his most sad and lonely and the thanks for allowing the transition to happen slowly, in God's timing. But most of all, the thanks for loving Sarah enough to buy her a gift, to understand that she deserved a party the same as any other baby.

Though she couldn't find the words, Ashley was certain deep in her heart that Elaine understood at least some of what she was trying to say. As she was handing Sarah to Elaine, the door opened.

A deliveryman walked in. "This the Baxter party?"

Ashley smiled at the question. *The Baxter party.* "Yes." She laughed even through her tears. "This is the Baxter party."

"Well, I've got more flowers and balloons than I know what to do with." He looked around. "No way they're gonna fit in here with all of you."

A chorus of laughter came from everyone in the room.

"I guess just bring in what you can." Landon took Sarah from Elaine. He nodded to the delivery guy. "You can leave the rest out in the hallway."

The man brought in four bouquets of pink helium balloons and three vases bursting with pink roses. When he was finished, he wiped his brow and looked at Landon. "I got lots more out there. Looks like congratulations are in order."

"Yes." Landon grinned. "They are. Thank you."

"Who are they from?" Ashley asked the

question almost as an afterthought. Every-one they knew and loved was here.

The guy looked at his clipboard. "Says here they're from Dayne and Katy. No last name."

Ashley noticed then that her older brother and his wife were in the corner, grinning.

"I told them this was one special little baby girl and to bring us all the pink balloons and roses in the shop." Dayne's eyes grew deep, and they locked onto Ashley's. "Because this is the sort of welcome every baby should have."

A sob caught in her throat, and Ashley closed her eyes tight. Another miracle was at hand. The idea that Dayne—whose first child had been lost to an abortion, an abor-tion he had known nothing about—would find healing in celebrating the short life of lit-tle Sarah.

Once more, Landon handed Sarah to Ashley. His expression told her that things were worse, and immediately Ashley noticed it too. Sarah's little chest was working harder than before, rising dramatically with each breath. Her eyes would close, and then she would startle, her hands jerking out to the sides and her eyes opening wide once more.

"She's fighting it," Ashley whispered. She brushed her cheek against Sarah's and kissed her nose, her hands. "She doesn't want to leave us."

All along, Landon had been telling Ashley that she was the brave one and that he admired her courage. But here, with Sarah slowly slipping away, Landon cleared his throat and stood straight by her side. In a voice both calm and compassionate, he explained what was happening. "Sarah's leaving us."

A somber air fell over the room, and the quiet conversations grew silent.

"Wait!" Cole ran from the room, and when he returned, he had a folded piece of craft paper in his hand. He was out of breath, panicked as if he might've missed his chance. "I made this for Sarah!"

He worked his way past Ashley's father and Kari and Ryan and their kids to the spot between Ashley and Landon. Then, suddenly, he seemed to notice that all eyes were on him. For a moment it looked like he might hide behind Landon and wait on the gift altogether.

But Cole set the homemade card on the

table, and he motioned for Ashley. "Come closer. This is private."

She slid over in the bed as best she could. Sarah wiggled in her arms, and again she let her arms out in a start. "Shhh, Sarah." Ashley kissed her daughter. "It's okay, baby."

When he could reach, Cole cupped his hands around his mouth and pressed them on either side of Ashley's ear. "I was praying to Jesus last night." His words were breathy, but they were clear enough to understand. "And Jesus gave me a picture in my head. A really happy one. I'm not that good a drawer, but I colored it the best I could, okay?"

Ashley was touched. Her competitive son taking the risk of drawing something for Sarah even when drawing wasn't his strongest gift. And a picture in his head from Jesus? Ashley was curious. She leaned back. "Can you show me?"

Cole nodded. He took the paper from the table and opened it up.

Across the top in crayon, he'd written, *I love you, Sarah. Tell Grandma hi for me.* Beneath that was a picture of an older woman, a smile stretched across her face. And in her arms was a tiny baby girl, wrapped in a pink and white blanket.

Ashley felt her heart skip a beat as she stared at the picture. "Cole?" She lifted her eyes to his. "Jesus gave you this picture?"

He looked around the room again, clearly embarrassed. And once more he cupped his hands around his mouth and leaned close. "Because He told me Sarah's going to be with Grandma."

In a rush, the Bible story came back. Ashley had asked for a miracle, and there had been many today. But here was the Lord . . . in the gentle whisper of her oldest son. His drawing would be more precious to her than anything else that could mark Sarah's life. And later, when she was ready, she would put the image on canvas—where all things that touched her heart eventually wound up.

Sarah coughed, and Ashley felt the urgency of the moment. She handed the picture back to Cole. "Thank you, Coley. Sarah loves your picture. Hold on to it, okay?"

"Okay." He cast a worried look at Sarah.

At the same time, the others moved in closer, watching the baby, holding on to the moment.

Cole blinked. "She's dying, isn't she?"

"Yes, buddy." Landon sighed and picked up where he left off. "Ashley and I would like us all to pray for Sarah."

Around the room, the Baxter family held hands. One at a time the voices filled the space, asking God to give Sarah a painless journey home and praying that she would know how much she was loved. Even the children prayed, thanking God for Sarah and telling Him that they wished she could stay here. Hayley added, "But heaven is so much better."

When they finished praying, Landon started to sing. It was the song Ashley had sung again and again over the years, one that the CKT kids had sung in the face of the worst possible announcement.

And now, others joined in. "'Great is Thy faithfulness, O God my Father, there is no shadow of turning with Thee. . . .'"

Every word rang out true and right. And as their song built and filled the room, Ashley leaned close to little Sarah. "It's okay, baby. You don't have to fight anymore." Her tears fell onto her daughter's cheeks, and she brushed them with her own. "Go to Jesus, baby. . . . Go to Jesus. He's waiting for you, Sarah." She remembered Cole's picture, the picture God had given him. "And Grandma's waiting for you, sweetheart. Tell Grandma we love her, okay?"

Sarah took a long gasp, and one last time, their eyes met. She seemed to hold on another few heartbeats, and in Sarah's eyes was all the love that would last Ashley a lifetime. They told Ashley thank you . . . thank you for giving her life and thank you for giving her love. And finally, they told her good-bye.

Landon leaned in closer and kissed Sarah's cheek one last time.

The others were still singing, most of them with tears in their eyes. "'Morning by morning new mercies I see; all I have needed Thy hand hath provided. . . .'"

As they reached the last line, as they sang about the greatness of God's faithfulness, Sarah finally closed her eyes. She breathed one more time, and then she was still. Forever still.

One at a time, the people she loved filed past and bid farewell to the little girl they'd known for only a few hours.

Cole was last, tears streaming from his eyes. But he gave Ashley a shaky smile. "She's with Grandma now. Grandma and Jesus."

"Yes, Coley." Ashley kissed her son and hugged him with her free arm.

When Ashley and Landon were alone with Sarah, Landon put his hands along either side of Ashley's face. "People worried that we couldn't do this, that it would be too hard and it would change us." His eyes were filled with equal amounts of pain and joy. "And it has. It's changed all of us. That's the miracle of Sarah's life."

"Yes." She looked at her daughter. "The Lord was here today. He was in the gentle whisper, just like He promised."

Landon gave her a look like he didn't quite understand, and she realized that he hadn't heard about Cole's picture yet, that Jesus had given him that picture and told him that Sarah would be with her grandmother. She smiled.

Ashley's mother loved children, loved being a grandma. But now she would have a grandbaby of her own, one she could rock and love and sing to until it was time for everyone else to join them. Sarah Marie belonged to Jesus, and she belonged to Ashley's mother. That was what God wanted Ashley to understand.

Long after they'd taken Sarah, yet another

miracle happened. Dr. McDaniel confirmed that against the odds, Sarah's heart valves had been saved and flown to New York, where they would save the lives of two babies. Then and weeks later, when only a small picture in a silver frame sat on the kitchen counter as a reminder of Sarah, Ashley remembered the message God had given her. It was her way of knowing that the Lord had heard her prayers and that indeed something good had come from their unforgettable summer. And that He was with them through it all. The proof wasn't in a dramatic healing or a misdiagnosis. That wasn't where they had seen God. Rather, He was in the dozens of miracles that Sarah's life had brought about all around them.

And most of all, He was in the gentle whisper.

A WORD FROM
KAREN KINGSBURY

DEAR FRIENDS,

Whew . . . that was a tough one! Even halfway through the writing of *Summer*, I wasn't sure if I was going to let Ashley's baby die. I thought about going back and having the diagnosis be something less serious—something where a misdiagnosis might be more possible. But every time I doubted myself, I went back to my research.

In writing this chapter of the Baxters' story, I studied the cases of real babies diagnosed with anencephaly. I looked at photos and read personal accounts. I learned that many times these precious souls are aborted at the suggestion of a well-meaning doctor—a doctor like Brooke—because the experience of embracing life and death in a single afternoon is a daunting one, one that without God could very nearly destroy a person.

But my research found many couples who decided to let their baby live, to enjoy the pregnancy and celebrate the child's life—however short. Life is God's to give and God's to take. This was the message repeated again and again by these couples. I spent days crying as I read about the treasured short lives of these babies and the impact they made on the families who loved them.

Anencephaly happens to one in a thousand babies, but most of them miscarry before a diagnosis can be made. Only one in ten thousand live to the sixteen-week mark, when the birth defect is most commonly found. I didn't write about anencephaly because I thought you could relate to it. In fact, very few of us will ever know a real experience with this type of birth defect.

Rather, I wrote about anencephaly because it forces us to look at life.

In our day, people take life very lightly. Whether the issue is one of euthanasia or abortion, cloning or stem cell research, life and its value are being called into question, redefined by our legal system.

My father, Ted Kingsbury, is in a skilled nursing facility as I write this. I want to tell you a little bit about him. Three months ago, his doctor gave him a choice. My dad's kidneys were failing, and he could either let the failure happen—a choice that would give him a month or two at the most—or he could choose dialysis.

The doctor was brutally honest. "Dialysis is painful and difficult. It leaves you cold and weak, and it will be wearying on you emotionally and physically."

And so for a short while, my dad thought about forgetting the whole thing. "I've lived a good life. . . . Maybe this is all God has for me," he told me.

All of us siblings—four girls, now that my brother is up in heaven—agreed that Dad had to fight this thing; he had to choose dialysis. Now it was a matter of convincing him. His birthday came up around that time, and I gave him one of those blankets with an enormous photo silk-screened onto it.

A color photo of all his grandkids.

My dad's chin quivered, and tears filled his eyes as he looked at that blanket.

"It's to keep you warm," I told him, "while you're at dialysis."

And then we talked about my dad's earlier days. One of my first memories of my dad is back in the early seventies. I was maybe eight or nine years old, and I remember him coming in on a rainy afternoon soaked to the bone. He set a stack of wet brochures on the counter, and I picked one up. On it was the image of an unborn baby.

"What's this?" I asked him.

"Some people are thinking of making it legal to kill babies." His voice was soft, kind. It held no judgment. "I helped some friends from church pass out brochures so people would understand better. So they would want to choose life for every baby."

The realizations for me that day were many and lasting. And decades later as my dad held his photo blanket, I reminded him of that rainy afternoon. "You taught us to choose life, Dad." I hugged him. "How can you do anything but choose life now?"

His change of heart was fast and sure. He made an appointment with his doctor and had a shunt placed in his arm, where it will stay as long as he lives. Three days a week he must go in for up to five hours of dialysis, so a machine can clean his blood the way his kidneys no longer can.

The doctor was right. Nothing about dialysis has been easy. Three times my dad's blood pressure dropped so low that he went into seizures and had to be rushed to the emergency room. And six weeks ago he was finishing up with dialysis when he passed out and fell. The fall broke the tibia bone in his right leg.

And so now he lies in a skilled nursing center, praying along with the rest of us that his leg will heal.

Across the hall is a man with early signs of Alzheimer's. When no one is nearby, this man often yells out, "Harry? Harry, are you there? Harry, come on in! Harry?"

A few doors down is a woman whose frail cries punctuate the afternoon. "Help me! Someone help me!"

"What do you need, Beth?" we'll hear one of the nurses say.

"Weeds . . . there're weeds everywhere."

"Okay, dear. . . . We'll take care of the weeds."

A skilled nursing facility is the sort of place where you are forced to take a hard look at life. But my father has no qualms whatsoever. He beams at me and my family when we visit and makes no reference to the days we've missed. He holds my hand and tells me how he's finally finding time to read my books—the large-print versions.

"And I'm reading Acts in the Bible!" His tone is happy and upbeat, his hope endless.

The reason? Because he has recommitted himself wholeheartedly to the truth that life is God's to give and God's to take. I treasure this time with my dad, time we wouldn't have gotten if he hadn't chosen dialysis. If he hadn't chosen life.

If you've struggled with this issue, and if you've made choices in your life that don't line up with God's mandate to choose life, then please . . . don't despair. God is merciful and gracious. He waits even now for you to turn to Him, run to Him. As long as you have a heartbeat, you have the chance to make a new start, to seek forgiveness the way all of us must seek it, and to choose life.

If you've found hope in Jesus Christ for the first time while reading this book, then please know that I am praying for you. Your next step is to find a Bible-believing church in your area and get connected. Go to a Sunday service, take in a Bible class, attend a small group. And if reading Scripture is new to you and you can't afford a Bible, write to me with the words *New Life* in the subject line. I'll make sure my office sends you a Bible so you can get started on that new life in Christ.

I pray that this finds you well and walking in His truth and light. And most of all, I pray that you will join me in looking for the miracles around us and in celebrating life! Remember, sometimes His greatest message to us comes in the most gentle of whispers.

Until next time, in His light and love,

Karen Kingsbury

PS—I still love hearing from you! Your prayers and letters remain a very great encouragement to me as I write stories that God might use to change your life and mine. You can contact me at my Web site—www .KarenKingsbury.com. While you're there, catch up on my latest journal entry, see photos of my family, and connect with other readers. You can also learn about the next installment in the ongoing story of the Baxter family. See you there!

Discussion Questions

1. Were you surprised that Ashley's baby wasn't healed? What did you expect would happen?

2. What did you think about Ashley's decision to avoid doctor's appointments through much of the summer? What do you think you would do in such a situation?

3. Brooke handled the news of Ashley's troubled pregnancy the way many doctors might handle it. Explain your stance on abortion.

4. Read Psalm 139. If you don't have a Bible, you can find a copy of Psalm 139 online at www.Bible.com. What do you think this chapter of Scripture says about life? According to these verses, when does life start?

5. What did you think about Ashley's reaction to Brooke's advice? Do you think this sort of situation could've ruined their relationship forever?

6. Tell of a relationship you are in or one that you're aware of in which well-meaning actions on the part of one person created a seemingly unfixable rift. How did healing come for this relationship? If it hasn't come, what steps would you need to take to help see that healing does come?

7. Ashley was struck by the fact that she had begged God for a miracle, yet God chose not to heal her daughter. What did this do to Ashley's faith along the way?

8. Has there been a time when you prayed for something, but God chose

to say no? Tell about that experience. What did you learn from it?

9. Against the backdrop of Ashley's ordeal, Katy and Dayne's marriage was strained badly. What are some events and choices that led to this strain?

10. Though your issues will be different, has your marriage or the marriage of someone you know ever been seriously strained? What led to that strain?

11. What could Katy and Dayne have done differently so that the news on the covers of the tabloids didn't hurt them so badly? In your opinion, why didn't they do this?

12. How important is communication to a marriage? How important is communication to a friendship or a sibling relationship? Give examples.

13. Ashley was looking for a miracle when she first received the diagnosis of a neural tube defect. By the end of *Summer*, what miracles had occurred because of little Sarah's life? What

other miracles might still happen in the months to come?

14. Ashley had a breakthrough in her relationship with Elaine. Describe that breakthrough and the importance of Elaine's decision to buy baby Sarah a gift.

15. John described himself as feeling tired and discouraged by the impending loss of Ashley's baby. What else was troubling John? How did the miracle of Sarah's life affect his attitude?

16. Cole talked about seeing a picture from Jesus. In the Bible, Jesus tells us to have the faith of a child. How have you seen a child's faith serve as an illustration in your own life?

17. Ashley took time to meet with God alone so she could question Him. Talk about her questions. Do you think it was right of her to question God? Why or why not?

18. Tell about a time when you or someone you know has questioned God. What

was the net result to your faith or to the faith of the other person?

19. Ashley heard God tell her to look for Him in the gentle whisper. Read 1 Kings 19. What lesson was God trying to teach Elijah in this section of Scripture?

20. What lesson was God trying to teach Ashley from that same Bible story? What touched you most in the final chapter of *Summer*? How did the lesson of the gentle whisper bring healing to Ashley?

Please turn the page for an exciting preview of

the third book in the

SUNRISE SERIES

by Karen Kingsbury

Available Spring 2008
www.tyndalefiction.com

From

S O M E D A Y

By Karen Kingsbury

CHAPTER ONE

JOHN MADE HIS decision as his family was leaving the hospital.

Elaine had shared a moment with him and his family that had bonded them like nothing else had. He held her hand as they walked silently to the car. In a few hours, everyone would meet back at the Baxter house for dinner. They needed to be together, needed to share about the ways little Sarah had touched them, changed them.

But in the meantime, he couldn't shake the certain feeling inside.

Elaine noticed it. Her car was parked not

far from his, and before she went to it, she stopped. "You're thinking about something."

"Yes." He smiled. He was worn-out and weary. But he was no longer discouraged, not after all he'd just witnessed. "I'll tell you later."

She would be coming over for dinner too, but for now she was going home. They all needed some downtime. "Tell me tonight, okay?" She angled her head, curious.

He wouldn't tell her tonight, but he didn't want to keep her guessing. "It's just something God brought into focus for me." He hugged her. "About how much I need you in my life."

She looked surprised and touched and maybe a little shy.

They said their good-byes, but when John was alone in his car, the decision in his heart took root, writing itself across his soul and forever changing his picture of the future.

When he reached home, he went inside and took a long, slow breath. The house still held Elizabeth's memories, the way it always would. He walked upstairs to their room and stopped in front of the photo of her on his dresser. "You were there today, dear. I felt you."

Before he left the hospital, Ashley had shown him Cole's picture. It brought him as much comfort as it brought Ashley and Landon. Because nothing could be more fitting than the image of Elizabeth holding little Sarah in heaven, taking care of her until they could all be together again.

He moved to the card table he'd set up at the end of his bed. Elizabeth's letters were spread across it, and on one end was a stack of letters already copied. Six copies each—one for each of their children. He was almost finished with the project, almost ready to put the letters into scrapbooks and pass them out. He had a feeling there was something in those letters that would make a dramatic difference to all of their kids—one way or another.

Even with Sarah's funeral planned for later in the week, he would focus his energy on the letters. It was time, and it was the right thing to do. When he was finished, he would know he'd finally found closure, finally walked through everything left of the woman he had so dearly loved. He would need that closure, because of the decision he'd made an hour ago.

The decision that one day very soon he

would take the step he had been certain he would never take.

He would ask Elaine Denning to be his wife.

The **Best-Selling**
Firstborn Series
by Karen Kingsbury

Catch up with your favorite Baxter characters from the best-selling Redemption series. Dayne Matthews is an A-list Hollywood actor with a bright future. But his heart is pulling him toward a woman and a family who have no idea how their lives are tied to his. Katy Hart, the director of Christian Kids Theater, finally feels content and at home in Bloomington, Indiana. But that changes when she meets Dayne Matthews and he promises a future she left in her past. Meanwhile, John Baxter struggles to fulfill a promise he made to his dying wife—a promise to reconnect the entire family, including the one child they never spoke of.

Fame
A story of hope, healing, and God's divine leading—even in the face of impossible circumstances

Forgiven
A story of God's divine leading and the realization that peace comes only after forgiveness

Found
A story of God's divine leading and the truth that God rewards those who seek Him with all their heart

Family
A story of the search for renewed hope and the desperate need to be loved and to belong

Forever
A story about surviving tough times and drawing strength and hope from family and deep faith

Other Life-Changing Fiction by

KAREN KINGSBURY

To see what readers are saying about Karen Kingsbury's fiction, go to www.KarenKingsbury.com and click the guest-book link.

REDEMPTION SERIES
Redemption
Remember
Return
Rejoice
Reunion

FIRSTBORN SERIES
Fame
Forgiven
Found
Family
Forever

SUNRISE SERIES
Sunrise
Summer
Someday (Spring 2008)
Sunset (Spring 2008)

RED GLOVE SERIES
Gideon's Gift
Maggie's Miracle
Sarah's Song
Hannah's Hope

SEPTEMBER 11 SERIES
One Tuesday Morning
Beyond Tuesday Morning

FOREVER FAITHFUL SERIES
Waiting for Morning
A Moment of Weakness
Halfway to Forever

WOMEN OF FAITH FICTION SERIES
A Time to Dance
A Time to Embrace

STAND-ALONE TITLES
A Thousand Tomorrows
Oceans Apart
Where Yesterday Lives
When Joy Came to Stay
On Every Side
Even Now
Ever After
Divine
Like Dandelion Dust

CHILDREN'S TITLE
Let Me Hold You Longer

MIRACLE COLLECTIONS
A Treasury of Christmas Miracles
A Treasury of Miracles for Women
A Treasury of Miracles for Teens
A Treasury of Miracles for Friends
A Treasury of Adoption Miracles

GIFT BOOKS
Stay Close Little Girl
Be Safe Little Boy

www.KarenKingsbury.com